La

GU01018699

LAURA

Noreen Riols

eagle

Guildford, Surrey

Copyright © Noreen Riols 1992

British Library Cataloguing-in-Publication Data. A
catalogue record for this book is available from the British
Library

Published by Eagle, an imprint of Inter Publishing Service
(IPS) Ltd, Williams Building, Woodbridge Meadows,
Guildford, Surrey GU1 1BH

Typeset by Falcon Typographic Art Ltd, Fife, Scotland
Printed in the UK by HarperCollins Manufacturing,
Glasgow

ISBN 0 86347 080 7

CONTENTS

PART 1 – 1962 *Back to Ardnakil*

CHAPTER   1   Back to Ardnakil   11

2   Preparations   24

3   'Your Turn Will Come'   39

4   The Curtain Raiser   46

5   The Ball   50

6   Oh Sandy!   71

7   The Other Woman   86

8   Escaping   100

9   Rehearsal and Confusion   108

10   The Count Down   120

11   A Day Later   129

12   Breaking into the Stronghold   137

13   The Unexpected Visitor   150

14   The Open Road   163

PART 2 – 1973 *Revelations*

CHAPTER   15   Bolts from the Blue   183

16   On their Wedding Day   196

17   The Funeral   206

18   Anti-climax   220

19   Parting   231

20   Revelations   241

21   Moving Away   261

PART 3 – 1979 *Out of the Summer*

CHAPTER 22 Josh   275
        23 A Strange Feeling   285
        24 The Gathering Storm   294
        25 Reminiscing   304
        26 'What is it?'   323
        27 Rose   331
        28 The Telephone Call   339
        29 On the Edge of the Precipice   357
        30 Out of the Tunnel   373

To
my son Christopher
and
his wife Hélène
who fell in love with Scotland

PART 1

1962

Back to Ardnakil

1

Back to Ardnakil

A sudden jolt followed by the hiss of steam and raucous shouts as heavy metal wheels clattered over the hard concrete broke slowly into Laura's dream. The gentle swaying and the rhythmic clackety clack had stopped, and now as she drifted back to consciousness through the hazy veils of sleep, she heard doors slamming and the sound of footsteps in the corridor outside.

Leaning on one elbow, still not fully awake, she twitched a corner of the blind, letting a shaft of bright early morning sunlight stream in through the window.

'It's Edinburgh,' Cristobel yawned from the bunk below her. 'No need to panic, we've got bags of time.' And pulling the bedclothes over her ears, she turned on her side and immediately fell back to sleep.

Laura, now fully awake, dropped the blind in place and lay back on the hard pillow, gazing up at the dim ceiling, her hands behind her head. She knew every corner of the great echoing Waverley Station and could clearly picture the frenzied activity on the platform now that the night train from London stood panting at a standstill for a few brief minutes. It was almost two years since she had last accompanied Cristobel on this journey to her friend's home and the excitement which had been mounting inside her ever since Cristobel had arrived from Switzerland yesterday afternoon now threatened to burst like a great overflowing dam and drench her in its flow.

Sleep was out of the question but she didn't want to disturb Cristobel so she turned on her side and gazed at the shadows flickering on the opposite wall. The train shunted, more footsteps, hurried this time, ran along the platform, the guard's whistle sounded, last doors were hastily slammed and, with a hiss and a snort, they were off again. Laura sighed deeply as she listened to Cristobel's soft, regular breathing in the bunk above, but it was a sigh of pure joy laced with tingling excitement. She was going to see Alasdair again! And with this blissful thought in her mind she drifted into a fitful doze.

There was a sudden rapid knock on the door of their compartment.

'Perth in fifteen minutes,' announced the attendant as, he passed on along the corridor.

'Cristobel?' Laura called anxiously.

'I heard,' she yawned. 'Ugh. Why is the night so short? It only seems to be ten seconds since we stopped at Edinburgh.'

'It seems like a lifetime to me,' Laura laughed, as she gingerly negotiated the steep ladder from her bunk. 'I'm SO excited I thought we'd *never* arrive.'

Cristobel joined in her laughter.

'*I'm* the one who should be excited,' she called, throwing back the blankets.

'Aren't you?' Laura enquired, now standing upright in the narrow compartment, looking down at her friend.

'Of *course* I am,' Cristobel smiled, wriggling out of her nightdress and reaching for her underclothes. 'Can't be bothered to wash, I'll have a bath as soon as we arrive.'

'Cristobel,' Laura reproved as she leant over the narrow washbowl and splashed her face with water.

She paused and looked up.

'You did say *all* your brothers will be home?'

'Yes, ALL of them,' Cristobel replied.

Laura reached for the towel.

'Do you think one of them might come to meet us?'

Cristobel laughed and crawled from her bunk, small and slim and already dressed.

'Not a hope,' she said. 'They'll all be in bed at this time of the morning. All except Sandy, who can't drive anyway. He's bound to be up looking for some mischief to get into.'

'How does he manage to be at home in the middle of June?'

'Half term, unfortunately,' Cristobel grimaced. 'No, Father will send Donald, I expect.'

She dug Laura in the ribs as she squeezed past her.

'Get a move on. Stop dreaming or you'll find yourself in the train on the way to Aberdeen.'

Laura quickly threw down the towel and began to cram her overnight things into a small suitcase.

Cristobel stepped out into the corridor and leant against the window watching the rolling countryside flash past, the heather covered mountains sloping away in the distance.

'It's good to be home again,' she breathed as Laura joined her. 'It's been a long time since Christmas.'

Laura smiled but didn't reply. She understood her friend's feelings perfectly and yet, at the same time she couldn't help feeling a tinge of jealousy. She envied Cristobel her roots and her sense of belonging; emotions which were totally alien to Laura.

And, suddenly, lulled by the rhythm of the gently swaying train she was in her small room in Oxford again, a drowsy twelve-year-old girl floating gently back to earth on puffy clouds of sleep. Through half-open eyes she saw her father's sister sitting by her bed and, as Edwina leant forward to take her in her arms,

Laura knew that her mother's long struggle with death had ended.

She had felt no violent emotion, just a hollow emptiness and isolation. But now, gazing through the train window at the scenery flashing past, the terrible wave of hopelessness and desolation, the feeling of rejection which had later overwhelmed her on that hot July morning seven years before when she learned that she had been left to sleep whilst her sisters watched at their mother's bedside, slowly began to trickle through her body once again. She shuddered.

Cristobel looked round and smiled.

'What's the matter,' she enquired. 'Someone walked over your grave?'

Laura shook her head slowly.

'No,' she answered quietly. 'Over my mother's.'

Cristobel shifted uncomfortably.

'Don't think about it,' she said, squeezing her friend's arm. 'Think about tomorrow evening instead.'

And, closing her eyes she let out a long, voluptuous sigh.

Laura continued to gaze through the train window. It was difficult for Cristobel, brought up in a warm secure family, to understand. Laura had been a solitary child. Mary and Philippa, her elder sisters, were both married and living their own lives when their mother was taken ill, so that when the cancer had finally claimed her life the one person Laura loved most had been torn from her leaving her shattered and alone, her roots cut from beneath her.

The train jerked, began to slow down, then picked up speed, and as the wheels regained their rhythm, clattering over the rails, she seemed to hear her father's name, Henry Denning, Henry Denning, repeated monotonously over and over again. And she began to wonder about the tenuous links which held her to her one remaining parent.

Henry Denning had always been a remote father, unable to relate to his three daughters, almost bewildered by them. After his wife's death he had buried himself even more deeply in his books and his writing, and Laura had been sent away to school.

The train flew through a small country station, and the cluster of people waiting on the platform gazed blankly at the faces at the window as they flashed past. Laura brushed a hand across her eyes to prevent the tears which were stinging behind her eyelids from spilling over and tumbling down her cheeks as she thought back over the seven years since her mother's death. She realised what a small part her father had played, had ever played in her life, and her mind turned to Robert Hamilton, Cristobel's father, so alive, so vital, so very much a presence in his home and in both their lives. And once again that emptiness crept over her and a feeling close to jealousy threatened to choke her. She wondered if she and her own father would have grown close had she not been sent away to school.

Cristobel lurched against her as the train rounded a bend.

'Do you remember that first day at Rosemead?' Laura reflected, almost to herself, as they both staggered to regain their balance.

Cristobel grimaced.

'*Do* I?' she laughed, pressing herself against the window as an elderly lady with a Pekinese in her arms gingerly negotiated the long corridor.

She leant backwards on her heels as the woman teetered past.

'Could anyone forget?' Cristobel went on. 'All those prim, archaic mistresses and bossy prefects pandering to mothers wearing home-spun skirts and Peruvian woolly caps.'

She giggled. 'I wondered what on earth I'd been dumped into.'

'Me too,' Laura mused. 'I don't know how I'd have survived if I hadn't met you that first afternoon.'

'Oh, you'd have survived,' Cristobel said airily.

'I'm not so sure,' Laura ended.

Cristobel slipped her arm through her friend's.

'What's all this mooning about?' she teased. 'People walking over your grave and now resurrecting our ghastly schooldays. Thank heaven they're over. I don't care if my children never learn to read and write: I'm certainly not putting them through all that.'

Laura smiled but didn't reply.

Meeting Cristobel on that first day when they were both new girls had forged a bond of friendship which had become an anchor for Laura the following summer when she had been invited to Cristobel's Scottish home. She had accompanied her friend every summer since, back to the place where she recaptured that sense of belonging she so sorely needed, and which she had lost the day her mother died. And gradually, in her dreams, Cristobel's family had become her family and Cristobel's four brothers her brothers.

Laura smiled to herself as she watched the country-side with the low grey stone walls, the shaggy Highland cattle and black faced sheep flash past. She was think-ing about Alasdair, the one brother who had never really taken much notice of her and the one she had never considered as a brother; and her heart began to beat unreasonably.

She hadn't seen him for almost three years.

He had always been away, doing his own thing, travelling with friends from University since that first grown up ball she had attended at Ardnakil when she was sixteen. Alasdair had danced with her and that evening had been engraved on her memory ever since. Graeme and Ninian, Cristobel's other brothers, had also danced with her, but Alasdair had been different.

And she felt again that surge of something which she could not then explain which had rushed through her when she saw him approach.

'I believe this is my waltz, little one,' he had said as he swept her into his arms.

He had smiled down at her, a crooked, quizzical smile.

'You've got freckles on your nose,' he'd teased. 'Just like a soft powdering of brown sugar.'

And she had felt mortified. Now she was going to see him again and she wondered what her reaction would be: whether she would still feel that surge of warmth go pulsating right through her. And at the remembrance, she blushed.

The countryside was giving way to straggled houses and then the outskirts of the town came into view. The train snaked round a corner, snorting and whistling and gradually began to slow down.

'Here we are,' Cristobel announced, turning back into the compartment to pick up her case. 'Got everything?'

Laura nodded and the train slithered into the station with a shuddering sigh.

They jumped down onto the platform and walked towards the exit. Suddenly Cristobel began frantically waving and Laura's heart missed a beat. COULD it be Alasdair who had come to meet them?

But it was only Donald.

He came forward and took their suitcases.

'Morning Miss Cristobel, Miss Laura,' he said. 'Did you have a good journey?'

'Splendid,' Cristobel replied enthusiastically, as he opened the door of the car. 'How's everything and everybody?'

'Very well, thank you, miss. All very happy about tomorrow, and very busy.'

Cristobel smiled. To-morrow her engagement to

Lindsay Fraser would be announced, and there was to be a great ball at Ardnakil in the evening.

'I can imagine the panic,' she giggled.

'Not panic, Miss Cristobel,' Donald reproached, starting up the engine. 'But everyone is very excited and busy.'

Cristobel laughed gaily.

'Oh Donald, please hurry,' she exclaimed. 'Don't worry about the speed limit or anything, I'm DYING to be home again.'

Donald smiled indulgently into the driver's mirror.

'And I'm *starving*,' she added.

Laura settled back in her corner and looked out of the window as the town once again gave way to the soft green and mauve of the distant hills and the countryside filled with drifts of wild flowers, and clumps of yellow gorse.

'Has everyone arrived?' she asked diffidently.

'Everyone, Miss Laura?' Donald enquired.

'Well, all the family.'

'Mr Ninian and Captain Fraser will be arriving tomorrow and Mr Alasdair is coming up late this evening.'

Laura's heart missed a beat and then dropped to her boots, remembering about the freckles.

'I'll bet Sandy's there,' Cristobel chuckled.

'Yes, Miss Cristobel, Master Sandy's there. He arrived last night from school and will be home for almost a week.

'Glory,' sighed Cristobel, 'how are we going to stand it? Has he improved at all?'

'He's grown much taller,' Donald hedged.

'Oh Donald, you know what I mean,' Cristobel chided. 'Is he still as GHASTLY?'

'He's certainly full of life,' replied Donald conservatively.

'Enough said,' Cristobel groaned. 'But he hasn't brought any appalling friend to help him in his antics?'

'No, Miss Cristobel, not this time,' Donald answered, obviously thankful.

Sandy was a handful all on his own without any outside help.

As they turned in at the great wrought iron gates and began to sweep up the wide tree lined drive, the overhanging branches forming a canopy above them, Sandy appeared out of a bush, a catapult in his hand and flung himself on the car.

'Sandy,' Cristobel shrieked in alarm as Donald swerved and slowed down.

'Hi, Sis,' he yelled, banging on the window before jumping off and disappearing back into the bushes.

'I don't think I can stand it,' wailed Cristobel. 'Not for a whole *week*.'

Laura smiled. She revelled in this family.

'If you'd ever spent your holidays in Oxford with my father you'd appreciate Sandy,' she murmured. 'At least you know you're still alive.'

'Can't imagine *anyone* appreciating SANDY,' Cristobel answered as the car drew up in front of the wide open door.

Cristobel jumped out and ran the few paces which separated them from the hall's dark interior.

'Hallo dogs,' she called. 'I'm home.'

Immediately there was a scuffle and a slither of feet as three black labradors, till then sleeping peacefully on the half landing of the great oak staircase, heard her voice and came hurtling down the stairs, barking and whining as they did so.

Laura, who had never owned a pet, could not understand the Hamilton family's passion for their dogs. Every time they returned it was the same: the first thing Cristobel did was to shriek for the dogs, causing

chaos and uproar at no matter what time of day or
night it happened to be.

Cristobel dropped to her knees and hugged the three
excited beasts who howled with delight and jumped up
and down clawing at her hair and licking her face.

'Sam, Joey, Sally, I'm so PLEASED to see you,' she
cried, ruffling their coats and returning their wet
caresses.

Then she suddenly looked up.

'Where's Sara?'

At the sound of her name, a very old, lame dog
lolloped slowly down the stairs, flopping on each step as
she advanced. Cristobel disentangled herself from the
damp hugs and went over to greet the matriarch. Sara
was almost fifteen years old, the mother, grandmother
and great grandmother of the other three.

'Sara,' Cristobel crooned softly, sitting down on the
bottom stair and cradling the dog's slavering head in
her arms.

The other three now turned their attention to Laura
as Donald came into the hall carrying the suitcases.

From a small turret at the side of the front door a
growl emerged and an elderly white West Highland
terrier waddled out to join the welcome committee.

'Isn't anyone up?' Cristobel enquired, bending down
to pat her mother's own pet, who growled again
in reply.

'Cook's in the kitchen,' Donald replied. 'Mr Hamilton
went out very early, I saw him as I was leaving.'

He crossed the hall and opening a green baize door
went down some stairs to the kitchen. As he did so a
shadow passed on the upstairs landing, a gliding black
shape moving slowly like a ghost, a pale, lined face with
a cloud of very white hair peeping out from under a frilly
mob cap appeared above the banister. Cristobel looked
up and, releasing Sara, suddenly rushed up the stairs
two by two.

'Morag,' she cried delightedly, hugging the frail figure. 'Oh, Morag, I'm *so* pleased to see you.'

The diminutive woman smiled, bringing a thousand wrinkles swarming across her face to fill the creases, her crinkled old eyes lighting up as they gazed at Cristobel.

Laura walked slowly up the stairs.

'Hallo, Morag,' she said shyly.

The old woman turned and offered her withered cheek to be kissed. As Laura bent and brushed her lips across its cold surface she felt the same fear she had always had of Morag. Not exactly fear, but awe. Morag was like the frowning portraits which lined the walls, arrested in a moment of time. She had been nurse to not only all the Hamilton children but to their mother and grandmother before them and had accompanied Lady Flora when she came to Ardnakil as Robert Hamilton's bride almost twenty-eight years before. No-one knew, or dared to ask, her exact age, but she was by now very old, and had become part of the fabric of Ardnakil, woven into it, never leaving the house for more than a few minutes, always gliding stiffly, silently along the upper galleries, watching everything, taking everything in.

'Cristobel,' she said sternly in her wavering voice. 'Ye have na' washed your face.'

Morag was the only one of the servants to call the Hamilton children by their Christian names.

'No Morag, I haven't,' Cristobel laughed. 'But I will soon. At this minute I'm STARVING. Have you any toast left over from your breakfast?'

Morag always rose early and had her breakfast before anyone else appeared.

'Ye'll no' ha' a crumb to eat in this hoose till ye've washed.'

'Oh Morag,' Cristobel pleaded.

But she knew it was useless, Morag was unflinching. They had all learned that very early on.

'Laura, Cristobel, you're here. How lovely!'

The two girls turned and looked down into the hall.

Lady Flora had just walked in through the open front door, a large flat basket brimming with fresh-cut flowers over her arm. She laid it down on the dark oak table and walked swiftly across the hall to the stairs, holding out her arms.

The girls ran down happily.

'Darlings,' she said, warmly embracing them both at once, 'I'm *so* pleased to see you. Let me look at you.'

She held them away from her at arm's length.

'I'm sorry I wasn't here when you arrived,' she went on, 'but I just went into the garden to cut some flowers for your rooms.'

She looked down at the tiny gold fob watch hanging on a chain round her neck.

'Donald must have done the journey in record time.'

'I told him not to bother about the speed limit,' Cristobel laughed. 'I was in such a hurry to get home.'

At that moment Sandy and his catapult catapulted themselves into the hall.

'Isn't breakfast ready?' he called. 'I'm absolutely STARVING.'

Cristobel turned.

'I don't suppose HE'S washed since he came home,' she accused.

'There's talk of a drought,' Sandy replied smugly. 'I'm helping the war effort.'

Cristobel caught him by the arm as he attempted to brush past her and into the dining room.

'The war's over,' she hissed, 'and drought or no drought, if I can't have breakfast in all my dirt neither can you.'

And she twisted his arm, pinning it behind his back.

'Ow, Sis, lemme go,' he yelled. 'All right, I'll pass my face over the wash-bowl.'

Cristobel released him and he grimaced behind her back then chased her up the stairs, the dogs yapping in hot pursuit.

Lady Flora bent to pick up the little West Highland terrier as he slithered past.

'They don't change do they?' she remarked.

Laura smiled.

'I love it,' she answered warmly. She turned impulsively towards Lady Flora.

'You don't know what it means to me, coming here. I feel part of a family and it's wonderful.'

'We consider you as part of the family, Laura,' Cristobel's mother said gently, putting her hand on Laura's arm.

Laura's blue eyes darkened with emotion and as Lady Flora stooped to put the little dog back onto the floor she turned and fled up the stairs, her heart thudding wildly. Were those words prophetic? Would she one day really be part of this family? Cristobel would soon be leaving to make her own life with Lindsay Fraser, creating with him another family, her own family. Dare she hope that she might, in some small way, replace this precious only daughter? And, as this thought surfaced and embedded itself in her mind, so did Alasdair's face.

2

Preparations

The following day dawned with a perfect blue sky hanging low over the towering, mist-capped mountains. Laura woke in her turret room next to Cristobel's and lay gazing out of the oblong window as a lone pink-tipped cloud (like a piece of fluffy swansdown) sailed into view and floated slowly across the morning haze.

Slipping out of bed she walked over and knelt on the cushioned window seat looking down at the wide terrace with the flight of steps leading to the lawns and the banks of multi-coloured flowers crowding the borders.

She breathed in deeply: the early morning air was fresh and cool and fragrant with the scent of heather mingled with a pot-pourri of roses and lavender which drifted upwards on the gentle breeze. She knew that beyond the banks of trees at the bottom of the garden a mountain stream would be rippling and rushing, clear as crystal, over the smooth pebbles. As she imagined its music so her heart sang in tune.

Leaning her elbows on the wide sill Laura looked sideways at the curtains of Cristobel's room which were billowing gently through the next-door window. She wondered whether her friend was awake, but nothing stirred.

How can Cristobel sleep on today of all days, she mused. She knew that if it were she who was to celebrate her engagement this evening she would have been up with the lark, unwilling to let one precious minute of this special day be wasted in sleep.

When Cristobel had written in great excitement from her Swiss finishing school to tell Laura of her forthcoming engagement, she had been delighted for her, but not entirely surprised. The Frasers had an estate a few miles away from the Hamiltons and the two families, like so many of the surrounding families, had practically been brought up together. Lindsay had been the special friend of Ninian, the Hamilton's second son, since childhood and that friendship had continued when they joined the same regiment. At Easter, when Laura had received the news, the engagement was still a secret and should not have been officially announced until August: but the regiment had been ordered to Germany, so the date had been advanced to June.

'Why all the rush?' Laura had enquired two days before when she met Cristobel at the station on her friend's arrival from Switzerland. 'Couldn't you have waited for Lindsay's next leave?'

'Goodness knows when that will be,' Cristobel had exclaimed. 'And when it does come, I want to get MARRIED not ENGAGED.'

Laura had looked at her and understood. Had it been she and Alasdair, she would have felt the same; but apart from telling her she had freckles on her nose, Alasdair had scarcely looked at her.

As this thought struck her, so did a sudden sadness.

Ever since her first visit to Ardnakil, when she was thirteen, she had worshipped Alasdair. At that time he was at Oxford and didn't appear to be aware of her existence. Their one dance three years ago had been the nearest they had ever come to intimacy and yet, as that schoolgirl infatuation didn't abate but gradually turned into something deeper, Laura had this strange feeling that perhaps, one day, he would look up and realise that she was there.

Propping her chin in her palm her eyes wandered down along to the line of mullioned windows behind one of which Alasdair was sleeping.

She had hoped to see him last evening but he had been delayed in Edinburgh on business and arrived late, so that when Lady Flora had said that they must both be tired after their night in the train, she had felt obliged to follow a yawning Cristobel up to bed.

But she would see him today, at breakfast, in a very short time. She reached for her watch and squinted at it: just gone seven, perhaps she could start getting ready. Breakfast at Ardnakil was a formal affair, at eight thirty sharp, nine o'clock on Sundays. Everyone was expected to be up and dressed and on parade for it, no matter how late a night they had had. Robert Hamilton was an indulgent father but one of the old school and a stickler for etiquette and discipline. Sometimes Laura wondered how he and Lady Flora had ever married, they were such opposites.

The story of their breathtaking romance was a legend in the area. Robert, a confirmed bachelor firmly wedded to the estate had, at forty-seven, suddenly fallen madly in love with the beautiful twenty-year-old Lady Flora and, after a whirlwind romance and a magnificent wedding, brought her back to be mistress of Ardnakil. Everyone had been left gasping: and yet it had worked. Theirs had, in fact, been the happiest of marriages. Robert adored his beautiful, vague, artistic wife and with Graeme's arrival just one year after their wedding, he had become a strict, but doting father. Ninian and Alasdair had followed at annual intervals but when Cristobel had appeared five years later something changed in the fifty-five-year-old father and he had become her devoted slave. Alexander's arrival when Robert was almost fifty-nine had surprised everybody. Sandy, as the red-faced screaming baby had been called right from the start, was completely different from his brothers, completely different from everyone in the family, in fact. Had it not been for his fiery red hair and hazel-green eyes, so like Robert and Alasdair's, one might have wondered whether he had not been switched at birth.

Suddenly, the stillness of the morning was shattered, as from far below came the sound of shouting. The kitchen window was flung open and Sandy's high-pitched laugh, followed by shrieks and dire threats from cook rent the air. Sandy darted round the corner of the house, a plate of ice-cream in one hand and a large piece of cake in the other. He looked back over his shoulder and blew kisses to the invisible but voluble cook, and Laura smiled to herself imagining cook's angry face. She looked like Mrs Noah with her stiff black hair plastered on her head, bright red cheeks, teeth like tomb-stones and a moustache.

'Master Sandy,' Laura heard her shriek, 'I'll no' have ye comin' into ma kitchen and helping yerself. Ice-cream's no good fer a body at this hour o' day.'

Sandy laughed and, still blowing kisses, settled down on the terrace with his spoils.

'It's all right cookie,' he shouted back, 'I've got a cast-iron stomach.'

'Och, ye'll be the death o' me,' Laura heard cook exclaim as she slammed down the kitchen window.

But already her tone had softened and Laura smiled. No-one could resist Sandy for long. She looked at him as he lounged back on one of the wicker chairs, his feet stuck out in front of him on the table, spooning great heaps of chocolate ice-cream and cake into his mouth at the same time. As she watched, the drawing-room door leading on to the terrace opened and Laura's heart jumped and fluttered like a frightened caged bird. Alasdair walked through it and, picking up Sandy by the scruff of his neck jerked him to his feet, sending the plate crashing to the ground.

'There, *now* look what you've done,' Sandy howled.

'Get that mess cleared up immediately and then go and apologise to cook, you little blighter,' Alasdair barked, giving his unfortunate brother a shake. 'I heard the goings on.'

Sandy howled even louder.

'And you can shut that row,' Alasdair concluded.

Sandy escaped from his brother's grasp and ran off into the bushes.

'Sandy,' Alasdair menaced, striding after him.

Sandy dodged and ducked but it was no use, Alasdair once more had him by the scruff of the neck.

'I said shut that filthy row,' Alasdair threatened, 'you'll wake the entire household.'

And he frog-marched the squealing Sandy round the side of the house to the kitchen.

A few minutes later Alasdair reappeared and Laura quickly withdrew her head as she heard him whistling for the dogs before striding off across the lawn and into the wood.

Laura's heart was pounding loudly. Getting up from the window seat she walked across to the mirror and looked carefully at her reflection. The freckles were now gone and the image which gazed back at her was of a slight, blonde girl with deep blue eyes, fair skin and a soft upward-curving mouth. She pinched her cheeks to give them more colour and then laughed at herself.

'He probably won't even notice you,' she said ruefully. 'Don't count too much on this evening or you're likely to be very disappointed.'

But all the same she dressed carefully. There were already the sounds of stirring coming from around the house and she was surprised to hear the breakfast gong send great thundering blows into the morning stillness as the notes bounded and rebounded echoing through the empty downstairs rooms. Immediately, everything was activity as doors opened and shut, feet sounded in the long galleries and voices greeted each other as their owner's paths crossed.

Glancing once again in the mirror and patting her hair in place for the tenth time since she had finished dressing, Laura opened her bedroom door and bumped into Cristobel coming out of hers, yawning.

'Sleep well?' she enquired, as they walked together along the corridor overshadowed by the frowning portraits in their heavy gilt frames.

'Very well,' Laura answered. 'But I woke early, it was such a gorgeous morning. I wonder you didn't wake too. Did you hear that fearful row going on between Alasdair and Sandy?'

'Didn't hear a thing,' Cristobel replied, yawning again. 'But that's nothing new. Everyone's always having a row with Sandy. He's obnoxious and he seems to get worse as he gets older.'

'He's only fifteen,' Laura reproved.

'Yes, but –' Cristobel interrupted, then quickly changed the subject. 'So Alasdair arrived did he?'

Laura's heart jumped at the mention of his name.

'Yes, I saw him going off with the dogs about an hour ago.'

'There's only Ninian to come, then, for the family to be complete,' Cristobel grinned.

'AND Lindsay,' Laura laughed as they swung down the last flight of stairs and into the hall.

'He's not family YET,' Cristobel smiled dreamily.

Then she flung her arms wide and danced around the vast echoing domed hall, her head thrown back, her eyes shining.

'Oh, I'm so *happy*,' she sang, 'so *happy*.'

Sandy, coming in through the front door at that moment, stood stock still and looked at his sister in amazement.

'You gone loopy?' he remarked.

29

Cristobel caught him round the waist and swung him round with her.

'No,' she sighed. 'Just wonderfully, delightfully, deliriously happy.'

Sandy escaped from her grasp.

'Well I'm hungry,' he announced, striding across to the dining room. 'You can have your epileptic fit later.'

Laura smiled wistfully as she watched the two of them, a tinge of envy in her eyes. It was so long since she had known what it was to have a real family: even before her mother's death she had been very much an only child, Mary ten years her senior and Philippa twelve. For a moment she almost resented her friend. Cristobel had everything . . . and now she had Lindsay.

'Come ON, Laura,' Cristobel cried over her shoulder. 'Breakfast's ready!'

Laura smiled, all resentment suddenly wiped away. How could anyone not love the carefree, generous, happy-go-lucky Cristobel? After all, it was because of Cristobel that she had been practically adopted into this warm, loving, warring clan. And she ran lightly across the hall to join her friend.

Lady Flora looked up from her place at the end of the long table as they went in and smiled vaguely, stirring her tea thoughtfully as she sorted through her pile of letters.

Graeme was hidden behind a newspaper and Robert was at the sideboard, helping himself to smoked haddock. He looked round, his bushy eyebrows bristling, and his moustache quivered with pleasure when he saw Cristobel.

'Come along girls,' he said jovially. 'Big day ahead. You know what they say, "breakfast like a king." You're going to need all your strength.'

He stopped and peered at them fiercely.

'You're not on any of these slimming things are you?'

Cristobel rushed across and kissed him.

'Of course, Father,' she teased. 'We only ever touch black coffee and grapefruit in the morning.'

'I'll have your share then,' Sandy remarked, already back at the sideboard for a second helping.

Robert's face had dropped.

'No darling,' Cristobel laughed gaily. 'Just teasing you. We're both ravenous, aren't we, Laura. Here Sandy, move over, leave something for the rest of us.'

'The rest of us have almost finished.'

The newspaper rustled as Graeme's voice came out from behind it.

'Yes, but the rest of us are not having a ball in their honour this evening,' Cristobel rejoined, putting her heaped plate down on the table.

'Touché,' said Graeme, without looking up.

'Children, children,' said Lady Flora absently, 'why must you always bicker? Sandy dear, don't gulp,' she ended mildly.

Laura looked from one to the other. She knew that they were all loving every minute of the backchat, that it was all part of the family closeness which bound them together. She glanced surreptitiously around the table. Alasdair's place was empty. His napkin in its silver ring lay untouched beside the plate, and a sudden hollow feeling of disappointment swept over her as she sat down beside Cristobel and dug her spoon into the grapefruit.

For a few minutes no-one spoke. The only sound was the rustle of pages turning and the sharp slit as Lady Flora's paper-knife bit into the envelopes.

'There's an invitation here from the McFaddens, they are having a ball for Catriona on the 24th July.' She looked enquiringly at Laura and Cristobel. 'Would you like to go?'

'*Can* I, now I'm a staid betrothed woman?' Cristobel mocked.

'Of course, darling,' Lady Flora replied vaguely. 'Maybe Lindsay will be able to come for the weekend?'

'MOTHER,' Cristobel groaned. 'Lindsay will be in GERMANY.'

Lady Flora looked up absently as if she was surprised to find them all sitting there.

'Come back to earth,' Cristobel chided patiently. 'Lindsay's regiment is going to Germany next week. Remember? Ninian's going too, that's why we're having the ball tonight instead of in August.'

'If you say so, dear,' her mother replied, going back to her letters. 'Never mind, Graeme can take you and Alasdair can come up from Edinburgh for the weekend and escort Laura.'

Laura choked on her toast.

'Oh Lord,' Graeme groaned, putting down *The Scotsman.* 'I thought now we'd palmed her off on Lindsay we'd all be relieved of the burden of carting little sister around.'

'PIG!' Cristobel spat across the table, her grey eyes dancing with laughter.

'Children, please,' Lady Flora chilled. She glanced down at the watch hanging from her neck.

'Oh dear, I really must go and see cook about lunch, and Malcolm is sure to already be in the kitchen fussing about flowers and vegetables.'

She gathered her pile of letters together and got up from the table.

'Such a busy day,' she said dreamily. 'We'll talk about the McFadden ball later. By the way, who's here for lunch?'

Her voice was drowned by a commotion in the hall. It sounded as if a male voice choir accompanied by a howling pack of beagles had burst in, as to bellows of 'down boy, down' the dining room door was flung open and Uncle Hamish stormed in.

'No-one,' he roared.

Uncle Hamish was a caricature of his elder brother. Almost as tall as Robert who, at six feet five towered over his already tall sons, he was twice as broad, weighing in at at least twenty stones. Above his moustache, his nose had been broken countless times during official and unofficial boxing bouts at school and had ended by spreading over his face in every direction, giving him a slightly frog-like look of permanent surprise. He now stood like an inverted pear, his vast form almost entirely blocking the dining room doorway. He wore an ancient pair of greenish tweed plus fours and enormous brown brogues.

'Down Archie, down,' he bellowed to his black and white spaniel who was leaping and howling, turning somersaults round and round his master. Then, producing a large red spotted handkerchief, he proceeded to blow his nose with a series of explosive honks.

'Mornin' Flora,' he nodded, stuffing it back in his voluminous pocket. 'I've come to invite you all to lunch.'

Uncle Hamish was a bachelor who lived in a house at the other end of the estate. He was in charge of the local fire brigade and when on duty carried a large axe and wore a brass helmet which made him look like Boadicea. The brigade was purely decorative and rarely called out, although they rehearsed with great pomp every other Thursday evening. But if the worst ever came to the worst and their bell did ring, by the time he and his brigade had climbed into their antiquated equipment they invariably arrived after the house had burned down.

He now stood glowering fiercely at them.

'Well?' he bellowed.

Cristobel rushed from the table and hugged him round his gigantic waist.

'*Lovely*, Uncle Hamish,' she cried delightedly.

He looked down at her warmly.

'Quarter to one then,' he barked. 'Don't be late.'

Graeme folded his newspaper.

'It's not one of your picnics, is it?' he enquired suspiciously.

Their uncle was addicted to picnics and, when the Hamilton children were younger Hamish had frequently burst into his old home and piled his niece and nephews and any of their friends who happened to be around into his ancient Daimler, which he'd left chugging noisily at the front door, and roared off with them to some remote spot in the Highlands. Having decanted them into a glen he would then unload kettles and blankets and kerosene cooking appliances and set up camp for the day, polluting the air with the smell of sausages which were black on the outside and raw on the inside, and handing out sandwiches the texture of a damp bath mat.

They had all loved it, but in the last few years their enthusiasm had somewhat waned.

'PICNIC?' roared Hamish, aghast, his eyes popping in horror. 'Certainly *not.*'

He glared through the window at the brilliant June sunshine.

'Not the weather,' he muttered, 'most unsuitable.'

Uncle Hamish, for some reason known only to himself, never went on picnics between April and October.

'How kind of you, Hamish dear,' Lady Flora murmured. 'One thing less for cook to worry about.'

'Not at all, not at all,' Hamish replied gruffly. 'How many, then? Jeannie will want to know?'

'Well,' his sister-in-law replied, 'I don't think I'd better come. Cook is sure to have one of her fits if I do. Robert?'

She looked enquiringly across at her husband.

'I'll stay with you, my dear,' he said gently, 'you might need some help.'

'Just the young people then.'

Flora turned to Hamish with a sweet smile and began ticking them off on her fingers.

'Laura, Cristobel, Graeme, Sandy and Alasdair . . .'

She looked up suddenly.

'Oh, where *is* Alasdair? He hasn't come down to breakfast.'

'I saw him earlier on,' Sandy remarked casually and Laura couldn't help suppressing a smile, 'going towards the wood carrying a gun. Hope he went to commit suicide.'

'He drove over to the Farquharson's,' Robert broke in, glancing at Sandy. 'I met him as I was coming in for breakfast. Said he wouldn't be here for lunch.'

'I expect he's gone to see Colin,' his wife remarked.

'To see Fiona more likely,' Graeme put in. 'Colin's just a smoke screen.'

Laura's heart began to thump against her ribs.

'Oh, do you think so?' Lady Flora replied. 'How nice.'

'So that makes how many?' Hamish glared.

'Just the four of them,' Lady Flora smiled. 'It IS kind of you Hamish.'

'Nonsense,' he growled, turning on his heel, then remembering something he glared back at them all, his hand on the door knob.

'That young fella o' yours not arrived yet?' he barked at Cristobel.

'Not yet, Nunkie darling,' she replied, pirouetting round him.

'So he won't be comin' then?'

'Afraid not.'

'Very decent sort,' he grunted. 'I like him. Knew his grandfather well, we were at school together.'

He smiled indulgently down at his niece.

'Lucky fella' he growled.

Uncle Hamish cleared his throat, obviously longing to make his exit but heavy with the weight of a duty he had to perform before doing so. He fished in his overflowing pockets then cleared his throat again.

'Thought this might come in useful for you,' he muttered, as his great fist shot out and pushed something into his niece's hand.

Cristobel cried out in delight as she snapped open the faded blue velvet box and held up a heavy gold locket. Putting down the box she slipped the clasp and caught her breath as the portrait of a beautiful young woman lay revealed on her palm, the delicate oval face surrounded with pearls intertwined with locks of dark brown hair.

'Uncle *Hamish*,' she whispered, looking up at him, her deep grey eyes misty.

He cleared his throat yet again, red with discomfort, looking as if he were trying hard not to burst a blood vessel and not really succeeding.

'Belonged to your great-grandmother,' he muttered. 'Dunno how I came to have it.'

Lady Flora had come to her daughter's side and now looked up at her brother-in-law.

'You know perfectly well how you came to have it Hamish,' she said softly. 'Your grandfather wore that locket on his watch-chain all his life, and when he died your grandmother had it made into a pendant and gave it to you for your future wife.'

Hamish was now puce in the face and positively squirming with embarrassment.

'Yes, well,' he growled, 'not much hope of that now. Cristobel might as well have it.'

His niece reached up on tiptoe and kissed his perspiring cheek.

'Are you quite sure, Hamish?' Flora asked gently, glancing up at her brother-in-law affectionately. 'You

were ALWAYS your grandmother's favourite and I
know how much that locket meant to you.'

Hamish nodded and looked desperately around, like
a caged animal, crazy to escape.

'Archie,' he roared. 'Archie, blast you, where are
you?'

There was a sudden scuffle and Archie appeared
from under the table where Sandy had been feeding
him bacon rinds.

'Now he'll be thirsty on the walk back,' Hamish
blasted, his fierce blue eyes glaring daggers at Sandy,
obvious relief flowing over him at this means of escape
from the emotional outburst. He stomped angrily over
to the table and grabbing a large jug of milk, poured
the entire contents onto the parquet floor.

'There, Boy,' he said, pointing to the opaque puddle
which was rapidly spreading in all directions.

No-one batted an eyelid. They were all accustomed to,
and seemingly oblivious of, their family's eccentricities.
Robert did exactly the same thing each evening for his
dogs with the milk and biscuits which were always
left behind a screen in the drawing room after dinner
as a night-cap. Laura never ceased to be astonished
every time she saw this extraordinary gesture which
everyone else appeared to consider perfectly normal.

Archie lapped noisily, chasing the milk as it spread
across the floor until every trace had gone. Then,
leaping and yapping, he waltzed to the door in a
grotesque ballet with his master.

'Twelve forty-five, then,' Hamish bellowed, turning
to glower at them all in the doorway.

'We'll be there,' Cristobel laughed.

Lady Flora had already drifted into the hall, murmuring about lists and vegetables and refreshments for
the band.

'Mother,' Graeme called after her, 'is Morag coming
down this evening?'

His mother turned with a startled look on her face, as if her eldest son had just announced that he intended to go and live on a raft in the middle of the North Sea for the rest of his life.

'Oh no, dear,' she said absently, collecting her thoughts with an effort. 'I don't think so. She's so frail now, the people and the noise would be too much for her.'

'Then can you lock her up somewhere,' Graeme went on. 'Otherwise she'll be roaming around the galleries like Banquo's ghost, terrifying all the guests.'

His mother opened her mouth to protest, but Graeme forestalled her.

'Or poor old Morag might get killed in the crush,' he hinted darkly, 'especially if some of the young bloods mistake her for the Phantom of Ardnakil and chase her into a turret.'

'Oh Graeme,' Lady Flora wailed, 'I do wish you wouldn't discuss our ghost in front of the servants. You know how it upsets them! Now, where was I? Oh yes, refreshments for the band.'

And she drifted off with her lists through the green baize door leading down to the kitchen.

3

'Your Turn Will Come'

'Let's go and sit in the old schoolroom,' Cristobel suggested as she and Laura left the dining room and sauntered across the hall, 'it's always full of sunshine at this time of day.'

She put her arm briefly round Laura's waist and hugged her.

'Oh, I'm so *happy*,' she whispered as they wandered towards the schoolroom wing along one of the many galleries which seemed to meander through the old house without any rhyme or reason or apparent plan at all. 'And I'm so pleased you're here to share it.'

Laura looked at her friend and smiled.

'Me too,' she murmured.

'I just wish *you* had someone,' Cristobel mused, flopping down in one of the schoolroom's sagging armchairs.

Laura walked across and looked out of the window.

'Oh, my turn will come, I suppose.'

'But I want it to be someone I know,' Cristobel went on. 'I'd hate us to lose touch Laura, we've been friends for so long.'

'We won't,' Laura replied without looking round, and in her heart she desperately hoped that it was true.

'Perhaps there's someone invited tonight who is just right for you,' Cristobel announced, swinging her slim legs over the arm of the old chair. 'Let me see now, there's the Buchanans, the Chisholms, the Scott-Campbells. No, they're none of them any good.'

'Oh Cristobel, stop it,' Laura cut in irritably.

Cristobel's wide grey eyes opened even wider.

'I'm sorry,' Laura said, turning round. 'But you can't just organise marriages like that.'

Cristobel's face relaxed and she grinned.

'No, I suppose not,' she sighed. 'Still, it would be nice if there were someone.'

Her face suddenly brightened.

'Perhaps the Erskines! Now *they've* got an eligible son, I haven't seen him for ages, but I know they're coming.'

Then she caught sight of Laura's face and she stopped.

'Don't take any notice of me,' she went on contritely. 'I just want you to share my happiness, that's all.'

She pursed her lips thoughtfully.

'And if you DID meet someone perhaps we could have a double wedding!'

Laura turned abruptly back to the window and stood looking out over the lawn and into the wood through which she had seen Alasdair disappear earlier that morning.

'Perhaps you can have a double wedding anyway,' she answered tightly.

Cristobel looked up in surprise, checking eligible bachelors off on her fingers.

'But how?' she enquired.

'From what Graeme said it seems that Alasdair is pretty involved with the Farquharson girl.'

She paused.

'He must be to have rushed off to see her without even having breakfast,' she ended bitterly.

'Oh *her*,' Cristobel said.

'Well, isn't he?' Laura insisted.

'Maybe,' Cristobel replied vaguely. 'I don't know.

She's all right I suppose, but I wasn't thinking of Alasdair. Though it would be fun if you did marry one of my brothers, then you'd be my sister.'

She looked up and smiled brightly at the idea, then shrugged her shoulders.

'But not a hope,' she ended. 'They're all so horrible.'

Laura couldn't help laughing in spite of the tight knot which had tied itself deep down inside her stomach.

'You don't mean that!'

'Oh, I do,' Cristobel said airily. 'They're all right, but not good enough for *you*.'

Cristobel stopped talking and cocked her head on one side.

'I can hear hammering,' she shrieked delightedly, swinging her legs off the side of the armchair and grabbing Laura by the hand. 'Let's go and see what's happening.'

They arrived, breathless, in the sunlit drawing room just as Lady Flora put her head around the door.

'Has anybody seen Sandy?' she enquired, stooping to pick up Laird who was whining and pawing at her feet.

'The last time I saw him he was at the end of the long gallery kicking a football against the wall in between the portraits of the Marquess of Bute and Great-Uncle Willie,' Graeme remarked matter-of-factly, still deep in his newspaper.

Lady Flora sat down abruptly on the piano stool, absently stroking her pet. She looked bewilderedly across at Laura and Cristobel who were rolling about the sofa with laughter.

'There are times,' she sighed, shaking her head sadly, 'when I simply don't understand you children.'

And with Laird still wriggling in her arms she went back to wandering through the house, reciting her lists.

41

* * *

The two girls crossed the lawns and went into the wood sauntering round the still, pewter-coloured lake shining in the morning sunlight. Laura breathed deeply and looked across at the purple-topped mountains, a feeling of pure joy surging through her. And suddenly, from somewhere deep down in the hidden recesses of her mind words long since forgotten floated into her mind, and she stopped abruptly.

Cristobel looked round at her inquisitively.

'I was just looking at the mountains,' Laura said breathlessly. 'They're so beautiful. And, strangely enough, some verses we had to learn by heart at school came into my mind.'

She sat down on the soft grass at the side of the still lake, her eyes gazing into the distance.

'"I will lift up mine eyes unto the hills, from whence cometh my help,"' she recited quietly. 'Do you remember?'

Cristobel nodded and flopped down beside her.

'Old Glory in divinity lessons,' she remarked. 'Wasn't she a sight?'

Laura smiled, her eyes still fixed on the distant mountains.

'She always reminded me of a worn-out hymn-book,' Cristobel giggled. 'She was so frightfully dowdy.'

Laura giggled too.

'Weren't her lessons ghastly?' Cristobel went on. 'Oh, how I hated them: it was all so boring and she made everything sound as if it had been doused in vinegar.'

'But those words are beautiful,' Laura murmured. 'And so appropriate this morning.'

'I suppose so,' Cristobel remarked. 'But Old Glory really put me off Christianity, didn't she you?'

'I don't know,' Laura answered reflectively, fiddling with a clover leaf.

'If that's what being a Christian is,' Cristobel announced, lying back and closing her eyes against the warm rays of the sun, 'drooping dusty old black skirts and a pork-pie hat skewered with a pearl pin, I'd rather be a heathen!'

Laura looked down at her friend reflectively.

'I don't think that anyone with Lady Flora for a mother could ever be a heathen,' she said quietly. 'To me she epitomises everything a Christian should be.'

Cristobel sat up slowly, a frown creasing her brow.

'What do you mean?' she enquired. 'Mother doesn't go around giving out texts or spouting verses from the Bible at everyone. She doesn't even expect us to go to church with her anymore.'

'No,' Laura replied. 'She allows you to be yourselves and doesn't try to force you into her way of thinking.'

'Oh, Mother lives in another world,' Cristobel said airily lying down again, a blade of grass twirling between her teeth.

'That's just it,' Laura went on. 'A world I've often thought I'd like to explore, but I've never found the way. Your mother seems to have the key.'

She sighed.

'I wish I could explain it.'

'So do I,' remarked Cristobel, closing her eyes. 'Maybe Mother has got this key you're looking for but she's certainly not Old Glory's idea of a Christian.'

There was a sudden shriek and Sandy roared out of the wood and into view followed at a more leisurely pace by Graeme. It was obvious they had been having a row.

'Wish I were an only child,' Sandy grumbled, slithering to a halt beside them.

43

'So do we,' said Graeme grimly, coming up behind. 'One who'd been strangled at birth.'

'Oh come on Sandy,' Cristobel laughed, 'cheer up. Jeannie's bound to have cooked all your favourite dishes. For some reason she likes you – though I can't think why.'

'There you go again,' Sandy wailed. 'Everybody's on at me.'

Graeme caught him roughly by the scruff of his neck, much as Alasdair had done earlier that morning.

'You snivelling little blighter,' he hissed. 'Another word out of you and I'll . . .'

But with an agonised howl Sandy had wriggled from his grasp and raced round the lake and out of sight.

Graeme looked after him and sighed.

'I can understand Sandy in a way,' Laura put in quietly, getting slowly to her feet.

'Oh, you always were his champion,' Cristobel cut in. 'Accompanying him on the piano whilst he bellowed on that ghastly trumpet.'

'It wasn't ghastly,' Laura replied. 'Actually he plays quite well and . . . I enjoy accompanying him. Perhaps later on he'll follow in my footsteps and study music full time.'

Both brother and sister looked at her in amazement.

'It's not always very amusing being the youngest,' she continued. 'You're bait for everyone.'

Graeme laughed shortly.

'Bait?' he hooted. 'Mother dotes on him.'

'That's perhaps it,' Laura answered softly. 'And you all take it out on him because of it. Maybe he wishes she didn't dote on him quite so much.'

Graeme looked at her strangely but didn't reply.

'Oh, Sandy's unique,' Cristobel grinned, brushing strands of grass from her frock as she scrambled to her feet.

Then she laughed and turned towards them, her eyes sparkling.

'I'm going to run on ahead and say hallo to Jeannie, you two can follow at your own pace.'

'I suppose there'll be no holding her today,' Graeme remarked, giving Laura one of his slow, rare smiles as he fell into step beside her.

'She does seem to find it difficult to stay in one place for long,' Laura replied, returning his smile. 'But then I suppose it's understandable.'

As the words left her mouth she suddenly thought of Alasdair and a great aching emptiness crept into her heart.

Graeme looked down at her curiously; then looked away.

'I imagine so,' he murmured quietly.

And they walked on in silence through the soft, shining green mist which hung over the clustered trees leading to Hamish's house.

4

The Curtain Raiser

Hamish lived in Findlay's Fortress, a jumble of old grey stones quite unlike anything Laura had ever seen before. It had been built a few centuries earlier by an eccentric Hamilton ancestor who had modelled it on the Norman castle which William the Conqueror, his hero, had abandoned to cross the Channel and subdue the English.

When Findlay Hamilton's wife had presented him with a fifth daughter, he had retired to his fortress in fury and exasperation and remained garrisoned there for the rest of his life, after installing twin cannons outside the front door to discourage any visits from his female relations. Since then the second son had always inherited it, though few of them had actually lived in it, until Hamish retired from the Army and took up residence.

From the outside it resembled a fortress in a fairy tale, inhabited by giants and ogres and wicked witches spinning devilish charms and brewing evil potions. Inside it was chaos. No two rooms seemed to be on the same level and endless stairs meandered up and down without seeming to have any clear idea of where they were meant to go. If countless stories told about the Fort, as it had become affectionately known, were to be believed, skeletons clanked in cupboards the minute the sun had set.

Although under Flora's gentle urging some improvements had been made, basically it hadn't changed over the centuries and was just as draughty and uncomfortable, even menacing, with the cannons now rusting, as the 1066 ruin on which it had been modelled. Getting through to the Fort on the telephone was slightly more difficult that attempting to have a direct line installed to the Dalai Lama.

Over this confusion Jeannie, Hamish's housekeeper, reigned supreme.

She looked rather like an understanding goat, with a tuft of whiskers bristling on her chin, boot-button eyes and a face like a Bath bun. As far as anyone could gather she spent her days boiling dusters and her evenings concocting lampshades out of old carrier bags, living a strange, disconnected existence inside the Fort's massive walls, totally oblivious to anything that might be happening in the world outside, with she and Hamish shrieking at each other all winter in an attempt to make themselves heard above the howling gales which rattled under every door and window.

But on that June morning when Graeme and Laura approached it, the old stones were mellowed by the shimmering light radiating from a buttermilk sky, clean washed and transparently blue. The windows winked welcomingly in the sun's flashing rays and a gentle cooing of doves drifted on the still air. Graeme pushed open the immense studded door and they entered the lofty dark hall. The floor sloped precariously, giving the impression that the furniture was crippled and about to collapse. It was crammed with stags' heads, trophies of all kinds, bits of armour, a selection of assegais and blow pipes, dusty family portraits and faded prints of faithful spaniels panting through the rye with glassy-eyed hares dangling from their jaws.

From Hamish's study came the crackle of his prewar wireless set, tuned to full blast, which had just finished wheezing out its lunchtime entertainment of massacres, bombs, riots, tribal wars and financial disasters. As Laura and Graeme entered the study, a chirpy voice was announcing that tomorrow morning the temperature would be minus ten in Stornaway and the rest of the country blanketed in thick fog by noon. Laura vaguely wondered whether he wasn't listening to the weather forecast for Siberia by mistake.

Like Jeannie, Hamish was impervious to anything happening outside his own four walls. Ensconced in a sagging leather armchair, he was drinking whisky and puffing away at his pipe, which was making noises like a geyser about to explode. He was addicted to a strong, particularly pungent brand of tobacco and liked to blow his smoke where he pleased without consulting anyone, which was probably why he considered women, who usually objected to this unsavoury habit, as a dratted nuisance.

The study looked like the headquarters of the War Graves Commission with turbaned, battle-scarred heroes standing rigidly to attention scowling down from every available space on the walls. It was so cluttered that any furniture it might once have boasted had disappeared from view. Hamish rose from amidst the debris, a broad smile on his face, his extraordinary nose and sandy-coloured moustache twitching in unison as he greeted them. Laura noticed that he had discarded his ancient tweed jacket for an even more decrepid, monstrously shapeless woollen cardigan of vast proportions, the corners of which drooped almost to his knees.

'Down, Archie, down,' he roared, the golden liquid sloshing about in his glass and spilling on to the faded carpet as the dog yapped excitedly, leaping frantically about in an attempt to catch one of the corners of the cardigan and drag it even further down.

'Whisky?' he enquired, holding up the decanter in one hand whilst fighting Archie off with the other.

They both declined and Uncle Hamish's haycock of a moustache drooped in disappointment.

'A glass of sherry, perhaps?' he wheedled, looking appealingly at Laura.

'No thank you,' she smiled.

'We're saving ourselves for this evening,' Graeme put in.

Hamish attempted to smile back with the result that his expression became even more ferocious.

Nodding sadly, he balanced the decanter on a toppling pile of newspapers and downed the rest of his glass in one gulp.

'Well then, if you're ready,' he said, 'we may as well go to the table.'

He fished in his waistcoat pocket and pulled out a large gold hunting watch.

'Jeannie's late sounding the gong,' he said irritably.

'That's Cristobel's fault,' Graeme smiled. 'She went on ahead to receive her congratulations.'

'Oh I see,' he grunted. 'Then I'd better sound it myself.'

And so saying, he ambled across the hall and struck three thunderous death blows at an ancient Burmese gong hanging on the wall, sending Archie into howls of anguish as he pranced and leapt, slithering around the floor.

Laura didn't really see the point of sounding the gong since they were all there. As the echoing booms disappeared trembling into the distance, Sandy appeared seemingly from nowhere, followed by the clatter of Cristobel's footsteps on the back stairs; and with Uncle Hamish leading the way they all trooped across the hall and into the dining room.

The dining room was dark and smelled of mutton. Laura doubted whether Jeannie, who had served as cook-housekeeper to Hamish for as long as anyone could remember and was now almost as ancient as her employer, ever opened a window or even aired the room. The immensely long table, at the head of which Hamish usually sat in solitary state, was overshadowed by an enormous sideboard resembling a Burmese temple. It groaned with silver salvers, decanters and an assortment of bottles all jostling for place. The walls were covered with what must once have been dark red brocade, but time, damp and cigar smoke had weathered them to a dirty reddish brown.

Uncle Hamish enjoyed his food and ate solemnly and reverently, not wasting time in small talk, leaving the young people to make conversation amongst themselves and totally ignoring Sandy's appalling table manners, which he always adopted in the hope of provoking one of his uncle's choleric outbursts.

At one point during the meal a flock of geese nosed their way through one of the long low windows which Graeme had surreptitiously opened before they sat down, and proceeded to flap their way to the floor, honking madly, before lining up in formation and waddling solemnly round the table to the accompaniment of shoos from Cristobel and frantic napkin waving from Sandy, who was obviously hugely enjoying the parade. Hamish didn't appear to notice anything amiss until the weird procession arrived back at its point of departure when he looked up from his beef and nodding towards the window said to Graeme in a tone which suggested that this was the most normal occurrence during a perfectly humdrum meal:

'Let 'em out, will you, there's a good fellow.'

Graeme got up, thrust up the window sash and with a final flapping and squawking they disappeared by the way they had arrived. As they left Laura felt that she wouldn't have been in the least surprised had Uncle Hamish suddenly got up and stood on his head in the middle of the table.

But the unusual interlude must have triggered something in Hamish's brain. He suddenly looked up and glared at Cristobel.

'D'you know which band your mother's engaged for this evening?' he growled, chomping on his roast beef.

''Fraid not,' Cristobel replied.

'Not one of those Sassenach groups I hope?' he snorted.

They all looked at him in astonishment.

'Uncle Hamish,' Cristobel spluttered in surprise. I didn't know you felt like that about the English.'

'I don't,' he muttered. 'Damned nice chaps some of 'em, but don't care for their music, that's all. Had one of their new-fangled bands at the Farquharson girl's coming out ball last month. Terrible show, terrible.'

Even Sandy stopped eating and stared at him.

'Dunno what came over them,' Hamish mumbled on, 'though old Farquharson always was a queer sort of fella. We were at school together.'

Uncle Hamish appeared to have been at school with everybody's grandfather and to have somehow missed out on the intervening generation. And his criteria for their worth had obviously been assessed at that time and not revised since.

'Must've passed his odd ideas on to his son,' he muttered. 'All that heathen dancing.'

Hamish glared round the table and threw a lump of gristle to Archie.

'Wouldn't be surprised if there wasn't something between Alasdair and Fiona Farquharson,' he spluttered. 'Never left her side all evening. Jiggin' around with her in a most improper manner.'

Laura looked down at her plate desperately hoping that no-one would notice the slow blush which she could feel gradually creeping up from her neck to suffuse her face. She suddenly felt hollow and scraped out, as if she had just come round after a major abdominal operation

51

and, looking up, it seemed to her that the sunshine had vanished and the day had turned dark and overcast.

'So it was true what you said this morning about Alasdair and Fiona?' Cristobel said incredulously, turning to Graeme.

'Looks like it,' he replied.

Hamish picked up his napkin and wiped his moustache furiously.

'Only hope we have the old dances this evening,' he trumpeted, 'not those modern things. Never saw anything like it. Women hopping one way waving things, men hopping the other way, stamping.'

Sandy began twirling his napkin wildly round his head, totally ignoring the staccato signs across the table from Graeme telling him to behave himself. But his antics were mercifully brought to a halt by the arrival of a wobbly pink blancmange on a magenta plate. As it was ceremoniously placed before Hamish he bent his head and glared down at the pudding, then poked at it with a spoon.

'Dunno what this is,' he grunted. 'Jeannie produces the most extraordinary puds these days.'

He sniffed disgustedly.

'All the fault of that pig!'

Four pairs of eyes swivelled towards him in astonishment.

'The *pig*?' Cristobel repeated. 'What *do* you mean?'

Hamish snorted.

'Jeannie's got a pig. Her nephew, dratted fellow, gave it to her. A throw-out from his last litter.'

He paused and added menacingly.

'The sickly one . . .'

He glared ferociously round the table, as if his guests were responsible for the pig's arrival. Then snorted again.

'Rickety looking thing. Keeps it in a basket by the kitchen fire. Most unhealthy.'

'But what has that got to do with the pud?' Cristobel laughed.

Hamish looked at her sadly, his vast moustache drooping.

'Mind's no longer on her cooking,' he answered mournfully. 'Spends her time singing the wretched thing to sleep.'

An explosion of laughter from the guests rocked the table. Hamish stared at them uncomprehendingly.

'Can't think what you all find so amusing,' he growled. 'It's most offputting to hear Jeannie mooing "The Eriskay Lovelit" every time the wind blows the back stairs door open.'

He gazed unhappily at the sagging blancmange.

'Used to enjoy her puds,' he sighed, then held up a large spoon enquiringly. 'Anybody want any?'

Nobody did. Not even Sandy.

'In that case, I'll ring for cheese,' Hamish went on, picking up the small Hindu cowbell on the table in front of him and agitating it furiously.

The meal over, Uncle Hamish retired to his study and Laura and Cristobel wandered off into the garden. Flora always called it the 'Shakespeare Garden', probably because it looked as if nothing had been done to it since the time of the bard.

'Oh bliss,' Cristobel sighed, sinking down onto an old stone bench. 'Perhaps when we get back home Lindsay will have arrived.'

'Don't you know what time to expect him?' Laura enquired.

'Around tea-time I think,' Cristobel replied dreamily. 'He's coming with Ninian.'

She stretched up her arms ecstatically and as Laura sat down beside her, once again that awful feeling of envy crept over her.

'I always thought Lindsay was a girl's name,' she went on, in an attempt to fight it off.

'It is,' Cristobel answered, her eyes closed, 'his first name is Ewen, Lindsay is his mother's maiden name, but no-one has ever called him Ewen. Probably because Lady Fraser is an only child and Lindsay, being the second son, will inherit Grandfather Lindsay's estate one day.

'Does that mean he'll leave the Army?' Laura asked.

'I suppose so,' Cristobel yawned. 'And we'll go and live in the beautiful Highlands right up at the farthest edge almost toppling into the sea and have lots and lots of children and live happily ever after.'

She laughed delightedly and looked across at Laura. 'Isn't life *wonderful*,' she breathed.

Laura smiled but didn't reply.

'Let's go home,' Cristobel cried, jumping up and dragging Laura to her feet.

'Already?' Laura enquired. It's only a quarter to three.'

'Never mind,' Cristobel grinned. 'I just can't stay still, I'm so excited.'

'So I've noticed,' Laura grinned, following her across the lawn at a more leisurely pace.

When they entered the hall Uncle Hamish was in the corridor leading to the gun room, enthusiastically practising golf shots into a large net strung across the entrance to the butler's pantry. His niece rushed perilously into his line of fire and flung herself at him, causing the ball to catapult into the glass eye of a stag's head staring from the opposite wall.

'Darling Uncle,' she cried, 'it was a lovely, lovely lunch and you will excuse us, won't you, if we're awfully rude and rush off, but Laura and I must look our best for this evening and will take us hours and hours.'

'Of course, of course,' he muttered. 'I'll drive you back.'

'No,' Cristobel insisted, 'we'll walk.'

54

'Wouldn't dream of it,' he snorted. 'I insist. Where's the other two?'

'Don't worry about us,' Graeme's voice came out of the depths of an armchair in the drawing room. 'We'll walk back later. I want to keep Sandy out of the way as long as possible, mother's got enough to do without having to wonder what he's up to. And, with any luck, I'll exhaust him so that he's in a coma by this evening.'

'Oh,' said Hamish, looking startled again. 'Where *is* Sandy?'

'Best not to ask,' Graeme went on.

Hamish grunted and handed his golf club to Jeannie, who appeared to have been keeping score, then walking over to a heavy brass hat-stand to which, caps, deerstalkers, bowlers and straw boaters clung for dear life, he carefully selected a brightly coloured tam-o'-shanter perched, like a triumphant peony, in their midst. Anchoring it firmly on his head, he ushered them through the front door.

He settled the two girls comfortably in the back of his car insisting, despite their protests and the brilliant sunshine, on smothering them in a mohair rug. Then, having carefully tucked it round them as if they were made of Bohemian glass, he eased his vast frame into the driving seat and started the engine with an explosion which would have shattered the Forth Bridge.

Laura and Cristobel stifled their giggles as, with a series of erratic jerks the car began to chug away from the front door, only to immediately collapse with a terrible bang in the middle of the drive.

Hamish glared angrily through the windscreen, his moustache twitching. Then, grabbing a shooting stick from under his seat, he stamped round to the front of the car and jerked open the bonnet. After peering intently at the engine for a few seconds, he gave it

55

a tremendous blow with the shooting stick, slammed
down the bonnet and returned to his seat. With an
appalling smell and clouds of dust the car roared into
action.

His passengers, almost convulsed by now, waved
to Sandy who, hearing the series of explosions had
thrust his tousled head through the kitchen window.
He had doubtless been commiserating with the pig,
and was now galloping after the car yelling frantically
for them to stop. Remembering Graeme's instructions,
Uncle Hamish took not the slightest notice but swept
majestically on to deposit Laura and Cristobel, with
a loud screeching of brakes, at the front door of
Ardnakil.

'Won't come in,' he grunted as he opened the car
door for them. 'Give my regards to young Fraser.'

And with a great slamming of doors and another violent explosion the car roared off back down the drive.

The two girls walked slowly into the silent hall.

'Wonder where everybody is?' Cristobel said, looking
round.

'You mean you wonder where Lindsay is,' Laura
teased.

Cristobel grinned at her.

Sounds of hammering and of furniture being pushed
and heaved around came from the ballroom at the far
end of the house, and from downstairs cook's wails and
the scuffle of feet could be heard as everyone raced
frantically around.

'Don't dare go down to the kitchen,' Cristobel grimaced. 'Everything is *always* perfect on the day, but
beforehand cook is impossible and only Mother dares
go near her. We'd be blasted out if we so much as set
our feet on the back stairs.'

Laura sat down on a dark oak settle as Laird
wandered out of his turret hidey-hole at the side of
the front door and sniffed around her feet. She bent

and picked him up but he growled and snapped and she hastily put him down on the floor again.

'Another one whom only Mother can handle,' Cristobel remarked. 'Bad-tempered little beast,' she hissed as he scuttled back to his warren in amongst the golf clubs and tennis racquets which were stored there. 'Oh, I'm so restless,' she continued. 'Everything seems strange today. Have you noticed how even the dogs don't dare to move?'

They both looked up the wide curving staircase to where the four dogs lay snoozing, their heads on their paws, on the half-landing.

'Well, for goodness sake don't disturb them,' Laura said as she got up.

When they entered the drawing room Lady Flora was kneeling in front of the huge fireplace carefully arranging an enormous sheaf of flowers in its wide black aperture. She looked up with that vague air of enquiry she always had, as if she wasn't quite sure where the two of them had come from, or why they were there at all.

'Any news of Lindsay?' Cristobel asked.

At the mention of his name something obviously clicked in Lady Flora's brain.

'Yes darling, he arrived about half-an-hour ago, but as you weren't here, he's gone to Killistrathan to see his parents and will be back later.'

Cristobel sank into a chair with a groan.

'Oh no,' she wailed.

'But Ninian's here,' her mother went on brightly, as if that piece of information would immediately dispel any disappointment her daughter might have felt at just missing the fiancé she had not seen for almost three months. 'I think he's in the old schoolroom. Do go over and see him, I've ordered tea to be sent up there, everywhere else seems to be in a state of siege.'

Laura looked around her. The drawing room did

not appear to be in a state of siege at all. In fact, she thought that she had never seen the gracious room looking more lovely, its long windows open to the sunlight, the turrets at either corner with their cushioned window seats where tea was so often served, bathed in the golden afternoon haze.

Leaving Lady Flora to her floral arrangements, the two girls wandered over to the schoolroom to await tea. In spite of all the titbits she had heard during the day about Alasdair and Fiona Farquharson, Laura's heart, was jumping like a frightened sparrow round and round in her throat, at the thought that she might soon see him again.

But Alasdair did not appear for tea.

As she sat toying with a scone, Laura's spirits slowly sank, leaving her limp as a wet rag and longing only to get away from all the signs of joyful expectancy which hovered over the whole house. As soon as she could she escaped, saying that she wanted to rest before the evening.

'I'd better come too,' Cristobel grumbled. 'Perhaps if I try to sleep the time will go quicker. You will call me the *minute* Lindsay arrives Mother, won't you? Promise?'

'Of course, my darling,' her mother soothed.

'I'll be in my room, so don't let anyone pretend they can't find me,' she threatened as they went out of the door.

'Really try to sleep,' Laura said as they parted outside her bedroom. 'You need to look your best for this evening.'

'I'll try,' Cristobel smiled, 'but I don't think I'll be able to. I'll probably curl up on the window seat and rush down the stairs every time I hear a car in the drive – just in case it's Lindsay.'

'Would you like me to come and sit with you?' Laura ventured.

Cristobel smiled and pushed open her door.

'No point in both of us feeling like wrecks this evening, is there? I'll probably look so ghastly he'll put the ring on *your* finger instead.'

And with a gay laugh she skipped into her bedroom and closed the door.

5

The Ball

To her surprise Laura did fall asleep and woke to see a shimmer of midges dancing across her open window in the early evening haze. Movements from the room next door indicated that Cristobel either had not slept or was already up and preparing for the evening's festivities.

Slipping off the bed she went through to see if the bathroom they shared was empty. A thin film of warm condensation over everything told her that Cristobel had already had her bath so, bending down, she turned on the taps and stood watching as the water gushed through, her thoughts once again on Alasdair.

'You're being utterly ridiculous,' she told herself as she slid into the foamy depths. 'It's almost three years since you saw him, you were only sixteen then – you're infatuated with an idea.' But as she swirled her toes round and round in the perfumed bubbles, she knew that it wasn't true. Alasdair's face had never stopped haunting her.

'Laura,' Cristobel called from the adjoining room. 'Are you nearly ready?'

'Won't be long,' she called back, rising from the foam and stretching for a fluffy pink towel hanging on the wooden stand beside the huge, old-fashioned bath. 'Has Lindsay arrived?'

'No,' Cristobel groaned. 'What *can* he be doing?'

She paused and her head appeared round the bathroom door.

'You don't think he could have changed his mind, do you?'

Laura laughed.

'Idiot,' she smiled, discarding the towel and sliding her feet into her slippers. 'Not a hope. He'll be here any minute now.'

Walking back into her room, from one of the turrets she heard a clock chime the hour.

'Gracious,' Laura exclaimed, 'I'd better hurry.'

The soft folds of the blue silk dress slid undulated over her slim young body and, smoothing it into place across her hips, a glorious voluptuous feeling swept through her. She turned this way and that in front of the long mirror, revelling in the way the dress glided round her, flowing over her ankles in ripples like clear sparkling blue water.

As she sat down at the dressing table to put on her earrings, the deep apricot light of the early summer evening streamed in through the window and touched her long blond hair with gold. There was a knock on the door and, with a rustle of tulle, Cristobel entered. She stood, framed in the doorway, a thousand diamonds shining in her eyes; Laura caught her breath.

'Oh, Cristobel,' she breathed. 'You look *lovely*.'

Cristobel walked slowly into the room, the flowing folds of white tulle whispering round her, emphasising her tiny waist, her shoulders rising creamy and rounded from the froth of tulle which rested softly across her breast.

'So do you,' she smiled.

'What a gorgeous dress,' Laura went on, walking round her admiringly. 'Wherever did you get it?'

'In Paris,' Cristobel answered, sitting down gingerly on the side of Laura's bed, the dress flowing out around her and almost entirely covering the narrow surface. 'When Mother came over to Switzerland to spend Easter with me we rushed to Paris for a few days and chose it then. They were marvellous, made it in record time, and Mother brought it back with her.'

She stood up, and pirouetted around, her head thrown back, her dark hair caught up in a soft fold at the back with a beautiful old pearl comb.

'I was supposed to wear the pearls Father gave me for my eighteenth birthday,' she went on, 'but I decided to wear the locket instead.'

She opened it and looked once again at the tiny exquisite portrait inside.

'Isn't it lovely?' she breathed. 'You can borrow my pearls if you want.'

There was another knock on the door and Lady Flora entered, dressed in a long pale mauve dress. The colour suited her delicate beauty and highlighted her silver grey eyes and soft dark hair. At her throat she wore a fine web of gold filigree sprinkled with diamonds like a cluster of dewdrops sparkling in the rain. Laura was struck, not for the first time, by the remarkable likeness between mother and daughter.

'I thought I'd find you here,' she said, coming in. 'Lindsay has just arrived. He's waiting for you in the library.'

'Lindsay!'

Cristobel's hand flew to her mouth and the diamonds shining in her beautiful grey eyes suddenly leapt and flashed.

'Oh *Mother*,' she breathed, and picking up her dress in both hands, she ran from the room without another word.

'Be careful on the stairs,' Lady Flora called after her. 'Mind you don't trip.'

But Cristobel had already turned the corner of the long corridor and was oblivious of anything but the fact that Lindsay was downstairs waiting for her.

Lady Flora smiled across at Laura.

'How lovely you look, my dear,' she said sitting down

on the bed her daughter had just vacated. 'The guests will be arriving any minute, but we'd better give the two of them a little time together before they go on parade.'

Her grey eyes became dark and dreamy.

'I well remember the evening of my engagement ball,' she mused.

Laura sat down on her dressing table stool, not knowing what to say, only one thought uppermost in her mind.

'Has everyone arrived?' she ventured.

'Everyone?' Lady Flora came unwillingly back to earth.

'Well . . . all the family. Graeme and Sandy . . . and . . . and Alasdair,' she stumbled, her eyes glued to the carpet on which her small blue silk shoe was slowly describing concentric circles.

'Oh Alasdair,' Lady Flora said vaguely. 'Now you come to mention it, I don't think he has. At least I haven't seen him. Oh dear, how tiresome. I wonder what's keeping him?'

And she got up and walked towards the door.

Laura had a very good idea what, or rather who, was keeping him and she bit her lip in an attempt to hold back the tears of disappointment which had risen to the back of her eyes.

'He can't be coming with the Farquharsons,' Lady Flora mused, turning with her hand on the door knob, 'he must have time to change . . .'

She looked across at Laura.

'Do come down whenever you're ready, darling. We'll all be in the hall.'

'Thank you,' Laura replied in a strangled voice, without looking up. 'I won't be long.'

Lady Flora smiled her vague sweet smile and drifted through the door, leaving a scent of summer roses behind her.

But Laura had no intention of going down into the hall and forming part of the reception committee. At that moment she wished she had never come. All she wanted to do was run out of the house and away from them all.

From far below the sounds of the band tuning up and then beginning to play soft lilting music drifted up to her. A man's voice throatily crooned, 'They say that falling in love is wonderful', As the refrain fell in gentle waves around her, a great surge of loneliness swept over Laura, and she burst into tears.

'Oh *blast*,' she said, looking into the mirror when her weeping had subsided. 'Now I've ruined everything. My eyes are red and puffy and I'll have to put my make-up on all over again.'

And she stumbled to the bathroom.

When she finally did appear, most of the guests had arrived and the sound of voices, laughter and the swish of feet dancing across the ballroom floor rose to meet her.

Cristobel waved her hand excitedly.

'Laura!' she cried. 'Where *have* you been? You were ready when I came down.'

Laura smiled and said nothing as she walked across the hall towards her radiant friend.

'I wanted to send someone up to see what had happened to you but they're all so busy.'

Cristobel broke off and gazed up adoringly at Lindsay, standing tall and erect beside her in his kilt.

'You remember Laura, don't you?' she breathed.

'Yes of course,' he answered politely, and Laura wondered whether he really did.

'My adopted sister,' Cristobel trilled. 'We've got to find someone for her tonight.'

'Cristobel!' Laura exclaimed, feeling her cheeks turn crimson.

'Look,' Cristobel squealed, holding out her hand at

arm's length to reveal a beautiful diamond surrounded by a circlet of tiny rubies glittering on the third finger of her left hand. 'Isn't it gorgeous?'

Laura took her friend's hand in hers and bent to examine the ring.

'It's beautiful,' she breathed.

'That's why Lindsay couldn't stay this afternoon,' Cristobel confided, 'he had to rush off home and collect it.'

She held out her arm again and cocked her head on one side admiringly as the ring sparkled and flashed on her finger.

'It belonged to Lindsay's great-grandmother,' Cristobel went on, turning her hand this way and that to catch the light. 'His grandfather had it cleaned, or whatever you do, and only arrived with it yesterday evening. You haven't met Grandfather Lindsay, have you? Oh you must, he's a darling. Go into the ballroom – Graeme's there, he'll introduce you.'

She suddenly broke off . . .

'Catriona, how lovely,' she exclaimed as a tall young woman with flaming red hair picked up her long skirts and swished into the hall.

Laura moved away towards the ballroom as a car decanted more guests. The floor was already crowded with dancers and she stood in the doorway admiring the colourful scene. Ever since that first ball at Ardnakil, when she was sixteen, Laura had been fascinated by the way, unlike in London, here it was the men who outshone the women with their brightly coloured swinging kilts and velvet jackets, lace ruffles peeping at throat and wrists.

She noticed Graeme leaning over the back of a delicate Louis XV sofa listening politely to Lady Entwhistle, a fat old lady whose body flowed across both seats. At first sight she resembled a beer barrel wound around in maroon silk, the top half of which was draped in yellowing lace. A large half-submerged diamond glittered helplessly through its folds, flashing frantic SOS signals for survival every time its owner breathed. Her make-up, to put it mildly, was horrendous. After having had each eyelash tugged violently into position, she appeared to have dipped her face in flour. On her head was a glittering tiara clamped down on hair which bore a close resemblance to a scouring pad. It was the colour of Dundee marmalade and there was enough of it to stuff a cushion. As she agitated an ivory fan the tiara sent friendly signals to the diamonds which danced and sparkled on her plump fingers. Laura began to wonder just how much longer the exquisitely carved gilt legs of the sofa would be able to stand the strain before giving way under her weight.

As she watched, fascinated, Graeme looked up and saw her standing there. He hailed her across the room then, walking round to Lady Entwhistle's side, offered her his arm.

Her small satin shod feet had been dangling in mid-air and, as she tentatively felt for terra firma and slithered to the floor there was a shuddering sigh of silk and her entire body shook like a gigantic raspberry jelly.

Stretching up and grasping Graeme's proffered arm, her tiara bobbing about somewhere in the region of his waist, they began a rather lop-sided polka across the floor, her wobbly gait making her look like someone who was running for her life from an approaching tidal wave wearing her shoes on the wrong feet.

Graeme steered her towards Uncle Hamish who was standing stiffly to attention, in his thin enormous kilt, glowering at everybody. Lowering his charge on to a more substantial piece of furniture, Graeme made entreating signs to his Uncle above Lady Entwhistle's head: signs which Hamish chose to ignore. As the sofa groaned and sagged beneath her weight Lady

Entwhistle, glanced coquettishly up at Hamish and
patted the seat beside her invitingly. But Hamish,
declined her offer and stared stonily ahead, mumbling
to himself like an angry tartan volcano on the point of
erupting. He was so ill-at-ease at parties and receptions
that he either shut up like an oyster or, after an excess
of whisky, said all the wrong things, shrieking like
an ageing prima donna in a series of high-pitched
arpeggios.

Graeme escaped and hurried across the room to
Laura.

'There you are at last,' he said, offering her his arm.
'Now let me introduce you. Who don't you know?'

Looking nervously around her, Laura felt that she
didn't know anyone amid this sea of laughing faces
and, in a sudden fit of panic, decided that she didn't
want to know anyone.

She fiddled with the little blue tasselled pencil
dangling from her ball card.

'Oh forgive me,' Graeme exclaimed. 'What dances
have you left free?'

Laura had just about every dance left free!

'May I have the next waltz?' Graeme enquired.

Laura nodded, quickly pencilling in his name.

The music stopped, everyone clapped politely and
began drifting towards the chairs clustered round the
sides. As the band struck up again Graeme held out
his arms and swept her on to the floor.

Once the dance was over he guided her towards a
group of young people and made the introductions.
Then, excusing himself, he returned to his filial duties
entertaining the many elderly ladies scattered on sofas
around the room. Laura's ball card began to fill up
rapidly and when a quickstep was announced one of
the kilted young men took her hand and led her back
on to the floor. As they twirled round and round, her
head pressed lightly against his shoulder, Laura caught

sight of Alasdair, twirling in the opposite direction with Fiona Farquharson in his arms. Suddenly she felt as if the ground had been removed from under her feet, and a dreadful wave of nausea swept over her.

Looking up at her partner who gazed steadfastly over her head, she tried to tell him that she wasn't feeling well but although she opened her mouth, no words came. At that moment Alasdair wheeled in her direction, his head thrown back obviously laughing at something Fiona had just said, and their eyes met.

For a second Alasdair looked blankly at her and then a brief spark of recognition flashed into those hazel eyes in which the green and gold lights were shining brightly this evening. He inclined his head in a slight bow and then she was whirled around again out of his sight, feeling weak and helpless, like a balloon which has been pricked and deflated, leaving it shrivelled up and empty. Her feet became like lead and began to drag.

Her partner looked down at her.

'Splendid party, isn't it?' he said conventionally.

'Yes,' Laura replied faintly, 'but would you mind awfully if we sat out the rest of this dance, I feel rather weak.'

'No, not at all.' He dropped his arms and taking her elbow, guided her to a sofa.

'Would you like me to get you something to drink?' he enquired solicitously.

She nodded and he skirted the ballroom and disappeared into the adjoining room.

The music stopped. From under her lids she saw Alasdair escort Fiona back to their party, then bending to say something to her, he obviously excused himself and made his way across the ballroom in Laura's direction.

'Oh God,' she breathed, 'please, *please* don't let him come.'

But her prayer was uttered too late. Alasdair had

arrived at the same time as her partner with a glass
in his hand. Taking it from him, Alasdair handed it to
Laura and sat down beside her.

'It *is* little freckle-nose, isn't it?'

Her partner discreetly disappeared.

Tears of humiliation smarted behind her thick lashes
and she nodded blindly, her eyes on the tip of her
shoes.

Alasdair put one finger under her chin and drew it
upwards until she was looking directly at him.

'They've gone,' he announced, smiling his crooked,
quizzical smile.

He tilted his head to one side and examined her
face.

'What a transformation,' he breathed. 'Cristobel's
little schoolfriend has turned into a beautiful fairy
princess!'

Laura removed his finger from under her chin and
looked away, angry and mortified by his teasing. The
band broke into another waltz and Laura heard the
swish of a kilt as her next partner came to claim his
dance. She half rose, but Alasdair gently pulled her
back into her seat.

'Hang on a moment, Angus,' he said to her expectant
partner. Then without waiting for her to comply, he
removed her ball-card from her gloved hand and
proceeded to scribble his name against most of the
free spaces.

'Please,' Laura began.

'I want all those you have left,' he smiled.

'I've promised to save one for Sir Adam. And I
must dance with Lindsay's father and his brother
and,' she cried desperately, 'Cristobel wants me to
meet Lindsay's grandfather, and I'd like to save one
for him too.'

'Well,' Alasdair replied smoothly, 'mark me in for the
rest. All right, Angus,' he said getting up and reaching

down to help Laura to her feet. 'Sorry to have encroached on your time with this ravishing partner.'

And handing her over he crossed the ballroom and went to enfold an elderly dowager in his arms.

Laura danced woodenly and could think of nothing to say. Suddenly, there was a peal of drums, the dancers melted to the sides of the floor and, with a flourish and a whisper of tulle and violins the happy couple entered the ballroom. As the band broke into 'I'll be loving you always', Lindsay turned towards his fiancée whose head barely reached his shoulder and, gazing adoringly down at her, swept her into his arms and waltzed several times round the deserted floor. They had eyes for no-one but each other and hardly seemed to notice when other couples gradually took to the floor and joined them. The music seemed to go on and on and Laura, now being twirled by another Angus, tried to empty her mind and merely float on the soft, lilting refrain, wishing that it would never end and that when it did she could fade into oblivion. This evening which she had anticipated with such hope and excitement suddenly seemed grey and drab. She dreaded being in Alasdair's arms, being guided across the floor by him whilst he teased her, his mind obviously on Fiona Farquharson.

The music gently wound down, the dancers drifted apart and formed into groups as the ballroom's double doors were flung open and supper was announced.

Laura was to be escorted into supper by Lindsay's elder brother who now came to claim her. He would introduce her to Grandfather Lindsay, and after that she would see that her ball card was filled up before Alasdair had a chance to approach her again. Out of the corner of her eye she saw him walking towards the doors with Fiona on his arm and vowed even more fiercely to keep away from him for the rest of the evening . . .

6

Oh Sandy!

'It was a perfectly *lovely* ball,' said Lady Flora dreamily as, rather bleary-eyed, Cristobel and Laura sat down to breakfast the next morning. 'Quite reminded me of our engagement almost thirty years ago, didn't it you, Robert?'

He husband appeared from behind the Sunday paper and smiled affectionately across at her.

'And *so* wonderful to have the house full and the ballroom in use again.'

There was no post to occupy Lady Flora's attention this morning, so she had taken to musing instead.

Cristobel yawned and then hastily stopped herself as her mother looked at her in surprise.

'It *was* rather late when I went to bed last night,' she murmured apologetically.

'Of course, darling,' Lady Flora smiled, 'and I imagine you're going to have another busy day today?'

She raised her eyebrows enquiringly.

'Lindsay's collecting me soon after breakfast,' Cristobel sighed happily, 'we're having lunch with his parents. Grandfather Lindsay will be there, and then . . .'

She paused and her eyes clouded.

'What time do you have to leave?' she said dully, looking across at Ninian.

'Not late,' he replied. 'Got to be back on duty first thing in the morning.'

'The night train then?' Cristobel wailed.

'Oh earlier,' Ninian answered, looking round the corner of a newspaper. 'The eight thirty I think. It arrives in the middle of the night, but it means we'll be back in barracks on time.'

'Oh *no*,' Cristobel groaned as if all the joy had suddenly seeped out of her.

'Afraid so, little sister,' Ninian laughed. 'But cheer up, you'll soon be married, then you can come with us.'

He lowered his newspaper and looked affectionately across at her.

'Have you decided on a date?' he asked.

'Helen Fraser and I were discussing it last evening,' Lady Flora broke in. 'If Lindsay is able to get leave we thought mid-September would be a lovely time.'

'Should be possible,' Ninian mused. 'The regiment's moving off before the end of the week, that'll give us almost three months. Oh yes, I should say go ahead.'

'We've tentatively suggested the twenty-second,' Lady Flora intervened,

Graeme pushed back his chair.

'Well, I'll leave you to your nuptials,' he said, 'I'm off to play golf.'

He paused and looked across at Alasdair with a faint smile.

'Doesn't give you any ideas?' he enquired.

Alasdair looked up.

'What, golf? No, not today thank you.'

'Not golf,' Graeme insisted. 'Nuptials!'

Alasdair grinned.

'Not for the moment.'

'Oh, seeing you last night,' his brother went on, 'I rather thought it might.'

'Seeing's not always believing,' Alasdair answered enigmatically, picking up the newspaper Graeme had discarded.

Graeme walked towards the door.

'I won't be here for lunch, Mother,' he said, pausing with his hand on the knob.

'Oh dear, how sad,' Lady Flora replied vaguely. 'What about the rest of you?'

'I don't think so,' Ninian replied.

Lady Flora looked enquiringly at Alasdair.

'Oh, I'll be here,' he said, wiping his mouth with his napkin.

'How strange,' Graeme put in. 'Thought you'd be racing over to the McFaddens again.'

'Not today, old boy,' Alasdair replied, unperturbed. 'They're having a family party to celebrate Grannie Farquharson's seventy-fifth birthday.'

'And you're not considered family?' Graeme taunted.

'Not yet,' Alasdair grinned.

'Can I come and play golf?' Sandy shouted, jumping up from the table with a clatter.

'No, you *can't*,' his brother replied and firmly shut the door behind him.

'Miserable blighter,' Sandy growled flopping back into his chair. 'Might as well have some more kedgeree, then.'

'Come to church with me instead,' Lady Flora said soothingly.

Sandy looked at her as if she'd just made a lewd remark.

'No thank you Ma, not today.'

Sandy was the only one of the children to call Lady Flora Ma and get away with it.

Laura looked desperately round the table.

Graeme had gone, Cristobel would soon be off, Ninian had said he wouldn't be here for lunch, that just left herself, Sandy and Alasdair. And she panicked.

'I'd like to go to church with you if I may,' she said unexpectedly, looking across at Lady Flora who had risen in her turn.

'Laura, how nice,' she smiled.

73

Laura hastily pushed back her chair. Robert was leaving, Sandy was still munching ravenously but would soon be bounding off, and she dreaded being left alone with Alasdair who didn't seem to be in any hurry to leave the table or to have any definite plans for the morning.

'No hurry, dear,' Lady Flora said placing a hand on Laura's arm. 'The service isn't till half-past ten. Let's meet in the hall in about half-an-hour and then we can walk slowly over: it's such a lovely morning.'

She looked out of the window at the birds hopping and twittering on the clustered branches of an overhanging tree, and sighed happily.

Laura followed her hostess out of the room. She hadn't the slightest desire to go to church, but anything was better than being left closeted alone with Alasdair.

After lunch as she sat in the drawing room Laura tried to concentrate on the Sunday crossword puzzle, but somehow the solutions wouldn't come.

Lady Flora looked up from her embroidery.

'I can never fathom those things,' she remarked. 'I think they must set them just for menfolk, *they* always seem to be able to find the answers. Perhaps Alasdair could help you.'

He glanced over the edge of his paper enquiringly.

'Laura's having trouble with the crossword,' his mother explained.

Alasdair put down his paper and, crossing over to Laura's side, picked up hers. He stroked his chin thoughtfully and began studying the squares. Laura held her breath. Except for their one dance the previous evening he had never been so close to her before, and the very feel of his hands brushing hers as he held the paper sent her heart scurrying back to her throat. Then she remembered Fiona Farquharson, and she stiffened.

Alasdair looked down at her with that same crooked,

quizzical smile, causing a deep blush to creep up her cheeks.

'I do hope Cristobel's wedding won't mean that we'll lose you,' Lady Flora smiled.

Laura smiled back, confused, unable to say anything.

'Of course it doesn't,' Alasdair said, quickly pencilling in a few letters. 'She's part of the family, aren't you Laura?'

Again Laura was at a loss for words.

'Will the wedding be here?' Sandy enquired from the turret where he was sitting hunched on the window seat, watching the dark clouds form and race across the sky and waiting for the first drops of rain to fall. The glorious promise of early morning had gradually deteriorated and as she and Lady Flora had walked back from church together Laura had looked up at the trees waving menacingly above them in the drive and felt them give off an almost perceptible chill.

'Of course it'll be here,' Alasdair replied without looking up. 'Where did you expect it would be, Edinburgh Zoo?'

Lady Flora leant forward and threw a handful of pine cones from a basket in the hearth on to the merrily crackling wood fire.

'Who'd have thought yesterday that we'd be sitting round the fire this afternoon?' she said pleasantly, picking up her embroidery again.

Laura watched the cones catch light and join in the blaze, and thought how different the great fireplace looked without its magnificent spray of flowers.

'Did you say something, Sandy?' his mother queried.

'Only asked where the wedding would be,' he answered sulkily. 'And Alasdair informed me it would be at the zoo.'

Lady Flora turned her bewildered gaze on him.

'Oh no dear, it will be here: in the garden I hope.'

'Perhaps this time we can have *my* band,' Sandy muttered, swinging his long legs off the window seat and strolling over to the fire.

Alasdair looked at his brother in amazement.

'*Your* band? Heaven save us, the monster's not running a band now.'

Sandy lunged out at him with his foot but Alasdair skilfully caught it and held it in his grasp.

'Ow, lemme go, you blighter, lemme go,' Sandy yelled, hopping furiously up and down whilst his brother held him in a vice-like grip. Alasdair suddenly complied with his wishes and Sandy staggered back and ended up on the floor.

Lady Flora looked from one to the other of them in total bewilderment, then bent down, holding out her hand to her youngest son.

'Sandy, darling,' she soothed, 'what *are* you doing on the floor?'

'Ask *him*,' Sandy grumbled as he scrambled to his feet.

Alasdair laughed and leant back on the sofa, putting the pencil behind his ear.

'I want to hear about this BAND,' he teased.

'Oh, I believe it's very good,' Lady Flora said. 'Sandy took up the drums as well as the trumpet at school last year, and four of them have formed a little orchestra.'

'BAND,' Sandy corrected as Alasdair threw back his head and roared with laughter.

'To think we could all have reeled to the rhythm of the Gordonstoun goons last night,' he spluttered.

'Been better than that lousy lot from Perth,' Sandy spat out.

'Oh Sandy, they were very good,' his mother chided.

'Yes, but so are WE,' Sandy broke in, '*and* we'd have been cheaper.'

'Oh so you even expect to be PAID for the racket?' Alasdair spluttered and went off into another laughing fit. 'Mother, do tell me what else the young get up to at school these days.'

'We could have had *my* band AS WELL AS the other one,' Sandy sulked.

'But darling, there simply wasn't ROOM,' Lady Flora comforted.

Sandy turned towards the door, mortally offended by his brother's slight on his musical abilities.

'It wouldn't have taken up any more room than Lady Entwhistle,' he blurted out, standing in the doorway and letting in a howling draught.

'Perhaps not, dear,' Lady Flora replied mildly, 'but she's such a dear.' She added as an afterthought, 'Sandy do please shut the door.' Sandy did and shut himself out.

Alasdair looked down at Laura, the lights in his hazel eyes dancing with merriment.

'He's probably right,' he smiled. The tension momentarily leaving her, Laura smiled back.

'By the way,' Alasdair remarked looking across at his mother. 'What was the matter with Grace Entwhistle yesterday? She didn't seem pleased at all.'

Laura suppressed a giggle. Grace was the last name she'd have given to Lady Entwhistle.

'Oh dear,' Lady Flora sighed. 'Is she still cross? I was afraid she would be.'

Alasdair frowned. 'Cross?' he queried. 'What about?'

'Oh darling,' his mother answered, 'I'm afraid it's Sandy.'

'Not surprised,' Alasdair sniffed. 'What's he been up to now?'

'He upset her terribly at the New Year's Eve party she gave for her grandchildren.'

'Oh?' Alasdair raised his eyebrows and leant back on the sofa. 'How?'

'You know she always has these marvellous fancy dress balls for them every year,' Lady Flora went on, 'you all used to go. Well, this year she invited Sandy.'

'He's hardly old enough to go to that sort of do is he?' Alasdair asked.

'Not really,' Lady Flora went on, 'but her youngest granddaughter Rose Livesey, who's the same age as Sandy, was there. Grace felt it was hard for her to be the only one not to go, so she asked if Sandy would partner her.'

'And?' Alasdair raised his eyebrows in enquiry.

Lady Flora sighed and put down her embroidery.

'He can be terribly stubborn. Perhaps he didn't really want to go, I don't know, but when he heard it was fancy dress he insisted on going as a radish.'

'A radish!'

Alasdair threw back his head and laughed, slapping his thigh in amusement.

'A RADISH?' he went on, still laughing helplessly. 'I can't believe it.'

'It's true,' his mother said mournfully. 'I didn't take very much notice because I knew we'd never find a radish outfit at the costumiers in Perth so I just went ahead and ordered a Bonnie Prince Charlie one, which is what Grace expected. Rose was going as a Quaker Maid.'

'So how did he get it?'

'The radish suit? Oh he persuaded Janet to make it. You know how devoted she is to him.' Janet was the teenage nanny who had arrived when the children were young to help Morag and had since married Donald and now lived at the gate house. 'She conjured up this frightful outfit for him behind my back.'

Lady Flora shook her head sadly.

'I can't tell you how dreadful he looked.'

Alasdair had gone off into more peals of laughter and Laura found herself joining in. Lady Flora looked at them as though they had just been caught singing bawdy songs at a funeral.

'It wasn't funny, I can assure you. When I went up to tell him we were ready to leave, there was the Bonnie Prince Charlie outfit on the bed where it had been laid out for him: and there was this ghastly apparition.'

Lady Flora sighed again.

'He'd even got Janet to tie his feet together in an enormous white sock, because apparently radishes don't have legs. You can imagine the effect he had on everyone when we arrived. Merely getting him down the stairs was a feat in itself. And of course he ruined the evening for poor Rose. How on earth can a radish dance an eightsome reel?'

Alasdair was by now convulsed.

'Oh Mother,' he spluttered, 'I can't believe it.'

'Not only that,' his mother went on. 'Janet had made him some waving green foliage to put on his head as he'd told her he wanted to be a living radish not one in a salad. You know how tall he's become; they kept getting in everybody's way and tangled up in the chandeliers. It was quite dreadful. He jumped around all over the place like a frog: what else could he do with both feet tied together? And poor Rose ended the evening in tears. I'm very surprised that Grace accepted our invitation for last evening. If it weren't that she's so fond of Cristobel she certainly wouldn't have done. Or perhaps the fact that she's a distant cousin of your Father's.'

'Hardly that,' Alasdair broke in. 'EVERYONE'S related in some way to Lady E. She's got cousins receding into the distance almost to vanishing point.'

Laura giggled.

'Tell me,' Alasdair went on, leaning back and clasping his hands behind his head. 'What else has our hero been getting up to?'

Lady Flora stared at him with a vague, troubled gaze, as if she was not quite sure just how she'd managed to produce Sandy and was looking to Alasdair for an explanation.

'You weren't here during the Easter holidays, were you?' she replied. 'No, of course not, you went up to Fort William with Colin. Sandy brought a very strange boy home from school with him and they shut themselves up in his room in the dark for the whole of Good Friday and most of Saturday. Hardly appeared until Easter morning.'

Alasdair frowned.

'What on earth were they doing?' he enquired suspiciously.

'Photographing a BEETROOT,' Lady Flora wailed. 'He seems to be very vegetable these days.'

'Photographing a beetroot?' Alasdair exclaimed, the laughter now gone from his voice, replaced by a tone of annoyance. 'Whatever for?'

'I wish I knew dear,' Lady Flora sighed. 'Your father was away in Glenfall and Graeme had gone with him so I had no-one to turn to. But it was really very distressing, especially as the weather was fine and it rained for the rest of the holidays.'

She sighed again and looked down at her hands.

'Janet looked through the keyhole at one point and said Sandy was lying on his back on the floor under the washbowl, you know the one which leaks, holding a camera with a torch pointed at Crispin, that was his friend's name, who was perched on the top of the wardrobe dangling this beetroot about on a piece of string.'

She looked across at Alasdair.

'I really can't see why it should have taken almost THREE DAYS,' she said sadly. 'A beetroot can't be as complicated as all that.'

'But why on earth did he want to waste his time photographing a beetroot in the first place?' Alasdair exploded.

'Something about a competition at school,' Lady Flora went on. 'They didn't get a prize. Sandy was MOST annoyed.'

She sighed and bent to pick up Laird who was sitting on a tapestry cushion at her feet, gnawing his way through an ivory chopstick.

'In fact, now I look back, he behaved very strangely all through the holidays. He refused to wear a tie or stand up for "God Save the Queen", and even came down to breakfast on Easter morning wearing a yellow kimono saying he intended to become a Buddhist.'

Lady Flora stroked Laird absently.

'Mercifully, your father had returned the night before otherwise I don't know *what* would have happened.'

Alasdair got up and walked over to a basket beside the hearth and, bending down, threw two large logs on to the fire.

'I don't know how you managed to produce such a monster,' he smiled, kicking the logs into place with his foot.

Before his mother had a chance to reply, the drawing room door burst open and Sandy, who had obviously been listening behind it, thrust round his shock of red hair.

'*Old seed,*' he announced.

They all three looked at him in surprise as he sauntered into the room, hands in pockets.

'OLD SEED,' he said again pompously, gazing loftily down at them. 'Don't forget Dad was nearly FIFTY-NINE when I was born.'

Laura gasped and felt Alasdair stiffen on the sofa beside her.

'Alexander,' Lady Flora said weakly, using his real name for the first time in years.

Alasdair got to his feet.

'Sandy,' he barked, 'that's *enough.*'

81

He took a step menacingly in his brother's direction, but Sandy was too quick for him and, darting through the door, slammed it loudly in Alasdair's face.

Alasdair turned and walked over to his Mother.

'That little bounder needs a lesson,' he said angrily.

'Oh Alasdair,' she whispered. 'I don't understand him. You others NEVER behaved in such an atrocious fashion. I can't think what the school is coming to, though of course he doesn't have the same housemaster as you three did. Things must have changed drastically since Mr Harris retired.'

'The school's got nothing to do with it,' Alasdair replied grimly. 'Sandy is one on his own, and even old Harris would have found his match in him.'

Lady Flora got up from her chair and looked around her with a vague, troubled expression.

'Perhaps we should play canasta,' she suggested diffidently. 'Or shall I ring for tea?'

She picked up the fob watch lying on her breast.

'No, it's only half past three.'

She paused and seemed uncertain what to do.

'I think I'll go up and see Morag,' she said quietly. 'She may be feeling a little neglected; everyone has been so busy these last few days.'

'You do that, Mother,' Alasdair said, knowing that Morag had always been Lady Flora's bolt-hole in times of stress.

He got up and opened the door for her.

'Don't worry about tea, I'll take Laura out for a drive and we'll stop and have tea somewhere. That little blighter Sandy can go without.'

'Oh really dear, do you think so?' his mother demurred, then went on. 'Yes, that would be nice. I'm sure Laura would enjoy a drive.'

And she walked unsteadily from the room.

As Alasdair closed the door and turned back into the

room Laura's aura of calm suddenly evaporated like a Scotch mist.

'I've got rather a headache,' she lied, struggling to her feet. 'If you don't mind, I'd rather not go out, I'll go up to my room and try to sleep it off.'

Alasdair looked out of the window at the darkened sky, curdled and menacing, strewn with ashen clouds slowly turning a ragged anthracite grey.

'It's not raining yet,' he said slowly. 'Don't you think a drive would help blow it away? We could get out and walk a little and drop in for tea somewhere later on.'

'Thank you,' Laura replied, averting her eyes from his gaze, 'but not this afternoon.'

And she too began to walk unsteadily across the room; but Alasdair caught her arm.

'Laura,' he said softly, 'are you avoiding me?'

At his touch Laura felt the same voluptuous sensation which had swept over her the evening before as she stood in front of the mirror and smoothed the soft siken folds of her dress over her warm body.

The blood rose behind her ears and spread slowly across her cheeks.

'Why should I try to avoid you?' she answered tightly, drawing her arm away.

'I don't know,' he answered thoughtfully looking down at her and willing her to meet his gaze. 'Only one dance last evening, and now this sudden malaise.'

As the first drops of rain began to patter against the window panes she hesitated and almost gave in, then the memory of Alasdair's laughing face as he swung Fiona Farquharson round in his arms rose before her eyes and she turned quickly towards the door.

'I'm sorry,' she said tightly, 'but all I feel like doing at the moment is lying down and going to sleep.'

Alasdair crossed the room and opened the door for her. He said nothing, but his lips were pressed together in a tight line and he gave her the strangest look as she passed through:

Laura walked slowly up the stairs feeling as if her legs were about to give way beneath her. Reaching the half landing she stopped, her breath coming in short, sharp gasps, almost sobs, as the woman blossoming inside her struggled to escape, to claim her right to fight for the man she loved. In that instant Laura almost spun round and raced back down the wide staircase, into the drawing room where Alasdair was standing, one elbow perched on the high mantel of the great fireplace, staring moodily down into the leaping flames. Her woman's instinct told her to claim him, to grasp his hand and run with him across the silent echoing hall, through the great oak door, laughing and carefree out into the rain.

But then the frightened twelve-year-old girl still lurking inside her took over, and the pain and anguish, the terrible sense of rejection she had felt when the bedroom door had closed on her mother's wasted body from which all life had now been extinguished once again enveloped her like a thick grey flannel blanket of fog from which she could find no avenue of escape. Her sisters, loving but always remote because of the age gap between them, had their husbands and their separate lives; her father had his books and although they tried to comfort her as best they could, she felt that they had already distanced themselves from the still warm body lying motionless beneath the sheet. And Laura had felt herself alone, suspended in nothingness, shrouded in misery as she wandered, lost, in an endless tunnel with no light at either end. For her, at that moment, there was no hope: her mother had been her refuge and her anchor, and now that she was gone she could only see herself trapped for ever on an endless treadmill of despair.

And as these violent, adolescent emotions, only half

buried, gained command, insisting that she could not face the pain of rejection yet again, the young woman crying for escape and release from her tortured mind was brutally pushed below the surface as Laura gripped the heavy banister and rounded the bend of the stairs.

'Anyway,' she muttered bitterly to herself, 'how can I compare to Fiona? She's so vivacious, so amusing, so full of life, and she's a great sportswoman; she hunts and shoots and does all the things Alasdair enjoys doing. Not like me. I'm terrified of horses, can't bear the thought of handling a gun and have never fished in my life, except for fun in the Ardnakil lake with Cristobel. I'm useless in their world. I don't know whether salmon swim upstream at Christmas or Easter, it might even be on Bonfire Night. I must have been mad to even imagine that Alasdair could be interested in me, except perhaps as a toy it amuses him to tease.'

And she miserably turned the corner of the corridor leading to her bedroom. As she did so she heard the front door slam and, looking out of the turret window saw huge brooms of rain sweeping across the lawn and Alasdair, hands thrust deep into his pockets, striding hatless down the drive, his head bent against the rising storm.

She assumed that, having been relieved of any further hospitable duty towards herself, he was off to see Fiona.

7

The Other Woman

Laura did not appear for the rest of the day.

At about half past six Lady Flora tapped tentatively on her bedroom door.

'My dear, I do hope it's merely tiredness,' she called softly, 'and you're not really unwell.'

'No,' Laura called back without inviting her to enter. 'I think I must have been too greedy at the buffet last night, and drunk too much champagne. My tum's all queasy and I've got a headache. I just want to sleep it off: I'll be perfectly all right in the morning.'

'Shall I have some clear soup and a rusk sent up?' her hostess enquired.

'No thank you,' Laura replied. 'I really don't want anything to eat. Just sleep.'

'I'll leave you then,' Lady Flora said. 'But don't hesitate to ring if you change your mind.'

'I won't,' Laura answered, feigning a yawn.

'I'll see to it that you're not disturbed,' Flora ended, moving quietly away.

Laura turned over on her side and closed her eyes and suddenly it seemed as if her Mother was very near. Her mind drifted back to the last time she had seen her, that warm July evening when Edwina had taken her to the sick room to say goodnight. Margaret Denning's pinched white face had smiled up at her daughter from amongst the mound of pillows and her emaciated hand had felt for Laura's as she stood awkwardly by the bed. Her mother's long illness, instead of embittering her, seemed to have brought her into a new spiritual dimension and, in spite of the pain, she had never lost her peace.

'Don't worry Laura darling', she had whispered, as if sensing that this was their goodbye, 'your Heavenly Father will look after you.'

Laura had looked up at her aunt in bewilderment then, bending to hastily kiss her mother's paper-thin cheek, she had backed away.

As these memories churned round and round in her mind she understood why she had immediately felt as if she'd come home when she had first met Lady Flora and the conversation they had had as they walked back from church that morning began to take shape and form and meaning.

'Don't you mind going to church on your own every Sunday?' Laura had enquired. 'Wouldn't you be happier if one of the family came with you?'

Lady Flora had smiled across at her.

'I'm delighted to have you with me to-day Laura,' she replied gently, and Laura had blushed recalling the reason for accompanying her hostess. 'But faith is a personal commitment between God and each one of his children, sadly not something we can inherit or pass on. The children must each come to him in their own way and in their own time: I cannot force them.'

They had stopped and looked at each other and for a split second Laura was tempted to ask how she could get to know this God who seemed so real to Lady Flora, and how she could have this faith. But just then Sandy roared past them on an ancient bicycle, frantically ringing the bell, almost scattering them into the bushes.

And the moment had passed.

Laura opened her eyes and gazed out of the window. The sky was leaden and heavy with rain, the mountains almost obliterated by a thick mist which hung damply over everything. The downpour had ceased but dark sullen clouds were chasing each other menacingly across the curdled grey sky: the whole outlook was ragged and threatening and exactly suited to Laura's present mood. For one crazy moment she contemplated ringing the bell and asking if Lady Flora would come and talk to her and continue the conversation which Sandy had so abruptly terminated that morning. But her innate reserve and shyness took over and once again the moment past.

Closing her eyes once again she reflected on how quickly light can change to darkness, happiness to despair. It didn't seem possible that her window, which now had a dank, rain-sodden wind rattling angrily at its mullioned panes could, only twenty-four hours before, have been wide open to admit the soft perfumed breeze which had danced through it in dazzling sunshine.

Propping a pillow behind her head and reaching for a book, Laura heard the sounds of a car in the drive followed by Cristobel's voice and feet running up to the front door. She knew that Cristobel and Lindsay would soon be saying goodbye, perhaps until their wedding in three months time. Her friend would need her after he had gone. Laura laid down the book and closed her eyes, feeling that she had nothing to give: her own melancholy was different from the melancholy Cristobel would shortly be feeling, because Cristobel's was temporary whereas hers was without hope. With a half sob she buried her face in her pillow and tried to sleep.

She heard Cristobel come up to bed, but did not move. Her friend made no attempt to come into her room: Lady Flora had obviously warned her. And, as the great house finally settled down for the night Laura felt the sleep which her tired brain so desired gradually begin to creep over her.

'Tomorrow is another day,' she murmured to herself.

'Alasdair will have gone, life will return to normal and I shall be able to comfort Cristobel.'

But her consciousness was dimming and as the veils of darkness slipped softly over her she yielded to them and slept.

* * *

When Laura opened her door to Cristobel's knock the next morning she found her friend looking pale and jaded.

'Are you feeling better?' Cristobel enquired.

'I'm perfectly all right now,' Laura said, forcing a smile. 'But you're the one who looks as if she needs a doctor.'

Cristobel grimaced.

'Miseryitis,' she wailed. 'Never thought it would be so hard to say goodbye to Lindsay.'

Laura slipped her arm through hers as they walked along the gallery.

'Not for long,' she comforted.

'Long enough,' Cristobel answered mournfully. 'And just *look* at the weather. It really doesn't help!'

They both stopped at the turning and gazed through the turret window.

The rain had cleared but the clouds were still threatening and a damp mist hung over everything. The dark sky looked as if it were perched on top of the mountains blackly outlined against it.

'Ugh,' Cristobel shuddered. 'Looks the way I feel.'

She turned to Laura suddenly.

'Do you think it's easier to part with someone you love if you live in a hot climate like Italy or the south of France? Somewhere where the sun always shines.'

'According to Philippa, the sun *doesn't* always shine in Italy,' Laura laughed.

Laura's elder sister was with her husband at the Embassy in Rome.

'And anyway she says she sometimes wishes it wouldn't, and longs for a rainy day.'

'Oh, how CAN she?' Cristobel exclaimed.

But it was difficult for Cristobel to be mournful for long. The tempting smell coming out of the open dining room door as they reached the bottom of the stairs immediately revived her spirits.

'In Italy we wouldn't be having eggs and bacon for breakfast, would we, just coffee and an old roll.'

And grabbing Laura's hand she skipped gaily across the hall.

'I suppose there are some compensations for living in the Arctic.'

As they entered the dining room, Laura stood frozen in the doorway. There, carefully wiping his mouth with his napkin, was Alasdair. He looked up and smiled, then picked up his cup and raised it to them in a mock salute.

'"Hail to thee, blithe spirits,"' he quoted.

'Hail,' Cristobel replied, helping herself lavishly at the sideboard.

Laura felt a blush mounting up behind her ears again and, before it could reach her cheeks, quickly turned towards the sideboard and began fiddling with dish covers. She suddenly didn't want anything to eat. Pouring out a cup of coffee she sat down and reached for the toast.

Lady Flora looked up from her letters.

'Laura *dear*,' she reproved. 'Is THAT all you're going to have?' You had nothing to eat last night. Are you sure you're not unwell?'

Laura kept her eyes rivetted to her plate.

'I think my stomach's shrunk,' she joked. 'But after yesterday I'd rather be careful. I made a pig of myself at supper on Saturday night.'

Alasdair looked up, smiling his crooked, quizzical smile.

'If you did nobody noticed it,' he remarked. 'I certainly didn't.'

'You were otherwise occupied,' Laura almost replied, but stopped herself just in time.

Cristobel rose to pour herself some coffee and seemed to notice Alasdair for the first time.

'Hallo,' she said. 'What are you doing here on a Monday morning?'

'I've been here all the time,' he answered. 'I even greeted you when you came in, *and* you replied.'

'Oh did I?,' replied Cristobel, sitting down at the table again and reaching for the toast. 'How long are you staying?'

'Not long. I've got an appointment in Perth at eleven, so it wasn't worth going back to Edinburgh last night.'

'Perth,' Cristobel said, brightening up. 'Oh good. Can Laura and I cadge a lift in with you?'

'Certainly,' he answered, getting up from the table. 'I'll be leaving in about forty minutes.'

Laura opened her mouth to protest but Cristobel got in before her.

'Lovely,' she cried, turning to her friend. 'A day in town is just what we need, to clear up your headache and blow away my doldrums. We can do some shopping, have lunch at the Royal Oak and see if there is a good film on in the afternoon,' Oh goody-good,' she laughed, clapping her hands like an excited child.

'I wonder if the cinema is a good idea if Laura has just got over a nasty headache?' Lady Flora queried.

'Oh just the thing,' Cristobel replied gaily. 'Come on Laura, let's put on our best bibs and tuckers and dazzle the local yokels.'

'Do you want Donald to come and meet you later on?'
her mother called as Cristobel danced out of the room,
all signs of depression gone.

'Oh no, Mother, don't bother, we'll take the bus.'

She turned to Laura and caught her hand, dragging
her across the hall.

'I love that old country bus,' she cooed happily.
'It takes hours but it's a splendid ride and it stops
everywhere, which is fun. And I always meet *everybody* on it.'

Half an hour later, with a heavy heart, Laura walked
back down to the hall where Alasdair was shuffling
some papers into his briefcase.

'All ready?' he said, lifting his eyebrows.

She nodded as Cristobel pirouetted down the wide
staircase holding out her left hand and admiring her
engagement ring yet again as she did so.

'Right then,' he said, snapping his briefcase shut.
'Goodbye, Mother,' he called.

Lady Flora appeared at the door of the morning room,
Laird cradled in her arms.

'Oh goodbye, darling,' she said vaguely as her son
bent to kiss her cheek.

'By the way, what's happened to that lout Sandy?'
he enquired, straightening up. 'He's kept a pretty low
profile since yesterday afternoon, I see.'

'I think he's upstairs arranging his Brazilian beetle
collection,' Lady Flora replied, stroking Laird who was
yapping in her arms.

'His *Brazilian beetle collection*?' Alasdair gasped.
'Heaven preserve us. A radish, a beetroot, the Ardnakil
honkytonks and now a beetle collection. Mother, I despair of your youngest offspring.'

He placed his hand affectionately on her arm and
Laird promptly bit him.

'Blighter,' Alasdair gasped.

Lady Flora smiled her sweet smile.

'How naughty you are,' she said gently to her growling pet.

Alasdair turned to the two girls.

'Let's go,' he said briskly.

'You sit in the front,' Cristobel said to Laura, jumping into the back of the car as her brother held the doors open for them.

'But no,' Laura panicked.

'Oh go on,' Cristobel said, 'don't *fuss*. I'm just going to lie down flat and dream of Lindsay, so there won't be any room for you even if you wanted to sit here.'

Without comment, Alasdair settled Laura into the passenger seat then climbed in beside her.

Laura smiled frozenly at Lady Flora standing on the step then, gathering herself together so as to avoid any contact with Alasdair, she sat stiffly on the seat beside him.

As they turned down the drive Alasdair waved out of the car window to his father who was striding towards the house with the dogs. Then, gathering speed, he rushed through the wide open wrought iron gates and into the deserted road.

'She hasn't wasted much time getting down to dreaming,' he said quietly, jerking his head towards the back seat where Cristobel was curled up along its length, fast asleep.

Laura glanced into the overhead mirror.

'I expect she's tired after all the excitement,' she replied stiffly.

'And you?' Alasdair said, looking quickly at her. 'Are you completely recovered?'

Laura thought she detected a hint of irony in his voice.

'Yes, thank you,' she answered primly, staring straight in front of her.

Alasdair slowed down and manoeuvred over a small

bridge crossing a rushing stream, its waters swelled with yesterday's rain.

'So I'm to be your escort to Catriona McFadden's coming out ball,' he announced, pressing his foot down on the accelerator.

Laura looked at him, her eyes wide with fright.

'Oh no, I don't think so.'

'That's what mother said last night.'

He paused and she panicked again.

'Graeme as the eldest son is to give his arm to his betrothed sister as is right and proper, and I'm to offer mine to you.'

He smiled down at her.

'Will you accept it?'

For a moment Laura could think of nothing to say.

A week ago she would have been deliriously happy at the mere suggestion of being escorted to a ball by Alasdair, but in the last few days everything had changed.

'I – I don't think I'll be here,' she stammered.

'What do you mean?' Alasdair enquired. 'I thought you were staying for the summer?'

'Er – not this time,' Laura rambled on, words dropping haphazardly from her lips without her seeming to have any control over them. 'I've promised to go to Italy to stay with my sister Philippa.'

'But I thought she was in Cairo?' Alasdair remarked.

Laura was taken aback. How could he possibly have remembered?

'She *was* when I was thirteen,' she replied coldly. 'They've been in Paris and Moscow since then.'

Alasdair smiled across at her.

'And how old are you now, little lady?' he asked softly.

Laura felt she was about to burst into tears.

There he was with that same mocking tone, laughing at her again: and she couldn't bear it. She looked

desperately round to the back seat, praying that
Cristobel would wake up and extricate her from this
tête-à-tête. But Cristobel was lying there wrapped
heavily in the folds of sleep, a sweet smile on her
lips.

'I'm THREE months younger than your sister,' she
blurted out, then fell abruptly silent.

The humiliation she felt at his teasing remark had
made hot tears spring up behind her eyelids and she
knew that if she attempted another word they would
gush out.

The narrow mountain road began to climb and
Alasdair kept his eyes fixed on it in concentration.
Looking through the window down into the valley
below, willing the tears not to flow, Laura caught her
breath as a ray of sunshine suddenly broke through
the dark clouds and flooded a little chain of blue tarns
twinkling below like a many-faceted sapphire necklace.
But, almost immediately, the road twisted and they
vanished from sight. As the descent began Alasdair
relaxed his grip on the wheel and looked down at her.

'You can't go to Rome in July,' he said. 'You'll die
from sunstroke, the heat's absolutely ghastly.'

'I shan't be going to Rome,' Laura answered,
swallowing hard before she spoke in order to gain
some sort of control over her voice. 'Philippa is taking
the children up to the Lakes, she might even already be
there, and I shall join them. I haven't seen my nieces
since Christmas.'

'Your family goes in for girls in a big way, doesn't
it?' Alasdair smiled. 'Does your other sister only have
daughters too?'

'No,' Laura replied. 'Mary and Edward don't have
any children.'

'We'd make a good couple,' Alasdair smiled. 'Break
the terrible bias towards male offspring which seems
to predominate in the Hamilton family.'

95

Laura felt a swift hot blush surge across her face, and she turned to look out of the window, annoyed that she had allowed herself to be upset by his teasing.

'That blush is so endearing,' Alasdair went on, ignoring her embarrassment. 'I think it was the first thing I noticed about you – after the freckles.'

She bit her lip tightly, her head averted, her mind going round and round in circles. She simply could not understand this man. What was he trying to do? Why did he delight in making her squirm?

'You'll come back in August for the shooting, won't you?' he went on, turning to her as the outskirts of Perth came into view.

'I don't shoot,' Laura replied coldly, her face still glued to the window.

'How refreshing,' he remarked. 'But we don't have to join the shoot: it would be quite a relief not to, as a matter of fact. We could do something else.'

'Do you fish?' he went on, after a pause.

'No,' she said tightly, picturing Fiona's athletic body standing knee deep in an ice-cold lake, or striding over the hills with a gun. 'And I'm not sure Cristobel will be here in August. She said something about Lady Fraser taking her on the Rhine, with the possibility of Lindsay being able to join them for a few days.'

Alasdair swerved sharply to avoid a dog which had just jumped over a low stone wall.

'But you don't always have to be Cristobel's guest,' he blurted out.

Laura looked at him in surprise.

'You could be mine,' he murmured, turning that quizzical crooked smile on her: and for a brief moment he took his hand off the steering wheel and placed it lightly on hers lying clenched together in her lap.

'And we could do anything you like,' he said softly. 'What do you enjoy doing?'

Once again that wonderful, overpowering, voluptuous feeling which she had felt at his touch in the ballroom and on the sofa yesterday afternoon came over her. She felt captured, encompassed with its warmth, and the trembling, rippling sensations pulsated throughout her body. She half turned towards him, her lips parted, her eyes bright. But suddenly, the old fear caught her in its grip, the fear of being alone and rejected, lost in that dark, deserted, endless tunnel. As it overpowered her she remembered him gazing down into Fiona Farquharson's smiling face, and her lips tightened as the feeling drained away, leaving her stiff and frozen once again.

Alasdair had sensed the warmth and now he felt the abrupt, inexplicable change in this tantalising, bewitching girl who had so suddenly captivated him. As a feeling of utter incomprehension took hold of him he slowly removed his hand and fixed his eyes on the road ahead.

'I'm tied up in Edinburgh next weekend,' he said as they entered the town, 'and the weekend afterwards I've promised to escort Fiona to a cousin's wedding, but in three weeks I'll be back.'

He paused and glanced down at her.

'I hope you'll still be here,' he said softly.

Laura could scarcely believe her ears.

What was he trying to do? Make a fool of her? He was certainly laughing at her.

For one wild, crazy moment, when his hand had touched hers, she had allowed her feelings to soar. Even when Fiona's face had floated into her memory she had still hoped: but now, here he was, on the one hand asking her to stay at Ardnakil as his guest, and on the other flaunting his relationship with another woman.

She opened her mouth to make a scathing remark; a remark which, had she only known it, would have

97

cleared the air and uncluttered the ground which lay between them. But at that moment Cristobel woke up and looked sleepily through the car window.

'Oh yippee,' she said, bouncing up on the seat, 'we're running into Perth. Can you drop us at the Royal Oak, Alasdair? We can have a quick cup of coffee and book a table for lunch.'

She peered at her face in the driving mirror.

'Heavens, what a sight! Yes, you'd better drop us at the Royal Oak,' she went on, taking a small gold powder compact out of her handbag, 'even if it means you're late for your appointment. I CAN'T face the town looking like this.'

She snapped the compact shut and ran her hands distractedly through her thick dark hair, yawning as the car drew up in front of the hotel.

'I'd like to give you both lunch,' Alasdair said as he opened the door for Laura, 'but I'm afraid this meeting I'm attending will run into lunch.'

Laura sent up a quick prayer of thanks.

'Not to worry, big brother,' Cristobel said, falling out onto the pavement.

'I'll see you in three weeks,' he said softly as he bid Laura goodbye.

'No,' she hissed.

He looked taken aback.

'Well, I hope you'll at least deign to come to Cristobel's wedding,' he replied stiffly as he climbed back into his car.

'My wedding?' Cristobel said, turning round. 'Whatever are you talking about? Of course you'll see Laura before then. She's here for the summer.'

Alasdair raised his eyebrows enquiringly at Laura.

'I wouldn't count on it,' he remarked as he turned the key in the ignition and, gliding smoothly away from the pavement, waved his hand through the side window.

'What's bitten him?' Cristobel said taking Laura's arm as they walked into the hotel.

'Cristobel,' Laura began, meaning to get this settled once and for all.

'Oh, weddings,' Cristobel cooed excitedly. 'Let's order some coffee and I'll tell you about the arrangements for mine: we got just about everything organised yesterday, all we have to do now is make sure Lindsay can have leave and that he has his Colonel's approval.'

She grinned.

'It would be a funny wedding if he couldn't,' she laughed. 'But I met his Colonel at the New Year's Eve ball, so there won't be any problem there.'

She grimaced.

'Lindsay tells me I'm approved. Even by *Mrs* Colonel.'

And, dropping into a deep armchair she went back to admiring her ring, whilst the waiter stood patiently waiting for them to give their order.

8

Escaping

It was not easy for Laura to get away from Ardnakil. Both Cristobel and her mother put up strong opposition to her leaving but, in the end, she hardened herself to Cristobel's woebegone face and announced that she simply had to go: Philippa was expecting her and she had promised to accompany Edwina to Ireland in August.

'But you've *never* not stayed the whole summer,' Cristobel wailed when she saw that Laura was adamant.

'I wasn't here last year,' Laura reminded her.

'All the more reason to stay this year,' Cristobel went on. 'And you *should* have been. It was only because that beastly peritonitis blew up the morning we were leaving. I *never* understood why Edwina insisted on taking you to Cornwall to convalesce, you could have convalesced here just as well, and NOW she's carting you over to Ireland on our last summer together.'

'Don't be ridiculous,' Laura replied sharply. 'Our *last* summer, indeed, You're not going to *die*.'

'No,' sulked Cristobel, 'but once I'm married it won't be the same: and anyway I won't be here all the time like I've always been.'

She looked at Laura with such deep gloom etched on her delicate features that Laura burst out laughing.

'Oh come on, Cristobel,' she chided, 'marriage is hardly a death sentence. Yesterday you couldn't wait and now you're behaving as if it's your funeral everyone's going to such trouble to arrange.

Cristobel looked up and her and grinned.

It was difficult for her bubbling spirits to remain downcast for long and, jumping up from her chair, she held out her hand to pull Laura up.

'You're right,' she laughed, twirling round and dragging Laura after her.

'But,' she said stopping suddenly and almost colliding with her friend, 'you *will* be in London at the beginning of September won't you? Mother and I are coming down to see about my dress and the bridesmaids' outfits, and you'll need to be there for fittings and things.'

'Oh CRISTOBEL,' Laura sighed. 'Do you really want me to be a bridesmaid?'

Cristobel sat down abruptly.

'Of course,' she answered in astonishment, her enormous grey eyes opening wide.

'But I'm going to look so ridiculous in the middle of that flurry of children,' Laura went on lamely. 'There'll be Lindsay's niece and nephew who can't be more than seven between them and all your little Sutherland cousins who are scarcely any older. I'll be like a runner bean in a field of daisies.'

She sat down beside Cristobel knowing that she had hurt her yet feeling helpless to do anything about it. What she had really wanted to say was: I don't want any official role which could possibly bring me into close contact with Alasdair. But in spite of their intimacy, a certain reticence she had inherited from her father prevented her from revealing her true feelings.

'But Laura,' Cristobel wailed. 'Of *course* you must be my bridesmaid. You're like a sister to me: it never occurred to me that you wouldn't want to.'

Laura bit her lip, entangled not only in her own emotions but now in Cristobel's, knowing she had wounded her friend yet incapable of finding a way to relieve the tension which had sprung up between them.

'I just thought . . .' she began helplessly, 'it might be better to leave it to small pages and bridesmaids instead of me in the middle standing out like a hat peg.'

Cristobel looked down at the floor and began describing circles on the carpet with her small foot.

'I suppose I *could* ask someone to keep you company so that there'd be two of you,' she mused. 'But I don't know WHO.'

She paused and frowned reflectively.

'Mother was the youngest in her family, a bit of an afterthought like Sandy, so all the Sutherland cousins are married and it's *their* offspring who'll be tripping up the aisle behind me – all very small. Uncle Hamish has no children', she went on making an obvious remark, 'and Father's elder brother was killed in the First World War before he had time to get married, so we've no first cousins on the Hamilton side.'

She caught her breath as a thought suddenly struck her.

'Just *imagine*,' she gasped, her mind leaping like a grasshopper from one subject to another, 'if Uncle Alasdair' – Laura's heart missed a beat – 'Alasdair was named after him, if he hadn't been killed we wouldn't be here at all.'

Cristobel looked up, her eyes wide.

'We'd probably be in *India*,' she whispered hoarsely.

Laura frowned.

'Why India?'

'Father was in the Army and that's where they all end up, isn't it?' she asked matter-of-factly.

'The British Army left India fifteen years ago,' Laura remarked drily.

'Oh well, whatever,' Cristobel went on unperturbed.

'But we wouldn't be *here*; Ardnakil would belong to Uncle Alasdair and his family.'

Her luminous eyes suddenly widened with fright.

'Oh *Laura*,' she gasped, 'just think how awful it would have been. We'd probably be living in some terrible slum!'

'Hardly,' Laura smiled. But Cristobel took no notice.

'I'm so glad he was killed,' she sighed thankfully.

'Cristobel,' Laura cut in sharply. 'Do you realise what you're saying?'

Cristobel looked across at her friend in amazement.

'Oh well,' she shrugged, 'you know what I mean . . . Where were we? Oh yes, bridesmaids.'

And her mind went hopping off again.

'There's Catriona McFadden,' she mused, leaving Laura, still aghast. 'No, she won't do, she's too tall, then you really *would* look ridiculous, like Laurel and Hardy.'

She swung her foot backwards and forwards across the arm of the chair, sucking in her lower lip thoughtfully.

'I suppose I *could* ask Fiona Farquharson,' she mused, 'she's not much taller than you . . .'

She paused, and this time it was Laura who caught her breath.

'But I don't really *want* her,' Cristobel blurted out at last. 'Oh Laura, what's the matter with you all of a sudden? We always said that whoever married first would have the other as a bridesmaid.'

'That was when we were sixteen,' Laura retorted.

'We're only *nineteen* now,' Cristobel breathed. 'Does it make such a difference?'

She leaned across towards Laura and, putting her hand beneath her chin tweaked it upwards.

'IS something the matter?' she asked softly. 'You've been so strange since we arrived. It can't JUST be the fact that we haven't seen much of each other during the past year which has made you change so much. Sisters don't grow apart.'

Laura looked up and forced a smile, words crowding into her throat longing to be spoken, longing to be shared with Cristobel the one person she had shared so much with in the past. But as she opened her mouth to bring into the open those words which would have cleared the air and brought her hope and joy, suddenly she saw Fiona's face float into her mind and Alasdair smiling down at her. And she closed her lips tightly. Getting up, she walked towards the empty fireplace and stood gazing into its cavernous depths.

'It's nothing,' she lied. 'You're just imagining it.'

'Then you will be my bridesmaid?' Cristobel wheedled, coming to stand beside her.

Laura nodded dumbly, not daring to look at her friend.

'Oh cheers,' Cristobel cried, clapping her hands like an excited schoolgirl. 'Now let's go and look at some dress patterns.'

And grabbing Laura's hand, she dragged her from the room.

* * *

Cristobel had won on that point, but as to the date of her departure, Laura was adamant and no amount of pleading would make her change her mind. Alasdair was due to arrive at Ardnakil for the weekend on the following Friday evening, so Laura insisted on taking the afternoon train. Although Cristobel wailed that it would be so much easier to travel by night Laura held her ground: she didn't want to run any risk of crossing Alasdair's path again.

As the train drew out of Perth station, Cristobel raced along beside it.

'The minute we arrive in London in September I'll telephone you at Edwina's,' she cried.

Laura nodded and waved, then withdrew her head as the small figure became even smaller and the train swerved round the bend and out of sight.

Edwina was not only her father's sister but also Laura's godmother and had become her surrogate mother ever since her own mother had died. If she was surprised to see her niece return from Scotland so soon, she made no comment, just welcomed her as warmly as ever to her Kensington home which, in the last seven years, had also become Laura's home.

'I'm afraid you'll find London very hot after Scotland,' she said as Laura dropped her suitcase in the hall and turned to greet her.

Her aunt kissed her lightly on the cheek then held her away from her.

'You seem tired,' she said gently. 'Perhaps it's the journey. Would you like something to eat, or do you just want to go to bed?'

Laura smiled at her, grateful not to be plied with questions.

'I think I'll go to bed if you don't mind. I'll give you all the news in the morning.'

Edwina looked at her niece shrewdly, then nodded and accompanied her to her small room overlooking the courtyard.

'Philippa telephoned yesterday evening,' Edwina remarked, walking across to the window and drawing the curtains. 'And wanted to know when to expect you.'

'Oh, I'd like to stay a few days with you before going to Italy,' Laura answered listlessly, her mind and her heart still in Ardnakil where she was imagining the family sitting on the terrace after dinner watching the midges dance in the northern twilight haze.

Her aunt's gaze rested on her thoughtfully for a few seconds.

'You'll feel better after a warm bath and a good night's sleep,' she said, removing the apple green silk coverlet and turning down the sheet.

Laura looked at her aunt gratefully and suddenly her eyes filled with tears and she longed to throw her arms round Edwina's neck and cry her heart out, telling her about the misery of the last few weeks and the emptiness she was now feeling.

Edwina stood silently waiting for the outburst. But it didn't come. Once again, the words dried up inside Laura and, kicking off her shoes, she turned away, letting the pent-up emotion escape in a great gaping yawn. Instantly, she covered her mouth with her hand in a childish gesture.

'I'm sorry,' she said looking across at her aunt, 'but the yawn kept coming.'

Edwina smiled at her.

'I thought we might drive down to Oxford for lunch on Sunday,' she said. 'I'm sure your father would like to see you.'

Laura nodded. She wasn't so sure. Since his wife had died Henry Denning had plunged himself into his books and hardly seemed to be aware of the world outside, thankful that his two elder daughters had their own lives and grateful to his sister for taking his youngest one off his hands.

And once again Laura's eyes brimmed with tears.

Edwina squeezed her arm affectionately.

'I'll run you a bath,' she smiled.

Within a few seconds Laura heard water gushing in the room next door, and climbing out of her clothes she pushed her feet into soft fluffy slippers and walked into the warm caressing steam. Lowering her body into the fragrant suds she told herself that now she was back in London she would see things differently, she would feel different. Alasdair would become the dream he always should have been: she could confidently file him away and forget about him as one does with photographs in an old album or acquaintances met on a cruise who have neither substance nor reality once back on dry land. There was her visit to Philippa and the girls to look forward to, the Donkey Derby in Connemara and the Dublin Horse Show with Edwina: Oh, life was full and exciting and beautiful and she was young, on the threshold of adventure. She did not need Alasdair.

Laura lay back voluptuously in the perfumed waters and relaxed. And, as she did so, out of the mist, his face slowly rose up before her, smiling his crooked quizzical smile.

And she knew, without the shadow of a doubt, that she did.

9

Rehearsal and Confusion

Lady Flora and Cristobel arrived in London at the
end of August, earlier than expected, and Laura was
not there.

'Where've you *been*?' Cristobel wailed down the
telephone when she finally managed to track down
her friend.

'In Ireland,' Laura replied. 'I told you I would be.'

'But,' Cristobel shrieked, hysterical with excitement,
'I've been ringing for absolutely *ages*, and your aunt's
maid kept saying she didn't know *when* you'd be
back. I've been paralysed with fear thinking you'd
deserted me.'

Laura laughed.

'You said you'd be here at the beginning of September and it's only the second.'

'Oh, is it really?' Cristobel sounded surprised. 'It
seems like at least December to me. You *must* see my
dress, it's . . .'

Her voice disappeared and Laura could imagine the
scene, Cristobel waltzing round the room, the telephone
clutched to her bosom.

'. . . Oh, it's a *dream*' she heard, as Cristobel's voice
reappeared.

'Cristobel,' Laura said sternly, 'DO STAND STILL.
I can't hear a thing.'

There was a sudden silence and she thought they
had been cut off.

'Oh sorry,' Cristobel's voice came down the now stationary line. 'I find it difficult to stand still. I'm so excited!'

'So I gather,' Laura put in drily.

'Can you come round this very minute?' Cristobel pleaded.

'Yes, but where are you?'

'At Madame Zoe's. She's getting quite *frantic*, your not being here for fittings and things. Says your dress will NEVER be ready on time.'

'Sounds very French,' Laura grimaced.

'Yes, but the most marvellous dressmaker,' Cristobel cooed. 'Do come now. I *must* show you what my dress is going to look like and we MUST choose a pattern for yours.'

'It would help if you'd tell me where to come to,' Laura cut in.

'Madame Zoe's, don't you know?' Cristobel sounded as surprised as if she'd suggested meeting her friend in front of Buckingham Palace and Laura had replied Buckingham what?'

'I wouldn't ask if I did. Just give me the exact address – if you can stand still for long enough.'

'Well, it's a small street off Piccadilly, almost opposite the Ritz, not far from Old Bond Street . . .'

'Please, Cristobel,' Laura broke in exasperatedly, 'don't give me a tour of London. Just the EXACT address.'

'Of course,' Cristobel said, contrite. 'Oh horrors, I don't KNOW. Look, I'll pass you to one of these nice assistants, she'll tell you where we are.'

Laura was thankful to be handed over to someone who wasn't dancing along on cloud nine.

'Goodness knows where I'd have ended up if I'd had to rely on Cristobel for directions,' she said to herself as she climbed out of the taxi. 'Probably in a back street on the other side of Wapping.'

109

* * *

The next few days flashed by at lightning speed. It was impossible to hold a normal conversation with Cristobel or to hope to receive a coherent answer if one did. She appeared to float through life oblivious of everything around her. Fittings became a major ordeal for the dressmakers as she seemed incapable of standing still for more than two seconds at a time.

Lady Flora smiled her sweet vague smile and, as usual, appeared to be apart from all the frantic activity going on around her. She collected the girls from their fittings, took them to lunch or tea at the Ritz afterwards, talked absently of lists and flowers and invitations and all the other paraphernalia attached to marrying an only daughter and, in a quieter and less agitated way than her daughter, drove Madame Zoe and her assistants crazy as she drifted gracefully through the whole procedure.

When they at last returned to Scotland on the last lap before the great day, Laura was exhausted.

'I really don't see WHY you can't come back with us,' Cristobel pouted as they had dinner together before she and her mother caught the night train to Perth. 'I've hardly seen you this summer and it would be nice to spend these last two weeks together before I disappear in a gown of gossamer silk.'

Laura laid a restraining hand on her arm as Cristobel's eyes clouded over and became dreamy, a sure sign that she was about to leap to her feet and dance. It was becoming slightly embarrassing, this twirling about in public places.

'I've told you why I can't come,' she said patiently.

'But only to come THE DAY BEFORE,' Cristobel sulked. 'It's positively CRUEL.'

'I promise you I'll be there on the Thursday morning,' Laura soothed, 'in time for the rehearsal in the afternoon and the family party at the Fraser's in the evening.'

She looked affectionately across at Cristobel.

'You'll be a wreck by Friday,' she murmured.

'Oh, it's only a small family dinner party,' Cristobel said, 'and early so that I can get to bed, though I shan't sleep a wink, and Lindsay and the others can have their stag night.'

She giggled.

'It's a funny world, isn't it? He's the one who'll be dead the next morning.'

Laura smiled.

'I do hope you will be able to stay on with us after Cristobel goes off on her honeymoon,' Lady Flora smiled.

Laura smiled back, but didn't reply. She didn't want another argument. But, mercifully, the car arrived to take them to the station and the situation resolved itself.

* * *

After a series of wailing telephone calls from Cristobel, Laura finally capitulated and took the night train on the Tuesday so as to give them what Cristobel described as a final day of giggling together before the last minute count down and preparations on the Thursday. To her great relief, she discovered at breakfast on the morning of her arrival that Alasdair would only be arriving the following afternoon.

'Does he really have to rehearse?' Laura enquired. 'He's not the best man or anything.'

'No, but we need him for the procession after the service,' Cristobel announced, her eyes shining. 'The

111

verger wants to make absolutely sure everyone knows who they'll be walking with so as to avoid all the family scrambling about in the aisle looking for their partners.'

Laura sighed and tried to put the whole thing out of her mind until the wedding party was gathered in the ancient village church, already beautifully decorated for the following day's ceremony.

'Now,' intoned the verger nasally, when they had all trooped down the aisle with one partner, done a quick swop and about turn and were waiting to troop back up it with someone else.

Nobody took the slightest notice of him.

He coughed discreetly, then a little more loudly and finally clapped his hands, eyeing the surging mass of pages and bridesmaids with distaste.

They had all spent a delightful morning racing along the endless passages and galleries at Ardnakil, sliding down the banisters, thoroughly upsetting Laird and Sarah and generally making a nuisance of themselves with the help of the three younger dogs who had added their barks and yelps to the children's excited shrieks. They now obviously considered the church to be merely an extension of the old house and were trying to recreate the earlier pandemonium.

'If you PLEASE, ladies and gentlemen,' bleated the now totally bewildered verger as Robert grabbed a handful of wriggling, giggling small attendants and sorted them into pairs once more.

The verger coughed again, then cleared his throat loudly to heighten the effect.

'Now,' he repeated for the second time, taking a deep breath, as under threat the pages and bridesmaids were once again lined up. 'For the processional march AFTER the ceremony, Lady Flora will walk with Sir Charles directly behind the bridal party. Yes, that's right,' as Lady Flora and Sir Charles took up their positions once more in the aisle.

Everyone else then either walked backwards or shuffled up.

The verger raised his eyebrows authoritatively making him look like a startled guinea pig.

'Now, if you please, Lady Fraser and Mr Hamilton.'

But Robert had gone back to threatening the pages who were starting up their antics again. Lady Fraser looked helplessly round and the group disintegrated once more. The whole thing was threatening to turn into a glorious free-for-all, with the verger completely out of his depth.

Nobody seemed to know where they were supposed to be or what they were supposed to be doing when suddenly, wondering what the hold up was all about, Cristobel looked round. Seeing the total confusion reigning behind her with bewildered adults and small warring children who, having exhausted themselves during the morning's antics had now become fractious and obstructive, she slipped her hand from Lindsay's arm and immediately, and quite uncharacteristically, assumed command.

'Mr McIntyre,' she cooed to the helpless, perspiring verger. 'We are being QUITE dreadful and tiring you out.'

She pushed him gently into a pew.

'You just sit there and tell me what you want us to do.'

And, so saying, she proceeded to completely ignore him and take over.

'Now where were we?' she called. 'Ah yes. After Father and Lady Fraser, Grandfather Lindsay and Grannie Sutherland.'

At this point Lady Fraser began signalling frantically to Cristobel.

'Grandfather Lindsay doesn't want to be in the

113

procession,' she mouthed. 'He has trouble with his hip.'

'Oh dear,' Cristobel replied. 'But won't he look very odd standing there all by himself in the front pew when everyone else gets up and walks out?'

She turned appealingly to her fiancé.

'What can we do Lindsay?'

But before he had time to think of a solution Cristobel hailed her future brother-in-law, who had been milling in and out of the procession ever since the rehearsal began, never really sure where he and his wife were supposed to be.

'Oh *Niall*,' she pleaded, 'would you and Emma mind *awfully* staying in the pew with Grandfather Lindsay, just so that it doesn't look as if we've left him behind?'

Niall and Emma dropped out of line gratefully, knowing at last what they were supposed to be doing.

'All settled,' Cristobel announced brightly.

Then a sudden thought struck her.

'Oh no,' she groaned. 'that leaves Grannie Sutherland by herself.'

She creased her forehead thoughtfully whilst everyone stood obediently waiting.

'Oh well,' she shrugged. 'Graeme you'll just have to walk with Grannie.'

She beamed on them all.

'That's it, I think.'

They all shuffled up again. All but Graeme.

'Come on, Graeme,' Cristobel called exasperatedly. 'Now it's you and Grannie Sutherland.'

Graeme raised his hands expressively, pointing to the empty place at his side. Grannie hadn't turned up.

'Oh, just walk by yourself for today,' Cristobel said impatiently. 'We didn't ask Grannie to come to the rehearsal, she's resting.'

Graeme shrugged resignedly and stepped into place as his sister turned to the waiting verger, giving him one of her sweetest smiles.

'I don't think there's anything else, is there, Mr McIntyre?' she cooed. 'We're all lined up. Now the wedding march can start.'

The organist, who had been hanging over the organ loft waiting patiently for a signal from someone, climbed thankfully back onto the seat and had just broken into a loud chord when there was a piercing shriek from Cristobel.

'Oh no,' she cried. 'Stop everybody, stop.'

She looked desperately up to the organ loft.

'Please, Mr McNabb.'

Mr McNabb's hands fell abruptly from the keys and the organ gave a loud gasping groan.

'It's LAURA,' Cristobel wailed. 'We've forgotten LAURA.'

All eyes turned to where the chief bridesmaid was standing in splendid isolation.

'POOR Mr McIntyre,' Cristobel soothed, patting the shoulder of the defeated verger who had thrust his head into his hands. 'You thought that as Ninian is best man HE'D be walking with the chief bridesmaid, but of course he'll be outside organising the guard of honour.'

She sighed deeply.

'NOW what do we do?'

Everyone looked around hoping someone else would come up with the solution. Everyone, that is, except Hamish who had been prowling up and down the aisle on tiptoe all afternoon in the opposite direction from everyone else. Now that the entire wedding party was facing the door, he was standing to attention facing the altar.

'That only leaves Alasdair,' Cristobel said thoughtfully, shooting out a hand, grabbing Hamish and

anchoring him firmly in the pew beside the distraught
Mr McIntyre.

Laura's heart began to pound as Cristobel turned
her dazzling smile on her.

'Darling Laura,' she cooed. 'Do you mind awfully?
Alasdair's all that's left.'

She suddenly looked round.

'By the way, where IS Alasdair?' she enquired.

'He should be here by now,' Lady Flora ventured.

As she spoke, there was the sound of brakes
scrunching on the road outside and Alasdair dashed
into the pool of sunshine flooding through the open
church door.

'Sorry,' he said, hurrying up to his sister. 'Got held
up at the last minute. Am I very late?'

'Yes,' she answered. 'But never mind. We're just
about to process out – we processed in before you
got here but as you're an usher at the beginning it
doesn't matter. Graeme will tell you where you're to
stand for that.'

Cristobel suddenly spun round and grabbed a small
bridesmaid, pushing her firmly back into place.

'Now,' she said, frowning in concentration, then
broke off again.

'Oh *do* stand STILL, Kate,' she snapped at the
protesting bridesmaid. 'It doesn't matter if Nigel
trod on your foot.'

'Now where was I?' she wailed. 'Yes, of course, I'd left
out the chief bridesmaid. Laura, you should be in front
of Mother and Sir Charles, immediately after all these
little horrors. And Alasdair, good thing you've finally
turned up because as Graeme is escorting Grannie
Sutherland and Ninian will be outside with the guard
of honour you must walk with Laura.'

Laura looked up in a panic and caught Alasdair's
amused gaze on her. Walking over to her side, he
offered her his arm with a mocking bow. Without

looking at him she took it as, like a pack of cards, they were all shuffled into place again.

'Ready?' Cristobel called, putting a restraining hand on Hamish who was about to resume his prowling.

'No do stay there with Mr McIntyre just for a minute, Nunkie darling,' she pleaded. 'Or go and talk to Grandfather Lindsay if you must change places. Now,' she breathed, taking her place at her fiancé's side. 'Are we all ready?'

Everyone grunted or nodded furiously.

'Right,' Cristobel commanded. 'Off we go.'

And as Mr McNabb, who had by now also joined the ranks of the defeated, slithered round onto the organ seat again, a triumphant Cristobel looked rapturously up at Lindsay and, with majestic chords thundering out above them everyone took up their places yet again and began to walk in slow procession back down the aisle.

Tentatively, as if she were touching red hot coals, Laura placed her hand on Alasdair's arm. As she did so, he looked down at her and she felt the muscles stiffen inside his grey pinstripe jacket. Then, suddenly, in a roaring flood, the same wonderful, crazy overwhelming feeling of voluptuous warmth coursed through her again, almost drowning her in its torrents. The music echoed round the empty church in thunderous crashing chords and Laura closed her eyes, letting it wash over her. She felt safe and secure in the shelter of Alasdair's protective arm and, for one wonderful moment let her imagination have free rein as, stepping lightly beside him, she dreamed that it was he and she who were heading the procession out of the dimness of the old church into the sunshine of a new life together.

'We've reached the step,' she heard him whisper, and opening her eyes, looked up to see him beaming down at her.

'Don't know where you were,' he went on, 'but with

your eyes closed you risked catapulting us both head first into the graveyard.'

Laura felt the blush rise once again and knew that there was nothing she could do to prevent it spreading in a deep red stain all over her neck and face. Quickly letting go of Alasdair's arm, she turned away.

'Hey, wait a minute, not so quickly,' he said, pulling her back. 'We've got to manoeuvre our way through this arch of swords I think. Or is it only the bride and groom?'

'Only the bride and groom,' Graeme called from the back. 'We now have to hang around and say "cheese" for the photographers. I must say I feel slightly idiotic standing here with my arm crooked and nothing in it. Only hope Grannie doesn't pass out tomorrow after all the excitement.'

'She won't,' Alasdair said, glancing back over his shoulder at his brother. 'She's like Mother. Looks as frail as a buttercup but in actual fact is as tough as an old boot.'

As there was no photographer present to capture the bride in her old tweed skirt and faded twinset standing beside the groom in crumpled cavalry twills, the little group broke up on the steps of the church.

Cristobel clapped her hands imperiously.

Whatever has come over her, Laura thought. I've never known her bossy like this before.

'Now then everybody,' Cristobel called, the verger seeming to have taken early retirement. 'Are you sure you all know your places for tomorrow? We don't want a rugby scrum when it comes to processing out, do we, Mr McIntyre?'

The verger nodded bleakly, obviously convinced that tomorrow would be a disaster.

There was a general chorus of 'yes', led loudly by the youngest members who had been standing still for long enough and had now begun a hilarious game of hide and seek among the tomb stones.

'Oh, someone catch them and tie them up somewhere,' Cristobel wailed.

'I think perhaps we could go home to tea now, dear,' Lady Flora put in mildly. 'Cook is being frantic about all the preparations for tomorrow so the sooner she has the kitchen free, the better.'

She turned to Lady Fraser and the two of them walked away deep in conversation.

10

The Count Down

'Do you think Lady Entwhistle will wear the Red Indian headdress she sported at the Buchanan wedding in June?' Alasdair enquired of his mother halfway through breakfast the next morning. 'She looked as if she'd been on a duck shoot and was carrying the booty home on her head.'

'Oh Alasdair,' Lady Flora reproached, 'I'm sure she looked very charming. I can't think why you're always so unpleasant about dear Grace.'

'Dear Grace, indeed,' Alasdair sniffed. 'You obviously weren't butted in the midriff by her "save the cuckoo" display.'

Laura looked down at her plate and bit her lip, trying hard not to laugh.

'I wish I'D seen her,' Cristobel said enviously. 'Just my luck to be in Switzerland and miss all the fun.'

'You didn't miss much,' Alasdair retorted. 'The buffet was modelled on one of Hamish's picnics, aged trout wilting on damp cotton wool and cockroach pâté.'

'Alasdair *darling*,' Lady Flora broke in and, smiling across at Laura, skilfully changed the conversation.

'Did Cristobel tell you about the arrangements for this evening?' she enquired.

Laura shook her head.

'It's always such an anti-climax for the younger members of a wedding party, once the bride and groom leave,' her hostess went on. 'So we've arranged a little dinner party for you.'

She stopped and looked across at her husband.

'It's all arranged, isn't it, Robert?'

Her husband smiled indulgently at her over the top of his newspaper.

'Yes darling,' he replied. 'Don't you remember you and Dorothy Farquharson spent the whole of Monday afternoon working it out?'

'Yes, of course,' Lady Flora smiled back, 'how stupid of me.'

She turned back to Laura, still with that same sweet vague smile.

'You'll enjoy it Laura. The Farquharsons have very kindly invited you all for dinner and an informal dance afterwards. I think Dorothy said she was hiring a pianist. I can't remember. Anyway, Graeme will escort you. Ninian . . .'

Her second son looked round a corner of his newspaper.

'As you're the tallest I've arranged for you to escort Catriona McFadden. One has to be so careful whom one chooses for her, otherwise she ends up with a partner who only comes up to her hip.'

'Oh thanks,' Ninian retorted drily.

His mother smiled at him, oblivious of his sarcasm.

Crumbling a piece of toast between her fingers, Laura kept her eyes fixed on her plate. She noticed that no mention had been made of whom Alasdair would accompany: but since the party was to be at the Farquharsons, it was obviously a foregone conclusion.

'That's all settled, then,' Lady Flora sighed happily. 'I'm sure you'll all have a simply lovely time.'

Alasdair reached for the marmalade and smiled across the table at Laura.

'Why can't Graeme take Grannie Sutherland to the party this evening and leave me Laura?' he teased.

'After all, the chief bridesmaid is my wedding partner, not his.'

Lady Flora looked up at him in bewilderment.

'Oh no, darling,' she replied. 'Grannie will be too tired.'

She cast a glance round the crowded table.

'Has anyone been in to say good morning to Grannie yet?' she enquired.

Nobody had.

'You can have Catriona McFadden if you like,' Ninian put in without taking his eyes off his newspaper.

'Oh NINIAN,' Lady Flora wailed, 'you *can't* do that to poor Catriona. You *know* how shy she is and I've told her that you're so looking forward to accompanying her.'

'Thanks *again*,' Ninian muttered.

'Oh dear,' Lady Flora sighed, 'why do you children have to be so difficult?'

Her husband put down his newspaper and looked across at her.

'Is something the matter, my dear?' he enquired.

'No, yes, oh ROBERT, now that everything is arranged, they ALL want to start changing partners at the last minute. It's really very trying.'

Her husband smiled his slow smile, which was so like Alasdair's.

'Not Cristobel, I hope?' he teased, raising his bushy eyebrows. 'At this late hour that really would be trying.'

Flora looked at him helplessly.

'Don't worry my dear,' he said soothingly. 'Everything is always all right on the day.'

At that moment, Sandy looked up from his plate, his mouth full of kippers.

'What about me?' he blurted out, showering everyone around him with half masticated bits of fish.

'Sandy, you're DISGUSTING,' Alasdair cried angrily, wiping lumps of Sandy's breakfast off the sleeve of his jacket. 'Mother, can't he be locked up somewhere out of sight at mealtimes?'

'I HAD thought of asking him to have breakfast in the old schoolroom with the little bridesmaids and pages,' Lady Flora replied absently, which remark brought further howls from Sandy, 'but it slipped my mind.'

'Heaven save us,' Graeme exclaimed, turning the pages of *The Scotsman*. 'Goodness knows what tricks he'd have taught them. They'd probably all have trotted down the aisle disguised as turnips and cucumbers.

'You're probably right,' his mother replied.

'But what ABOUT me?' Sandy insisted loudly. 'I'M ushing too. I should be invited to the party.'

'*Not* a hope,' Alasdair put in. 'Radishes are definitely *not* on the menu this evening. And anyway, who would want to partner you?'

'We could always ask Rose Livesay,' Graeme said mildly. 'I'm sure she'd jump at the chance.'

Alasdair burst out laughing and Lady Flora, once again oblivious of everything that was going on around her, smiled sweetly across at him.

'I went to Cristobel's engagement ball,' Sandy pouted.

'Merely because it was safer to have you where we could keep an eye on you,' Alasdair answered. 'The Farquharson's don't have that problem.'

'But why should I have to come home to a rotten boiled egg when you lot will be stuffing yourselves with caviar?' Sandy protested, waving his fork in the air.

'Sandy dear,' Lady Flora cut in mildly, looking up from her letters. 'Don't be so tiresome. You know perfectly well that no-one goes to a grown up party at fifteen. And leave your fork on your plate.'

Laura not only kept her fork but her eyes fixed

firmly on her plate. As she heard the inevitable wrangling and repartee going on around her she wondered at Robert Hamilton's seeming indifference. He was a man of authority and yet he rarely intervened in these frequent altercations between his children. Perhaps he realises that they none of them mean it, she thought, and once again felt a pang of envy for Cristobel's tremendous good fortune in being part of this warring, teasing but basically happy and united family. Yesterday afternoon, when she had let her imagination run away with her, she had almost felt that she might one day be part of it. Now the immense happiness which had swept over her at Alasdair's touch in the church drained slowly away, leaving her with only the fragments of her fragile dream, as she told herself miserably that he was merely being nice to his little sister's friend.

'Oh, they're talking about our little lass!' Graeme's voice broke in on her thoughts. He laughed, shaking the pages of *The Scotsman*.

'Ooh,' squealed Cristobel, 'let me see.'

And she leapt from her place and flew round the table to grab the newspaper from her brother's hands.

'Hey, steady on,' he chided.

She rustled the paper impatiently, looking for the announcement.

'Here,' Graeme laughed, taking it from her anxious hands. 'Let me find it for you.'

And, slowly turning the pages, he folded the newspaper in half and pointed out a paragraph to her.

Cristobel gazed enchanted at the black print and sighed with delight.

'I can't *believe* it,' she purred. 'It's really happening . . . It's *today!*'

And throwing down the paper she grabbed Graeme from his chair and began her inevitable twirling.

'Wait a minute, steady on,' he laughed.

But there was no stopping her: she twirled him round and round the table until her brother cried out for mercy.

'If you want me to ush' he gasped, 'then you'd better let go, or I won't even be able to stand up, let alone show your illustrious guests to their seats.'

Cristobel dropped her arms and stood stock still.

'Oh WHY isn't it half past eleven NOW?' she cried.

'It soon will be,' Robert Hamilton smiled affectionately at his only daughter.

Laura looked at him and thought she detected a note of sadness in his voice. He caught her glance and, perhaps sensing that she had understood the undertones behind his remark, quickly masked his face with his newspaper again. Laura thought of her own father so remote and distant, and contrasted him unfairly with Robert.

'Perhaps we should be thinking of getting ready?' Lady Flora suggested.

Cristobel grabbed Laura, hauling her to her feet.

'Come on,' she squealed excitedly, 'let's go on up.'

'The bouquets have just arrived,' Lady Flora announced, as she joined the two girls on the half landing where Cristobel had stopped to commiserate with Sarah over all the uproar her bridesmaids and pages had wrought upon the dog's peaceful old age. 'They are absolutely lovely. Jock organised them all.'

'Jock?' Cristobel looked up, her arms round Sarah's thick neck.

'He insisted on coming back and coping with the flowers,' her mother said.

'Oh, DARLING Jock,' Cristobel breathed. 'Is he downstairs now?'

'No, he's gone home, but he'll be here when you come back from the church.'

'Isn't he going to the church?' Cristobel asked in surprise.

'He's ninety-two, darling,' Lady Flora reminded her. 'He might find the crowd and the standing too much, but he wants to be the first to congratulate Lindsay when you return.'

Cristobel's luminous grey eyes filled with tears. Jock had come as an apprentice gardener to Ardnakil before Robert was born. He had risen to head gardener and had taught Malcolm and a succession of younger men their skills. He was now very frail but had always sworn that he would not die until he'd seen his Miss Cristobel married.

A terrible wailing came from the floor above.

'Oh dear,' said Lady Flora. 'I do hope Alasdair isn't being too unkind to Sandy.'

Laura and Cristobel looked at each other and grinned.

'You will stay until Lindsay and Cristobel come back from their honeymoon, won't you?' Lady Flora said to Laura as they walked up the wide oak staircase together.

'I'm afraid I have to go back to London,' Laura mumbled. 'My classes start early next week.

Laura was a talented pianist and, against her aunt's advice and in spite of Cristobel's pleadings and protests, had decided not to accompany her friend to the finishing school in Switzerland but to concentrate on her music instead. She was now about to enter her second year at the Academy.

'And . . . I'm taking up the harp as well this term,' she added. 'I can't possibly arrive late.'

'Oh Laura, how sad,' Lady Flora said. 'I was so hoping you would be able to stay on. Robert and I will find the house terribly empty once Cristobel has gone.'

Laura knew that this was not true. They were utterly wrapped up in each other, but the lonely child she had always been was pleased to feel wanted.

'We're only going to be away a week,' Cristobel

complained. 'Can't you just wait till next Friday?
Lindsay has to be back on duty in Germany on
Monday morning so we shall be leaving here on
Saturday afternoon and taking the boat from Hull to
somewhere or other over there, can't remember where,
then drive on to our new home.'

Lady Flora looked intently at her daughter.

'I do hope you won't be disappointed,' she remarked
thoughtfully. 'Married quarters can sometimes be
rather primitive.'

'DISAPPOINTED?' Cristobel exclaimed, her eyes
shining. 'Oh NEVER, no matter WHERE we end
up. I'd be happy living under the bacon counter at
Sainsburys as long as Lindsay was there.'

Her mother and Laura exchanged amused smiles.

'Oh do change your mind,' Cristobel pleaded, grabbing her friend round the waist. 'You simply must
stay. You can practise your old scales twice as hard
the week after.'

Like her elder brothers, Cristobel was not musical.

'The entire family will be here,' she added, 'and
we're going to have a lovely wedding party all over
again next Friday evening, only this time with Lindsay
and me present.'

They had reached the long gallery and Cristobel
began dancing Laura round from side to side. Had
Laura been wavering, this last remark would have
decided her. She had no desire to be part of any more
family gatherings as long as Alasdair was around.

'Say yes,' Cristobel whispered looking directly into
her eyes, as they slithered to a standstill.

Laura smiled and said nothing, and Cristobel assumed
that she had won. When she gets back from her
honeymoon she'll have other things to occupy her
mind, Laura said to herself, she won't even notice
I've gone.

'Your dress has been laid out on your bed,' Lady

Flora said coming up behind them. 'So pretty, the same blue as your eyes. You'll look enchanting, Laura dear.'

Laura smiled and opened the door to her room.

'Mother, come and help me,' squealed Cristobel as she pushed open her own door. Then she gave a gasp.

'Oh Laura,' she swooned, 'just come and look.'

She reappeared in the corridor holding in her arms a frothing mass of ivory satin and old lace.

'Cristobel, don't,' Laura cried. 'You'll crease it or get it dirty.'

Cristobel grinned and waltzed back into her room.

Her mother smiled affectionately after her and made to follow her daughter but, turning in the doorway saw Laura still standing in the long gallery. Sensing the bitter-sweet emotions which inevitably mingle in the mind of every chief bridesmaid as she sees her best friend go to the altar before her, Lady Flora walked back towards her.

'Do call if you need anything,' she said softly and, drawing Laura to her enveloped her in a warm embrace.

11

A Day Later

In spite of the pandemonium and almost total confusion
which had reigned at the rehearsal, as her father had so
wisely stated, everything was all right on the day and
Cristobel's wedding had been the wedding that every
young girl dreams she will one day have.

A perfect September morning, a dance of flowers
against cloudless blue sky and the autumn foliage
brushstroked with glorious wild slashes of rust and
gold. As the shimmering sunbeams filtered in through
the open church door and Lindsay and Cristobel walked
out on to the sunlit porch, the great bell pealed, the
organ boomed, the waiting crowd cheered and, feeling
Alasdair's protecting arm against her hand, Laura
momentarily felt the flame of the bridal couple's blaze
of happiness set her alight.

'That dress exactly matches your eyes,' Alasdair
whispered as they stood in the sunshine posing for the
photographer. 'Has anyone ever told you that they are
like forget-me-nots?'

Laura felt that wretched blush rise up and stain her
cheeks again.

Alasdair pressed her hand against his arm.

'Now they're shining,' he murmured, 'like deep blue,
unfathomable pools.'

But, at that moment, just when she was beginning
to feel that perhaps her imagination had not deceived
her, Fiona Farquharson ran towards them.

'Laura,' she called, 'you're to go with Lady Entwhistle in her car.'

And, grabbing Alasdair's hand possessively, added, 'You're coming with us.'

Laura's blush faded, and with it the sparkle in her eyes. She felt like an unwanted parcel with 'not known at this address' written boldly across it in Fiona Farquharson's handwriting.

'Just one minute,' Alasdair said, retrieving Laura's hand and tucking it back under his arm. 'I'd like to see Laura to her car first.'

'All Mother's carting arrangements seem to have gone haywire,' he remarked, as they walked over to where Lady Entwhistle's chauffeur was waiting.

He laughed.

'But then that's Mother. Unfortunately, out of the muddle you've picked an unlucky number: only hope the old girl doesn't bite you!'

Laura looked up at him, not understanding.

'Her fancy dress,' he smiled. 'She's swopped her Minnehaha headpiece for a bright purple flue brush festooned with feathers. Looks like an angry cockatoo that's been left out in the rain all night, and she might have developed their nasty pecking habits! Mercifully the journey won't take too long, but I'm sure the old girl will find time to tell you all about the riots in Injah and how her gairls tore up their underwear to make bandages for dying Sikhs.'

And he squeezed her hand encouragingly as he handed her into the waiting car.

Lady Entwhistle leant forward to greet them, her vast form flowing over the entire back seat. Her dress appeared to have been made from pleated aluminium and her small head literally drooped with a profusion of feathers.

'Hope there'll be room for you as well as the hat,' Alasdair hissed out of the side his mouth.

Then turning to Lady Entwhistle he smiled.

'How charming you look,' he remarked. 'So kind of you to take Laura with you.'

Lady Entwhistle made a not very successful attempt to liberate a few square inches for her passenger and Laura squeezed in beside, or more accurately, on top of her. As the car glided off with its heavy cargo, Lady Entwhistle leant forward and waved. As she did so, a few stray feathers detached themselves and flew about in every direction.

In spite of her sudden onset of gloom on the church steps, Laura could not help but be amused by Lady Entwhistle's outrageous outfit. Her hat continued to moult for the rest of the day; so that by the time the happy couple left for their honeymoon in a shower of rice and confetti and old boots, thoughtfully provided by Sandy, the drive at Ardnakil had taken on the aspect of the city dump.

'It won't make any difference to our friendship,' Cristobel had whispered as she hugged Laura warmly before being whisked away by her handsome bridegroom to the Lindsay estate in the Western Highlands which would one day be theirs. 'You must come to Germany to visit us very soon, and promise you'll come back and meet me here next summer.'

Laura had promised. It would have been impossible to refuse the radiant Cristobel anything at that moment. But once the kisses, the hugs, the good wishes, the last minute recommendations and the frantic waving had subsided and Sandy had been hauled from inside the boot of the bridal car, Laura escaped to her room, ostensibly to rest. Sitting on the deep window seat she looked out across the lawns which until such a short time ago had teemed with more than three hundred people laughing and chatting as they strolled over them. She knew that unless a miracle occurred this would be the last time she would come to Ardnakil: at least until her feelings for Alasdair, which now seemed to be deeper and more intense than ever had faded or died, or perhaps even been replaced by something stronger.

But as she gazed at the last guests straggling across the lawn she knew that this was unlikely, if not impossible. Alasdair had filled her thoughts and her dreams for so long, and that adolescent infatuation had slowly changed into a deep certainty that he was the one man who could bring her to that awakening which she had seen in Cristobel's eyes, and supply her every woman's needs.

Laura sighed, and rising from her low cushioned seat, wandered aimlessly around the pretty room, then flopped down on the bed, her hands locked behind her head, gazing at nothing in particular. Now, all that seemed impossible, and life stretched bleakly in front of her with Alasdair dancing slowly into the distance, Fiona Farquharson in his arms. But the excitement of the past twenty-four hours, combined with the gentle caressing warmth of the late afternoon sunshine beaming into her room through the wide open window finally overcame her. In spite of herself, she slept, to awaken with a start as the clock in the tower struck six.

When she walked into the drawing room an hour later, as she expected, only Graeme was waiting for her.

'How charming you look,' he said politely, offering her his arm.

Laura smiled, remembering that these were the very words Alasdair had spoken to Lady Entwhistle as he handed her into the car after the wedding; and knowing that he had meant just the opposite.

The evening was a success as far as everyone else was concerned. Graeme was an attentive escort. Ninian was his usual quiet, charming self and Alasdair came over to her the minute they arrived and made the same remark Graeme had made half an hour before, thereby plunging Laura into an agony of gloom and uncertainty. And she determined that no matter what pressure was put on her to stay, she would cut short her visit and return to London the following morning.

*   *   *

'It's another beautiful day,' Lady Flora announced happily at breakfast the next morning, 'and we're all going to Pitlochry for lunch. A lovely family party.'

She looked vaguely round the table where several Sutherland and Gordon relations were having breakfast.

'You will all come, won't you?' she smiled. 'It's going to be like the wedding all over again, only nicer in a way because it will be just us. How many shall we be, Robert?'

'I've told them we'll be twenty,' her husband answered, 'but I can always telephone and say we'll be more.'

Like Hamish, Robert Hamilton had a habit of speaking in short staccato bursts. He now raised his bushy eyebrows and smiled affectionately across at his wife.

Laura looked from one to the other of them and, remembering her own parents, felt a lump rise in her throat. They had been happy in their way, although there had never been any visible sign of their love for each other. But seeing the way Robert's eyes rested on his wife, and how she returned his smile as their eyes met, Laura realised that at that moment in time they were alone together, wrapped warmly and securely in a loving world of their own. A world which no-one could ever penetrate or destroy.

And she wondered whether she would ever know

that absolute certainty of love given and returned, that complete oneness with another human being which she now witnessed between this couple who had been married for nearly thirty years.

Laura was tempted to let herself be drawn into this post-wedding family gathering, even to pretend that she might one day see that expression in Alasdair's eyes as they rested on her. She had so many happy memories of Pitlochry, the gateway to the Highlands, and of that particular hotel to which Robert had often taken them during her annual visits. She smiled as she recalled the sensation they always caused as he marched in, towering above everyone else, with them all scrambling behind, to the large oval table set in a deep bay overlooking the glen which appeared to have been reserved for the family in perpetuity.

It would be fun, she reasoned, to discuss and dissect the events of the previous day. Then, looking up, Laura saw Alasdair remonstrating with Sandy who was wolfing eggs and bacon as if he'd had advance warning of a famine, and she knew that, as far as her emotions were concerned, the sooner she got away the better. Every glance he cast in her direction she misinterpreted, every word he uttered gave her hope, and although he had been kind and attentive the previous evening and indeed throughout the whole day she knew that she was only building up dreams which would in the end be shattered. For Alasdair, she was merely his little sister's friend, a guest in his parents' home to whom he was expected to be helpful and courteous.

'I'm afraid I have to leave this morning,' she announced, taking her courage in both hands.

Lady Flora looked at her as if she had just announced the end of the world.

'But Laura, you CAN'T', she cried.

Laura smiled at her hostess.

'I'm afraid I must.'

Alasdair grinned across at her.

'Going already?' he teased. 'It's positively cruel. I was just beginning to enjoy walking down the aisle with you.'

Laura coloured and felt wretched.

'Couldn't you just stay for the weekend?' Lady Flora pleaded. 'I had hoped you'd still be here next weekend, but to go now, is cruel.'

Laura knew that she had to just ride the storm.

'I'd love to,' she replied. 'But I really have to get back and start my studies. It would be easier for me to take the lunchtime train if it's not too inconvenient for you.'

'It's TERRIBLY inconvenient,' Lady Flora wailed. 'Oh Laura, how COULD you desert us like this?'

Then sensing Laura's discomfort, she smiled.

'But you'll come back again very soon, won't you?' she coaxed, reaching across and patting her hand. 'We've come to regard you as one of the family.'

Again Laura felt that dreadful lump rise in her throat.

'Thank you,' she mumbled, her voice beginning to break.

Lady Flora gathered her letters together and everyone left the table to go their separate ways.

'See you all in the hall at a quarter past eleven,' Robert said. 'And wear stout shoes, we're going for a walk afterwards.'

Everyone gathered around Laura, expressing their regrets, saying goodbye, showering her with compliments, telling her how perfectly lovely she had looked at the wedding. When she at last managed to escape and make her way towards the stairs, Alasdair was standing in the hall glancing through an old copy of the *Horse and Hound*. As she walked towards him he lowered it and smiled at her.

'It's possible that I may be in London in a few weeks' time,' he said. 'Perhaps I could have your address, or your telephone number. It would be nice if we could meet.'

Laura panicked.

'I don't have an address,' she answered stupidly. 'I live with my aunt.'

'I know,' he went on quietly. 'Edwina. Cristobel told me.'

Laura looked up at him in amazement.

Alasdair smiled his tantalising smile.

'But SHE must live somewhere,' he continued, putting down the magazine and walking towards her.

'Yes, she does,' Laura stammered. 'She lives in Kensington. Cristobel will give it to you.'

Alasdair stood directly in front of her, his head on one side.

'Won't you?' he asked softly and, taking a small leatherbound notebook from his breast pocket he stood there, holding his pen aloft, looking enquiringly at her.

12

Breaking into the Stronghold

Laura returned to London, her mind in a turmoil. Not
only was she physically tired from the hectic few days
she had just spent, but emotionally drained by the
series of bumps and jolts she had received during
those days. For her, they had been like a violent
thunderstorm pierced by intense lightning flashes of
unexpected joy, only to be immediately followed by
sudden plunges into the depths of despair. Alasdair's
behaviour towards her was now even more of an enigma
than ever.

Looking out of the carriage window at the countryside flying past, her emotions followed the same
pattern, rising abruptly like the distant purple-clad
mountains to impossible peaks of delirious happiness when she remembered the touch of his hand,
his whispered confidences, his quizzical smile in the
church, the look in his hazel eyes when he asked for
her address; only to be suddenly extinguished as the
inevitable image of Fiona Farquharson's laughing face
gazing into his and her possessive attitude outside the
church took their hold on her mind. By the time the
train finally steamed into King's Cross Laura wanted
only one thing: to sleep and to forget, to wake up
and not even remember that she had ever known the
Hamiltons, ever been to Ardnakil.

But, as she wearily dragged her suitcase from
the rack and stepped down onto the grimy crowded

platform she knew that even if such a thing were possible, even if one could wipe out the past and begin again, the memory of Alasdair's smile would continue to haunt her.

And so, in the ensuing days, she plunged into her music, spending long hours in front of the harp which Edwina had now had installed for her in the drawing room next to the piano. Every time the telephone rang and Effie came in to announce that it was for her, Laura's heart missed a beat.

But it was never Alasdair at the other end of the line.

Occasionally she found Edwina watching her with an understanding, almost protective look in her eyes and then she would long to throw herself into her aunt's arms and pour out all the ache in her heart but, always something held her back, and Edwina wisely made no comment, made no effort to force her niece's confidence. And again, Laura would envy Cristobel the easy intimacy which existed between her and her mother: an intimacy which seemed alien to her own family.

'I was wondering whether you would like to go to Vienna for Christmas,' Edwina remarked one evening as Laura sat musing at the keyboard.

Laura looked up.

'But what about Father?' she enquired.

Since her mother's death, she and Edwina had often gone down to Oxford to spend the two festive days with him, but they were anything but festive, although Henry Denning's old housekeeper did her best to make an extra effort as far as the cooking was concerned. But her father, after welcoming them cordially, usually seemed rather relieved when the time came for them to say goodbye.

'I really don't think he'd notice whether we were there or not,' Edwina smiled. 'It might even be a relief if we weren't. You've been looking very pale recently perhaps you're working too hard and need a change. You'd enjoy Vienna, there are always wonderful performances at the Opera during the winter season.'

Laura shrugged.

'Yes,' she replied half-heartedly. 'If you think it would be a good idea.'

'I do think so,' Edwina replied firmly. 'In fact, I've already made some enquiries.'

She got up and came to sit on the piano stool beside her niece.

'We could leave on the twenty-second,' she went on, 'that would fit in with your classes, wouldn't it?'

Laura nodded absently.

'I'll write to The Bristol later this evening to reserve rooms, and I can see about our train reservations in the morning, unless you'd rather go by aeroplane. It is much quicker but I do prefer to travel by train, especially in the winter and . . .'

She broke off suddenly.

'Laura, you're not listening!'

With an effort Laura jerked herself back to the present.

She had been thinking of Ardnakil, wondering whether Lindsay and Cristobel would be there for the festive season, seeing in her mind's eye the enormous Christmas tree twinkling with coloured lights which always stood in a corner of the great hall, the dining room decorated with garlands of holly and mistletoe and the laughter as the turkey was brought in. And then her thoughts had slipped on to Hogmanay. The Hamiltons have it all ways, she thought, they celebrate Christmas in style and then hardly have time to recover before they are plunged into the balls, the parties, the excitement of New Year's Eve. Laura suppressed a smile as she remembered Sandy and his radish outfit, wondering whether Lady Entwhistle would invite him to her young people's party this year or whether she

139

would seek a more suitable escort for her youngest granddaughter.

'I'm sorry,' she blinked, 'Do go on.'

'Never mind,' Edwina said serenely, getting up and going back to her book by the fire. 'We'll talk about it in a few days when you're less tired and the idea has had time to sink in.'

Laura twisted round on the piano stool and smiled at her aunt.

'Yes, if you don't mind,' she said weakly. 'I am rather tired. I think I'll go to bed.'

'You need to get out more,' Edwina said fondly as Laura closed the piano. 'There's a Polish pianist playing at the Albert Hall tomorrow evening. Would you like me to see if I can get tickets?'

'What's he playing?' Laura enquired, as she walked towards the door.

'I don't know. Chopin I should imagine. Poles usually do,' Edwina replied non-committally. You don't have anything else on, do you?'

Laura shook her head. Since she had returned from Cristobel's wedding she had not had 'anything else on'. She had plunged herself into her music, in an attempt to forget.

'Then I'll book tickets for us,' Edwina said firmly.

She looked at her niece as she turned in the doorway.

'It might be a good idea for you to get out of London at the weekend and breathe some country air,' she remarked. 'And it wouldn't hurt you to put on a little weight either. You've never been fat but these last few months you've become positively wraithlike.'

Laura nodded, her hand on the door knob, but didn't reply.

But the next evening when she returned home, Edwina greeted her with an unexpected piece of news.

'I had a telephone call from a friend of yours this afternoon,' she said, coming into the hall to greet her.

Laura dropped her music case and looked at her aunt enquiringly.

He asked for Miss Denning, Edwina went on and of course Effie thought he meant me. It was Cristobel's brother. He's in London for a few days, so I asked him to dinner this evening.'

'This EVENING?' Laura replied. 'But I thought we were going to that concert at the Albert Hall.'

'We were,' Edwina went on, 'but I asked him to accompany you in my place.'

Laura stood stock still, her mouth half open, her throat suddenly dry, gazing at Edwina.

'But none of the Hamiltons are musical,' she said, her voice sounding like a croak and added as an afterthought: 'Except Sandy.'

Edwina looked at her strangely, but made no comment.

'You do surprise me,' she answered, walking back into the drawing room. 'He seemed delighted by the idea.'

She sat down again by the fire and looked across at Laura standing gaping in the doorway; and her eyes twinkled.

'I asked Effie to iron your blue tafetta,' she smiled. 'I think you look particularly charming in it.'

She bent down to throw a log into the leaping flames.

'Now do go and change, he'll be here in half an hour.'

Laura turned back towards the hall not daring to ask the question uppermost in her mind. It could be Ninian in London for a few days ... or it could be Graeme. But neither had asked for her telephone number ...

'Do you know which brother?' she finally managed

141

to blurt out, keeping her face averted from her aunt's penetrating gaze.

'Yes,' Edwina replied calmly, 'he announced himself as ALASDAIR Hamilton.'

Laura looked at her in a panic and fled to her bedroom.

By the time she had shut the door behind her and glanced in the mirror above her dressing table, her face was crimson. She sat down abruptly on the bed, seeking wildly for some excuse not to appear at dinner: a headache, nausea, or perhaps sudden, unaccountable fatigue. But she knew that none of them would work. Edwina had seen the panic in her eyes and, at the same time, seen right through her. Laura understood that inviting Alasdair to dinner and offering him her place at the recital was not an uncalculated act on her aunt's part. Edwina knew her niece better than Laura realised, and had gathered that her listlessness over the past few weeks was not accidental or even physical, and certainly not due only to overwork.

'Oh, why did he have to telephone?' she groaned.

Her emotions were at last beginning to simmer down, or so she had thought, and she was busily engaged in carving out a niche for herself in which she could hide, a life which excluded everything but her music. Why had he come to break into this cosy stronghold which she had not yet finished erecting?

Then she remembered the look in his eyes when he asked for her address and, for a moment, her heart soared, only to sink again like a bird suddenly felled by a hunter's bullet.

'He said he was coming to London later on,' she muttered. 'I suppose he doesn't know too many people and thought his sister's little friend might fill an evening, instead of spending it alone at his club.'

And she hardened her heart to any other explanation as she walked steadily to the bathroom, her lips set in a firm line, hoping against hope that he would have a last minute hold-up.

But Alasdair arrived exactly on time.

Laura heard him in the hall as she sat stiffly in the drawing room with Edwina and her heart began to beat unreasonably. But by the time Effie had announced him she had set not only her lips but her thoughts into a straight hard line.

Edwina was obviously charmed by Alasdair and, good hostess that she was, made up for Laura's sullen silence, keeping the conversation flowing smoothly throughout dinner.

'I'll ask Effie to telephone for a taxi,' she said as she poured the coffee. 'I don't think you should leave it much later.'

Laura dreaded the moment when she would find herself alone with Alasdair, bowling towards the Albert Hall side by side. She steeled herself in advance to his touch.

As they sat together in the taxi he looked at her with that same quizzical smile.

'Your aunt is charming,' he murmured.

'Yes, she is,' Laura replied.

'Odd that she hasn't married,' he went on after an uncomfortable pause.

'Perhaps she didn't want to,' Laura said aggressively.

He looked down at her again and she trembled, feeling his nearness, longing for his touch, yet shrinking into the corner of the cab, fearful of what would happen if she surrendered to his closeness.

'Perhaps,' he answered thoughtfully, and lapsed into silence.

As the taxi drew up in front of the Albert Hall Alasdair turned to hand her down.

'And are you like her, Laura?' he enquired.

For a moment she didn't fully understand his meaning, then when she realised that he was merely finishing the sentence he had started a few minutes earlier, she blushed and stiffened.

'I don't know,' she mumbled, getting out and standing beside him, removing her hand from his. 'Yes, I suppose so.'

They walked in silence up the steps and into the crowded foyer.

When they walked back out into the dark night, it was raining. Standing amongst the milling crowd waiting for a taxi, Laura looked away from him, looked at anything rather than risk meeting his eyes. The glistening wet pavements, from which double decker buses, their streaming windows solid with heads, were lumbering away, spread out before her like a shining wet macintosh. The lights from passing cars dazzled with raindrops as they glided by into the rain-soaked darkness.

'Here we are,' Alasdair said as a taxi stopped beside them.

Laura was in an agony of apprehension as he opened the door and handed her in. She knew that she ought to invite Alasdair back to the flat for a drink to end the evening but, as he sat beside her, the slight damp smell rising from his clothes seemed to bring with it an odour which emphasised his masculinity. And she did not know how much longer she could keep up this pretence of indifference.

'I have to return to Edinburgh at the weekend,' he remarked casually, as he leant back against the leather cushion. 'But it would be lovely if we could meet again. Would you by any chance be free to have dinner with me tomorrow evening?'

Laura's heart was beating a tattoo inside her dress. Her defences were beginning to crumble, everything within her longed to say 'yes', but she remembered the last time they had met. Fiona Farquharson once again came and stood aggressively between them.

'No, I'm afraid not,' she said tightly.

'Oh dear,' he replied. 'What a pity.'

Alasdair looked intently out of the taxi window for a few seconds then turned to her.

'Perhaps Thursday?' he enquired.

'I'm awfully busy at the moment,' she answered stiffly, shrinking once again into the corner of the cab. Then, anticipating his next question, added. 'On Friday I'm going down to the country for the weekend.'

He did not pursue the matter further and they sat in a heavy silence as the taxi manoeuvred through the web of streets.

'I have the offer of a transfer to London,' Alasdair said quietly as they turned into her quiet road. 'That's why I'm here, to nose out the pros and cons.'

He cleared his throat.

'I have to make up my mind fairly quickly whether I shall accept it or not.'

It almost seemed as if he were asking her opinion: but, if so, she chose to ignore it.

'Really?' was all she could find to say. And the taxi drew up in front of Edwina's block of flats.

'I would like to ask you in for a nightcap,' Laura said as he prepared to pay off the driver, 'but it's late and I know you have a busy day tomorrow with all these important decisions to make. I have to be at the Academy early for a lesson, so I'll say goodbye now.'

Alasdair looked at her in surprise, too polite to comment.

He signalled to the driver to wait and, taking her arm, walked with her to the door.

'It's been delightful to see you again Laura,' he breathed. 'May I ring you when I am next in London?'

Flashes of electricity were shooting up Laura's arm and through her body at his touch.

'Perhaps – yes, no,' she stuttered. 'I am very busy.'

She quickly released her arm and plunging her hand into her little velvet evening bag, searched blindly for her key.

Alasdair held out his hand for the key and inserted it into the lock. The door swung open and an elderly porter shuffled out of his lodge.

'Good evening, Miss Denning,' he said, with a decidedly approving look at Alasdair. 'Good evening sir. Nasty night.'

He walked over to the lift and pressed the button.

'Don't worry, Sidney,' Laura murmured. 'I'll see to it.'

With a smile Sidney went back to his lodge and closed the door, leaving them standing alone together in the deserted hall.

Alasdair took Laura's hand in both of his.

'Thank you for this evening,' he said softly and, as the lift glided to a standstill, he leant slightly towards her. Laura felt his breath on her forehead and for a second leant towards him, then abruptly she stiffened and withdrew her hands. She felt him stiffen in his turn then, without a word, he opened the lift door and pressed the button for the third floor.

Without looking at him, Laura entered the lift. Alasdair closed the gates and, as it slowly mounted and she disappeared from view, he turned and walked across the hall and out into the street to where the cab was waiting, its engine gently throbbing.

Laura stood frozen in the slowly ascending lift, her head suddenly aching, longing to call him back. But her lips seemed to have locked themselves once again into that hard straight line. When the lift stopped at the third floor, she ran from it to the landing window.

Alasdair was just climbing into the waiting taxi. She watched it draw away and disappear around the corner, and tears began to tumble down her cheeks, spattering her dark blue velvet coat in sympathy with the rain spattering the window panes.

'Alasdair, Alasdair,' she wept softly. 'Oh why did you come back just as I was beginning to make some sort of sense, some sort of pattern out of my life?'

And, entering the quiet flat she crumpled, sobbing, onto the hall chair.

When the storm of her weeping began to subside, Laura became aware of the muted strains of a Beethoven symphony coming from the drawing room and she knew that her aunt had not yet gone to bed. Quickly wiping a hankie round her face she put her head round the door. The room was in darkness except for the roseate tints of the logs glowing in the grate and a pool of golden light streaming from the lamp by which Edwina sat reading. She looked up as Laura appeared.

'What a charming young man,' she smiled, wisely making no comment on her niece's red-rimmed eyes and woebegone face. 'I do hope he enjoyed the concert.'

'Yes,' Laura mumbled. 'Yes, I think so. I've just come to say goodnight.'

'Goodnight, darling,' Edwina murmured, her eyes back on her book as if she had noticed nothing amiss. 'Sleep well.'

As Laura closed the door behind her Edwina sighed and, switching off the peach-shaded reading lamp, walked across to the fire and stood gazing down into its glowing embers. She had heard the lift stop, the front door quietly open and then the broken sobbing, and her mind went back to that July morning when she had sat beside her niece's bed waiting for her to awake so that she could tell her as gently as possible that her mother's long battle with cancer had finally ended.

Laura had taken the news without comment, without

147

tears, without any outward sign of emotion. In fact, she had never spoken of it. But, always a shy, reserved child, she had seemed, from that day on, to have withdrawn more deeply into herself, to have become even more sensitive and remote. And Edwina wondered whether the storm of weeping she had just heard were not unshed tears which had been stored for over seven years, held back, waiting for release.

As these thoughts crossed her mind, Laura's words when she had broken the news of her mother's death to her took on a new meaning.

'Were *they* there?' her niece had asked.

She had been referring to her two elder sisters, both married and living away, who had come back home in the past few weeks. And Edwina heard for the first time the resentment in the young girl's voice and knew the rejection Laura must have felt, perhaps even the feeling that she was unwanted or unworthy, or in some way to blame for her mother's death.

'We thought it best to let you sleep,' she had replied.

And she knew that they had been wrong.

In isolating Laura from this traumatic event in her young life they had cut her off from the help and the healing she needed, leaving her alone to cope with a terrible feeling of rejection, insecurity and worthlessness: with a pain which had never been worked through and released from her body.

She sighed again and for the first time in her life felt at a loss. Then, recalling the last words her sister-in-law had spoken to Laura: 'Your Heavenly Father will look after you', words which, at the time, seemed to have bewildered her young niece, Edwina wondered vaguely whether there might not be something to be said for having a faith after all. Had she been a churchgoer . . . but she dismissed the idea. She knew dozens of churchgoers and she was sure they would have been as much at a loss as she had been. But, as her elegantly shod foot poked idly at the few remaining embers, she recognised that there were others, some she had met over the years who had a transparent quality, a radiance about them, oddly enough like her sister in law during the last few weeks of her life. They had been different.

Edwina straightened herself, desperately hoping that Laura could meet one of them: someone who would be able to help her where she herself felt so helpless, who would be able to give her the answers to life's problems and help her find the security she so desperately needed.

Could this young man, Edwina mused, be the catalyst needed to open the floodgates so that the torrent of pent up emotions could be released? She fervently hoped so. Gone were the days when she could make her niece's pain better with a hug and a kiss. Laura was a woman now and, as far as her aunt could make out, a woman in love, deeply in love.

Edwina smiled sadly as she walked across the gracious white-panelled room and out into the silent hall, feeling for the first time ever out of her depth before life's great mystery.

13

The Unexpected Visitor

Laura awoke the next morning with a splitting head-ache and, turning over with a groan, a feeling of hopelessness invaded her.

The remembrance of Alasdair's nearness the evening before and, with it, the resurgence of the emotions she had tried so hard to subdue during the past weeks had left her feeling drained and weary. Mercifully, Edwina always breakfasted in her room so, apart from a brief 'good morning' to Effie when she brought in her tray, Laura was spared any conversation or discussion.

When she returned to Kensington later in the day Edwina was standing by the fire reading a note.

She turned and smiled as Laura walked into the drawing room.

'Aren't they lovely!' she exclaimed, pointing to a beautiful spray of winter roses standing in a tall vase on the piano, the deep orange gold petals blending perfectly with the autumnal shades of the furnishings. 'There's a little posy for you beside them.'

Laura walked over to the piano and picked up a bunch of forget-me-nots tied with blue satin ribbon. Withdrawing the card from its envelope she suddenly felt her knees about to buckle under her and sat down abruptly on the stool.

'The colour of your eyes,' she read. 'Remember?'

It was simply signed, 'A'.

She did remember: Cristobel's wedding when she

and Alasdair had walked together behind the bridal couple. Recalling her brief, intense happiness that perfect September morning, her whole body tingled and she began to tremble.

Laura buried her face in the posy, hoping that its freshness would draw some of the heat from her cheeks before her aunt noticed that tell-tale blush. But if Edwina did notice she made no comment and, mercifully, at that moment the door opened and Effie came in with the tea tray.

'Such a charming young man,' Edwina repeated, sitting down on the deep sofa. She picked up the Georgian silver teapot and began to pour. How very thoughtful of him, she went on, as the pale gold liquid flowed into the delicate cups. Those roses are so beautiful.'

She glanced across at them, standing erect and regal in the crystal vase.

'And wherever did he find forget-me-nots in London in December?' she added, her eyes carefully avoiding her niece's face.

Laura hurriedly put down her cup and got up.

'I forgot to ask Effie to put them in water,' she mumbled, picking up the posy. 'I have some theory to work on for tomorrow so I'll go to my room and get down to it.'

Edwina looked at her intently over the rim of her cup.

'For a young girl not yet twenty,' she remarked, as Laura crossed the room, the posy clutched in her hand, 'you do not seem to be having a very exciting time: it's all work and no play.'

Laura turned in the doorway.

'I went out yesterday evening,' she replied belligerently.

'Merely because I suggested it,' her aunt answered smoothly, putting down her cup and smiling sweetly at her niece. 'It does seem to me that when I was your age

we took life a great deal less seriously . . . and enjoyed
it a great deal more.'

Edwina sighed.

'But then, that was another generation, I suppose.
Run along, darling, and do your theory. But remember
there are other things in life besides music. Don't
become so wrapped up in it that life passes you by.'

And she innocently picked up the evening paper and
leant back amongst the deep oyster satin cushions to
read it.

All the next day Laura was absent, her thoughts
distracted. Her mind refused to concentrate, but kept
focusing on Alasdair, wondering what decision he had
taken, whether he had opted to move down to London or
to stay in Edinburgh. And, as she left the Academy later
that afternoon she once again felt weary and drained.

But the Friday was even worse than the two preced-
ing days.

She knew that by now Alasdair would have taken
that vital decision and the thought that he might
reappear in London, perhaps even living nearby with
Fiona at his side, sent her into paroxysms of anguish.
She was now convinced that his telephone call and
resultant visit had been merely a stop-gap, a means
of passing the time, as was his wish to see her again
during that week.

And she resolutely erased from her mind any remembrance of warmth between them, of tenderness on his
part, convincing herself that she had imagined it all;
that she had read more into his innate courtesy than
was intended; that once back in Scotland, Fiona
Farquharson would occupy his thoughts, if indeed she
had not been occupying them throughout the evening
he had spent with her.

As these thoughts chased each other backwards and
forwards, round and round in her tired mind, she knew
that concentration was out of the question. Not only

her fingers but her eyes refused to obey her and she was making stupid mistakes with every partition she attempted. The notes on the sheet in front of her constantly faded, and Alasdair's or Fiona's mocking faces took their place. With an exasperated sigh she finally gave up any attempt at concentration and, closing the piano, gathered up her music and left the little cubicle.

Hailing a taxi, Laura gave the address in Kensington and, lying back exhausted against the leather cushion, she suddenly had a burning desire to see Alasdair again. Just to see him, if only in the distance. Scarcely realising what she was doing, she leant forward and, tapping the dividing window, asked the driver to go through St James, so that from the cab's sheltered interior she could pass in front of Alasdair's club and perhaps catch a glimpse of him walking in or out of it: or even striding across the park.

But although the driver changed his route and slowed down as they approached the club, there was no sign of Alasdair. Two businessmen wearing bowler hats were standing discussing on the steps and, for a moment, her heart leapt. But, as the taxi crawled by she realised that they were both of medium height, neither in any way attaining Alasdair's imposing stature.

Laura closed her eyes to hold back the tears, squeezing her lids tightly together as the hot pricking behind them indicated that the dam was about to burst and gush down her cheeks. And, suddenly she clenched her fists tightly together at her sides, angry with herself and hating Alasdair for coming back into her life, for coming into her life at all, and reducing her to this miserable state of slavery.

The taxi slowed down and, opening her eyes, Laura saw that they had arrived.

As she let herself into the flat Effie appeared.

'Madame told me to tell you she won't be in for tea,'

she said, 'and that there's a gentleman waiting to see you in the drawing room.'

Laura frowned. She wasn't expecting anybody and the last thing she wanted was company.

'Who is it, Effie?' she asked listlessly.

'I don't know, miss,' the maid replied. 'Madame didn't say.'

Laura dropped her things onto the hall chair, glancing into the gilt oval mirror on the wall above her as she did so.

'What a sight,' she moaned, passing her hands through her long golden hair as her pale heart-shaped face stared back at her, the wide-set deep blue eyes appearing even larger and deeper hued than usual.

Walking across the hall she opened the drawing room door. Twilight lay like a purple cloak over the gracious room, casting deepening shadows on the silhouette of a tall well-built man. He was standing framed in the window, looking down on to the mews below but as the door opened, he turned round.

It was Alasdair.

For a moment Laura stood where she was, stunned. Then she blinked in the half light, not believing the evidence before her eyes. This man who had haunted her dreams and her every waking moment for the past six months, and even before, whom she had so unsuccessfully tried to forget so many times, whom she had so longed to see, even just to catch a distant glimpse of not an hour ago, and whom she had since convinced herself she hated and never wanted to meet again, was standing there before her.

For a split second the warm, cosy, familiar room rose and swam in front of her eyes and she clung to the heavy brass door knob for support.

'Laura,' Alasdair said quietly, and as he stood there looking at her the whole room seemed to be filled with his masculinity.

She didn't reply. She couldn't. The words refused to come.

He started to walk across the room towards her, but she remained standing in the doorway, her hand tightly gripping the knob. And, since she made no movement towards him, and no reply, he stopped abruptly, taken aback by her silence.

'I'm sorry,' he said lamely. 'I wanted to see you before leaving for Edinburgh.'

He paused.

'I had to see you,' he went on. 'I rang Miss Denning and she said you would be home at about five.'

Laura looked pointedly at her watch.

'It's only just after four,' she remarked stiffly.

'I know,' he said lamely. 'But I couldn't wait.'

Alasdair took a step towards her, but she remained where she was, rooted to the spot.

'Won't you come and sit down?' he pleaded.

She advanced slowly into the room, testing every step, her legs feeling like lumps of cotton wool, and sat down quickly on a delicate, tapestry-covered chair, carefully avoiding the deep sofa.

He sat down opposite her, his joined hands hanging loosely between his knees. No words pierced the encroaching darkness in the room: they neither of them seemed to know what to say.

Laura stole a glance at him from beneath her thick, lashes. Alasdair's face was almost in darkness, only his rugged profile visible, reflected in the dancing firelight, his eyes cast down on a square of pale gold carpet between his clenched fists.

'Laura,' he murmured at last, without raising his eyes.

But at that moment the drawing room door opened and Effie came in with the tea tray. She set up the small table in front of Laura and placed the tray on it.

'Shall I draw the curtains, miss?' she enquired.

Laura nodded dumbly and Effie bent to switch on a small lamp on the table beside her, sending a soft peach glow onto Laura's pale features. Effie straightened up and, walking across to the window, drew the heavy gold curtains against the early winter's night. Suddenly, Alasdair's features were plunged into obscurity. Laura could see only the sharp outline of his cheek and the shadow made by the cleft in his chin. As the maid switched on a tall standard lamp behind him and he leapt into view, she noticed that his lips too were pressed tightly together.

Effie walked noiselessly back across the thick carpet and closed the door quietly behind her, leaving a silence which was so heavy it enveloped them like a suffocating grey blanket of fog.

Laura lifted the silver teapot and looked across at Alasdair enquiringly. He nodded absently and she began to pour, her heart pounding in her chest, the blood thundering in her ears. As she handed him the fluted Victorian cup he looked up at her and she tried to recapture the feeling of intense anger towards him which she had experienced in the taxi on her way home. But it had gone. Their eyes met briefly and she saw the green and gold lights, which usually danced so merrily in his, dampened and almost extinguished. An overwhelming wave of love for him washed over her with such force that she caught her breath, afraid of being drowned in its depths.

Looking quickly down, she lifted the lid from a silver salver.

'Crumpets?' she murmured, avoiding his eyes.

He took one, then placed it on his plate, untouched. Laura did the same and the heavy, dense silence returned.

Suddenly Alasdair put down his cup and looked

appealingly across at her, but she avoided his gaze, studiously cutting her untouched crumpet into tiny, ridiculous squares.

'Laura,' he said hoarsely, and there was a break in his voice.

She did not look up.

'Did you get my flowers?'

She nodded.

'Thank you, yes. I'm sorry, I should have written you a note . . .'

But he brushed her excuses aside.

'I didn't want thanking,' he said harshly. 'I just thought that perhaps forget-me-nots might touch off some spark . . . that you would remember . . .'

He made a helpless gesture with his hands.

'I've waited since Wednesday hoping that there would be a message from you at my club.'

'Remember what?' Laura asked coldly, and hated herself.

He suddenly seemed crushed.

Laura picked up her cup and pushed aside her mutilated crumpet, not daring to look at him. She could feel herself weakening, melting and she pressed her lips tightly together knowing she had to steel herself against this man or be completely submerged, lost in the avalanche of love which was roaring through her and which she was convinced could only lead to disaster.

'Have you made your decision?' she enquired with false brightness.

He looked up at her blankly.

'Whether to stay in Edinburgh or come down to London?' she went on.

He shook his head slowly.

'But I thought you had to do it before you left,' she pursued still in that same false tone.

He nodded.

'I have. I'm playing golf with the Chairman tomorrow morning and lunching with him afterwards. He expects an answer then.'

Laura could feel her heart hammering beneath her silk blouse and reaching gingerly up, she pulled her soft lavender wool cardigan closely round her, convinced that he could see the rapid staccato movement underneath.

She took a deep breath.

'And do you know what it will be?'

Her voice sounded in her ears like a parrot's screech.

A log dropped in the fire, then toppled into the grate. Alasdair bent forward and, picking up the tongs, retrieved it and placed it carefully back on the pile.

'No,' he answered dully. 'That's why I'm here.'

Laura's cup clattered into the saucer.

'What on earth do you mean?' she gasped.

And then it all came tumbling out.

'I can't take any decision until I'm sure about one thing,' Alasdair said.

He got up and stood looking down at her.

'Laura,' he pleaded. 'Please tell me. Is there anyone else?'

She looked up at him blankly, her blue eyes deepening as she saw the misery in his.

'I have to know,' he said. 'At first I thought if I were patient it would all work out. I knew you were shy and reserved but you seemed to be as drawn to me as I was to you when we met again last June. And then you became so strange.'

He ran his hands through his hair in a gesture of desperation.

'For the last six months you've been avoiding me,' he cried. 'Every time I tried to see you, you ... you ran away.'

Laura sat breathing deeply, trying to collect her

thoughts, unable to believe much less understand what she had just heard.

'When I first met you, you were just Cristobel's friend,' Alasdair went on, sitting down again, 'a freckled schoolgirl with pigtails, like she was. But that evening of her engagement ball when I saw you dancing with Angus Dunbar you took my breath away.'

He looked across at her with a wry smile.

'I'll admit, I didn't recognise you at first.'

He paused, his eyes back on his clenched hands and his voice dropped almost to a whisper.

'But then I suddenly realised who you were.'

Alasdair looked up again briefly, his face softened by his endearing smile, his hazel eyes moist and shining.

'Shy little Laura with the big blue eyes and thick golden plaits, who'd turned into the most beautiful woman I'd ever seen.'

Laura leant back in her chair, the tension slowly oozing out of her as a little ripple of happiness like a gently melting ice-drift began to trickle through her. She knew that this was a dream. Her tired, tormented brain had given up and was playing her tricks, feeding into her mind a series of sequences which she had imagined herself living through so many times during the past six months, and which had now taken over and replaced reality.

Closing her eyes she tried to shut out everything but this moment, willing the world to stop. She knew that what she was hearing was merely a figment of her imagination, that imagination which now seemed to have supplanted her reason. Even so, she wanted to savour and record every moment of it. She would worry about the consequences, the aftermath when the film ended and she returned to the real world with a bump.

'Since that day I haven't been able to get you out

of my mind,' she heard Alasdair say in this beautiful dream which was wrapping her like a shawl in its soft, silken folds. 'But whenever I tried to approach you, you froze.'

He paused and looked down at his clenched hands.

'And yet there were moments,' he finally went on, as if talking to himself, 'like that evening at the Fraser's before Cristobel's wedding, and the next morning as we left the church, when I felt an answering spark in you: and I dared to hope that perhaps you did care.'

He looked up at her and smiled his crooked smile.

'That I wasn't just Cristobel's big brother.'

Laura did not open her eyes. She could not bear to. She wanted the dream to go on for ever, and she knew that once she admitted the real world, once she looked up, all she would see would be the familiar room, the crackling fire, the curtains cosily drawn and Alasdair's empty place.

'Laura,' he pleaded. 'Please say something. Whether I stay in Edinburgh or move down to London depends entirely on you.'

Alasdair got up and came over to where she was sitting and, taking both her hands in his, he gently drew her to her feet. She opened her eyes and saw him looking down at her, his eyes pleading, but at the same time, out of the shadows Fiona Farquharson's laughing face rose up and danced mockingly above his shoulder.

With a cry like a wounded fawn Laura wrenched herself free from his hands, realising that it hadn't been a dream after all, Alasdair had been there all the time. The words she had heard had not been the meanderings of her fevered imagination. And as reality began to slowly flood back into her brain, anger and pain replaced the beautiful peace and joy which had flowed through her only minutes before.

'How dare you?' she cried. 'How *dare* you?'

Alasdair stood looking helplessly down at her.

'How DARE you come here and make a fool of me?'

Laura breathed deeply attempting to gain control of herself.

'Or has Fiona Farquharson thrown you over for someone else, and you're now looking for another victim?'

And she strode across to the window and, fiercely pulling the curtain aside stood there fuming, looking down on the lighted mews below.

Alasdair turned slowly round, gazing in bewilderment at her angry, shaking figure, too stunned to speak.

'Fiona?' he gasped at last. 'FIONA? But what on earth has SHE got to do with it?'

Laura clutched at the curtain for support as his words rang in her ears. She couldn't believe what she had just heard. Had she been completely mistaken in him? Was he such a philanderer, his conquests so numerous and so ephemeral, that he lost track of them when on to another trail?

She knew she had to try to remain calm, not on any account to lose her composure, which was badly shattered, to steel herself for just long enough to see him out of the flat. Then she could let go and collapse, let all the successive waves of misery which were now crashing over her have their way and drown her in their depths. Taking a deep breath, she tried to control her breathing, but her words when they came sounded like gasps.

'Everything,' she managed to get out, her hands tightly entwined in the curtain's thick folds. 'If *you* don't know what your relationship with her is, you must be the only one who doesn't. Your entire family was practically ringing the wedding bells for you both the last time I was there.'

For a moment there was, once again, that terrible

tense silence in the room. As Laura stood there, her chest heaving, it seemed to her that black slimy shapes which had been crouching in the far corners where the lamps had not yet been lit, slowly began to creep, like dumb grey shadows towards her, leering at her, laughing at her, sidling menacingly towards her, waiting to pounce and attack, to stifle her in their lethal grasp.

She bit her lip to hold back the cry which was clutching at her throat and, at that moment, as if they had all in one fearful leap converged on her, squeezing the breath from her slim body, the terrible electric silence was broken.

A tiny gold clock on the mantlepiece began to chime the hour ... and Alasdair threw back his head and laughed.

14

The Open Road

As his laughter echoed round the room, Laura stood stiff and tense, waiting for him to go, willing him to go, longing only to hear the drawing room door close behind him and the sound of the lift rising to carry him away.

But Alasdair didn't move. He just continued to laugh helplessly, and she began to wonder whether he had taken leave of his senses.

Utterly bewildered, she half turned from the window, letting the curtain fall from her hand and, as she did so, he held out his arms and striding quickly towards her grasped both her hands, pressing his face into her upturned palms.

'Oh Laura, little Laura,' he gasped, raising his head and looking down at her, the green and gold lights once again dancing merrily in his hazel eyes. 'So *that's* what it was.'

For a few seconds she remained stiff and taut then struggled desperately to free her hands, but he held them in a vice-like grip.

Still laughing he tried to draw her to him, but she resisted fiercely. As he released her hands and caught her tightly in his arms she struggled and kicked, pounding her clenched fists against his broad chest.

'How DARE you?' she cried, the tears now streaming unchecked down her cheeks. 'Let me go!'

But Alasdair held her even closer to him, so that her

Laura

hands were imprisoned and she felt as if all breath was
being slowly squeezed from her body.

'Laura,' he murmured, his face buried in her hair,
'little Laura with the forget-me-not blue eyes. What a
fool I've been.'

And he brushed his lips across her forehead. Then,
gently tilting back her head, he gazed down into those
blue eyes which were now swimming with tears.

'Darling,' he whispered, kissing her hot, wet cheeks.
'You're even more beautiful when you're angry.'

And, bending down, he kissed the tip of her nose.

She was now sobbing freely, all strength and resist-
ance drained from her, totally bewildered and confused
by the turn events had taken, but wanting only to
stay in this moment, never to move from this point
in time. She was in Alasdair's arms and the rest of
the world seemed to evaporate and no longer have any
substance.

He tenderly disentangled himself and, drawing her
towards the wide deep sofa pushed her gently into its
soft depths.

'Laura,' he said, sinking down beside her and taking
her back into his arms. 'I'm so sorry, so DESPER-
ATELY sorry. I didn't realise that you weren't aware
of the situation between Fiona and me.'

He laughed drily.

'Almost everyone else was!'

She looked up at him, her eyelashes wet and glistening against her pale cheeks.

Alasdair let his lips wander across her hair, idly
running his fingers through the long silken strands.

Laura relaxed. She felt as if she were melting into
him, becoming one with him and all she wanted was
for this magic moment never to end.

Alasdair released her gently and, leaning back on
the cushions, put his arm round her and drew her head
down onto his shoulder.

'I love you,' he said softly. 'I have ever since that moment I caught sight of you dancing with Angus Dunbar: it just hit me then right between the eyes and I couldn't believe what was happening. Do you remember how I rushed over and tried to book every dance on your ball card?'

She nodded dumbly and he tenderly stroked her cheek with his fingers.

'I won't pretend I haven't been in love before,' Alasdair went on, 'as you probably have.'

Laura snuggled up to him and shook her head.

'No,' she whispered. 'Never. There's only ever been you.'

He stopped stroking her hair and, gathering her to him gently placed his lips on hers. With a sigh Laura closed her eyes and yielded in his arms, soft and pliant and beautiful.

'Laura,' he whispered hoarsely, 'I could have lost you.'

And his arms tightened round her as he brushed his lips against hers, drawing them once more to his. But, suddenly, with a sharp agonised cry Laura broke away, fear and pain in her eyes.

'Alasdair,' she groaned. 'Alasdair. Fiona. What about FIONA?'

Alasdair took her back into his arms, settling her head once again on his broad shoulder. She nestled close feeling his masculine strength, her whole body suffused with a warm, tingling sensation.

'Yes, Fiona,' he went on. 'But before I clear that up I want you to know that I've never known anything like this before. Never known this intense feeling I felt for you when our eyes met at Cristobel's ball. Never. I thought it might fade with time, especially as you seemed to be so indifferent to me, but it hasn't, it's grown stronger and convinced me that this time it's the real thing. You are the only woman for me Laura, the only one I could ever ask to be my wife.'

Laura stiffened momentarily, then relaxed completely and began to cry.

'DARLING,' Alasdair cried, fumbling in his pocket for a handkerchief. 'Darling, don't cry. What's the matter?'

'I don't know,' she mumbled. 'I'm just so happy.'

And the tears welled up and overflowed once again.

'But I thought you wanted to know about Fiona and me?' Alasdair teased.

Laura nestled closer to him, her tear-stained face radiant with happiness.

'Not now,' she smiled. 'Not any more. It simply doesn't matter.'

Alasdair laughed.

'It does to me,' he said, holding her close. 'I want everything to be absolutely clear between us.'

He groaned.

'To think that this has been standing in the way for six months when we could have been together. Why ever didn't that idiot Cristobel tell you what was going on?'

'Tell me what?' Laura asked dreamily.

'The joke Fiona and I were playing on Graeme.'

Laura sat slowly upright and looked at him.

'Come back,' he whispered, holding out his arms and she snuggled into them.

'Fiona has been dotty about Graeme ever since she was at school,' Alasdair went on as Laura relaxed against his chest. 'Goodness knows why, and she's been hedging off all other admirers always hoping he'd come to heel. But he never did. So, this Easter when I was up at Fort William with Colin we decided to rouse Graeme's jealousy by my pretending, whenever Graeme was around, to be devoted to Fiona, in the hope of getting him moving in the direction of the aisle. We

put the plan into action at the McFadden girl's ball not
long before Cristobel's engagement and, of course, that
evening I fell in love with you we were in full swing.'

He sighed.

'Doing a pretty good job by the sound of things.'

Laura laughed softly.

'We called a halt after the wedding because there
really didn't seem to be any point in carrying on any
longer. The old bounder wasn't in the least perturbed
by our antics and, as neither Fiona nor I was even
remotely interested in the other, how could we be?
– she's dotty about Graeme and, by then, I'd fallen
hopelessly in love with you – it all seemed rather
pointless.'

Alasdair sat up and slapped his thigh in exasperation.

'But if *only* Cristobel had told me how you felt, or
at least told you the game we were playing.'

He shook his head in disbelief.

'We couldn't have too many people in the know or
otherwise Graeme would have got wind of it, but
Cristobel knew, and thought it hilarious. I wonder
why she didn't mention it to you and put your mind
at rest?'

'But wasn't it a secret?' Laura enquired.

'Yes,' Alasdair answered. 'But it never occurred to
me that she kept anything from you. You two were
always twittering together in corners like a couple of
sparrows.'

Laura smiled slowly.

'Cristobel didn't know how I felt,' she whispered.
'She was even trying to find someone suitable to marry
me off to at the ball because she wanted to keep me
around. Said she'd love to have me as a sister-in-law
but there was no hope of that because her brothers
were all too horrible.'

Laura giggled into Alasdair's chest.

He held her away from him and looked down at her.

'DID she now?' he mused. 'And do you agree?'

Laura nodded happily and he grabbed her back into his arms and playfully bit her ear.

'Ow!' she shrieked.

'Still think so?'

'No,' she whispered, holding her face up to be kissed.

As he released her and she lay back in his arms, a faraway expression in her eyes, she murmured blissfully, 'I am dreaming, aren't I? This can't really be happening.'

Alasdair fondled her hair.

'We're both dreaming,' he whispered. 'I can't believe it's really happening either.'

She gazed up at him, and Alasdair noticed that her eyes had darkened to a deep violet blue.

'Your eyes aren't like forget-me-nots any more,' he murmured, brushing his lips across them. 'They're like a deep sapphire sky studded with a thousand stars.'

His arms suddenly tightened around her, crushing her to him once again.

'Oh Laura,' he cried, 'you *will* marry me, won't you?'

She searched for his hand, too overcome to speak, and nodded her head.

'When?' he whispered. 'Say it can be soon.'

'Whenever you wish,' she whispered back, and closed her eyes, savouring the moment.

And they nestled close together, each dreaming their separate dreams which, up until a very short time ago, had appeared to both of them to be impossible. Then, slowly, gently, Alasdair released her and sat watching the firelight dancing on her now rosy cheeks, his eyes serious again.

'But what about your music?' he asked. 'Doesn't

it mean an awful lot to you? Am I asking too much, wanting to marry you so soon without waiting till you finish your studies?'

As he spoke, Laura suddenly realised that, in the past half an hour everything else in her life had ceased to matter, to have any importance at all. All had been obliterated in this tremendous outpouring of love she felt for him, this new awakening which was gradually blossoming deep inside her. Nothing mattered except that she and Alasdair should be together.

She gazed dreamily over his shoulder at her harp standing waiting in the corner and she knew she had work to do but suddenly, it wasn't important any more. Even her music, which till then had been her one passion, her driving force, receded into the background. The piano's shiny lid hiding the ivory keys seemed at that moment to be a symbol, a sign that a chapter in her life had now definitely ended. As her eyes rested on the closed keyboard the apricot tinted roses which Alasdair had sent to Edwina only two days before slowly moulted their velvet petals on to its polished surface, their heavy scent mingling with the pungent fragrance of the crackling logs.

Laura looked up at Alasdair adoringly and his face seemed to expand and block everything else from her line of vision, until all she could see was the love in his eyes, and she knew that all she wanted was him. He bent to kiss her, sensing the answer to his unanswered question, and her aunt's words of the previous evening came back to her. 'Don't become so wrapped up in your music that life passes you by.'

She shuddered.

Alasdair looked down at her, one eyebrow raised enquiringly.

'I was just thinking,' she mused, 'how near we came to passing each other by.'

'*Don't*,' he said sharply, drawing her back into his arms.

As he released her Laura became pensive and began fiddling with his tie.

'There's just ONE thing I don't understand,' she said slowly.

He lifted her chin and looked straight into her eyes, and she saw that his own were laughing.

'Speak now or for ever hold your peace,' he mimed.

'Do you remember the day of Cristobel's ball?' she began.

He frowned, obviously not remembering a thing.

'I was awake very early that morning sitting by my bedroom window about seven o'clock when you walked out of the house and disappeared. Someone said at breakfast that you'd gone to the Farquharsons and wouldn't be back for lunch. Your mother assumed you'd gone to see Colin but Graeme added that it was more likely to be Fiona, judging from the way you'd been dancing attendance on her at the McFadden ball.'

Alasdair let out a low whistle.

'The old devil,' he murmured. 'So he *did* notice after all.'

'Oh he noticed all right,' Laura went on, 'and his remark plunged me into the depths of despair.'

Alasdair leant forward and took her in his arms again.

'No, but wait, I must tell you,' she went on, slipping away from him. 'You disappeared all day, although you were expected back for tea. The next time I saw you you were dancing with Fiona and gazing into each other's eyes.'

'That's because Graeme was around,' Alasdair laughed.

'Yes, but Graeme wasn't at the Farquharsons all day,' Laura insisted. 'So why did you have to pretend then?'

Alasdair grabbed her by the shoulders and kissed the tip of her nose.

'You really should work for Scotland Yard,' he laughed. 'But I beg to inform Your Honour that my mother's surmise was right. The reason I was away all day was because Colin had telephoned me in Edinburgh about a legal problem and I'd told him I'd come over and sort it out for him on the Saturday morning. As we also wanted to play golf, we decided that we'd make an early start: which is what we did. Before breakfast in fact. Actually we finished even earlier than I'd expected, so we went to the club, had lunch and played golf until quite late. That's why I wasn't back for tea. Colin drove me over at about six and I didn't even see Fiona until they all arrived for the ball.'

He tweaked her nose.

'*Now* are you satisfied, madame?'

Laura gazed up at him, her eyes shining. Then, pulling him down towards her once again, she pressed her soft lips against his. She felt his grip on her tighten, and, sinking luxuriously back onto the satin cushions, yielded to his embrace.

'Alasdair,' she whispered at last, taking hold of the end of his tie and slowly twining it round her fingers, 'Why me?'

'The obvious answer to that question,' he laughed, 'is, why not?'

'No, please be serious,' she pleaded. 'You are surrounded by very attractive women in Scotland: women who would fit into your way of life in a way I never could. Why didn't you fall in love with one of them?'

'Perhaps,' he replied thoughtfully, 'because they WOULD have fitted in so easily. You were different. You utterly bewitched me.'

'But I don't hunt or fish or shoot,' she went on. 'I'm not "sporty" at all.'

'That's what I mean,' Alasdair answered quietly. 'I

was never attracted by "sporty" women, as you so aptly call them. To be perfectly honest, they rather bore me. And who says I want that way of life, anyway? If I did, I'd hardly be here.'

He went back to gently stroking her hair.

'You can't believe how you stood out amongst them,' he breathed into her silky tresses. 'Like a beautiful delicate orchid lost in a gorse bush. You were elusive and mysterious and ethereal and you had that incredible knack of drawing me to you and then slipping away.'

'You know why,' she interrupted.

'I know why now,' he answered. 'But I didn't then, and I've gone through absolute hell these past few weeks, thinking I'd lost you.'

'To think,' Laura mused, 'that I compared myself to Fiona and decided that I could never match up to her.'

'Thank heavens you can't,' Alasdair broke in. 'Fiona's a great girl, as a friend, but not as a wife. Not for me at any rate, horsey women leave me cold. Only luscious hot-house flowers have any power to attract me, beautiful delicate orchids. And only one particular orchid at that.'

He drew her to him once again.

'But let me return the question. Why me? Why not Ninian or Graeme? You saw much more of Graeme than you ever did of me: I was always away. And you must admit he's very charming. A thoroughly nice chap in fact, *and* he's the heir. A much better catch than I am.'

'You're right, Laura mused. He is very charming.'

'Want to change your mind and try your luck?' Alasdair teased.

Laura grinned and gave him a playful punch.

'Or there's Colin or one of the numerous Angus's littered about all over the place. Why not one of them?'

Laura smiled up at him.

'I don't know,' she said softly. 'I really don't know. There's only ever been you.'

Alasdair tweaked her nose.

'See what I mean,' he smiled. 'It was a silly question in the first place. There simply isn't any reason, any logical explanation as to why sparks fly the way they did for me at Cristobel's engagement ball: why this chemistry exists between us. So let's stop wasting time trying to find out. I just knew the moment I set eyes on you that evening that this time it was it, the real thing, and that you were the only woman for me. I felt as if I'd finally come home.'

He sighed happily and leant back on the soft cushions.

'Call it love at first sight if you like, call it what you will, it won't make any difference. It's there and neither of us can deny it. Even though for the last six months I've felt as if having at last come home, it was only to be kicked out to wander alone in the desert again.'

Laura sat up, her eyes shining, and gazed down at him.

'Oh, ALASDAIR,' she murmured.

The sound of the telephone ringing in the hall outside caused them to draw apart. They waited for Effie's tap on the door, but it didn't come.

'Must have been for Edwina,' Laura murmured, nestling back into Alasdair's arms. 'Oh, I just want to stay like this for ever.'

Alasdair rubbed his face against hers and she felt the rough stubble graze her cheeks.

'Darling,' he breathed, 'I have to go back to Edinburgh tomorrow night or Sunday morning at the latest to make a start at winding things up, but I'll try to come back next weekend.'

'Oh yes, please, *please* . . .' Laura interrupted.

'I'll do my very best. But you promise to come to

Ardnakil for Christmas, won't you? It's in less than three weeks. I'll have the ring then: Mother's got Great Grandmother's sapphire and I'm sure she'd want you to have it to match your eyes, and then we can make it official.'

Alasdair sat up and stroked his chin thoughtfully.

'I should be joining my new law firm towards the end of February or mid-March at the latest; we can look for somewhere to live and . . . Can we have a spring wedding?'

He grinned down at her.

'Early spring for preference.'

Laura didn't even bother to reply.

Had he suggested they marry that very evening, both standing on their heads in the middle of Kensington High Street, she would have joyfully agreed. At that moment she would have agreed to anything. The fact that Edwina had already made arrangements for them both to spend Christmas in Vienna had completely slipped her mind.

But Alasdair's next words brought her back to earth with a bump.

'And Edwina must come with you at Christmas, too.'

Laura's hand flew to her mouth and her eyes widened.

'Oh ALASDAIR,' she gasped, 'how awful!'

He looked at her in surprise.

'What's awful?' he asked.

'Edwina,' Laura went on. 'She's making all sorts of elaborate plans to take me to Vienna for Christmas, something about it being the opera season. She must already have booked our rooms at The Bristol, and even the train tickets for all I know. Oh, WHAT are we going to do? I can't possibly not be with you.'

And, like a frightened small girl she flung her arms round his neck.

'Darling,' he laughed, gently untangling himself. 'Don't worry, it can all be rearranged, I'm sure. Edwina seems to be a perfectly reasonable woman and, anyway, I can think of nothing more ghastly than spending Christmas listening to people screeching.'

Laura looked at him in surprise and suddenly his face fell.

'Oh Laura,' Alasdair groaned. 'I hadn't thought of it before, but can you *really* marry a man who is absolutely tone deaf? I can't tell the London Philharmonic from the Salvation Army Band!'

Laura burst into an uncontrollable fit of giggles.

'And can you REALLY marry a woman who is terrified of horses and doesn't hunt, shoot or fish?' she teased.

Alasdair joined in her laughter, then suddenly became serious again.

'No, but it's true,' he moaned. 'It's a family failing. Father's tone deaf and we've ALL taken after him. All except Sandy, that is, he seems to have some musical sense, hence his jazz band. Perhaps that's why Mother dotes on him so.'

And he added thoughtfully.

'And why she immediately took to you when Cristobel first brought you home.'

'I know,' Laura smiled. 'I remember Cristobel at school. We had to beg her NOT to sing in church, she sent us all off key.'

She turned to him with a radiant smile.

'If your mother can take it, so can I,' she announced happily. 'She and your father seem to have a blissful marriage in spite of the fact that she doesn't exactly spend her time leaping on and off horses and he does, and she's very musical whereas he doesn't know a 'cello from a tin whistle.'

Laura's smile suddenly faded and she became serious.

'Which reminds me,' she said quietly. 'I have a father, too.'

Alasdair seemed startled by this piece of news.

'Darling, I'm so sorry,' he exclaimed. 'I didn't know.'

'People rarely do,' she remarked drily. 'He's pretty remote most of the time and has become even more so since my mother died.'

'Perhaps I should ask his permission, or at least meet him before we go any further,' Alasdair hesitated, 'after all . . .'

But Laura cut him short.

'Don't worry,' she smiled. 'There'll be no problem from him. He scarcely knows I'm still around.'

'Poor darling,' Alasdair cried, drawing her tenderly back into his arms.

She snuggled closer to him.

'It doesn't matter any more,' she whispered. 'I'm going to have a REAL family at last.'

'My family, you mean,' he asked gently, looking down at her enquiringly.

She nodded her head and, as a slow blush crept up her cheeks, whispered.

'And OURS!'

Alasdair held her tight.

'Your mother always said she considered me as one of the family, but I never really felt I was,' she murmured against his chest, drinking in his strength, his masculinity, the faint scent of a sportsman's soap which clung to his skin. 'But now I shall be.'

She lay back in his arms, her eyes shining, the colour of bluebells in a sunlit wood.

'And oh, won't Cristobel be surprised,' she exclaimed.

And leaping up she clapped her hands delightedly, like a small child about to divulge a secret.

Alasdair caught her hands in both of his.

'Darling little Laura,' he smiled. 'How old are you?'

She immediately became serious and withdrew her hands.

'I shall be twenty on the twenty fourth of March,' she said primly, 'only three months younger than your sister. And *she's* already expecting a baby.'

Alasdair laughed.

'Well, we can soon remedy that.'

Laura looked quickly down as her cheeks suddenly flamed again. But he placed a finger under her chin and forced her to look at him, then bent down and kissed each crimson cheek in turn.

'Touché,' he whispered. 'But . . . isn't this where we came in?'

And, as they both suddenly remembered how mortified she had been when he had teased her about her age as she sat stiffly beside him on the drive to Perth that Monday morning, they broke into peals of such helpless laughter that neither of them noticed when the door opened and Edwina walked in.

She stood in the doorway looking at them, an amused smile on her face.

Alasdair jumped hurriedly to his feet, quickly smoothing his hair and straightening his tie.

Edwina affected not to notice.

'Mr Hamilton,' she smiled, coming towards him.

'How delightful. I didn't expect to have the pleasure of seeing you when I came back.'

Alasdair cleared his throat and looked down at the patch of carpet under his feet.

'Well – er – to be perfectly honest, when you left I wasn't sure myself.'

'But the situation has somewhat changed since then?' Edwina smiled.

He looked across at her and his face broke into a grin.

'I'm afraid you're going to have to get used to calling me Alasdair,' he went on, 'now that I've become your future nephew-in-law.'

Edwina raised her eyebrows enquiringly, looking from one to the other of them as Laura shyly took hold of Alasdair's hand.

'So SOON,' she teased. 'But how splendid.'

She looked archly at them both.

'So it WASN'T the lack of country air which was ailing you Laura darling?'

Laura smiled happily, but didn't reply.

'Oh gracious, yes,' Alasdair said, squeezing her hand and looking anxiously down at her. 'Weren't you supposed to be going to the country for the weekend?'

'That was before I learned the truth about Fiona,' she laughed, looking up at him roguishly.

Edwina glanced from one to the other of them.

'Just a little joke between us,' Laura smiled.

'Well,' Edwina exclaimed, going towards a small mahogany chest standing in a corner of the room, 'this calls for a celebration.'

'We were thinking of going out to dinner to celebrate this evening,' Alasdair ventured, 'since I have to leave tomorrow.'

'Of course,' Edwina smiled. 'Run along and change, Laura darling and *do* wear that blue frock which suits you so well.'

'The forget-me-not blue one?' Laura enquired, laughing across at Alasdair.

She skipped happily across the room and then suddenly stopped, her hand on the door knob.

'Edwina,' she ventured timidly. 'I suppose you've made all the arrangements for Christmas in Vienna?'

'Why do you ask?' Edwina enquired without turning round.

'Nothing. It's only that . . .'

'You no longer wish to go,' Edwina broke in,

straightening up from the chest and giving them both a dazzling smile. 'I'm so thankful. I must confess I wasn't at all looking forward to that long journey across Europe in the middle of winter. Changing trains in Paris in the rain – it always rains in Paris when one is changing trains and there's never a taxi in sight – then most probably being marooned for days on end in a wagon-lit outside Salzburg because there's been an avalanche. It happened to me once, before the war, I was much younger then and I can assure you it was extremely unpleasant.'

She sighed happily.

'Oh no, darling,', Edwina went on, 'I'm most grateful to you for changing your mind and sparing me all that. I shall be much happier toasting the New Year in with Effie in my warm little flat.'

'Edwina, you're an angel,' Laura shrieked and, running across to her aunt, threw her arms around her neck in a most unaccustomed and highly uncharacteristic gesture, kissing her warmly on the cheek.

It would be difficult to say which of them was the more surprised by this sudden, unexpected change in Laura. It seemed that Alasdair, in a few short hours, had unleashed the flow of pent-up emotions which had been dammed up inside her ever since her mother's death almost eight years before.

'Now do run along and change darling,' Edwina said, slightly breathless, releasing herself and patting her immaculately dressed white hair back into place.

Alasdair cleared his throat, but Edwina anticipated his question.

'Thank you,' she said turning towards him, 'you are very kind, but if you'll excuse me, I won't join you both for dinner this evening. I've had rather a busy day. Would you mind awfully celebrating by yourselves?'

Her eyes twinkled up at Alasdair.

'Now let me see,' she went on taking two delicate

crystal glasses out of the chest and placing them on a silver salver.

'A glass of sherry, Alasdair? Or would you prefer something else? We'll wait for Laura to join us to open the champagne.'

Alasdair's eyes twinkled back at her, their green and gold lights now positively dancing with happiness. Her use of his Christian name for the first time had subtly indicated her approval and complete acceptance of him as a future member of the family.

'A glass of sherry would be splendid, thank you . . . Aunt Edwina,' he replied.

Effie, coming in at that moment with olives and cheese straws, almost dropped the tray in surprise when, to her utter astonishment, and for no apparent reason, both Edwina and Alasdair suddenly burst out laughing.

PART 2

1973

Revelations

15

Bolts from the Blue

Laura leant forward on her dressing table stool and peered intently into the oval mirror, pulling gently at the delicate skin under her right eye as she did so. She grimaced at her reflection and sighed.

'The years are beginning to tell,' she murmured, turning her head this way and that discerning the faint tracing of lines which were showing like blue feathery strokes of an artist's brush beneath the skin's opaque surface. She propped her elbows amongst the assortment of glass jars and bottles and began to relive in her imagination the last weekend, her tenth wedding anniversary: lying in Alasdair's arms in that quiet country hotel where they had spent their honeymoon, listening to the distant sounds of the sea rushing, then whispering as its waves curled along the white beach. As they watched the spring moon tint the leaves outside their open window with silver, he had told her that she was even more beautiful now than on the day he had married her.

Laura sighed happily and, slowly rising to her feet, hugged herself at the remembrance of her husband's words.

'Ten years,' she sighed dreamily, walking about the familiar bedroom. 'Ten years, it hardly seems possible.'

She sat down in the deep armchair by the casement window.

'And now I'm thirty!'

Laura shuddered, realising that she had entered a new decade, and wary of the ravages of time. Then she leant back and remembered how happily she had entered the last one. That fine March day, with a gentle breeze blowing the early blossom off the trees in the Kensington square, her twentieth birthday, when she had run joyfully out of her teens to marry Alasdair.

'Why don't you two go off for the weekend and celebrate this double anniversary?' Ninian had said on the telephone the week before.

He was now in London, seconded from his regiment on what he called 'a stint at the War Box'.

'I'll take Jamie and play uncle.'

Laura had demurred. Ninian was still a bachelor and she wondered just how he would cope with her turbulent son for a whole weekend. But her brother-in-law had laughed.

'He's my godson, after all,' he replied. 'And goodness knows how long I'll be in London, might as well make the most of it. I'll pick him up on Saturday morning, or even Friday evening, if you like, and you two go off on a second honeymoon.'

Laura had been excited at the idea but when, that evening, she told Alasdair of his brother's suggestion, her husband had become pensive.

'Wonder what's up with Ninian,' he had enquired, 'wanting to cope with Jamie all on his own.'

And he had left his chair and gone to the telephone.

'Come for dinner tomorrow evening,' he suggested to his brother. 'I think you should know what you're letting yourself in for before committing yourself for a weekend.'

Ninian had laughed but when he arrived they had both noticed that there was something different about him. The normally quiet, reserved Ninian had changed. He seemed to be jubilant.

'What's going on, Ninian?' Alasdair had enquired, going straight to the point as soon as dinner was over and they were sitting round the fire in the cosy chintz-covered drawing-room. 'You may as well come clean. NOBODY in his right mind would want Jamie for a weekend.'

Jamie was the youngest of their three sons.

At seven he was a determined youngster and, since his two elder brothers had gone off to prep school, his presence in the house had become even more obvious.

Laura had always felt that Jamie was Alasdair's special gift to her. Iain, their eldest son, had arrived on Christmas Eve, that first Christmas of their marriage, and had been like a beautiful present for them both. A tiny replica of Laura, so blond that he had at first appeared bald, he was now a fair-haired, blue-eyed schoolboy with his mother's sensitive nature. Andrew, had been her gift to Alasdair, born scarcely more than a year later in early February, just a few days before Alasdair's own birthday, a sandy-haired grey-eyed child, a mixture of Hamilton and Denning. But Jamie, who had made his screaming presence felt just as the bells were ringing in the New Year was definitely Alasdair's gift to his wife. He had leapt from her womb fighting his way into the world with flaying fists and angry roars, his red face exactly matching his tufts of hair. No-one had had to give him a sharp tap on the buttocks in order to get his lungs going. And it seemed that, at seven, Jamie hadn't changed.

Ninian smiled his slow smile, so like Flora's, and lifted his grey eyes, looking at them both intently.

'You're right,' he said, fiddling with the stem of his glass watching the rich red port rise and fall as he twisted the glass round and round in his fingers. 'I suppose I want to see what it's like playing house.'

'You haven't decided to take the plunge at last?' Alasdair teased.

Ninian nodded.

'Did Sandy give you the idea?,' Alasdair went on. 'Or shame you into it?'

Sandy, who had now joined his brother in the regiment, was to marry Rose Livesey in ten days time, the 'Quaker girl' he had partnered as a radish and so upset at her grandmother's young people's ball all those years ago.

'Not really,' Ninian went on, his eyes staring intently at his glass. 'But I intend to introduce her at Sandy's wedding.'

He looked up, his grey eyes soft, and smiled across at them.

'You're the first to know,' he said quietly.

'Haven't you told the parents?' Alasdair asked.

'Not yet,' Ninian went on, 'but Deirdre will be coming to Ardnakil with me next week to meet them.'

He laughed briefly.

'Deirdre?' Alasdair queried. 'She's not someone we know?'

'No,' Ninian replied and went back to fiddling with the stem of his glass. 'I met her one weekend when I was staying with friends in Ireland.'

Ninian had just left the regiment in Northern Ireland where Sandy was now stationed.

'I'm not sure how the parents will take it. She comes from Eire and is a Roman Catholic.'

Alasdair let out a low whistle.

'Not easy,' he said slowly.

'It isn't as if I were the eldest,' Ninian went on. 'Graeme will inherit Ardnakil.'

'Yes, but Graeme doesn't seem to be in any hurry to produce an heir,' Alasdair said, 'and now that Fiona Farquharson's given up and married an Englishman there doesn't appear to be much hope.'

'I don't think he was ever very interested in Fiona,' Ninian continued slowly, 'it was all on her side. And, anyway, Graeme's a dark horse, you never know what he's got up his sleeve.'

He suddenly brightened. 'He'll probably be like Father and wait till he's past it.'

Laura smiled. 'I don't think your father made such a bad job of it, even if he WAS past it,' she remarked, looking adoringly across at Alasdair.

Alasdair smiled back at her and, for a moment, they were lost in a world of their own.

Ninian watched them.

'I intend to marry Deirdre,' he said quietly, 'no matter what happens.'

And for a moment, there was a silence round the hissing fire.

'Tell us about her,' Laura said gently.

She had always been particularly fond of Ninian, the quiet, reserved son so unlike the other brothers, and so like Lady Flora.

'She's a dancer with the Royal Ballet,' he said slowly. 'A very good one too.'

Alasdair let out another low whistle, then began to laugh.

'Graeme's not the only dark horse,' he remarked. 'Whoever would have thought it of you. How old is she?'

'Twenty-two,' Ninian replied, adding hastily, 'Fifteen years between us may seem a lot but, well, that's how it is. I'm like Father, I suppose.'

'Age doesn't *really* matter,' Laura said softly, 'not if you truly love someone.'

She looked across at Alasdair again.

'And, after all, there's almost twice as many years between your parents and look what a happy marriage theirs has been, and still is.'

Ninian nodded, but didn't reply. It was obvious that it wasn't Deirdre's age which was bothering him but the other contributing factors which were so contrary to what was expected of him. The Hamiltons had always married Protestants, and preferably Scots Protestants. But a Roman Catholic from the Irish Republic!

He sighed.

'We'll manage,' he said looking up.

'What is she like?' Laura asked.

'Very like Mother, as a matter of fact,' Ninian replied, brightening up. 'Small and dark, rather fragile.'

'Difficult for a ballerina to be hefty,' Alasdair put in, and Laura realised that he was embarrassed, envisioning the difficulties which might await Ninian and trying to minimise them for his brother's sake.

Ninian didn't reply, but turned to Laura instead.

'So you'll lend me my godson for the weekend,' he smiled. 'Deirdre and I would like to take him to the zoo for a start and then anything else which might amuse him.'

'I think it would be a splendid idea,' Laura said softly, her heart going out to Ninian, who had waited so long for the right woman and now saw his future happiness fraught with difficulties. 'Jamie will love it.'

'I'll pick him up on Saturday morning,' Ninian went on, 'and bring him back in time for bed Sunday, then you two can go and celebrate this double event. Thirty is quite an age. It's supposed to be when a woman really blossoms and comes into her own.'

He turned and smiled his slow sweet smile at Laura.

'And ten years of marriage shouldn't go by without some kind of celebration.'

'Thank you, Ninian,' she answered. 'It was sweet of you to think of it. Why don't you bring Deirdre with you and have dinner with us on Sunday evening?'

Ninian's eyes brightened, but he looked across at Alasdair, not sure how his brother would react.

'Yes, do,' Alasdair said reservedly. 'Never actually seen a ballerina off the stage.'

It was obvious to Laura that Ninian sensed his embarrassment. He excused himself soon afterwards.

'Got to be at the War Box early in the morning,' he said, 'and I suppose it's the same for you Alasdair. I'll be here about ten on Saturday to collect Jamie.'

And he left.

Laura turned back into the drawing room to put out the lights and Alasdair walked in behind her.

'Wonder if Ninian hasn't got himself into a real can of worms,' he remarked.

Laura looked round, suddenly irritated.

'Oh Alasdair,' she exclaimed. 'This is 1973, not the Middle Ages!'

'Exactly,' Alasdair said, bending to switch off a small lamp and placing a guard in front of the fire's dying embers. 'But Father doesn't know that. He's almost eighty-five, after all.'

Laura sighed.

'I suppose so,' she said, turning off the last lamp and plunging the room in darkness. Suddenly, she felt very tired: the elation she had experienced on hearing Ninian's news was inexplicably extinguished.

* * *

The weekend had been a tremendous success.

Jamie had returned dragging the diminutive Deirdre by the hand, obviously as besotted with her as Ninian was, his exuberance completely dispelling any tensions which might otherwise have arisen. When he had finally been persuaded to go to bed, Laura had had time to get to know this future sister-in-law and to appreciate her.

Deirdre barely came up to Ninian's armpit and was like an exquisite porcelain figure, reed slim with the smooth dark hair of the ballerina and a perfectly shaped oval face in which brilliant green eyes sparkled. Even Alasdair fell under her spell and, when they finally left, Laura sensed that Ninian was feeling more at ease about introducing his future wife to the rest of the family the following weekend.

'When are you leaving for Ardnakil?' he enquired.

'We're taking a 'plane on Friday lunchtime,' Alasdair had replied. 'The boys come on holiday on Wednesday evening so that will give Laura time to wash their necks ready for the wedding. We should be there in time for tea and for the family dinner Mother's giving. Pity old Grace Entwhistle won't be there. She always added a bit of local colour to these occasions.'

Lady Entwhistle had died very suddenly in early January shortly after the New Year's Eve ball she annually gave for her grandchildren. Typically, she had not noticed that her grandchildren were no longer 'young people' but were now mostly married with 'young people' of their own; ignoring the passage of time she had carried on in the same fashion year after year and her grandchildren had all played the game and loved every minute of it. This year at the ball Rose and Sandy's engagement had been announced, Sandy's earlier misdemeanour long since forgiven, and Lady Entwhistle had made Rose promise that she would be married from Eglinton Hall, the Entwhistle family home. Rose, whose parents were living in Hong Kong, had happily agreed.

Now that her grandmother was no longer there, the plans were going ahead as she would have wished and Rose, who up till then, had been nursing in a large London hospital, was back at Eglinton preparing for her wedding.

'We might even be on the same 'plane then,' Ninian said. 'The midday one from Heathrow?'

'I think so,' Alasdair replied vaguely. 'Oh good, I'll hand that monster Jamie over to you to look after.'

Ninian smiled down at Deirdre.

'Are you ready to face the family?' he asked tenderly.

She didn't reply just looked up at him, her eyes deep and shining like glittering emerald pools.

'Ninian's exaggerating,' Laura put in quickly. 'They're an absolutely delightful family: I'm sure you'll love them.'

Deirdre's eyes left Ninian's face and focused briefly on Laura.

'But will *they* love *me*?' she asked quietly.

Ninian had obviously explained to her the difficulties they were likely to encounter.

For a moment no-one spoke.

'I don't see how they could help it,' Laura said at last.

'Well, see you at the airport on Friday,' Alasdair broke in, putting a stop to further conversation.

'It's going to be a wonderful time,' Laura said as they walked with them to the car. 'Who ever would have thought Sandy would marry Rose after that dreadful radish incident.'

Deirdre looked enquiringly from one to the other of them.

'I'll explain to you on the way back,' Ninian said as he held open the door of the car for her.

'Everything is going to be all right,' Laura whispered, bending down as Deirdre opened the side window.

Deirdre nodded and the car moved off.

'I only hope so,' Alasdair sighed, throwing his arm round his wife's shoulders as they walked up the steps to the house.

Laura looked at him and they paused together on the doorstep.

'Kiss me,' she murmured, reaching up on tiptoe.

He looked at her in surprise then, bending down brushed his lips against hers.

'No,' she said, pulling his head down and twining her fingers into the curls which straggled on his neck, 'PROPERLY.'

Alasdair caught her to him with a laugh.

'You're a glutton for punishment,' he said softly, his lips closing on hers in a rough, hard embrace.

Laura nestled against his broad chest.

'Don't you want this for Ninian?' she whispered.

She felt his arms tighten round her.

'After ten years,' she breathed, snuggling up to him as she had done on her aunt's sofa that far off December afternoon. 'It's unbelievable.'

Alasdair picked her up in his arms and carried her across the threshold.

'After ten years,' he said, 'we don't have to kiss on the doorstep.'

He set her down inside the lighted hall and turned to close the door. Laura walked ahead of him towards the stairs then, turning on the first step she looked back at her husband, her eyes shining.

'Catch me,' she cried gaily, and began to run up the shallow staircase.

For a fraction of a second Alasdair hesitated, then with great strides ran across the hall and taking the stairs two at a time caught her in his arms just as she reached their bedroom door.

'Vixen,' he cried.

Laura laughed delightedly and, struggling from his grasp, dodged into the room ahead of him.

Now, as she sat contentedly in the deep armchair in front of her bedroom window dreaming of the past two days she realised that her second honeymoon had been even more wonderful than her first. And, remembering Alasdair's tenderness, she closed her eyes and relived those precious moments, floating away on wave after gentle wave of her husband's caresses, revelling, luxuriating in her happiness.

'Life is so beautiful, so perfect,' she heard herself murmuring as smiles chased each other across her softly parted lips and golden slanting beams of early spring sunshine floated in through the open window, bringing with them the damp, sweet smells from the garden below which was just beginning to wake up and blossom after the darkness of winter.

Laura felt as if she were waking up, too, waking up from one beautiful dream to another, which would be even more perfect than the one which had gone before. Recapturing in that moment the joy and excitement which she had felt when she left her girlhood behind and entered her second decade, she now put aside all thoughts of lines appearing beneath her eyes and looked forward with even greater joy and anticipation to her third decade. And, with all her heart, she wished for Ninian and Deirdre in their marriage the happiness and fulfilment which she and Alasdair had known in theirs.

It was Monday morning and she knew that there were countless things which she should be doing; but she didn't move, unwilling to let this exquisite moment go, to allow the deep, all-pervading happiness which tingled her every nerve to be troubled or broken or vanish into mist. She just wanted to sit and bask in the sunshine of her life, her love for Alasdair and the beautiful future which, she was convinced, stretched endlessly ahead without a cloud in the sky.

The telephone's sharp ring brought her back to earth. Gliding in a golden haze over to the bedside table, she reached down and picked up the receiver.

'Laura?', Graeme's voice came down the line.

'Graeme,' she exclaimed happily. 'How lovely to hear from you. We're so much looking forward to the wedding. Is everything going according to plan? I expect you're all run off your feet. When is Sandy arriving?'

There was a slight pause.

'Laura,' Graeme went on, and his voice sounded grave, but then Graeme had always been serious, and even a wedding seemed to fail to excite him.

He paused again and Laura could hear him breathing heavily at the other end of the line.

'Laura,' he went on at last, 'is Alasdair at home, by any chance?'

'ALASDAIR?' Laura replied. 'No, he's at the office.'

'I rang his office,' Graeme said dully, 'but he wasn't there.'

'Oh,' Laura replied, 'I think he said he had to go to court this morning.'

Alasdair was now a rising young barrister.

'Do you know when he'll be back in his office?'

'I've no idea,' Laura answered. 'Depends on how long the case lasts. He didn't say what it was. Could be there after lunch, or it could be some time during the afternoon.'

She frowned, wondering why Graeme was being so evasive.

'Is there something I can do? If it's about the wedding I'm more likely to be able to help than Alasdair.'

She laughed.

'I don't imagine you have a legal problem you want to discuss with him at this time?'

'No,' Graeme answered heavily, 'not exactly.'

He paused again.

'Graeme,' Laura said. 'Is something wrong?'

Suddenly it seemed as if a dark cloud had drifted aross the sky in front of the window blotting out the dancing sunlight.

'Yes,' Graeme went on. 'I'm afraid so.'

Laura sat down abruptly on the bed, all manner of thoughts racing crazily through her mind.

'What is it?' she whispered, a terrible fear suddenly creeping like a cold snake over her body. It couldn't be Alasdair, or Graeme wouldn't have asked to speak to him. Had anything happened to the boys it wouldn't be Graeme who was telephoning her. It must be Robert or Flora.

She paled at the thought. Oh no, not *now*. Not just before the wedding. Robert was in excellent health, but as Alasdair had reminded her only last night he WAS eighty-five.

'Graeme,' she cried, fear taking hold of her and strangling her voice. 'Graeme, what is it?'

That terrible fear had now invaded her entire body, clutching her like a vice in its deadly grasp.

'What's happened?' she gasped.

'It's Sandy,' he said quietly.

'*Sandy*,' Laura exclaimed and suddenly felt a piercing pain shoot through her as rapid and sharp as a burst of machine gun fire and just as shattering.

'What's happened to Sandy?' she managed to gasp, her voice hardly more than a croak.

There was a terrible pause during which darkness seemed to envelop the room as the sunbeams slowly faded and an inky rain-sodden cloud took their place, blocking all light from the window. In the distance the wind began to rise, bringing with it a sound like the sad wailing of gulls.

She heard Graeme take a deep breath in an effort to gain control of his emotions before he replied, and she stood motionless, her body stiff and taut like a block of ice.

'He was killed in an ambush last night,' he finally said, his voice toneless and devoid of any emotion, as if he were reading out the fat stock prices.

16

On their Wedding Day

The telephone trembled and almost dropped from Laura's hands.

'Oh NO,' she moaned.

'Laura,' Graeme cut in. 'I'm terribly sorry, I didn't want to have to tell you but I can't get hold of Alasdair so I had no alternative but ... Laura, *Laura*,' he shouted down the line when she didn't answer.

'It's all right,' she answered weakly. 'I'm here.'

'Oh Laura, there's absolutely nothing I can do from this distance. Is there someone who could come and be with you? Can't you get hold of Alasdair?'

Laura pulled herself together.

'I'm all right, Graeme,' she said, her hands gripping the telephone tightly. 'Don't worry, I'll get hold of Alasdair somehow.'

She paused, struggling to control her voice now that tears were racing down her cheeks. Sandy, her heart kept beating, Sandy, dear, darling, crazy Sandy ... oh NO, it wasn't POSSIBLE.

'How are they?' she managed to blurt out.

'Mother's being wonderful,' Graeme replied. 'It's Father I'm worried about. He's absolutely broken.'

He paused.

'He seems to have shrunk about six inches since we received the news,' Graeme went on, 'and all of a sudden to have become a very old man.'

Laura pressed a damp hankie to her mouth in an attempt to stifle her sobs.

'And Rose?' she stammered.

'Rose is on her way over. I don't think it's a good idea but she insisted, says she wants to be with us, she'll feel nearer to Sandy here than at Eglinton.'

'I understand,' Laura said bleakly.

'Do you?' Graeme queried.

And the line was pregnant with their grief.

'Does Ninian know?' Laura asked after a few seconds.

'I've just telephoned him,' Graeme said. 'He's trying to get permission to go over to Ireland and bring Sandy's body back.'

He paused again and Laura could feel that he was fighting for control of his voice.

'Looks as if we'll have a funeral on Saturday instead of a wedding.'

'Oh Graeme,' Laura cried brokenly.

'I have to go,' Graeme said abruptly. 'But Laura, I'm worried about you. Is there NO-ONE who can come and be with you?'

'Don't worry about me,' she assured him. 'You've got enough on your hands at Ardnakil. I'll get hold of Alasdair some way or other.'

'Well, see you on Friday as arranged,' he said grimly, 'if not before.'

'Probably before,' Laura choked.

'Oh good,' Graeme answered his tone almost brightening and Laura could feel the terrible strain he was under, coping not only with his own grief but also with Rose's and his parents. 'If you can I'm sure it would be a great comfort for Mother to have you here.'

'Give her my love,' Laura said softly.

'I will,' Graeme promised and rang off.

Laura lay back on the bed and looked bleakly up at the ceiling. The room, which only half an hour before

197

had been dancing with sunshine, a sunshine which was reflected in her heart, was now grey and cold. And suddenly all the happiness, all the joyful expectancy which had suffused her as she lay dreaming in the armchair by the window, all the certainty that life was on a bright and beautiful course which nothing could change, that her future and her love were secure and immortal, lay shattered in jagged fragments at her feet. One quick telephone call and her world had crumbled.

She dreaded having to tell Alasdair, dreaded seeing him suffer the terrible pain which was now searing through her like a wild, diabolical flame. The pain she had not felt since her mother had died and her little girl's world had crumbled around her, a pain which when she had married Alasdair and become part of the warm, loving security with which his family had surrounded her she was sure she would never feel again.

Laura glanced at her bedside clock. Just ten, there would be no point in even trying to get hold of Alasdair before lunchtime: for the next three hours, at least, there would be this terrible secret between them, they who for ten years had shared everything were now divided by a dreadful chasm of grief.

And as this thought struck her, so did an ominous wave of foreboding, and she knew that from this moment onwards nothing would ever be the same. Sandy had taken with him a part of their lives; a part of that wonderful mosaic which made up the family which had welcomed her and given her the security and the roots which she so badly needed. And, as this knowledge seeped into her bewildered brain, the floodgates opened and great gasping sobs wracked her slim body. And she knew that she was not only weeping for Sandy, whose laughter they would never hear again, for Rose whose life now lay in ruins but, in some strange way, for herself.

The sobbing finally subsided leaving her limp and exhausted and she lay back on the bed, knowing that she should get up, be busy, try to keep her mind occupied. But she also knew that however occupied she was nothing would be able to wipe from her memory the terrible tragedy which had just overtaken this young couple who, until this morning, had been so confidently looking forward to their future life together. As she lay there gazing once again at the ceiling, her heart bleeding for Rose and longing to hear Sandy's voice, to wake up and discover it had all been a bad dream, the telephone rang again. Listlessly she reached out her hand and picked it up.

'Laura,' Ninian's voice came down the line.

'Oh NINIAN,' she cried, and the tears started once more.

'Yes, I know,' he said tightly. 'It's dreadful isn't it?'

And, hearing his words she knew that she was not going to wake up from a nightmare, that she had been awake all the time, and Sandy was dead.

'Graeme is worried about you,' he went on. 'Are you all right? You don't sound it.'

'I'm as all right as you are,' she gulped. 'We can none of us be all right after hearing that piece of news.'

'No, I suppose not.'

He paused.

'Would you like to come to London and have lunch with me?'

'Oh Ninian, I don't think so.'

'Do come,' he broke in. 'We need each other. I'd come down to you but I'm afraid I can't at the moment, but we've got to have lunch so we might as well have it together. I don't want to be alone, and yet I don't much want to be surrounded by my colleagues either. Can you meet me at the Savoy Grill at one? It's about the nearest place for you if you're coming up by train.'

'Wherever you wish,' Laura replied bleakly.

'One o'clock then.'

As she walked along the Strand Laura watched the faces of the people hurrying by and she couldn't believe that they all looked so normal, so ordinary, even so happy. Didn't they know that Sandy was dead? How could they go about, continue their lives as if nothing had happened? Looking in shop windows, getting on and off buses, smiling and chatting.

She looked at them curiously, surprised that they didn't stare back, nudge or whisper to each other as she passed, imagining that they must all know about the terrible blow which had just struck her: she couldn't look normal and ordinary now, she must somehow look different. But nobody stared curiously at her or even glanced in her direction and she realised that, in spite of what had happened, she still looked the same, the same as she had yesterday or the day before.

And she pulled herself together.

The world had stopped for her, had collapsed for the whole Hamilton family at this moment, but these unknown people scurrying past could not possibly know about the tragedy they were all living through. And the thought came to her that perhaps they too were struggling under some heavy burden, some terrible blow: perhaps their lives had also been shattered, their hearts broken in the last few hours, but that outwardly there was no sign. Life went on. And as Laura realised this she raised her head and held it high to give herself courage, also to carry on.

Ninian rose to meet her as she walked in and led her to a quiet table in a corner.

'I left a message for Alasdair to join us if he can,' he said as they sat down.

He gave their order and for a few moments neither of

them spoke, then suddenly he leant forward and gently touched her hand.

'I know how fond you were of Sandy,' he said softly.

She looked across at him, her lashes wet and glistening.

'Weren't we all?' she choked.

'Yes, but sometimes we older brothers had an odd way of showing it,' Ninian said grimly. 'You were always his champion, even before you married Alasdair.'

Laura smiled down at her plate, idly crumbling a roll between her fingers, not daring to lift her eyes in case the tears which were gathering in force would suddenly spill over.

'I don't think he minded,' she answered softly. 'It was just family teasing.'

'Perhaps not,' Ninian remarked and shook out his napkin, placing it on his lap as the waiter arrived back at their table. 'At least, I hope not.'

Laura picked up her knife and fork and began pushing the food slowly round her plate without the slightest desire to taste it, hoping that by some magic method it would disappear.

'Poor Rose,' she whispered brokenly.

Ninian looked down at the untouched food on his plate, and Laura suddenly, instinctively knew that nothing would ever be the same again.

'Graeme said you'd be going over to Ireland,' Laura ventured.

'Yes,' Ninian replied. 'On Wednesday. I hope to be at Ardnakil on Thursday, probably not until late in the evening.'

His lips tightened.

'I imagine the funeral will be on Saturday.'

Laura's fork fell with a clatter onto the plate.

'Oh NINIAN,' she gulped, 'their WEDDING DAY.'

'I know,' he sighed. 'But I'm afraid it can't be earlier. There are all sorts of formalities to be gone through. Friday would have been better but just in case of a last minute hitch we have to make it Saturday. And anyway, the villagers will want to come and pay their respects. Everybody loved Sandy, it would be cruel to rush it through the minute we arrived. But leaving it over till Monday would be even more cruel.'

Ninian put down his knife and fork and placed his hand over hers once again, squeezing it tightly but saying nothing.

'And you?' she said at last, finally managing to control her emotions.

'Me?' Ninian asked.

He seemed surprised.

'It was to have been a special weekend for you, too, wasn't it?' she whispered.

He nodded and sighed again.

'Yes, well, I'm afraid for the moment any thought of introducing Deirdre to Ardnakil will have to be shelved.'

'Oh Ninian,' Laura cried brokenly. 'It all seems so unfair.'

'Life is unfair,' Ninian replied and smiled across at her. 'Have you only just realised that?'

'It's funny,' Laura mused, 'when Graeme rang I was just revelling in the fact that life was so wonderful.'

'Were you?'

Ninian smiled indulgently as if at a small excited child.

'For Alasdair and me,' she went on, 'there wasn't a cloud in the sky and then, suddenly, within the space of a few seconds, everything crashed; the world spun round and seemed to fall back into place upside down.'

She broke off and looked across at him, her deep blue eyes wide and glistening.

'But Ninian,' she pleaded, 'it is going to be all right for you and Deirdre, isn't it?'

'I sincerely hope so,' he said grimly. 'Some day. But certainly not for the moment.'

'Does she know?' Laura asked.

'Yes, I managed to get hold of her.'

'And what did she say?'

Ninian pressed his lips together in a hard straight line.

'She understands,' he said tightly. 'Or at least she said she did.'

He sighed and wiped his taut lips with his napkin.

'But for how long? She's very young.'

'Oh Ninian, she's so right for you, it *must* work out in the end.'

Ninian looked across at her.

'But for this, it most surely would have.'

He shrugged hopelessly.

'Deirdre comes from the Irish Republic. It would be a little hard for the parents to welcome her with open arms at the moment, don't you think?'

Laura nodded dumbly, tears once again welling in her gentle blue eyes.

Ninian reached across and covered her small hand with his and they sat together in an emotional silence.

'Well, what a surprise!'

They both looked up, startled, to see Alasdair standing above them. He was smiling, but Laura could see that he was not entirely at ease. The apparent incongruousness of their posture had obviously more than surprised him.

'I got your message, Ninian,' Alasdair went on staring down at them, 'but I never expected to find you holding hands with my wife.'

Ninian pulled forward a chair and signalled to the waiter.

'What are you two plotting during your lunch

together?' Alasdair enquired as he sat down, looking from one to the other.

Laura excused herself and got up. She couldn't bear to see the pain which would immediately extinguish the dancing lights in Alasdair's eyes when he heard the news. He caught her hand and smiled at her as she left the table.

When she returned Alasdair was sitting crushed, an untouched glass of whisky on the table in front of him. Ninian was stirring his coffee thoughtfully, purposely not looking at his brother.

'I'll take you home,' Alasdair said bleakly as he pushed Laura's chair back into position.

She began to protest but he silenced her.

'If you don't mind coming back to the office with me for half an hour whilst I see to a few things, or better still, why don't you wait here and I'll pick you up?'

'But you haven't had lunch,' Laura protested. Then, remembering her own scarcely touched plate she didn't insist when he said he wasn't hungry.

'Have *something*,' Ninian coaxed. 'I'll leave Laura to you. I ought to be getting back.'

Alasdair looked at him gratefully. Suddenly, the two brothers seemed to be much closer.

'Thank you for looking after her, Ninian,' he said quietly.

'My pleasure,' Ninian replied, bending down to kiss Laura's cheek. 'Well, see you at the weekend.'

Alasdair nodded bleakly as Ninian walked, imposing and upright, amongst the tables and out into the Strand. He looked across at Laura, then reached over and took her hand, drawing it towards him.

'You look whacked, darling,' he said tenderly.

She didn't reply: she couldn't. The raw pain she saw in her husband's eyes ricocheted off onto her and left her speechless.

'Let's go,' he said quietly, pulling her gently to her feet.

Alasdair smiled down at her, his same crooked, quizzical smile and, as he tucked her hand under his arm, the gesture brought with it a semblance of comfort after the series of blows she had received that morning. Laura managed to smile back.

17

The Funeral

It was arranged that Laura should go to Scotland the
following day, leaving Alasdair to collect the boys from
school and bring them straight up to Ardnakil on the
Thursday. They had been in two minds whether or
not to leave them behind but the children had been
looking forward to going to Ardnakil for the holidays,
and they both felt that as Sandy had been the young
uncle their sons had always had so much fun romping
with during holidays at their grandparents' home, they
would probably want to be there.

'If they don't,' Alasdair said as they debated the
question back and forth, 'they can always go to the
Frasers and fight with their cousins. Cristobel will
probably leave the girls there, so there'll be no problem.
And anyway,' he had added, gathering Laura in his
arms as they lay in bed that night once again endlessly
discussing the day's dramatic events and arrangements
for the days to come, 'I want them with us at this time,
don't you?'

In the darkness Laura had nodded, knowing of
Alasdair's nearness, longing for his touch and yet, in
a strange unfathomable way, feeling that they would
be betraying Sandy by expressing their love for each
other whilst he lay dead across that stretch of sea.

'Oh Alasdair,' she suddenly cried.

His arms tightened round her, and she felt a rush
of warmth pulsate through her slim taut body as

he did so. But, like her, he also felt guilty, afraid
to express his love because his young brother, who
had been on the brink of this bliss had been cut
down before he had had the chance to taste it. And
yet, in spite of everything he needed the comfort of
knowing that she belonged to him: that amid the
shattered ruins which lay around them, something
still remained.

As she melted in his arms, blotted against him, all
the pain, the weariness and the hopelessness which
they had both experienced in successive crashing waves
during the past twelve hours faded into the distance
and they were cradled on a gentle tide of love oblivious
of everything but each other: Momentarily they were
comforted and at peace.

* * *

When Laura landed at the airport the following afternoon, Donald was waiting to meet her. He took her
suitcase and wisely made no comment as they walked
towards the car.

'How is everyone?' she managed to enquire, as he
settled her into her seat.

Donald hunched his shoulders, and Laura felt for
him. He had been born at Ardnakil, he had seen Sandy
born and watched them all grow up. He and Janet
had never had children and the Hamilton children,
to whom Janet had been nanny until Sandy went off
to school, had, in a way, been their children. They had
lived their lives vicariously through them. And now,
like any parents, they felt the sharp cutting grief of
Sandy's untimely death.

'And Janet?' Laura asked, as the car began to
glide away.

'She's naturally very upset, Mrs Alasdair,' Donald

replied. 'Very upset. Master Sandy was her baby in a way.'

'I know,' Laura said softly, and there the conversation ended.

She could see that Donald's grief was raw, as raw in a way as hers and Alasdair's and she understood his need for privacy, above all his need not to be forced into a position in which his emotions might get the better of him.

It was the last day of March; spring was awakening, and the sky above the mountains was lit with a curious light: neither silver nor white but something in between. In the low hedges bordering the cottage gardens birds were twittering and fidgeting, flapping their wings as they flew in and out of the leaves. From the dark damp earth there rose a sweet, pungent smell. Everything seemed to be bursting into life after the long winter sleep and Laura felt an agonising jab of pain, remembering why she was here. She steeled herself into numbness, knowing that she couldn't let herself feel any more and still remain sane.

As the car turned in through the gates and began to cruise along the half mile of drive, the overhanging trees stood sentinel and through their awakening foliage she caught a glimpse of the sunset turning the lake to silver and outlining the woods behind darkly against the sky.

The house was strangely quiet when Donald drew up in front of it. Even the dogs seemed subdued and too lethargic to give their usual uproarious welcome. MacDuff, who had succeeded Laird when he died, wandered out from Laird's old hiding place but did not greet her, merely sauntered aimlessly across the hall in search of nothing in particular. The others stayed morosely in their basket on the first landing, eyeing Laura sorrowfully, not understanding and yet aware that something had happened, something ominous.

As she walked through the great door Cristobel came silently out of the drawing room and, running quickly across the hall, threw herself into Laura's arms.

'Laura DARLING,' she cried. 'How GOOD of you to come.'

Laura clung to her.

'I couldn't do otherwise,' she choked and they stood there together as their tears mingled and overflowed.

'How are they?' Laura asked at last.

Cristobel shrugged and tucked her hand in Laura's arm.

'Father's in his study. He's hardly left it all day. SIMPLY CRUSHED. I don't think he can take it in.'

'And your mother?'

'Amazingly brave,' Cristobel went on. I suppose its her faith that helps her to keep going. Otherwise she'd have become a Zombie like Father and Rose. 'She's in the drawing room making lists.'

Laura knew what that meant. Now that Morag was dead, lists had become Lady Flora's bolt-hole in times of stress.

'And Rose?' Laura asked as they sat down side by side on the old oak settle in the dim hall. 'Graeme told me she was coming here.'

Cristobel nodded.

'Yes, she arrived yesterday and hasn't left Sandy's room since. Not a word nor a tear. Just sits, dry-eyed on the window-seat looking out on the garden.'

She shuddered.

'Its awful. If ONLY she would cry. If only they would ALL cry.'

She turned and hugged Laura.

'I'm SO glad you're here. I felt dreadful being the only one to shed tears and I can assure you I've shed buckets since last night. I feel it should be ME comforting Mother, but it's Mother comforting me.'

A great gasping sob escaped Cristobel's lips and she threw herself into Laura's arms.

'Oh Laura,' she sobbed, 'I'm so thankful I've at last got someone to cry with. Poor darling Sandy, I can't believe it.'

She looked up, her beautiful grey eyes brimming with tears.

'And we were all so BEASTLY to him.'

Laura put her arm round Cristobel's shaking shoulders.

'You weren't, you know,' she soothed, 'not really.'

'But the things we said to him,' Cristobel sobbed.

A smile flitted briefly across Laura's lips.

'What about the things he said to you?'

Cristobel looked up, her beautiful tear-stained face still almost childlike.

'You were always special to him,' she whispered. 'He was TERRIBLY fond of you, even before you married Alasdair.'

Laura didn't reply, just sat thinking of Sandy. Sandy, the mischievous impossible young boy who had turned into such a poised, charming young man, as tall as Ninian, strikingly handsome but still with his thick unruly flame red hair and laughing eyes. And once again, she couldn't believe what had happened. Her mind told her that death is always hard to believe in for those left behind to grieve, always unacceptable. But her heart cried out that Sandy's death was so unexpected, so senseless. All that vital energy, that outgoing irrepressible young man bubbling with laughter and enthusiasm for life could not have been exterminated in a flash by a single sniper's bullet. This must be some terrible nightmare from which she would soon awake, from which they would all awake, and she would find herself at home in her sunlit bedroom.

'Do you remember how you used to help him with his

trumpet practice?' Cristobel said. 'Accompanying him on the piano for hours.'

As she heard Cristobel's voice, coming it seemed from a long way off, slowly pierce through the heavy veils of thick black gauze, and still talking about Sandy, she knew that an era in her life had come to an end. None of them would ever again hear Sandy's infectious laugh echoing through the great house or see him bounding into the hall, the dogs yapping hysterically at his heels.

And as this reality hit her with a terrible finality so did that dreadful premonition that nothing would ever be the same again. With Sandy's untimely death something had died in her life too, in all their lives. The beautiful mosaic which had fallen into place when she married Alasdair now seemed to be slowly disintegrating, with great gaps showing through the delicate pattern. With this awful feeling, this foreboding, wrapping itself round her like a deathly shroud she forced her attention back to what Cristobel was saying.

'. . . and we were none of us musical. Strange, isn't it? Only Sandy . . . and Mother, of course.'

She paused reflectively.

'He was different in so many ways. But you seemed to understand him better than any of us, and to have time for him.'

Laura reached out a hand to her stricken sister-in-law.

'Don't torture yourself,' she whispered. 'Sandy knew you all loved him.'

Cristobel nodded bleakly as the tears streamed down both their cheeks, each seeking comfort from the other, comfort which neither was able to give. And so they sat together in silence trying to put off the moment when they would have to go into the drawing room and face Lady Flora's bright, metallic smile.

'Where's Lindsay?' Laura asked at last.

'At home,' Cristobel replied. 'He insisted on my coming immediately.'

Lindsay had resigned his commission the year before, after Grandfather Lindsay's death, and he and Cristobel had returned to Scotland, with their three little daughters, to manage the estate.

'He'll be arriving with the girls tomorrow,' Cristobel went on. 'But I think they'll probably be staying at Killistrathan with their other grandparents.'

She sighed and passed her hand wearily across her blotched face.

'I don't think Ardnakil is any place for children at the moment.'

They looked at each other and smiled wanly.

Ardnakil had always been a paradise for children.

'Perhaps the boys should stay at Killistrathan with their cousins,' she ventured. 'We didn't think it right to leave them behind.'

'Why not?' Cristobel replied. 'They'll all have a wonderful time fighting together.'

She looked up and for the first time since they had met something like smiles flitted fleetingly across their tear-stained faces.

'I wonder why they do fight so,' Cristobel mused, glad for the moment to take her mind off the tragic event which had brought them together. The Fraser and Hamilton cousins had battled non-stop ever since they had met in their cradles. Flora, named after her maternal grandmother was only a few months older than Iain, Helen was the same age as Jamie and little Iona at four was able to give as good as she received when it came to tussles with her boy cousins.

'Different sexes, I suppose,' Laura smiled. 'They'll probably grow out of it.'

She looked down at Cristobel's rounded figure.

'Maybe you'll have a boy this time and even things out.'

For a brief moment the old twinkle came back into Cristobel's eyes.

'Jolly well hope so,' she answered. 'A fourth daughter would really be a bit much.'

Cristobel stroked her abdomen lovingly.

'It's due mid-August,' she said dreamily. 'Though after the shock we've all had I've been expecting it to arrive at any minute.'

She turned and squeezed Laura's hand.

'Come on,' she said. 'Mother will be pleased to see you, but don't be surprised at her brassy brightness, it's all a pose, I'm sure. She'll have to break down some time.'

The next few days for Laura were a living nightmare. The strangely quiet, subdued house nonetheless hummed with an undercurrent of activity. Lady Flora had been delighted to see her daughter-in-law but, far from being a comfort to her, Laura felt helpless in her presence. Lady Flora wandered around the house, pretending to be busy, just as she had always done, arranged flowers, received people who came to call, rang the bell for tea and made endless lists. Occasionally she could be seen coming quietly out of the study where her husband sat hunched and motionless, or from Sandy's room where Rose still remained dry-eyed, as if in a trance. Yet always, it seemed, upheld by some force more powerful than herself. A force which enabled her to carry on, to remain calm and bring comfort to those who came to comfort her.

Had it not been for Cristobel's presence, Laura felt she would have fled. It was like living in a haunted house, a house full of animated puppets, pulled by some invisible string, marionettes who had no connection with flesh and blood people at all. Realising that there was little that they could do but be there, she and

213

Cristobel spent most of their time together, either sitting silently in the old schoolroom or going for long blustery walks in the park, through the wood, round the lake, anywhere to get out of the nightmare which was being acted out at Ardnakil, trying to find some semblance of normality. Laura longed for Alasdair with a longing which had become a physical ache, and when on the Thursday afternoon he arrived with the boys, she too, had taken on the atmosphere of the house and seemed to be frozen.

The boys were subdued but also excited. Death was something which had not really penetrated their little minds and it was difficult for them to suppress the macabre excitement they obviously felt. When Lady Flora saw Jamie's flame coloured, windtossed hair as he jumped boisterously out of the car, for a brief moment her composure almost cracked. He was like Sandy had been as a little boy. So full of energy and mischief, unable to keep still, always dancing on one foot, and always untidy. She gathered the three of them to her, embracing them more warmly than she had ever embraced her own children, hugging them, seemingly not wanting to let them go. When they finally wriggled out of her arms and went racing across the hall, she stood looking after them as if she wanted to remain at this moment in time, have this memory etched deep in her subconscious.

After tea, Lindsay took them over to the Frasers and then the long wait came until, just after dinner which no-one ate, they heard the crunch of the cars on the drive and knew that Ninian had arrived with Sandy's coffin.

Hearing the cars, Robert opened the door of his study and walked heavily out, looking neither to right nor left. His wife went across and took his arm, but he seemed unaware of it. Hamish shuffled out of the drawing room, his ruddy, ham-like face woebegone, his moustache drooping lower than ever, as Rose, deathly pale, her face almost transparent with grief, walked down the stairs on Graeme's arm.

Laura clutched hold of Alasdair's hand, gripping it tightly as the cars stopped, the great door swung open and Sandy's body in a coffin draped with the Union Jack, was carried across the threshold and placed reverently on the wooden trestles. Ninian walked behind it, his face drawn with fatigue.

For a few tense seconds no-one moved, the only sound came from the ponderous tick of the old grandfather clock in a far corner of the hall. Then suddenly Robert lurched forward: his wife quickly caught hold of his arm but he steadied himself and, leaning heavily on his stick, stood upright and dry-eyed, motionless before his youngest son's earthly remains.

Laura felt Alasdair's grip tighten on her hand and she wondered just how much longer she could stand this charade, this silence, this complete control which everybody was showing. From behind her there came the welcome sound of muffled sobs as the door from the servants' hall silently opened and they stood, huddled together in a forlorn group, watching the silent grief. Suddenly Janet, standing in the doorway with Donald, buried her face in her hands and broke into heartbreaking sobs. Her husband put his arms round her and drew her away; and as they passed him, Ninian stretched out his hand to them and the dreadful moment was broken. Hamish took a large red-spotted handkerchief from his pocket and blew his nose loudly, Robert turned and leaning heavily on his wife's arm, shuffled like a sleep walker back into his study.

Loosening her tight grip on Graeme's arm, Rose moved forward as if in a dream and laid her hand gently on top of the coffin. She stood there for a few minutes, a faint, unreal smile hovering about her lips, as if she were alone, far away in some never-never land. Then whispering, 'Goodbye Sandy', she turned, and brushing aside Graeme's offer of his arm, walked swiftly back up the stairs.

Alasdair drew Laura to him and half carried her, sobbing quietly into his jacket, back into the drawing room. Lindsay followed with Cristobel and the two sat holding their wives in their arms on either side of the fire, waiting for their weeping to cease.

The door opened and Ninian walked in and sat down heavily on the sofa.

'Has it been like this all the time?' he enquired. 'This strange calm?'

Alasdair nodded.

'Afraid so. If only they would just let go of this iron control and break down.'

He sighed and looked across at Ninian.

'Graeme was right about Father. He looks twenty years older than he did at Christmas.'

Ninian nodded, and the five of them sat there not knowing what to say, longing for it all to be over and for normality to return.

All day Friday Sandy's coffin remained on its trestles in the great hall as the villagers who had known and loved him came to pay their last respects, to weep in front of it, to lay little posies of heather or other mountain flowers on the top. Rose appeared from time to time, still with that doll-like expression in her eyes as if she were not really there, as if she had already gone to join Sandy in a land where there was no more pain. Lady Flora remained upright and gracious, tight little smiles jumping erratically across her lips as her voice uttered mechanical phrases or comforted those who came to comfort her.

By the Saturday morning Laura was feeling so drained with grief and exhaustion that she wondered just how she was going to get through the day. But finally the cars arrived; they all gathered once again in the hall and Sandy's body was carried, for the last time, from the house in which he had been born, and down the long drive, under the canopy of trees standing erect and still, their fresh young leaves shining with moisture in the pale spring sunshine. At the gate a crowd of young men from the estate were waiting and the coffin was lifted reverently from the hearse and carried on their sturdy shoulders through the village and into the little stone church.

It was a glorious morning, the second of April, a perfect day for a Spring wedding Laura couldn't help thinking as she entered the crowded church and took her place beside Alasdair. The service was short and beautiful, the singing tearful but lusty, with Lady Flora's voice rising, full of assurance, strong and clear above the others. As the strains of 'Abide with me', the Soldier's Hymn, a last tribute to Sandy, died away the old clock chimed twelve, the hour at which Rose should have been walking, a radiant bride on her father's arm, down that very aisle to meet her bridegroom.

Laura stole a glance at her and, as she did so, a dazzling sunbeam pierced through the stained glass window and fell onto the coffin, bouncing off it to highlight the deathly pallor of Rose's face. For a moment, her dry eyes wandered briefly to the coffin and Laura thought Rose's composure was going to crack. But, gripping the pew in front of her for support, Rose steadied herself and stared straight ahead as the bearers came to carry the coffin back down the aisle.

The clock striking the last notes of twelve mingled with the tolling bell as Rose left the pew and followed Sandy's body out of the church and into the little graveyard.

As they all crowded round the freshly dug grave and the final words were pronounced, the poignant call of a

217

bugle playing the last post broke onto the soft clear air. Sandy's body was slowly lowered into the grave. The last broken note hit the air as the coffin disappeared, the silence in the graveyard was deathly; then the joyful reveille rang out.

Robert lurched forward, to be caught by Ninian. He shrugged his son away and, once again leaning heavily on his stick stood erect, looking down into the open grave as earth was thrown onto the coffin's shiny surface. At that moment the crushing silence was eerie. But, suddenly, in the distance, the sound of a lone piper playing 'The Flowers of the Forest' pierced the deathly stillness and as its mournful lament drew nearer suddenly Rose's composure broke and with a last long agonised look into the open grave she gave a terrible shriek, like an animal which has been mortally wounded, and fell weeping into Graeme's arms.

He gathered her to him and turned away and, as the lament rose and fell around them, the crowd parted and, the tension at last broken, the family moved through it and back to the waiting cars.

Laura clung tightly to Alasdair's arm, tears streaming freely down her face as they followed Lady Flora, upright and dry-eyed, walking with her husband, a shuffling, broken old man, to a house which would never again ring with the sound of Sandy's laughter.

'Thank God it's over,' Lindsay said, coming up beside them, supporting a weeping Cristobel. 'I don't think Cristobel could have taken much more, and I'm worried about her as it is.'

The four of them walked together out of the graveyard and through the church gate.

'Let's travel back together,' Lindsay said to Alasdair. 'I've got a suggestion to make.'

Alasdair looked at him in surprise as they climbed into a car.

Lindsay sat in front next to the driver and leaned over the seat as they drove away.

'Why don't you all come back to Lochincraig with Cristobel and me?' he asked. 'I honestly don't think there's any good to be done by staying at Ardnakil at the moment: your parents would be better left to work through their grief on their own. You were going to stay on here after the wedding, weren't you?'

Alasdair nodded.

'Well, as things didn't work out as we'd hoped, why disappoint the children? All of you come back with us and we'll try to make some sort of holiday for them. And, anyway it would be good for Cristobel and Laura to be together and try to wind down: this past week has taken a terrible toll on them both.'

Alasdair shrugged his shoulders.

'If you think it would be a good idea' he replied. 'It doesn't seem as if we can be of much use here for the time being. But,' he smiled, 'as for our children enjoying themselves together, that's a hope. They never do anything but fight!'

'Oh, Mother says they've been getting along splendidly these last few days,' Lindsay said. 'Perhaps they're growing older.'

'Or perhaps Jamie is so relieved not to have had to hold your Helen's hand and walk down the aisle with her that he's decided to be pleasant for a change.'

'Perhaps,' Lindsay laughed. 'It's agreed then?'

'Would you like that Laura?' Alasdair asked gently.

'Yes please,' she whispered, like a little girl who had been offered a treat.

And as she said it Alasdair looked down at her and his heart melted once again.

18

Anti-climax

In later years when Laura looked back on her life, she
realised that her thirtieth birthday and Sandy's death
had, in some strange way, precipitated the series of
events which were to follow. They had both been
catalysts for her, signposts with lights flashing, a
watershed out of which the life which flowed had
never been the same again.

When she replaced the receiver after Graeme's traumatic news, her world had crumbled. She knew that all
she had so lovingly built up, all she had put her trust,
her faith and hope: in her home, her husband, this
wonderful family which had received her with such love
were finite, ephemeral—they could all, at any time, by
some strange quirk of fate be lost, swept from her like
a leaf in the wind.

And all the old fears had begun to invade her
heart, together with the feeling of rejection which had
overwhelmed her when her mother died.

Although Edwina had done everything in her power
at that time to restore her niece's confidence and give
her the love and security she so sorely needed, her
sisters' absence and her father's seeming indifference
had left Laura feeling unloved and abandoned, causing
her to put up a wall and retreat behind it, lost and
bewildered, alone in a hostile world.

And, without even realising what she was doing, as
the subdued little party drove away from Ardnakil on

the day after Sandy's funeral en route for Lochincraig,
she once more retreated into her shell and began to
rebuild that defensive wall, that barrier against pain
and anguish, determined that never would she allow
her life to be shattered, her world to crumble again.

To all outward appearances the holiday at Lochincraig had helped and refreshed them. Lindsay's forecast about the children becoming older and wiser and
less inclined to fight had proved true, yet that dreadful
foreboding that something was irrevocably broken, that
some terrible shadow had fallen across their lives which
Laura had felt creeping over her when she heard the
news of Sandy's death, did not disappear. And in the
days and weeks after their return home it seemed to
loom larger and more menacing like a great black cloud
gathering on the horizon. All she had built up during
her years with Alasdair began to crack as she saw how
easy it was for life to be snuffed out, as the flame from
a candle disappears the minute it is extinguished. And
Laura's peace and happiness began to be slowly eroded
by a chilling fear.

'I wonder whether it mightn't be a good idea to send
Jamie to school with the others in September instead
of waiting till after Christmas,' Alasdair remarked
casually one evening in May when they were sitting
together in the garden after dinner watching the
midges shimmering in the twilight haze.

Laura turned to him, her eyes wide and uncompre-
hending, as something tightened inside her chest like
an iron band slowly compressing her heart.

'But WHY'? she cried.

'Well,' Alasdair went on, puffing contentedly at his
pipe, 'he's ready for it, always on about when is he
going to join his brothers.'

Laura took a deep breath in an attempt to free herself
of the constricting iron band.

'But he's only SEVEN,' she pleaded.

'He'll be eight in January,' Alasdair reminded her.

'Yes, but he's only seven NOW.'

Alasdair turned to her with his amused, quizzical smile.

'Do I hear the mother hen clucking in the distance?' he teased.

Laura rose angrily to her feet.

'Call it what you like,' she snapped. 'I STILL think he's too young.'

'All right, all right,' Alasdair laughed, catching at her hand as she flounced past him. 'It was only a suggestion.'

But, for Laura, the peace of the soft spring evening had been brutally shattered, and pulling away from him, she walked angrily into the house, not even sure WHY she was angry. Her husband had made a perfectly rational suggestion, and it WAS only a suggestion, and yet she had reacted as if he'd announced his intention of putting all the children into an orphanage the following morning!

She crossed the drawing room and sat down at the piano, but the gesture of running her hands along the keyboard, which usually soothed her, tonight only set her nerves jangling as the notes danced tantalisingly in front of her eyes, her fingers refusing to obey her brain. After a few futile attempts she closed the lid and, with a sigh, walked over to the curved window.

Alasdair had picked up the evening paper and was straining his eyes in the half light. She saw him put it down and sit puffing thoughtfully at his pipe as he gazed at the shadows of purple twilight creeping slowly across the garden. For a second Laura's heart softened and melted towards him and she almost ran out across the few yards which separated them and put her arms round the back of his neck and kissed the top of his head. But that tight feeling returned to her chest and she turned away from the peaceful view towards the stairs and went miserably to bed, lying stiffly in the darkness as she listened to the sounds of the May night whispering up to her from the garden below. She could smell the roses, and the lavender and the comforting, pungent odour of Alasdair's tobacco mingling with them; but this evening it brought her no comfort.

Laura turned on her side and tried to sleep, but a dazzling blackness flashed in front of her eyes and suddenly, for the first time since she had married, she felt that heavy dragging frightening weight of being alone slowly creeping over her.

When Alasdair came to bed her eyes were closed. She heard his step, heard him moving quietly about the room, heard the slight creak as he got in beside her, the click as he switched off the bedside light, the gentle heave as he leant on one elbow and bent over to lightly kiss her cheek. But she remained still and unresponsive. He turned over, and, within a few minutes she heard his regular breathing and knew that he was asleep.

Slipping out of bed she went across to the window and leant on the sill, drinking in the sweet, damp air. A waning moon like a baroque pearl hung low in the sky, lapping the garden with its opal light. She could just make out the faint outline of the white wooden chairs on the terrace below, the steps leading down to the small smooth lawn, the dim silhouette of the overhanging roof and the shadow of a wheelbarrow propped against the side of the house. All the familiar sights and sounds of this home she so loved, where up till just a few weeks ago she had felt secure and at peace. She couldn't understand this sudden misery which had descended on her.

Alasdair had brought her here as a bride. It was here that their three sons had been born. She loved the house because it was theirs, their home and her bolt hole; her protection against the outside world. Yet, inexplicably, this evening that protective shell had withered and fallen off leaving her exposed and vulnerable. She imagined the house without Jamie and suddenly felt empty and useless, her role in life usurped by a school matron. Laura heard again Alasdair's teasing words: 'Do I detect the clucking of a mother hen?' and she knew that he was right.

She had experienced a feeling of desolation when Iain had left for prep school, but there had been Andrew and Jamie who still needed her. Then when Andrew had joined his brother the following year, Jamie's lively, noisy presence had filled the empty space. But now it was Jamie's turn, and she knew instinctively that she could not bear to part with the last of her babies. His presence in the house gave her a sense of purpose, a feeling of being needed. She would not be able to face the tidy, quiet, echoing rooms once he had gone.

Her mind wandered to Ardnakil and she wondered whether Flora was now thinking back to the locust years, those years when Sandy, her baby, had only come home for the holidays, those years when he hadn't been growing up beside her, running to her with his cuts and bruises or to wipe his tears when the world had turned against him. He had been away from her, comforted by another woman who was not his mother.

And suddenly, with these bleak thoughts, Sandy's death hit her again in all its force.

As the muted night sounds lessened and the soft breeze wafting the variegated scents of a spring garden into the still room gently stirred the muslin curtains, she laid her head on her arms, folded on the window sill, and silently wept. And out of her weeping, words from her childhood, learned by rote and long since forgotten, floated back into her consciousness: 'Our lives are like a blade of grass, here today and gone tomorrow.' Laura realised in that instant that nothing was eternal and no-one was immortal and no matter what anyone did, there could be no guarantee of continuity, for nothing was ever completely safe. In spite of everything, she had once again come face to face with death in all its finality and once again she felt powerless and was afraid.

Her marriage to Alasdair had swept away the aching sense of isolation, of rejection, the insecurity which had overwhelmed her since her mother's death. The latent woman trapped inside her young body, yearning for release, had finally been allowed to surface and to blossom. The frightened young girl having at last been supplanted, she was able to face the future with hope, not with fear. Even her father's death from a sudden heart attack three years ago had not really disrupted her life, merely left a momentary sadness which had soon passed. And she had told herself that, secure in her marriage and her love for Alasdair, she was safe and protected. Nothing could ever shatter her world again.

But Sandy's death was different. It had not been 'after a long illness courageously borne', as the newspapers had described her mother's passing. He had been young and vibrant, on the threshold of life: he had also been part of this new life she had forged for herself, where everything was as solid as a rock and nothing changed. And yet, when she least expected it, that rock had suddenly splintered and she found herself slithering about in deep waters. And, in spite of herself, she began to ponder about life, about death and ask herself what it was all about. Raising a tear-stained face to the night sky she wondered if she would see Sandy smiling down at her, but there was only a monstrous strutting peacock striding across the heavens, its tail studded with a thousand twinkling stars.

Alasdair stirred and raised himself up on the pillows,

blinking in the darkness. He got out of bed and padded softly over to her.

'Darling,' he said gently, putting his arms round her shaking figure and leading her back to bed. 'Whatever is it?'

He tucked the blankets tenderly round her, his face full of concern. But she turned on her side and buried her head in the pillow, unable to speak, unable to explain because she did not understand what was happening herself. Her husband climbed in beside her and lay stroking her hair: she longed to turn and blot herself against him thereby blotting out all the eerie night shadows which seemed to be lurking in every corner of the room waiting to creep out and stifle her. She wanted to feel his nearness, his strength and be reassured merely because he was there. But the horror of the darkness with its black fantastic shapes suddenly engulfed her and she was afraid; afraid that this rock, the rock on which her foundations were built, on which her whole life and happiness depended, might not also one day crack and leave her drowning, totally out of her depth: like the blade of grass the Bible spoke of, here today and gone tomorrow.

And she stiffened and drew herself away, unconsciously refusing any contact which could render her vulnerable again.

Alasdair gently kissed her hair and, turning on his side, fell asleep almost immediately as Laura lay tense beside him feeling his warmth, his closeness, longing for his touch but held as if in a vice by the terrible, crippling fear which had suddenly and inexplicably overwhelmed her.

The next morning at breakfast her husband did not refer to their conversation of the evening before but he looked at her curiously as he got up from the table.

'You seem tired,' he said gently, waiting for her to reassure him.

But she didn't reply.

'Try to take things easily,' he went on stooping to kiss her. 'You've got a busy weekend ahead with the boys coming home for half term.'

Laura nodded briefly and walked with him to the front door then stood waving mechanically as he walked down the drive and out through the gate.

* * *

They neither of them broached the subject of Jamie's eventual departure again and it almost seemed as if they were both skating round the issue, afraid to approach it. But the question resolved itself the following week.

'Dad,' Jamie said moodily, kicking at a discarded paper cup left lying on the grimy platform as they turned away from the train which had just left taking his brothers and most of their friends back to school after the half term holiday. 'Why do I have to wait till after CHRISTMAS to go to school with Iain and Andrew?'

He looked angrily from one to the other of his parents.

'You can't go NOW,' his father answered mildly, 'because it's the middle of the term.'

'WELL,' Jamie plunged on belligerently, finding another discarded cup and giving it the full force of his anger, 'why can't I go NEXT term? I'm sick of that stupid day school and that twit Miss Fanshawe.'

Alasdair smiled at Laura across their youngest son's head.

'"Jamie, I've already told you haven't I dear, we don't pull little girls' plaits and make them cry,"' Jamie mimicked, taking a deep breath and pursing his lips into a sickly smile. '"And JAMIE, we MUSTN'T shut Amelia in the shoe cupboard, it isn't kind now, is it, dear? No, Jamie, please put that hammer DOWN, Cedric didn't MEAN to make a face at you."'

His voice rose to a staccato screech.

"'And now, Jamie, let us pretend we're little fishes ALL swimming in a great big pond, no NOT like that dear, I'm sorry if REAL fishes DO make rude noises with their mouths but we mustn't, must we dear. It's not polite. Oh JAMIE, I'm *sure* Mummie NEVER said you COULD Jamie. Ooh JAMIE,"' he ended, giving a perfect imitation of the spinsterish Miss Fanshawe who ran the small private school he attended.

'Honestly Dad,' he spat out, 'she's PATHETIC.'

He looked up at his father appealingly: then suddenly brightened.

'Iain said they had a terrific pillow fight the other night, Audley was knocked unconscious because Haddon had put a football boot inside his pillow-case and Sir William came and there was a dreadful fuss and they all got six of the best.'

His eyes shone at the exciting prospect.

'And all I get,' he continued moodily, his joy suddenly evaporating as he dragged his feet along the platform, 'is that nincompoop Miss Fanshawe saying, "Now Jamie we don't tease little girls and make them cry do we dear? It's not KIND. *Nice* little boys don't do it."'

He pranced in front of them, wriggling his hips and taking small mincing steps, his lips still drawn up into a Dorothy bag. In spite of herself, Laura couldn't help laughing. Jamie's imitation of the twittering Miss Fanshawe was perfect.

Alasdair tweaked his son's ear as he hailed a taxi.

'Your turn will come soon enough,' he smiled, handing them both in. 'Charing Cross,' he said to the driver and he smiled at Laura. 'I'll try to be home early.'

'But Dad,' Jamie protested as his father slammed the door.

But the taxi had already moved away.

Jamie sat moodily back in his seat and, there now being no discarded cups on which to vent his anger, began kicking at the cab's upholstery.

'You really want to go to school with your brothers, don't you?' Laura remarked diffidently, putting a restraining hand on his jerking leg.

'You BET,' he gasped and looked up at her with shining eyes. 'Oh Mum, CAN I?'

'We'll see,' she answered, her heart suddenly lurching over. But they had arrived at Charing Cross and their waiting train.

Alasdair didn't mention the subject that evening: it was Laura who brought it up.

'It seems that the question of when Jamie leaves for St Bede's has resolved itself,' she said quietly as they sat together in the drawing room, listening to the summer rain which was pattering furiously against the window panes.

Alasdair looked at her over the top of his newspaper.

'It's up to you, darling,' he answered. 'If you want arrangements to stay as they are, then he'll go after Christmas.'

'Do you think we could handle him till then?' Laura smiled. 'He's absolutely determined to go, and if he continues to behave at Windsmoor House the way he appears to be doing at the moment, I very much doubt whether Miss Fanshawe will take him back in September.' She sighed. 'So we really have no option.'

'Darling,' Alasdair said, putting down his paper and crossing over to her. But she got up hurriedly.

'The last few days have been rather tiring,' she muttered, 'I think I'll go up to bed.'

He looked at her curiously, but said nothing.

'I expect everything will look different after the

holidays,' she remarked, seeing the look on her husband's face and feeling guilty.

They were going to Ardnakil as usual that summer and, although Cristobel probably would not be there because her baby was due in August, Laura would be happy to be back, to be with Flora again in that familiar place where she had her roots; and to find the security which appeared to have deserted her, especially since the day she realised that Jamie was about to leave.

She paused in the doorway and smiled at Alasdair. 'I'm looking forward to it,' she said softly. 'Do you think Ninian will come?'

'I don't know,' Alasdair answered thoughtfully. 'I hope so. It would be nice if he could bring Deirdre, but I wonder if it isn't a little too early.'

Laura didn't reply. The old ache returned when she thought of Ninian having waited so long for this happiness, postponed, and now not even sure whether it would ever be his.

'I'll ask them to dinner next week,' she promised, trying to make up to Alasdair for her coldness. 'I expect they need cheering up.'

Alasdair looked at her intently.

'You look as if you do too,' he said slowly, and made a move towards her. But, suddenly, the old fear returned, the ugly shapes seemed to be creeping out of the shadowy corners once again and she was afraid. Quickly walking through the door she closed it behind her and turned to the stairs.

19

Parting

But the holiday at Ardnakil turned out quite differently from what Laura had expected.

When they arrived, everything appeared to be the same as it had always been: the terrible empty feeling of desolation which had enveloped the house in April had gone and normality seemed to have returned.

Flora was waiting for them in the great hall as the car drew up. She greeted them as she had so often, in the past, greeted Laura and Cristobel when they arrived from school, with a delighted cry of 'My darlings'. But this time Laura noticed that she bent and gathered her grandsons into her arms holding them to her as if she never wanted to let them go. As they hugged her and then scrambled from her grasp, Jamie looked up at his grandmother, his freckled face grubby from the journey, his fiery red hair awry. Laura saw her mother-in-law catch her breath, and a slight mist cloud her eyes. Jamie looked more like Sandy than ever. But Flora collected herself immediately and turned to greet Laura and Alasdair as they stood waiting for her usual, cool embrace.

'Is Helen here?' Jamie asked excitedly, referring to Cristobel's second daughter.

Lady Flora turned towards him.

'Why no,' she replied. 'I hadn't thought to ask her.'

She bent and ruffled Jamie's already haywire hair.

231

'The last time you were here together, you kept pulling her hair and making her cry,' she teased.

Jamie grinned up at his grandmother.

'That was at Christmas,' Iain piped in, 'we quite like the girls now. I wouldn't mind having Flora here to play with.'

'I s'pose that leaves me with Iona,' Andrew said disgustedly, looking from one to the other of them.

They all laughed.

'Can they come, Grannie?' Jamie pleaded.

Flora smiled down at him.

'I don't see why not,' she replied gently. 'Perhaps with the baby due very soon it would even be helpful for Cristobel if they were here. How stupid of me,' she went on. 'I should have thought of it before. I'll go and telephone Lochincraig immediately.'

And pausing to give Jamie another long look she turned quickly and walked from the hall.

The three Fraser girls arrived the next day and, much to Laura's relief, the truce between the cousins held and they all got on famously together. Andrew felt a bit out of things at times but he was an easy-going boy and Iona, now four years old, was a lively little girl, eager to keep up with her sisters, so he resigned himself to 'playing with babies', as he called it.

Robert seemed to have shrunk. His clothes hung on his once massive frame as if they were supported on the inside by coat hangers. But to all outward appearances the grave had been filled in, the ranks had closed and, whatever their private grief, neither Flora nor her husband allowed it to show or in any way to cast a shadow over the holiday.

But early one morning, about ten days after their arrival, Robert had a sudden, massive stroke which left him paralysed and speechless. The doctors were pessimistic, but said that if he survived the first few days there was a great likelihood that he would partially recover and live. Yet, as he lay there in the great bed in which he and his father and grandfather before him and all his sons had been born, a pathetic shadow of the man he had once been, Laura wondered whether he really wanted to live: whether he had not grown tired of the life which had once been so full, and yet had become a broken shell for him after Sandy's death.

Flora hardly left his side but sat holding his hand, talking softly to him. Through his sunken eyes which never left her face, he seemed to communicate back. The rest of the family tiptoed in and out from time to time but their parents appeared to be so peaceful, so happy in each other's company, that their presence seemed almost an intrusion.

On the first day Flora had agonised over whether to inform Cristobel or not. She knew the strong links which bound her to her father but she also knew that to travel with the birth imminent would be unwise, and she could not be sure that Cristobel, under the stress of emotion, would act wisely. Graeme convinced his mother that she must at least telephone Lindsay and let him decide. He had promised to break the news to his wife as gently as possible.

On the third day Graeme persuaded his mother to leave the sick room and come downstairs to have tea with them in the drawing room. It had been raining all day. But, as the tray was brought in a pale yellow sun was struggling to break through the ragged pile of curdled grey clouds and Flora decided to have tea on the little table in the west turret where they could look out on to the terrace and the damp garden and watch the rainbow which was just beginning to shimmer through on the horizon.

Just as they were finishing, the telephone rang and Kirsty came in to announce that it was for Lady Flora.

'I'll take it,' Alasdair said, fearing that Flora would seize the opportunity to return to the sick-room. But he returned a few minutes later, his brow creased.

'It's Lindsay,' he said. 'I'm afraid he won't give me a message: he wants to speak to you, Mother.'

Flora rose with her usual vague sweet smile and glided across the drawing room. Laura noticed that her slight figure had become almost wraithlike in the last few days, she seemed to have melted. And her heart went out to this mother-in-law who had been more than a mother to her.

Within a few minutes Flora returned and stood in the drawing room door.

They all looked up expectantly, no-one daring to ask the news. But Flora smiled.

'Lindsay telephoned to announce the arrival, half an hour ago, of Robert Alexander Hamilton Lindsay-Fraser,' she breathed. 'Eight pounds ten ounces, red hair and both mother and son doing well.'

They looked from one to the other, relief written all over their faces. In the last few months the house had weathered so many storms that they had almost come to expect bad news rather than good every time the telephone rang.

Lady Flora took a deep breath as if trying to gain control of herself.

'Cristobel sends her love,' she ended and her voice broke.

Laura looked across at her mother-in-law and their eyes met. In that split second it was as if something fused between them, something which had been hanging in abeyance for years: the tears which had been lingering behind Laura's eyelids ever since she heard the news, tears of joy and relief suddenly gushed from her eyes and cascaded down her cheeks. And, as Flora looked back at her, something broke deep inside her too. All the pent-up held-back emotion which had been building up into a crescendo since the day Sandy's coffin had been carried into the house rose rapidly to the surface, momentarily choked her and then, as the iron grip which she had imposed upon herself, that grip which had enabled her to face the world, snapped, the tears long held back, began to trickle slowly down her cheeks.

'MOTHER,' Laura cried, calling Lady Flora by that name which she had longed to use ever since she married Alasdair but which had always refused to come. And, leaping up from her chair she ran towards her, suddenly conscious of a great release within her, too, a tremendous surge of joy at being able to once again pronounce that word which had frozen on her lips the day her own mother died: the word which had been locked up inside her, longing for utterance ever since.

Flora held out her arms, the tears now coursing freely down her face and Laura blotted herself against her, weeping almost hysterically. Flora enfolded her daughter-in-law in her arms and led her gently towards the drawing room door.

Graeme and Alasdair said nothing. But as the two women passed into the hall beyond, Graeme slowly got up and walked across the room to close the door behind them, and caught a glimpse of them clinging together on the old oak settle, sobbing in each other's arms.

The brothers sat in silence for a few minutes, neither of them knowing what to say. This unexpected show of emotion on their mother's part had unnerved and upset them; and they each searched around in their minds for some phrase which would bring the situation back to normality.

'Perhaps someone should go and tell the girls they've got a baby brother?' Alasdair ventured at last.

They were all busy playing in the old schoolroom,

Janet having completely taken charge, happy to have little Hamiltons under her wing once again.

'Oh leave it for the moment,' Graeme said. 'I think I've had enough emotion for one afternoon. Haven't you?'

Alasdair nodded agreement, his eyes on the tip of his shoes.

'I wouldn't mind another cup of tea,' Graeme went on. 'Ring for Kirsty, will you, and ask her to bring some more scones as well.'

Alasdair got up and walked slowly across the room to pull the long, tasselled rope dangling at the side of the fireplace.

'The baby'll keep,' Graeme stated, settling himself back in his chair. 'They're quiet now: Janet's an angel the way she keeps them all amused and happy. We can save this choice piece of news for a time when they get bored or start fighting.'

Alasdair sat down and smiled at his brother, realising that Graeme didn't sense the importance in children's eyes of such news. And he marvelled at how much marriage and fatherhood changed a man. But, at the same time he didn't feel like being overwhelmed by six over-excited children either, so he leant back in his chair and gazed out at the sodden garden lying in the half circle of a deepening rainbow.

As their weeping gradually subsided, Lady Flora gently released Laura and began dabbing at her eyes with a sodden scrap of handkerchief.

'I MUST go and tell Robert,' she said. 'Such wonderful news, and early too, we didn't expect to hear anything for another week at least.'

'Perhaps learning of Father's illness brought it on,' Laura suggested slipping automatically into calling Robert Father for the first time, too.

'Perhaps,' her mother-in-law mused. 'But he's a fine baby and they're both well, so that's all that matters.'

Laura nodded.

'Robert Alexander Hamilton,' Flora murmured quietly, and hearing it, Laura choked again.

Flora put her arm round her shoulders.

'You go back into the drawing room,' she said gently. 'I saw some fresh tea being taken in.'

She looked down at the tiny old-fashioned gold fob watch, an engagement present from Robert, which she always wore pinned to her dress.

'Good gracious,' she exclaimed as Laura got up. 'I've been away for almost an hour. Robert will wonder what has happened to me.'

And with a final scrub of her handkerchief around her face she turned towards the stairs.

As she entered the sick room her husband was lying as she had left him, except that his eyes were now closed. His eyes always seemed to be closed as if he had already said goodbye to the world, except when his wife entered the room when, sensing her presence, he slowly opened them.

Lady Flora smiled at the nurse, who was busy at a small table in the corner.

'He hasn't moved since you left' she replied in answer to her unspoken query. 'He seems to be asleep.'

As the nurse tiptoed from the sick room Flora sat down in the chair which was perpetually there at her husband's side and took his thin white hand through which the blue veins showed beneath the dry skin.

'Darling,' she said softly.

Robert's eyes which, since she returned to the room, had never left her, seemed to move towards her until they were almost fused with hers. She noticed that the dancing green and gold lights which Alasdair and Sandy and now Jamie had inherited from him were dull and glazed. Only the hazel shell remained.

'Darling,' she whispered again, holding his frail hand caressingly to her cheek. 'The most wonderful

237

news. Lindsay has just telephoned to say that Robert
Alexander Hamilton arrived this afternoon.'

For a moment the old light flickered in Robert's eyes.
But it was a light of fear. These two people who had
shared so much had become so much a part of each
other that, even without words, she understood his
meaning. She gently laid his hand on the sheet and
covered it with hers.

'He's a fine boy,' she said softly, 'and he and
Cristobel are both very well.'

Immediately the fear went out of his eyes and it
seemed that a veil of peace dropped over them.

'Everybody is very happy,' Flora whispered.

And she had the impression that his head, with its
shock of hair now almost white, but with a few rebel-
lious streaks of red still running through it, nodded his
approval.

And then, as if a great weight had been lifted from
him for the first time since his stroke he appeared to
visibly relax. The arrival of Cristobel's son, seemed
to give him hope, hope for the future, hope even for
immortality, that his life would continue in this new
life, this grandson whose eyes had just opened to the
light of day.

Flora sat by his side, her hand cradling his as the
weak evening sun struggled in through the windows,
sending pale beams dancing across the foot of the bed
as the soft, washed-out light of a late summer's day
gradually began to fade.

She knew that this was the end, the end of their long
life together, the end of her life as mistress of Ardnakil;
as Robert Hamilton's wife, and yet she was at peace.
As the sun crept round the large old fashioned room,
highlighting the familiar furniture, the loved objects,
the pictures, lingering waveringly on her silver-backed
hairbrushes sitting stiffly on the mahogany dressing
table, it seemed to her as if he and she were saying

goodbye: goodbye to a life which was slowly ebbing away from him, carrying him gently through the door which divides us from the world to come. Robert had been waiting to hear the news of the safe arrival of Cristobel's baby and, now that he had received it, it was as if soft veils were slowly dropping over him, gradually but irrevocably hiding him from her sight for ever, carrying him away to a place where she could not follow.

Flora did not call the nurse. She did not call their children. She wanted this to be a farewell between herself and Robert, the man she had married against all good advice, the man who had been faithful and devoted, had given her hope and love and security more than any woman could ever wish for, and who was now about to drift gently out of her life.

She bent forward. His eyes were not as bright as they had been a few minutes earlier. She squeezed his hand, but there was not the faint feathery pressure with which he had acknowledged her in the past few days.

'Robert,' she murmured softly, leaning over him. 'Robert, my darling.'

With a great effort he raised his drooping lids and she saw once again the love in his eyes.

'Robert,' she whispered brokenly, 'Oh ROBERT, I love you so much.'

For a fraction of a second it seemed as if he were going to rise on his pillows but it was only a gesture. He opened his mouth but no words came: his eyes looked at her pleadingly, willing her to understand what he was trying so desperately to tell her.

'I know,' she said softly. 'I know Robert. You love me, too.'

Relief seemed to be written in his eyes and with a final effort, he opened his mouth and a soft fluttering sound so unlike his usual booming tones filtered through the dry lips.

'Flora,' he managed to whisper, his voice scarcely more than a ripple in his throat; and with another superhuman effort, 'my Flora.'

She gripped his hand more tightly in both of hers as the tears began to flow steadily down her cheeks. Almost imperceptibly his head moved from side to side as if he were trying to say, 'don't cry'.

Flora took a corner of the soft linen sheet and wiped her eyes, then, smiling through her tears, she bent her head and laid her cheek against his cold, withered one.

'I won't cry Robert,' she whispered. 'I promise. There's nothing to cry about, you've given me nothing but pure happiness all these years.'

Hearing her words he seemed to relax and they lay there side by side, his cheek touching hers, as they had done for so many nights in the past forty years.

The door opened slowly and Alasdair stood there. Seeing them together, their eyes closed, a look of ecstasy on his mother's face, he quietly closed the door and tiptoed away.

And, as the room slowly dimmed and the summer twilight faded, Flora felt Robert's hand slacken in hers, the bedclothes which had scarcely moved with his shallow breathing suddenly become still as her husband took a long deep breath and quietly slipped away.

20

Revelations

'Is there any news of Ninian?' Lady Flora asked later that evening. They were all sitting together in a rather eerie silence round the drawing room fire, feeling slightly unreal, trying to appear normal, to make plans and arrangements and not achieving very much.

As soon as she heard the news of Robert's death Lady Fraser had arrived at Ardnakil and swept up all the children taking them back with her to Killistrathan. They had not yet been told the reason for their sudden move and had whooped with joy at this unexpected bonus to their holiday. Hamish had bumbled over and was sitting glumly with them, his shaggy white moustache drooping even lower, his knee-length woollen cardigan, which he was still wearing, drooping in sympathy.

'I telephoned when Father had the stroke,' Graeme replied, 'and the War Box said they would contact him. I don't know where he is, somewhere secret it seems. Anway I telephoned again this evening and apparently he should be arriving in London about now. I daresay he'll be here tomorrow.'

'I see,' Lady Flora remarked, and they all fell silent again.

There didn't seem to be anything to say . . . or to do. Their minds reeled and no-one except his wife seemed to be able to take in the fact that Robert, the rock on whom they all depended, upon whose broad shoulders this vast house had rested for as long as any of them could remember, was no longer physically with them. And they silently turned to her in their shock and bewilderment seeking shelter beneath the aura of peace, which in spite of her fatigue, surrounded her.

'Mother,' Graeme said gently. 'You should try to get some sleep.'

'Yes, dear,' she replied automatically. And then realised that for the first time since she came to Ardnakil as a bride she would not be able to sleep in her own bedroom. Robert's waxen, inert body was now lying stiff and lifeless on the great bed which they had shared for so many years. 'I think I'll sleep in your father's dressing room,' she added quietly.

Alasdair frowned.

'Do you think that wise?' he put in. 'Wouldn't it be better if you went right away, to another part of the house?'

'No, Alasdair,' his mother replied with unusual firmness. 'I will sleep there with all your father's things around me. It will make everything seem more normal, less unreal, and help me to get used to this new situation.'

She looked across at Graeme.

'This is YOUR house now, Graeme,' she ended quietly.

'Oh *Mother*,' he interrupted.

'No, Graeme, it IS and I don't want to be a burden to you in any way. I want the necessary arrangements for you to take over to be made as soon as possible and then, of course, I shall move out.'

Graeme walked over to his mother's chair and sat down on the arm.

'Mother,' he said gently, putting an arm across her shoulders. 'It may be my house but I'm going to have enough to do running the estate on my own now that

Father's gone, I can't run the house as well. I want you to stay. I NEED you to stay.'

He paused and looked into the fire's dying embers.

'If I were married it would be different. But I'm not.'

'You may very well wish to marry one day,' his mother went on. 'After all, your father waited till he was in his mid-forties and Ninian doesn't seem to be in any hurry.'

She smiled up at her eldest son.

'Marrying late seems to be a Hamilton family trait.'

'Perhaps,' Graeme said patiently. 'If and when that happens, we'll rethink the whole situation but, for the moment, let's just stay as we are. There have been enough upheavals in this family in the last few months without adding more.'

Lady Flora looked as if she were about to argue with him, then suddenly changed her mind.

'Thank you, darling,' she answered softly. 'If that is what you wish.'

'It is,' Graeme said firmly and he looked across at Hamish who was sitting slightly apart, stunned and bewildered, his watery blue eyes staring in front of him at nothing in particular, his hands hanging loosely between his knees, like two great paws. Archie, now also showing signs of the advancing years, sat mournfully at his feet, his head resting on his crossed paws, his sad brown eyes looking expectantly at Hamish.

Laura's eyes followed Graeme's gaze and her heart went out to this old man who suddenly looked so bereft and alone. She, more than any of them, knew what he was feeling: that sense of total isolation, even in the midst of this close-knit group which was his family, and yet not his family.

Hamish and Robert had always been close, and now everything had abruptly fallen apart and it was his eldest nephew who was about to take over the place where he had been born and grown up, where he had doubtless dreamed his dreams, some of which must have come true but many of which would never now be fulfilled. And Laura understood his loneliness, the loneliness she had felt when she came with Cristobel and was accepted as one of the family and yet knew that she was not. Hamish must be feeling like that at this moment. Robert had been his last link with his childhood and now that he was no longer here Hamish was cut off and alone. Perhaps the same thought might have been going through Graeme's head as he got up and stood with one foot on the fender looking down at Hamish's face, usually so florid, but which tonight seemed to be drained of all life and colour.

'It's your home too, Uncle,' he said gently.

Hamish looked up at him balefully, but didn't reply.

'Why don't you just shut up the Fort and come and live over here?' he suggested. 'Back to your roots. Mother and I are going to rattle around in this place, just the two of us, and your help in running the estate would be invaluable to me.'

Laura knew that Graeme did not really mean what he was saying. Hamish had been a regular army officer until he retired and had no idea how to run the estate. All he had ever run was his dog. And Laura knew that Hamish knew it, too.

He looked up at his nephew but did not commit himself.

'Thank you, Graeme,' he said gruffly. 'Thank you, m'boy, very civil of you, very civil indeed.'

'Jeannie must be about on her last legs,' Graeme went on seeing that he had not convinced him. 'How long has she been with you? Certainly before any of us was born.'

'Since '34, when I retired,' Hamish said dully.

'Then it's time *she* retired,' Graeme continued.

'Yes, well, perhaps so,' Hamish muttered, 'we'll see, dunno about that.'

'Why don't you BOTH pack up and come over here?' Graeme said persuasively. 'If she doesn't want to retire she can always give cook a hand in the kitchen. But if she does, well she can spend the rest of her days haunting the galleries like Morag did until she faded into the woodwork.'

'Graeme,' Lady Flora reproached.

Her eldest son smiled down at her affectionately.

'Come on now, Uncle,' he coaxed, 'take the decision: I know Mother would be pleased to have your company.'

Hamish flushed and dropped his eyes and, as Laura looked at him she suddenly realised that not only had he lived vicariously through his brother's family but that he had also been in love with his brother's wife and probably still was. She smiled sadly to herself at the thought of those long years of unrequited devotion to Flora. And she wondered if Graeme also knew Hamish's secret.

'Wouldn't you, Mother?' Graeme ended.

Flora looked across at Hamish.

'Of course, Hamish,' she answered softly. 'And perhaps that is what Robert would have wanted, that we join ranks so that the dreadful gap in our lives doesn't hurt so much.'

She smiled her sweet smile, now tinged with an immense sadness, and seemed to be looking at something far away.

'One of the last things Robert said to me before he died was "don't cry",' Flora murmured.

Alasdair looked up.

'Did Father regain his speech before he died?' he asked in surprise.

His mother leaned across and put a hand on his arm.

245

'No darling, not really, but we were always so close sometimes words were superfluous between us.'

Alasdair picked up his mother's hand and squeezed it.

'Well now, that's all settled,' Graeme said quickly, and Laura sensed that the atmosphere was becoming too charged with emotion for him. 'Move in as soon as you like, Uncle.'

He smiled, and added,

'Your old room in the east turret is still empty, why don't you sleep there tonight?'

Hamish grunted and Laura realised that the old man did not trust himself to speak. Fumbling in his overflowing pockets he took out his red spotted handkerchief and blew his nose fiercely with his usual loud honking sounds. Then he slowly got to his feet.

'I'll be saying good night to you all,' he said gruffly. 'Come on, Archie.'

The spaniel looked mournfully up at his master and, lumbering to its feet, followed Hamish as he shuffled across the room, a bent, broken old man.

'And now, Mother,' Graeme said firmly, holding out his hand to Flora, 'I really think you should try to get some sleep, too. The next few days are going to be exhausting.'

Lady Flora rose and Laura rose with her.

'I'll see you to your room, Mother,' she said.

Flora looked at her.

'It's not necessary Laura dear,' she said gently. 'I'm perfectly all right.'

'I know you are,' Laura replied, 'but I'd like to, if you'll let me.'

And taking her mother-in-law's arm in a gesture which was totally uncharacteristic, she walked with Flora across the gracious drawing room. Graeme got up to open the door for them, then returned to the fire and sat down thoughtfully.

'I wonder why Laura did that?' he mused. 'Not like her at all.'

'I suppose she wanted to help Mother,' Alasdair replied vaguely, without mentioning that he also had been surprised by Laura's gesture. 'She's very fond of her and women are perhaps more sensitive than we are, Laura certainly is. She maybe felt that it was better not to leave Mother alone.'

'Perhaps,' Graeme sighed. 'Blowed if I understand women.'

He looked across at Alasdair.

'After ten years, do you?' he smiled.

Alasdair stroked his chin thoughtfully.

'I thought I did, but these last few months Laura has had some strange reactions.'

He frowned to himself.

'Come to think of it, she's been different ever since Sandy's death. Perhaps it affected her more than it did us. She's certainly not been herself since.'

He smiled ruefully at his brother.

'To answer your question . . . No, I don't think I do.'

And they both laughed, glad that the tension in the air had diffused and the conversation taken on a tone of normality after the emotionally packed evening.

As they reached the door of Robert's dressing room Laura paused.

'Do you think you'll be able to sleep?' she enquired.

Flora stood with her hand on the heavy brass knob.

'Probably not,' she replied. 'Why do you ask?'

'May I come in and talk to you?'

Flora squeezed Laura's arm affectionately.

'But darling, of COURSE,' she answered warmly and, opening the door, ushered her inside.

'I'm SO glad you're here,' she said quietly as she bent to put a match to the logs lying ready in the small grate.

'It's SUCH a blessing to have a daughter by one's side at a time like this.'

She stood warming her hands at the blaze as the dry logs spluttered into a violent hissing flame then, pulling a small armchair up to the fireside, motioned to Laura to take the one opposite.

'Sit down, darling,' she invited. 'Would you like some tea? I think Kirsty is still up.'

Laura shook her head.

'No, I just wanted to be alone with you for a while.'

The mention of Ninian's name earlier on had sparked off a thought in Laura's mind, but she wasn't sure she would be able to voice it. She leant back in the chair and looked around the room at the heavy furniture, the numerous silver trophies standing on tops of cupboards, the riding crops, the photographs of Robert as a boy at school, as a young subaltern. It was more like a study than a dressing room.

'Do you think Cristobel will come?' she enquired idly.

'I do hope not,' Lady Flora said as she too leant back and appeared to relax, letting the tensions of the past few hours slowly drain out of her. 'It would be most unwise, and there's nothing she can do.'

'She and her father were very close.'

'Yes,' Flora mused, 'but now she has another Robert in her life and one who, at the moment, can't do without her.'

She smiled across at Laura.

'You're a mother, Laura, you understand that.'

Laura nodded and again had a strange feeling that Flora was looking straight through her, could read her innermost thoughts. But she didn't feel it was the moment to bring up the subject which was eating at her heart, that of Jamie's imminent departure – especially as it would have meant talking about Sandy. The day had been sufficiently emotionally exhausting for them all and even more so for Flora who must now feel amputated after so many years with Robert by her side. And she wondered whether her mother-in-law would ever be able to walk upright again or whether she would go through the remainder of her life on crutches because he was no longer there.

For a while they sat together in a companionable silence, gazing into the red gold flames leaping against the logs, each thinking their own thoughts.

'"Cristobel" is not a Scottish name, is it?' Laura asked after a while, looking enquiringly across at Flora.

'No,' Flora smiled.

'Strange,' Laura mused; 'all the boys have typically Scottish names, and Cristobel is so unusual. What made you give it to her?'

Lady Flora leant her head against the back of the chair and, as the fire settled into a soothing purring blaze, in her turn allowed her gaze to wander around the familiar, very masculine room which had been her husband's.

'She was born during the war, at a time when I was very unhappy,' Flora began softly. 'Robert had been sent to the Middle East, to Cairo, actually, though I didn't know it at the time.'

She smiled across at Laura, the flickering flames lighting up her face and revealing the tired lines around her beautiful grey eyes.

'He went back into the Army as soon as war was declared, though he was really over age. But both he and Hamish had been regular soldiers. He only resigned his commission when his elder brother was killed in 1918 and he had to return home and take over the estate. He'd spent almost seven years in Egypt before the First World War, so perhaps he was useful to the authorities. I don't know: I believe he spoke Arabic.'

Laura suppressed a smile. The air of authority which
Flora had worn earlier that evening when they were
making arrangements had entirely dropped from her
and her old endearing vagueness returned.

'Is that why you were so unhappy when Cristobel
was born?' Laura pursued as Flora threatened to lapse
into dreaming.

'Yes,' she replied softly. 'I've always been totally
lost without Robert. And when he left I was alone here
with three little boys. The house had been turned into a
hospital and convalescent home for Allied officers and
we were occupying a very small part of it. Everyone
on the estate seemed to have gone to the war, news
was difficult to come by, if not impossible, the war was
going very badly, especially in the Middle East, and my
whole world seemed to have suddenly collapsed.'

She looked across at Laura.

'Then, not long after Robert left, I found I was
expecting another baby.'

'Were you pleased?' Laura enquired.

'I don't remember,' Flora answered vaguely. 'Yes,
I think I was. Robert had always wanted a daughter and this time I was sure that I was carrying
a girl.'

She smiled at her daughter-in-law.

'Funny how sometimes one is sure, isn't it? Did
it ever happen with you when you were expecting
the boys?'

Laura shook her head.

'Alasdair always wanted a daughter, too,' she said
softly. 'We were going to call her Elspeth.'

Flora leant across and gently touched her hand.

'It's not too late, Laura,' she said quietly. 'You're
still very young.'

Flora looked up at her mother-in-law but didn't reply.
The events of the past few days had shattered her
sensitive spirit once again and she had drawn even

more into herself and away from Alasdair, as if terrified of being hurt by anything else.

'Cristobel was born on the twenty-first of December that year, Robert's birthday,' Flora continued, tactfully ignoring Laura's silence, 'just as the winter dawn, the dawn of the shortest and the darkest day of the year, was breaking. When they placed her in my arms she looked like a tiny sculptured angel, so delicate, so perfect, quite different from what the boys had been as babies. She was very blonde – you'd never believe it to see her now, would you? As she lay there looking up at me, the sun broke through for a few minutes and shone on the trees outside my bedroom window. It was bitterly cold and they were covered in hoar frost and icicles, but as the sunbeams touched them they became quite magical, glittering and sparkling against the black branches. And from somewhere in the house came a peal of bells. It must have been a wireless or a gramophone playing – there weren't any church bells during the war, you know, they were only to be rung to announce an invasion or a final victory. It was strange the way the peal came just at that moment. But as it rang out, the glittering silver branches tapped gently at my window and the pale sun shone on the baby's golden head. It was all so beautiful and fairylike, and the name "Cristobel" came into my mind. And I knew that that was what I wanted to call her.'

Flora removed a scrap of handkerchief from her sleeve and dabbed at her eyes.

'What a foolish old woman I am,' she breathed. Forgive me, darling, but the last time I spoke of this was with Robert on the morning he arrived home after the war. Cristobel was three then and he'd never seen her. He couldn't believe that he had a daughter at last. When he picked her up in his arms the bells began to ring from the village church for morning service and the sun came out and glistened on the

snow which was lying fresh on the ground. I'll never
forget it.'

She replaced her handkerchief, her eyes still glistening with tears.

'And that's how she came to be called "Cristobel",'
she smiled. 'Funny, Robert was the only other person
ever to ask me.'

Laura fished for her handkerchief and blew her nose.
Flora's story had moved her deeply.

'You love your children very dearly, don't you,
Mother?' she said at last.

Flora looked across at her enquiringly.

'Of course, Laura,' she said in surprise. 'Like you
do.'

Laura nodded and wondered what Flora would think
if she told her of her present obsession with Jamie, her
possessiveness towards him, her terrible fear of letting
him go.

'Does their happiness mean more to you than anything else?' she pursued.

Flora seemed puzzled.

'I think so, darling,' she answered quietly. 'Why do
you ask?'

'I was thinking of Ninian,' Laura remarked.

'Ninian?'

Lady Flora raised puzzled eyebrows.

'You mentioned earlier on that neither he nor
Graeme seemed to be in any hurry to marry,' she
continued, now launched and not really knowing where
the words would lead her, or even whether Ninian
would thank her for what she was doing.

'Yes?'

'If Ninian isn't married it's because he wants to spare
you, or he wanted to spare both of you.'

Lady Flora sat bolt upright in her chair.

'Laura,' she said sharply. 'What are you hiding
from me?'

'I'M not hiding anything,' Laura said quietly. 'But Ninian is.'

Her mother-in-law leant back and closed her eyes.

'Go on,' she whispered.

'The Sunday before Sandy was killed Ninian came to dinner with us. He brought his fiancée.'

Lady Flora opened her eyes and looked across at her.

'He intended to bring her here and introduce her at the wedding.'

She paused.

'As things turned out, he didn't feel it was possible.'

Lady Flora looked into the dying embers of the fire.

'Perhaps not THAT weekend,' she said slowly. 'But why hasn't he brought her since, or at least told us about her?'

Laura looked directly at her mother-in-law, but Lady Flora kept her eyes on the last flickering flames.

'Ninian met Deirdre through mutual friends when he was stationed in Northern Ireland,' she ended quietly. 'She's an Irish Catholic from Dublin.'

For a moment there was a dreadful silence between them. Then Lady Flora looked across at her, her face stricken and grey.

'WHY, oh WHY, didn't he tell us?' she whispered brokenly.

'Would you have accepted her?' Laura asked tightly. 'In theory she's on the other side. The side that killed Sandy.'

Flora twisted in her chair.

'Laura,' she said at last, her voice still hardly above a whisper. 'Perhaps a year ago, perhaps even six months ago I would have been reticent, but now . . . of COURSE I will accept her.'

She gave a short sharp cry.

'Poor Ninian, what he must have been suffering and . . . how little he knows me,' she ended sadly.

'Would Father have accepted her?' Laura pursued.

Flora paused and sighed deeply.

'I don't know,' she mused. 'Yes, after what happened, I think he would.'

She sighed again, twisting that same scrap of handkerchief round and round in her fingers.

'As one gets older one realises the futility of all this strife, people taught to hate each other merely because they've been born on different sides of a man-made frontier. Oh Laura, just think, it COULD have been SANDY.'

Laura looked across at her enquiringly.

'He could so easily have met and fallen in love with a girl from Dublin instead of Rose. Imagine how I would have felt now if it HAD happened and WE had opposed the marriage.'

She gasped and her breath came in a sob.

'Just imagine,' she cried brokenly.

Laura saw what she meant.

'Oh NO, Laura,' she went on in a rush, 'we none of us know what tomorrow may bring. I want Ninian to be happy. Of course I'll accept his Deirdre . . . and love her. If Ninian loves her then there must be something very lovable about her, don't you think?'

Laura nodded.

'She IS lovable. She's also a very lovely person.'

And she added with a smile.

'Jamie adores her.'

Flora smiled back.

'And I respect Jamie's opinion,' she replied with mock solemnity, and for an instant there was a flicker of the old twinkle in her eyes.

'Isn't it wonderful Laura?' she said dreamily, leaning back in her chair with a sigh, 'when God closes one door He always opens another?'

Laura looked at her in surprise but Flora's eyes
were half closed and she seemed to be far away again,
back in that world of her own. She wasn't sure what
her mother-in-law meant and assumed it must have
something to do with losing Rose as a daughter-in-law
and gaining Deirdre. But she didn't see what God had
to do with it.

'Robert dies and the same day Robert is born,' Flora
murmured to herself. 'And now I am no longer Naomi
having lost husband and son, because God has brought
Deirdre to be my Ruth.'

Laura began to wonder whether the dramatic events
of the past few days had not affected Flora more than
they all realised and made her light-headed, talking
about people no-one had ever heard of. In her embarrassment before what appeared to be Flora's sudden
decline into senility, she did not know what to reply and
grasped at the first name which came into her mind.

'Have you any news of Rose?' she asked trying to
sound casual.

Rose had returned to Hong Kong with her parents
the previous May, ostensibly for a holiday to distance
herself from everything which reminded her of the
tragedy she was living through.

'Isn't she coming back?' she went on when Flora did
not immediately reply.

Flora opened her eyes and turned her gaze slowly
towards Laura.

'Well,' she sighed, 'she really has nothing very much
to come back to. She resigned from the hospital and
gave up her flat in London last March and, now that
her grandmother is dead she doesn't feel she has a
home at Eglinton any more.'

Flora bent down and poked the last remaining ashes
into a final spurt of flame.

'I'd love her to come here,' she sighed, 'but I don't
really think she'd want to, it would bring back too

many painful memories, especially at the moment with Ninian about to get married.'

She glanced down at the fire's dying embers.

'I think that's why Grace was so fond of her. Her parents being so far away she spent most of her school holidays at Eglinton. The last time I heard from her she had decided to stay on and nurse in Hong Kong for the time being.'

'Poor Rose,' Laura murmured.

Flora nodded, her eyes still on the fire's last flickering flames. Then, abruptly, she rose to her feet and held out her hand to Laura.

'I mustn't keep you up, darling,' she smiled. 'Alasdair will wonder what has happened to you.'

Laura slowly got to her feet, her mind a confused whirl, not only because of the day's events, but also because of her conversation with her mother-in-law. Flora seemed to consider God as a person, someone who actually had a part in her everyday life, and intervened in her favour: an idea totally foreign to Laura. Apart from their conversation that far off Sunday morning in the drive when Flora had spoken of a personal God, she had never heard anyone else talk like this, not even at her confirmation classes or divinity lessons at school; and for a second, as on that Sunday morning, she hesitated, wanting to know more.

She glanced across at Flora, uncertain whether to ask her to explain but, as she did so, she saw the tired lines around her eyes, the dark circles beneath them, and she changed her mind.

Flora slipped her arm through Laura's and walked with her to the door and, as she opened it, she caught her to her in a warm, unexpected embrace, holding her tightly for a few seconds.

'Thank you, darling, for telling me about Ninian,' she whispered. 'What a day this has been.'

She paused.

'I'm so glad he died when he did, Laura,' she said softly. 'He would have hated to be handicapped.'

Laura nodded, her throat too full to speak.

'But OH, how I'm going to miss him,' Flora choked.

Tears were now streaming down both their faces.

'You must come and stay with us,' Laura said lamely.

'We'll see, we'll see,' Flora soothed. 'But for now let's try to get some sleep. I'll telephone Ninian first thing in the morning if he hasn't already arrived and tell him how delighted I am with his news.'

She kissed Laura's cheek and quietly closed the door. Then, returning to her chair, sat gazing into the warm grey ashes. From somewhere in the dark, silent house a clock began to ponderously strike the hour. As the twelfth stroke echoed through the empty galleries Flora looked up and across at the heavy door separating her from her husband's body. It was already another day. With the last booming stroke yesterday had vanished for ever into the shadows of memory, a page had turned and a new life had begun for her. A life without Robert. Suddenly, the full significance of what had happened struck her with all its force and a strangled cry escaped from her lips.

'Robert,' she cried brokenly, 'oh ROBERT.' Cradling her head in her arms she wept, loud agonising sobs welling up from the very depths of her being.

21

Moving Away

Deirdre arrived at Ardnakil to meet her prospective family at the beginning of September, just two weeks after Robert's funeral, and her beauty, her simplicity and her obvious devotion to Ninian charmed and conquered everyone.

She and Ninian were married at St James', Spanish Place towards the end of November. Flora, Hamish and Graeme travelled down from Perth by train two days beforehand, Hamish having refused point blank to trust his vast bulk to 'one of those infernal flying machines'. Cristobel and Lindsay arrived by plane the morning before the wedding and they all stayed at the Ritz, simply because that was where Robert and Flora had always stayed on their rare visits to London; it would never have occurred to her to go anywhere else. Laura and Alasdair joined them there the evening before the wedding for the family dinner to meet Deirdre's parents and her younger brother, who had come over from Dublin for the occasion.

Throughout the short marriage ceremony Hamish glared fiercely in front of him, angrily flapping at whiffs of incense which he said got up his nose and made him sneeze, stating loudly that he didn't hold with popery, and muttering about people waving things around mumbling in Latin and all this bobbing up and down. Lady Flora, standing erect at his side looking frail and beautiful, took not the slightest notice of his antics but smiled her sweet vague smile, her eyes riveted lovingly on Ninian.

Deirdre, as a bride, was more beautiful than ever, and Laura thought what a pity it was that she had not had the traditional white wedding with pages, bridesmaids, guards of honour and all the other trappings. But Deirdre had shown a wisdom and a sensitivity far beyond her years in choosing this simple ceremony which could not in any way bring back painful memories to Ninian's family of the more sumptuous nuptials which had been arranged for Rose and Sandy only a few months before.

'Shall we have tea?' Lady Flora enquired as the little wedding party walked back into the foyer of the Ritz after waving goodbye to the happy couple who had just left for a short honeymoon in Switzerland before Ninian took up his new appointment as Military Attaché in Berne early in December.

'Not for us,' Cristobel smiled, grabbing Laura round the waist.

'Let's go up to my room,' she hissed. 'I don't seem to have seen anything of you for AGES and Lindsay and I are leaving at the crack of dawn.'

And the two of them walked quickly away before anyone could persuade them to stay.

'Won't you all come to Lochincraig for Christmas?' Cristobel asked as they sat down and tea was brought in. 'Now that our children at last seem to be on speaking terms we may as well make the most of it. It may not last!'

Her eyes twinkled as she handed Laura her cup.

'I'm going to persuade Mother and Co. to come as well,' she went on. 'It would be too painful for them to stay at Ardnakil after the year we've all had.'

She sighed and lifted the lid off a silver salver.

'Have a sandwich,' she said offering Laura the dish. 'They're nice but I'd rather have cook's hot scones!'

She looked appealingly at Laura over the rim of her cup.

'SAY you'll come,' she pleaded. 'Do you remember those wonderful Christmases we had at Ardnakil, the enormous tree in the hall, the turkey, the waits on Christmas Eve and all those scrumptuous things to eat and presents and fairy lights and games?'

Cristobel giggled.

'And the charades. Remember when Uncle Hamish was the fairy queen?'

They both burst out laughing.

'I want to make it like that for my children,' she went on dreamily. 'Something they'll always remember.'

Once again she turned her deep grey eyes appealingly on Laura.

'Oh DO come,' she coaxed. 'We all need to be together, and you and I can just spend hours sitting around and chatting like we used to do in the school holidays.'

'And the children?' Laura said caustically.

'Oh, it's bound to snow,' Cristobel replied nonchalantly. 'Alasdair and Lindsay can take them ski-ing or something.'

And so they all went to Lochincraig and Christmas was as they had remembered it at Ardnakil, a time of happiness and excitement and starry-eyed children. Edwina even agreed to accompany them, for the first time since that Christmas eleven years before when Laura and Alasdair had become engaged. Then she and Flora had taken to each other immediately and, now that Robert was gone, Edwina and Flora spent long hours together, much as Laura and Cristobel were doing, content to be in each other's company.

They returned home only just in time to get the boys off to school for the new term.

Jamie had joined his brothers at St Bede's in September but it had been autumn, a glorious autumn with a lot of work to do in the garden and golf at weekends. Alasdair and Laura had been busy helping Deirdre with her trousseau and Ninian with plans for the wedding. And once it was over, Christmas and all its attendant preparations had been upon them, so the full force of her youngest son's leaving had not immediately hit Laura. But when she waved the three of them goodbye as the school train left the station that cold January afternoon and returned to an empty house and the chaos left in their now silent rooms, a sudden hollowness, and a feeling of apathy overwhelmed her.

'Boys get off all right?' Alasdair smiled as she greeted him in the hall on his return home that evening.

She nodded.

'Sorry I wasn't able to get to the station to say goodbye to them,' he said bending to kiss her, 'but something turned up just as I was about to leave which had to be dealt with immediately, and by the time I'd finished it was too late.'

He followed her into the drawing room, rubbing his cold hands together.

'I wanted to take you out to tea afterwards,' he went on, sitting down and holding them out to the blaze. 'Thought you might be feeling rather down?'

He raised an eyebrow at her enquiringly, but she didn't react. Something inside her seemed to have gone cold, frozen over since she returned home, leaving her incapable of feeling. It was almost the same sensation she had had when she heard of Sandy's death, total disbelief and refusal to accept the evidence. But then the tears had flowed and she had had Alasdair to turn to.

Now she felt alone, isolated, shut off from him in this misery which had closed around her as she watched the school train draw away from the platform. Sitting down on the other side of the fireplace, she mechanically accepted the glass of sherry he offered her, incapable of sharing or of even explaining the desolation which now engulfed her.

'I'm rather tired,' she said when dinner was over. 'I think I'll go to bed.'

Alasdair smiled at her over the top of the briefs he was leafing through.

'You do that,' he answered gently. 'The holidays must have been exhausting for you: now I hope you'll be able to relax and take things easily.'

He got up to open the drawing room door for her.

'I won't be long,' he smiled as she walked through.

As Laura walked up the stairs, her whole body felt stiff and unyielding.

'How little he understands me,' she muttered tightly to herself.

She sighed, one hand clutching tightly to the banister.

'How little he understands,' she ended. 'Full stop!'

Entering their room she walked over to her dressing table and stood gazing down at the large oval photograph of her three sons and, as their animated faces laughed up at her, she crumpled on to the stool and wept. She knew that a gaping chasm had opened up between her and Alasdair, a chasm which, at that moment, was too deep for either of them to leap. She wondered if, with time, it would gradually close or grow even wider. And, as she sat there with her head on her arms, her shoulders gently heaving with sobs, she honestly did not know – and at that moment she didn't even care.

* * *

The long, dark January days dragged by and Laura's mood did not change. She had heard that the second term was always difficult, not only for the boys but for their mothers as well. The newness had worn off for them both and they were each returning to a life which had become routine, to things which had become familiar and no longer held any excitement. The summer holidays seemed very far away.

But she expected that once the first week had passed and their obligatory ink-stained letters, written after church on Sunday morning, had arrived, she would settle down to a term-time routine, like all the other mothers she knew whose children were away at school. But she didn't. The garden was sleeping, the house impeccably tidy and Alasdair was going through a very busy period entailing long hours away from home. Laura felt herself abandoned and useless, her mission in life suddenly snatched from her. She knew she had to find something to do, something to occupy the long lonely hours, but she didn't know what. Alasdair and the boys had filled her life so completely, had been all she had ever wanted, and now both seemed to have distanced themselves from her. As she wandered round the empty, silent rooms and watched the January frost turn into dreary February downpours she felt listless and desolate, as if all feeling had been drained away.

One evening as they sat together in the rather uncanny silence which now always seemed to lie between them, Laura took her courage in both hands. She knew that what she was about to suggest might upset Alasdair, almost certainly would upset him, that he might not even agree. But her desperation had reached such a point that she felt she could no longer go on as she was.

'Alasdair,' she said tentatively.

He looked up questioningly from some papers which he was checking through, slightly surprised: she usually called him darling.

'I've been thinking.'

He remained with his pen poised in the air.

'Do you think you could put those things down for a minute?' she said irritably, and immediately hated herself for it.

With a sigh he laid down his pen and piled the files on to the small table beside him.

'Well,' he smiled, raising his eyebrows in enquiry.

'I'd like to move,' she blurted out.

And suddenly she had his attention. He was stunned, and for a few seconds didn't speak.

'It seems silly for us to live out here now that the boys have gone,' she went on hurriedly. 'I thought we could go to London, it would save you hours of travelling.'

'I don't mind the travelling,' he cut in.

'But I mind it for you,' she said forcing herself to smile. 'And anyway, I find the time rather long now that Jamie has gone.'

Alasdair crossed one leg over the other and reached in his pocket for his pipe.

'So that's it,' he said slowly.

'What do you mean, "that's it"?' she retorted angrily.

'Nothing,' he answered briefly, pressing down the tobacco and looking directly at her. 'Go on.'

Laura was on the verge of tears.

'You don't seem to understand,' she cried, and then stopped.

'I'm trying to,' Alasdair replied calmly as he placed a match to the bowl of his pipe and began puffing.

He looked up at her through the smoke.

'I thought you were happy here?'

'I WAS,' she said defiantly, 'as long as I had something to do, as long as there was a REASON for my being here. But now . . .'

Her voice tailed away.

'There are lots of things for you to do if you want to,' he said levelly, lying back in his armchair and looking up at the ceiling through a haze of smoke.

'Oh, I know what you mean.'

She picked up a cushion and banged it angrily into shape.

'The WVS, the Mothers' Union, the village fête, coffee mornings.'

She gave the cushion another angry bash.

'But ALASDAIR,' she cried, her voice rising almost hysterically. 'That's just not ME. I'm not gregarious, I'm not terribly sociable, you know that. I don't want to spend the rest of my life on women's committees and presiding over the teapot at local charity fairs.'

She threw the cushion down onto the end of the sofa, almost beside herself, and gazed sulkily into the fire. For a few minutes neither of them spoke.

'All right,' Alasdair said at last, uncrossing his legs, 'what DO you want to do?'

Laura looked up at him gratefully.

'I thought we might move to London: when the boys leave St Bede's it would be easier for them to come home for weekends.'

Alasdair had wanted his sons to follow the family tradition and go to Gordonstoun but Laura had pleaded with him not to send them so far away. Finally he had given in and they were all down for Westminster.

'And I could see more of Edwina,' she hurried on. 'She's not getting any younger and since my father died she has no-one but me in the world.'

'You seem to be forgetting Philippa and Mary,' Alasdair put in drily.

'Mary's in VANCOUVER,' Laura cried.

'But Philippa isn't,' Alasdair pointed out, 'she's living in Sloane Street, practically on Edwina's doorstep. And when Polly gets married in April she'll be living in London, too, so Edwina will not only have a niece but also a great-niece living round the corner. And, anyway,' he ended tersely, 'Edwina's never been averse to coming out here to visit you. On the contrary, she always seemed to enjoy it.'

Laura knew that she had lost that round.

'Hugo's in London at the Foreign Office NOW,' she went on, 'but for how long? He and Philippa could go off to the other end of the world at any time.'

Alasdair gripped his pipe between his teeth. He had been aware of the tension mounting in Laura during the past few months, since Sandy's death, in fact. He had noticed her preoccupation, her apparent indifference to him since Jamie had left, but he had believed it to be merely the result of the traumatic year they had all lived through and that it would pass. Now he realised that it had not, and he was faced with a crisis which he had never envisaged.

When they had first seen the house a few weeks before they were married, Laura had exclaimed that it was too big for the two of them.

'We won't be two for very long,' he had teased throwing his arm lightly round her shoulders and drawing her to him. 'I intend to fill it up very quickly.'

And he remembered how Laura's cheeks had become suffused with that tell-tale crimson blush, and how embarrassed she had been when it happened. He had found it a very endearing trait, but she never blushed nowadays. Something which passes with age, he thought sadly as he stared at the glowing logs. He wished once again that they had had a daughter, one looking just like Laura, so that he would always be able to recapture that innocence and freshness, that fawn-like timidity which had first drawn him to her.

Alasdair sighed. He had always hoped that this house would be their permanent home, one where they would build memories, like he had of Ardnakil, and where their children would grow up and their grandchildren come to visit. But in the light of Laura's present state of mind it now seemed that his hopes for the future had gone up in smoke, like the softly weaving spirals mounting from his pipe towards the ceiling.

'I'd like to take up my music again,' she said quietly, not looking at him.

He leant forward to take her hand, but she drew away.

'But you can take it up here, can't you?'

'No, I mean go back to the Academy.'

Alasdair frowned.

'You're not thinking of becoming a professional pianist are you?' he asked sharply.

She laughed briefly.

'Of course not, it's far too late for that, even if I wanted to. But if I DO take it up I want to do it properly, not have second-rate lessons from the music teacher at the local convent.'

Alasdair said nothing, just sat thoughtfully puffing at his pipe. It suddenly seemed that his world was slowly beginning to cave in on him, unbelievingly and weightlessly, like a pack of playing cards. He looked across at her, but she was fiddling with a tassel on a cushion and not looking at him. Seeing her sitting hunched there, looking so young, so helpless, he knew that she mattered more to him than the home they had so lovingly created together, more to him than any house, more to him than anything in the world in fact. In order to keep her and recapture that wonderful closeness which had existed between them for almost eleven years and which seemed to have elusively disappeared since Sandy's death, he was ready to sacrifice the house, to sacrifice anything.

'All right, Laura,' he said slowly, taking his pipe from his mouth and knocking it against the edge of the grate. 'If that is what you really want, let's look around and try to find somewhere to live in London.'

She glanced across at him, her eyes suddenly alight, and he could see from the damp traces on her face that she had been crying. He put down his still smouldering pipe and went to sit beside her.

'What about the boys?' he asked gently. 'The holidays?'

'We hardly ever spend our holidays here,' she answered. 'And now that your mother is alone we'll probably go up to Scotland more often. And,' she turned to him eagerly, 'since the boys have developed this passion for their girl cousins there's always Lochincraig. We don't need this house.'

Her lips tightened and she stiffened.

'They'll hardly be in it any more anyway,' she rasped. 'Once they've gone, they've gone.'

Alasdair turned away, feeling the chasm widen slowly between them once again. And he sighed.

'All right, darling,' he said quietly. 'You win. But this is no time to house hunt, too miserably cold. I promise you, though, once the Easter holidays are over we'll start looking in earnest and we'll move before the autumn. Then you can enroll for all the courses you want at the Academy.'

He threw his arm round her shoulder, drawing her gently to him. She didn't resist.

'Any idea whereabouts in London you want to live?' he smiled.

He felt her tension evaporate and she turned to him, her beautiful blue eyes shining like many faceted sapphires in which the golden flecks of firelight were now dancing.

'Oh Alasdair,' she breathed, 'thank you.'

He tentatively drew her closer and she did not stiffen or turn away but relaxed and melted against him as she had done on that December afternoon in Edwina's flat when he had finally convinced her that he loved her.

'Happy?' he asked softly.

She nodded ecstatically, her eyes closed.

'I had thought of Chelsea,' she whispered. 'It would be near Edwina.'

Alasdair smiled, brushing his lips through her soft hair.

'And near the tube station which connects with Westminster,' he teased.

Laura snuggled close to him, warm and soft and yielding.

'Yes,' she murmured happily. 'And the tube for your office too.'

She looked up at him roguishly and he pulled her head roughly backwards and gazed into her laughing eyes

'Mother hen,' he whispered, 'don't think you fool me.'

Laura smiled radiantly up at him.

'I don't want to,' she whispered back as his mouth closed over hers.

She sighed contentedly, completely and utterly at peace, all tension, all anguish washed away as she lay back in her husband's arms happy once again. The past months were wiped from her mind and only the memory of Alasdair's embrace was imprinted upon it. She was convinced that she had found the solution and that the road now lay straight and unwinding ahead, even strewn with roses.

'What about those case sheets you were studying for tomorrow?' she teased.

Alasdair sat up, looked down at her and then closed his arms more tightly round her again.

'Blow the case sheets,' he said quietly, carrying her across the room towards the door. 'They can wait.'

* * *

Soon after the boys returned to school in September they moved to London. Throughout that spring and summer Laura had been her old self again, all anguish and irritation gone, happy and at one with Alasdair as she had been for the first ten years of their marriage. And, once they were finally settled in the tall house in the leafy Chelsea Square, she convinced herself that she had been right to insist on the change of surroundings. Contrary to expectations and Alasdair's fears the boys did not appear to be in the least affected by the upheaval. Jamie even admitted to being delighted not to have any more social contacts with those 'nerds' – a new word which he'd learned at St Bede's and overworked mercilessly – at Miss Fanshawe's. The other two were absorbed in their school life and friends, and the fact that their garden now consisted of a small patch the size of a pocket handkerchief didn't seem to bother them one iota. And once the move was finally accomplished even Alasdair seemed to be relieved that he no longer had to have his life dictated by a train timetable.

Laura enrolled herself at the Academy again and ran happily up and down the steep stairs playing house in her spare time, convincing herself that she had done the right thing and that their being so close would be good for Edwina.

Edwina, on the other hand, when coming to tea one afternoon once the curtains were up and the house was at last in order, was not so sure. She wondered just what lay behind this sudden upheaval in what she imagined had been up till then her niece's apparently idyllic marriage. As she sat sipping her tea, she was strangely silent, looking curiously at Laura, waiting for her to say something. But Laura avoided her aunt's gaze and talked of other things. And Edwina went away shaking her head and waiting for the bomb she knew would one day explode and reveal the deep crater beneath.

If there had, initially, been more to this move than

was apparent, Laura was not herself aware of it. She busied herself with her new home, her music, the concerts she was now able so easily to attend and was completely and utterly happy, convincing herself that that deep gaping chasm which had opened up between she and Alasdair the year before was now finally closed. But it had only been temporarily patched over, and as Laura became more and more absorbed in her outside interests and her life in London so, gradually, the cracks began to re-appear. Little by little the close links which had once bound her and Alasdair so tightly together slowly loosened, as Laura scurried back to her old bolt hole and buried herself in her music making the piano her god.

Alasdair noticed it, but said nothing. His devotion to Laura was absolute. She was his whole life and he was prepared to sacrifice anything just to keep her by his side. And so he ignored the mounting signs, of which all but Edwina seemed oblivious, of their gradual growing apart. And as Laura, in her own eyes fulfilled herself in her new life and, in Alasdair's eyes, became even more beautiful, he immersed himself in his work, trying to pretend it wasn't happening. Until suddenly, as he watched her thirty-fifth birthday fade into the distance he realised that, although nothing had been said, the woman he had loved for so many years, the only woman he had ever really loved and whom he still loved deeply, was someone he no longer knew.

The shy young girl who had yielded so eagerly, so joyfully to his touch, who had blossomed into womanhood as they became one, no longer responded, no longer gave herself willingly to his embrace. Gradually, without anything being said, without any outward sign of the subtle change in their relationship, she had distanced herself from him, as if a key had suddenly been turned on her emotions locking them tightly out of reach, until her love-making became lifeless, mechanical, a duty to be performed and dispensed with as quickly as possible.

And Alasdair sadly acknowledged the cynical truth that often in a marriage there is one who loves and one who allows herself to be loved: because that was what was being enacted in his own life.

PART 3

1979

Out of the Summer

22

Josh

Laura looked up from the piano as the postman mounted the steps to the house. Hearing the gentle plop of letters, she took the pencil from between her teeth and, placing it on the music stand, walked into the hall.

There were three envelopes lying on the mat. Stooping to pick them up, she turned them over in her hand and saw that two were bills for Alasdair but the third bore a Vancouver postmark. It was from her sister Mary.

She tore it open eagerly. Since her father's funeral she hadn't seen Mary and Edward, although they promised with every Christmas card to visit England the following year. Somehow it had never happened and with time their links had gradually loosened. Neither she nor her sister were very good correspondents and Laura sometimes wondered whether had it not been for birthdays and Christmas their links would have been severed altogether.

But it was only February, her birthday wasn't till next month: she was intrigued as to why Mary should be writing to her at this time.

'Edward and I are still very busy,' the letter went on after the first few lines of formal greetings and enquiries after the health of each member of the family, 'though we haven't given up hope of visiting London later in the year . . .'

Laura grimaced: that was what Mary always wrote.

'The real reason I am writing,' the letter continued, 'is to introduce you to Josh Faraday. His mother is a great friend of mine and Josh will be going to Europe very shortly to study for a few months. He's a very talented pianist and has won a prize which will enable him to have lessons with someone famous in London, I'm afraid I can't remember whom, and give some concerts. I wondered whether you would be awfully kind and give him a meal occasionally and perhaps be his bolt-hole if he gets homesick. I don't think he will, he's an outgoing sort of fellow, but one never knows, and Lois (his mother) is rather concerned about him as this will be the first time he's been in Europe for any length of time on his own. He's bound to feel lonely at first, and he'll fit in easily with your family of boys.'

Laura frowned. How typical, she thought. Mary and Edward had no children of their own, though whether by choice or not she had never discovered, so her sister obviously didn't understand that her nephews, not being in the same age group, would have little in common with this young man – especially as they had all three inherited Alasdair's tone-deafness and thought of nothing but rugger – hardly likely to be the passion of a rising young musician.

She turned to the last page and finished reading.

'Knowing your interest in the piano – how's it going by the way? – I thought this wouldn't be too much to ask. Anyway, I've given him your address and telephone number and told him not to hesitate to contact you. Bless you!'

Laura sighed. Her preoccupation with music had already had an effect on her relationship with Alasdair, who could not understand her total absorption with it. So the last thing she wanted was someone else around the house pounding the keyboard as well.

She glanced back to the second page.

'"Josh",' she said to herself. 'What a strange name, short for something, I suppose. Why on earth do North Americans have to shorten everything?'

She wondered whether her brother-in-law was now called 'Ed', and winced at the thought.

'Oh well,' she shrugged, 'perhaps he won't telephone.'

And putting the letter in a drawer of her small desk, which stood in the window overlooking their patch of garden, she went back to the piano. She never for one moment dreamt that her emotions and her peaceful ordered existence would be shattered as a result of it, that those few pages would prove to be a catalyst in her life leaving her standing at a perilous crossroads bewildered and afraid, not knowing which way to turn.

* * *

'I had a letter from Mary,' she said to Alasdair over dinner that evening.

Although outwardly nothing had changed in their relationship, there was all the same an underlying tension between them. They didn't share as freely and openly as they had once done and, each being preoccupied with his own life, subjects of conversation were sometimes thin on the ground these days, especially when the boys were not at home to fill the gaps. So Laura was glad to have some news to animate their evening meal.

'Oh?' he looked up at her with interest.

'She's given our address to a young man whose mother is a friend of hers and who happens to be coming to spend a few months in London.'

She purposely omitted to mention that he was a music student.

277

'Mary didn't say WHEN, but I imagine it must be soon or, knowing her, she would have waited and added the request that we offer him a bolt-hole to the bottom of my birthday card.'

She smiled across at her husband.

'Mary was never one for writing a letter unnecessarily.'

Alasdair smiled back.

'And will you?' he asked.

But something in his tone irritated Laura.

'If he telephones and asks to come and see us, yes, of *course* I will,' she replied testily. 'I can't do anything else.'

'I suppose not,' Alasdair answered. 'Hope he doesn't ring this weekend, I'd hoped we might be able to get out of London for a game of golf.'

Golf seemed to be the one thing which Laura and Alasdair enjoyed doing together these days. Recently she had begun to wonder about their relationship and to be afraid. She still loved Alasdair as much as ever, or believed she did, but since they had moved to London, it seemed that her links with her husband, once so strong, had loosened. She opened her mouth, wanting more than anything to re-establish those links, to slip back into their old, easy intimacy, wanting to say something which would bring those green and gold lights dancing back into his eyes and see that crooked, quizzical smile which had always made her heart beat faster and which seldom touched his lips nowadays.

But no words came. The barriers were up and, although they talked and even, occasionally, smiled, it was all on the surface and they didn't communicate.

'You did warn the boys that we wouldn't be home till tea-time?' Alasdair enquired, as he tossed their golf clubs into the car on the following Saturday morning.

They were all three of them now at school in London

278

and often came home on Saturday afternoon for the weekend.

Laura nodded and, as Alasdair slammed down the boot and climbed into the driving seat, he smiled diffidently at her. She smiled back and placed her hand lightly upon his knee, telling herself that she had been imagining the tension, it was simply that her husband was working very hard and was over-tired: everything was as it had always been between them. And, closing her eyes, she leant back in her seat, determined to enjoy their outing.

It was a perfect winter day, dry and blustery with a mild west wind blowing. When they re-entered the house late that afternoon, relaxed and happy, once more seemingly at peace with each other, a stranger was sitting at the piano running his hands up and down the keyboard, with all three boys hanging around him admiringly.

'I'm Josh,' he said shyly, getting up to greet her. 'I hope you don't mind my dropping by like this. I did ring and Iain said to come on out.'

'No, no, of course not,' Laura said, slightly confused and then suddenly her mind went back to Mary's letter. 'Josh Faraday, is that it?'

'Sure,' he answered and a smile broke across his lean, taut features.

Later Laura remembered thinking that he looked as if he needed feeding up.

'Do sit down,' she went on. 'We've been expecting you to telephone. I'm sorry we weren't here when you arrived.'

'Oh, no problem,' Josh said, sitting back down on the piano stool, 'the boys and I have had a great time.'

He grinned across at them.

'He doesn't play the same stuff as you do, Mum,' Jamie piped in and began wiggling his hips and grimacing. 'He plays ROCK.'

Laura looked slightly taken aback and all four boys laughed.

'Just to get acquainted,' Josh grinned. 'But I do play other things.'

At that moment Alasdair, having put away the car, walked into the room.

He looked enquiringly towards the piano stool and Jamie leapt up and dragged Josh to his feet, pushing him in front of him across the drawing room towards his father.

'No need to let yourself be dragged off to concerts any more, Dad,' he announced. 'You can snore at home instead. Mum's got a resident pianist now.'

Alasdair turned a bewildered gaze on Laura and they all laughed.

'You'll stay to dinner?' Laura smiled, getting up.

'Well, I'd like that,' Josh demurred, 'if you're sure it won't be an imposition.'

'No, of course not,' she answered, warming to his frankness, his apparent ingenuousness. 'Let's have it early, I expect you're all hungry.'

'STARVING,' Jamie shrieked. 'Come on, Josh, play that tiddlede-dee dee dee dee bit, you know the Gary Glitter song you were playing when Mum walked in.'

Josh looked uncertainly across at Laura.

'Go ahead,' she smiled, 'I'm going to the kitchen and I'll shut both doors.'

'I'll come with you,' Alasdair said as Josh swung round on the piano stool and crashed down on the keyboard in a series of discordant notes.

* * *

'Do come back whenever you wish,' Laura heard herself saying as they bid Josh goodbye later that evening.

He was living in central London, so it would be easy for him to pop in if he felt like it.

'Yes, tomorrow,' Jamie piped, jumping up and down on the step.

Josh smiled and ruffled his red hair.

'I gotta work,' he laughed. 'You guys don't seem to realise that.'

'Well, come back next weekend,' Andrew pleaded.

Josh looked expectantly at Laura.

'I DID say whenever you wish,' she smiled. 'And now, you boys, it's high time you went to bed.'

'Thank you Mrs Hamilton,' Josh answered, turning on the step. 'I DO appreciate it.'

Laura clasped his outstretched hand, surprised at herself for having given the invitation and suddenly realising that she meant it.

'I hope you don't mind,' she said looking anxiously at Alasdair as they walked back into the drawing room.

'Why should I mind?' he said gently. 'He seems to be a splendid fellow and the boys certainly appear to enjoy having him around.'

He laughed.

'Maybe he'll babysit sometime!'

Laura laughed too as they sat down together in a warm, companionable silence. And Josh Faraday became part of their family from that moment on.

The weekend of her birthday he arrived almost invisible behind an enormous pale pink camellia singing 'Happy Birthday To You' as he walked through the door.

The boys began flapping their hands, gesticulating and shushing, but it was too late. The secret was out.

'Oh JOSH,' Iain groaned, 'it was supposed to be a SURPRISE.'

'Gee, you guys, I'm sorry.'

And he looked so crestfallen that they had all rushed to reassure him.

'But how did you KNOW?' Laura enquired, when tea had been served, the iced cake brought in, the candles blown out and she was sitting in the middle of a heap of crumpled coloured wrapping paper.

Josh looked across at Alasdair and winked.

'Alasdair told me to be sure to come this Saturday,' he replied, 'because it was to be a special celebration. I'd no idea it was a SECRET.'

'Are we having a celebration,' Jamie squealed, 'another one?'

'We're all going out to dinner this evening,' Alasdair replied, 'to somewhere special ... that is, if you can manage to behave yourself.'

Jamie leapt to his feet and dragged Josh from his chair.

'C'mon,' he ordered, 'play "Happy Birthday" for Mum.'

Josh sat down and ran his fingers up and down the keyboard, then broke into a complicated version of the old song. The boys and Alasdair started to sing but Josh quickly covered his ears with his hands.

'Gosh, that's AWFUL,' he laughed.

He pronounced it 'arful'.

They all laughed with him, well aware of their musical shortcomings.

'*You* sing it for Mum, then,' Andrew cut in.

Josh placed his hands back on the keys and softly sang the refrain.

'But she's NOT your "Mother,"' Jamie cried. 'You should have sung "Laura."'

Josh frowned thoughtfully.

'You're right. But it wouldn't have sounded the same.'

He swung round on the piano stool to face Laura.

'You are my Mom in a way,' he said appealingly. 'My English Mom.'

Laura smiled, touched by his remark.

'How old are you?' Jamie piped up. 'Come on, Mum, come clean.'

'You don't ask a lady her age,' Alasdair reproved.

'Thirty-five,' Laura answered. No, I'm not, I was thirty-five yesterday, TODAY I'm thirty-six. Oh, how ghastly!'

And she covered her face in mock confusion.

'Wow,' whistled Josh, 'you *could* almost be my Mom.'

'How old are YOU?' Jamie pursued.

'I'll be twenty-two in the fall,' Josh answered.

'What's the fall?' Jamie asked.

'Don't you know ANYTHING?' Andrew hissed at him. 'It's American for autumn.'

'And Canadian,' Josh corrected.

'I thought it was the same language as ours,' Jamie harped on.

Everyone laughed.

'It is sometimes,' Josh smiled.

'When in the fall?' Jamie persisted.

His brothers sighed deeply casting their eyes to the ceiling.

'That's enough, Jamie,' Alasdair said sharply.

'Thirty-first of October,' Josh whispered.

'Ooh, Hallowe'en,' Jamie mooed. 'GHOSTIES!'

And he spread his arms and dangled his fingers looking like an animated coat-hanger as he tiptoed heavily around the room emitting weird hollow sounds.

And that was how it had all began.

Josh fitted very easily into their family life, arriving on the doorstep when he was free, hungry or downcast, mostly at the weekends to begin with. But as he got to know them better, he would sometimes drop in during the week and sit improvising at the piano, talking to Laura about his home, his family, his hopes for the future, or follow her into the kitchen, lifting off the saucepan lids and sniffing appreciatively.

The boys always made a tremendous fuss of him: he was like a big brother to them. To Laura, to begin with, he was just another son.

It was all so innocent.

Then subtly things had changed, and she couldn't pinpoint when.

23

A Strange Feeling

One warm May afternoon Laura was sitting at the piano struggling with Listz's original version of 'Liebe-straum', the window open onto the quiet square, when Josh walked in, softly humming the refrain.

'Gee,' he said, as she looked up and smiled. 'You sure don't take the easy way out. I sweated blood over that last year when I was working up for the concours.'

And, sitting down on the stool beside her he took over.

Laura remained motionless beside him, her eyes closed, her hands idle in her lap as the cascade of chords flowed beneath his talented fingers, letting the haunting strains ripple over her like a warm, caressing wave. As the last note faded away in a soft, melancholic whisper, Josh reached down and, taking her hands, placed them gently on the key-board.

For a brief instant, she was startled: his touch had sent a tingling thrill coursing through her whole body, the same overpowering, voluptuous sensation she had first felt when Alasdair had danced with her at that long-ago ball at Ardnakil, a sensation which had been ever present in their relationship for the first ten years of their marriage but which seemed to have gone cold since Jamie had left for school and they had moved to London.

And, suddenly, Laura was afraid.

'Come on,' Josh laughed, 'don't look so startled. Your turn now. Play it with me if you like.'

But she had risen abruptly from the stool and walked over to the window, seeing once again that terrible chasm from which her marriage had rescued her, with herself hanging precariously on the edge about to be plunged into its roaring depths.

'Whatever's the matter?' Josh had asked. 'Have I goofed it?'

Laura turned and forced a smile.

'No Josh, of course not,' she said trying to sound casual. 'It's just that you're too good for me: I can't play that after you.'

He began to protest but she cut him short.

'Play it again, will you, whilst I put the kettle on. You'd like some tea?'

Josh nodded but didn't reply.

'I can hear you in the kitchen if I leave the doors open, and it will help me for my own practising. I can try to copy your technique.'

She turned in the doorway and smiled at him, but he had already swung round on the stool and the cascade of notes went echoing round the room as his supple fingers careered up and down the keyboard.

Laura glanced at herself in the hall mirror as she passed through. She half expected to see someone different gazing back at her, some visible change in her appearance, but apart from a slightly heightened colour, the face which was reflected was exactly as it had always been. She felt reassured.

'How stupid,' she said to herself as she walked into the kitchen. 'Whatever came over you?'

And she smiled once again.

Things had improved enormously between her and Alasdair during the past few weeks: it seemed almost as if Josh's arrival had been the catalyst needed to draw them back together and open up the lines of communication. In fact, he had been good for all of them, and the boys certainly enjoyed his company.

She picked up the tray and went back across the hall, telling herself that Josh was just a fourth son.

'You have an unusual name,' she remarked, as she passed him his cup. 'Is it short for Joshua?'

He grimaced.

'No, St John,' he replied grimly. 'Ghastly, isn't it?'

He pronounced it 'gastely'.

'I don't think it's ghastly at all,' Laura smiled. 'In fact, I think it's rather nice. I like it better than "Josh".'

'You wouldn't if you were a kid in school in Canada,' Josh laughed. 'Dunno what came over my Mom, euphoric with her first child I guess. The ones who came after did better.'

'What are their names?' Laura enquired.

'My brother's Dan.'

Laura shuddered at this mania for cutting the tail off everything.

'And my sister's Mary-Ellen.'

'They're younger than you? Yes, of course, how stupid of me.'

'And luckier too,' Josh grinned. 'Got good plain old fashioned names. My Dad realised I was going to have one hell of a time being saddled with a handle like St John even before I went to school and he nicknamed me Josh. My Mom didn't hassle him too much, I think she'd got over her passion for St John by then and I've been "Josh" ever since.'

'Even when you're billed?' Laura asked.

'Even when I'm billed,' he replied.

'I still think it's a pity,' Laura said sipping her tea thoughtfully. '"St John" is quite theatrical, it would look good on a programme.'

Josh laughed.

'Talking of programmes, I've got your tickets for my

concert next week. Almost June, I can't believe it, then in July I go on tour in Europe with the orchestra for almost two months.'

He laughed again.

'The Grand Tour before I go back home.'

Laura put her cup down abruptly, that old fear which had shot through her only an hour before suddenly coming back. Angrily, she tried to shake herself free, but it refused to go away, just clung to her like a writhing twisting boa-constrictor, twining itself lethally around her body.

'How lovely,' she echoed faintly. 'I do hope the concert is on a Saturday, the boys would love to come.'

'I'm not sure,' he said, 'I rather think it's a Thursday. But you'll come won't you?'

He looked at her appealingly and her stomach seemed to turn over.

'Of course, Josh,' she stammered. 'We'll both come. I'll look forward to it.'

Josh smiled roguishly.

'I'm sure YOU will,' he said, 'but I wouldn't bet my boots on poor Alasdair.'

He put down his cup and stood up.

'I gotta go,' he announced. 'I have a lesson at five thirty.'

Laura walked with him to the front door.

'Shall we see you this weekend?' she asked.

'Probably,' he smiled. 'I'll let you know. Bye, Mom.'

And with a wave he was gone.

She remained on the steps, looking after his lanky frame until it disappeared round the end of the square. Then she walked slowly back into the hall and sat heavily down on the chair by the telephone, unable to understand what was happening to her.

As she sat there the telephone rang and, mechanically picking up the receiver, as if from a long way away, she heard Alasdair's voice at the other end of the line.

'Laura,' he said, and then repeated her name anxiously when she did not reply.

'Oh Alasdair,' she gasped out at last.

'Laura,' he said again, his voice now genuinely concerned, 'whatever's the matter?'

She took a deep breath and tried to compose herself.

'Nothing, darling,' she managed to reply. 'I was thinking of something else, that's all. The telephone startled me.'

'Were you practising?' he enquired.

The mention of the piano nowadays did not bring a note of tension into his voice, and she relaxed, telling herself that she was imagining things. Josh had been like a wonderful remedy bringing her and Alasdair back close together again.

'Yes,' she lied, 'and you interrupted the sonata.'

He laughed.

'Darling,' she said suddenly. 'Would you like to invite me out to dinner this evening?'

For a moment he seemed taken back.

'Well,' he hesitated, 'actually I rang to say I might be rather late.'

'It doesn't matter,' she cut in breathlessly. 'I can meet you somewhere. I – I just feel like going out that's all. Do say yes.'

'Yes,' he laughed. 'Look, I have to go but I'll give you a ring when I'm almost through. Book a table wherever you like, half-past eight should be all right. Then when I telephone we can both leave at the same time.'

'Lovely,' she breathed, and to him she sounded just like a young girl again, the young girl he had married.

Laura put the telephone down and walked into the drawing room.

'You're a stupid idiot, Laura Hamilton,' she murmured, 'and you're letting your imagination run away with you.'

And slipping onto the piano stool she began to play the music which Josh had played for her earlier that afternoon, feeling a thrill of pleasure as she heard some of his expertise escaping through her fingers.

* * *

'The concert was a HUGE success,' Laura said to the boys on the following Saturday. 'SUCH a pity you couldn't come.'

'Was it rock?' Jamie asked.

'Not exactly,' Laura smiled. 'But Josh was superb. He had a five minute standing ovation.'

'What's a standing ovation?' Jamie asked.

'When everyone in the audience gets up and claps,' his father explained.

'Did YOU?' Jamie went on.

'Had to,' Alasdair grimaced, 'I was dragged to my feet.'

He grinned across at Laura.

'Actually,' he confided, 'I'm not surprised it lasted five minutes, the racket your mother was making, shrieking "encore, encore" and jumping about in her seat almost before it finished. I thought at one point she was going to fall into the pit.'

'What's the pit?' Jamie piped in.

'Oh no,' Iain groaned. 'Go and look it up in the dictionary if you don't know.'

He was sure his young brother didn't really care what the pit was or a standing ovation either, but Jamie had got into this awkward habit of questioning everything. He'd been thoroughly sat upon at school and now he was trying his luck at home.

Laura smiled at Alasdair.

'Doesn't he remind you of Sandy?' she asked. 'Funny how families repeat themselves.'

Alasdair leant back in his chair and filled his pipe. 'Is Josh coming this weekend?' he enquired.

'I don't know,' Laura answered thoughtfully. 'I think he's busy with rehearsals for his European tour.'

Alasdair bent his head towards the bowl and inhaled deeply, holding a flickering match to the flame as the tobacco spluttered into life.

'It'll be strange next year without him, won't it?' he commented looking at her through the rising smoke. 'Perhaps we could advertise for a lonely music student willing to serve as bait for three horrors.'

Laura looked across at him but said nothing.

Then, suddenly, a terrible wave of anguish swept through her, catching her like a sharp pain beneath her heart.

'I'd better go and see about dinner,' she said tightly.

Alasdair caught her hand as she walked unsteadily past him.

'Laura,' he said anxiously. 'Are you all right?'

But she withdrew it, the memory of Josh's hand on hers now burning into her flesh.

'Of course I'm all right,' she said sharply. 'But the boys are used to having dinner early at school and they're always ravenous the minute they arrive home.'

She stopped abruptly and stood transfixed as the front door opened and a step sounded in the hall.

'Hi, you guys!' Josh called.

Laura remained frozen in the middle of the drawing room as Josh's face appeared round the door. Alasdair got up and, knocking out his pipe came slowly towards her, putting his arm round her shoulders. She leant gratefully back and closed her eyes.

'Dear Alasdair,' she murmured, as Josh withdrew his head and the boys thundered down the stairs to greet him.

He rubbed his hand gently against her cheek,

sensing that something was wrong but not able to discern what.

'Don't bother about dinner,' he said quietly. 'I'll take you all out.'

Laura looked up at him, her beautiful blue eyes wide with fear.

He tipped her chin towards him and gazed deep into those eyes which still seemed to him to be like shining sapphire pools.

'What is it darling?' he asked tenderly.

She stared at him, anguish in her face, and dumbly shook her head. Then, collapsing in his arms she began to quietly weep.

He led her back to the sofa and sat down beside her, cradling her in his arms like a lost lonely child. After a while her tears stopped and she gazed bleakly in front of her.

'Can't you tell me what's the matter?' he said softly.

She shook her head dumbly.

'I don't know,' she whispered. Her emotions and her mind were so confused she truly didn't.

Alasdair gathered her to him once again, holding her close and suddenly all the warmth drained out of the perfect June day: the wide iridescent sky which up till then had been china blue and cloudless seemed to darken menacingly and the walls of the familiar room to close in around them, crushing them, shutting out the light. He bit his lip as a dreadful feeling of foreboding crept up his spine. He had not been unaware of the rift which had been slowly widening between he and Laura since Jamie went to school and they had moved to London; but lately it had appeared to be so much better, the communication lines had opened and he felt that he had found his Laura again, the girl he had married all those years ago.

But in that moment, he sensed the protective covering which had always bound them so close together slowly slipping off and he knew that not only she but he was vulnerable to some outside influence, something which threatened their happiness: but he couldn't fathom what.

As they sat there, mute and lonely, each trying to work their way through their own private fears, the door burst open and Jamie fell in.

He stopped abruptly when he saw them.

'Oh hallo,' he piped, 'what are you two doing sitting there like statues? Isn't it time we had dinner? I'm STARVING!'

Laura drew away from her husband's arms and attempted to smile.

'It won't be long,' she started to say, but Alasdair cut her short.

'Tell the others to make themselves tidy,' he said, 'we're going out to dinner.'

'Yippee!', Jamie shrieked and, with a deafening crash slammed the door. Yelling the good news so that the entire neighbourhood could hear, he roared off back up the stairs as if all the demons in hell were after him.

24

The Gathering Storm

'Isn't this perfect?' Alasdair said, glancing down at Laura lying in the deckchair beside him.

She smiled but didn't reply.

They were relaxing by the Serpentine on a glorious summer day, lazily watching the ducks float past. Although they both had books in their hands neither was even pretending to read, just enjoying the peaceful hum of bees and the gentle lap of the water.

It was early August and the boys had left on holiday. Iain and Andrew had gone with a party from school on a climbing expedition in Switzerland, and Jamie had rushed up to Lochincraig to be with Helen, for whom his passion had not abated with the years. Cristobel had added Roddy to the family three years earlier and was now expecting her sixth child, so Laura had been loathe to send Jamie. But Cristobel had insisted and, from what she had heard, the cousins were all having a wonderful time together. Helen was the tomboy of the family and she and Jamie suited each other admirably.

'Next week at this time we'll be at Ardnakil,' Alasdair said sleepily. 'Looking forward to it?'

'You know I always do,' Laura murmured, smiling affectionately at him.

Alasdair yawned, laid his book face downwards on his chest and, tipping his hat over his eyes, went to sleep.

Laura sat gazing out over the expanse of gently flowing water, looking at nothing in particular.

Josh had left to go on tour almost a month before, just as the boys came on holiday. She had imagined that once he had gone, her world which appeared to have been turned on its end in the past few months, would slowly right itself and normality return. But it hadn't happened. Instead she had felt an ache and a loneliness which she had never known before: a sense of desolation and pain which was totally out of proportion, not at all like the emptiness she felt when the boys went back to school and the house echoed their absence. Then it was momentary and passed: but this hollow despair was different. And, as the weeks went by, it didn't go away: it slowly became worse.

As she sat there in the sunshine turning over the events of the summer in her mind, trying to analyse, to reason with herself, to pretend that everything was normal and that Josh hadn't happened, a young girl in a pretty flowered dress walked by, a transistor slung over her shoulder. From it flowed the last haunting bars of 'Liebestraum', the piece of music which Josh had played for her on that late May afternoon when he had walked in and found her practising. Hearing it brought a sudden stab of pain and the remembrance of the touch of his lean hands as they took hold of hers and placed them on the keyboard: Suddenly Laura knew without any shadow of a doubt that she no longer loved Josh as a son.

She looked over at Alasdair, peacefully sleeping, his hat well over his eyes, only the tip of his nose and his slightly open mouth visible beneath it. To her anguish, was added the knowledge that this time she could not turn to him for comfort.

A half stifled cry burst from her lips. Alasdair stirred and, pushing back his hat, looked up at her enquiringly.

'It's becoming chilly,' she said, getting up and smoothing down her frock, 'let's go.'

Her husband rose lazily from his seat.

'If you say so,' he smiled and, taking her arm, fell into step beside her as they walked together across the thick springy turf.

'Do you mind if I go up to Scotland ahead of you?' she asked as they left the park.

Alasdair looked at her strangely.

'If you wish,' he replied slowly. 'But it's only a WEEK.'

'I know,' Laura went on, 'but since Cristobel won't be there this year it might be nice for your mother.'

Alasdair's grip tightened on her arm.

'Of course, darling,' he said quickly. 'When would you like to go?'

'I – I thought perhaps Monday?'

She looked up at him, her eyes soft and strange. She suddenly felt that she had to get away from her husband. She could no longer bear their intimacy, she loved him but couldn't bear to think of his touch, and suddenly she wanted to run away and hide as she had wanted to do all those years ago when she had imagined he was in love with Fiona. Laura realised that she was behaving like an hysterical schoolgirl, but she seemed helpless in the face of this terrible rising tide of emotion which was sweeping through her body and threatening to submerge her in its depths. And she knew that in order to keep her sanity, to try to preserve their relationship, her's and Alasdair's, she had to get away from him to somewhere where she could be alone and think.

'Very well, darling,' he said quietly. 'I'll join you on Saturday.'

'Edwina's coming to lunch tomorrow,' Laura reflected, 'otherwise I could have left in the morning.'

Alasdair dropped her arm and looked down at her.

'What's the matter, Laura?' he asked sharply. 'Why this rush? Are you trying to get away from me?'

She dropped her eyes.

'Don't be silly,' she muttered.

'If I may say so,' he replied coldly, 'I think you're the one who's being silly.'

And, without another word, he held open the car door.

The evening was a catastrophe. Alasdair seemed cold and distant: that awful fear which had gripped him once before suddenly descended on him again and caught him in a vice. He did not know what was the matter with Laura: she had always enjoyed these early August days, with the boys gone and the holidays to look forward to when they could wind down and be together. But now she seemed edgy and irritable and quite unlike herself. He knew that something was wrong and yet he couldn't for the life of him fathom what. Mercifully, Edwina saved the situation at lunch the following day merely by being there. But she wasn't deceived. She knew Laura too well and she sensed that something was desperately wrong but, like Alasdair, couldn't fathom what. But she had the feeling that her niece's total absorption in her music had something to do with it.

'Why don't you go with Laura to Ardnakil tomorrow?' Alasdair said as he carved the joint.

'Is Laura leaving tomorrow?' Edwina queried. 'I thought you were going together on Saturday.'

'We were,' Alasdair replied tightly, 'but Laura wants to get away.'

He looked down at his plate then savagely plunged his fork into an unprotesting slice of beef.

'Oh ALASDAIR,' Laura pleaded. 'I just thought perhaps your mother . . .'

'Yes, I know,' he answered testily, 'but I really don't see what difference a few days will make.'

He sighed, without looking up.

'However, you've made up your mind and I've got your reservation for the morning train. But if Edwina would like to accompany you?'

He looked across enquiringly at her.

'It's rather short notice,' Edwina demurred. 'I think I'll stay and keep you company, Alasdair.'

She kept her eyes fixed on her plate as memories which had been buried for twenty-five years rose unbidden to her mind. The deep hurt and rejection in Laura's life stemming from her mother's death which Edwina believed had been washed away the day Alasdair asked her to be his wife, seemed to be resurfacing: and not gently, nostalgically, but in an ugly, menacing flow, threatening to destroy this tight web of happiness which had been spun around them since their marriage.

Edwina realised that something had to be done, and done quickly, to avert disaster in what had, up till then, always appeared to be a perfect marriage, but which now seemed to be floundering desperately. But she felt helpless, and couldn't think what.

Her mind went back to that evening when she had first met Alasdair and she wished once again with all her heart that she had had a faith which she could have passed on to this niece whom she loved so much. Something to bring her hope and peace and comfort in the midst of what now appeared to be a threatening storm in her life. Something, or someone, to cling to as she went through the deep waters. In desperation she laid down her knife and fork and smiled across at Alasdair.

'Will you come and have dinner with me tomorrow evening?' she enquired.

Maybe a little tête-à-tête with Alasdair would reveal the true problem: he was down to earth and sensible and there was no doubt that he was devoted to Laura.

Perhaps by a little gentle probing, without interfering, she could get to the root of the matter. Edwina looked across at Laura and saw her bottom lip quiver slightly. For the first time in her life she felt irritated by this beloved niece.

Alasdair raised his head and his face broke into a smile.

'Perhaps not tomorrow,' he answered. 'I'll take the opportunity of being alone to clear up some backlog at the office ... I may even get away a day or two earlier.'

He paused and his eyes directed their sharp green gaze on his wife's face.

'That is, if Laura would like me to,' he ended with a touch of sarcasm in his voice.

'Darling,' Laura pleaded, 'you KNOW I would.'

'Just needed to be reassured,' he answered grimly.

'I'll leave it to you then, Alasdair,' Edwina broke in. 'Any evening when you feel like company, do telephone me. I'd be delighted to have you.'

Alasdair put down his knife and fork and, leaning across the table, lightly touched her hand.

'Thank you, Edwina,' he said warmly. 'I'll do that.'

Their eyes met briefly and he saw the unspoken question in Edwina's. Dropping his own he felt suddenly helpless and vulnerable and wide-open to view: as if he were about to finally lose his footing and crash over the edge of the chasm which he now knew had never closed but had been yawning hungrily between he and Laura ever since Sandy's death.

He did not understand what had happened to them at that traumatic time, he only knew that, ever since, his life had been like a yo-yo regularly tossed over a precipice and then momentarily caught up into safety again. He had been aware of the chasm and the danger but his love for his wife had blinded him to reality, to the fact that the string on the yo-yo would one day become thin and snap: and he felt that this was what was now about to happen. And yet he still refused to believe that they could one day plunge into that yawning blackness. Up till today he had imagined that he alone was aware of their precarious situation but, seeing the look in Edwina's eyes, it appeared that the mounting tension in their lives had been apparent to others as well.

And so Laura left for Ardnakil, an atmosphere of strained politeness between them. The communication system appeared to have completely broken down and the wonderful feeling of unity and closeness which had crept back into their marriage during the past few months to have entirely vanished.

When the train slowly drew away from the station the next morning and Laura saw Alasdair's tall figure walking from the platform, she sat back in her seat, her mind in turmoil. She felt as if a steel band were being screwed on to her forehead forcing out every happy memory and leaving only a feeling of intense pain. Looking out of the window at the conglomeration of railway lines meeting, joining, separating, dancing before her eyes, she saw them gradually give way to a tangled web of sordid streets. The fine weather had broken in the night and heavy rain was falling on the slimy black pavements which spread out endlessly like a vast wet macintosh.

And suddenly, for no apparent reason, Flora's deep shining faith, her utter trust in an unseen God came to Laura's mind, and gazing at the derelict factories, the tattered hoardings and the depressing rows of ill-kept grey streets straggling in every direction, Laura wondered whether, in the midst of it all, there were really people whom God had made in his image.

Since she married Alasdair, and up until Sandy's death, she had never given the question a thought. Her future had risen like a gently sloping heather-covered mountain before her, its heights disappearing into soft shell-pink mists of snow-capped beauty. But in the past few weeks it seemed to have turned into a long black tunnel, a place where she had to gasp for air, with only occasional glimpses of a welcoming light beckoning and flashing at the end of it.

Sitting huddled in her corner of the empty compartment, she felt like a kaleidoscope shaken impatiently and jerkily up and down by an excited child, so that the thousand coloured mosaics which made up the pictures of her life kept whirling round and round, almost touching ground then being tossed helplessly into space again.

Deception was totally alien to Laura. Her life had always been as transparent as a bubble but now she felt trapped, enclosed, suffocated by it, struggling desperately to escape, yet pinned down on every side. She shut her eyes and tried to wrap herself round in nothingness, safe in some haven where everything was as it had always been, where life was ordinary and orderly and crystal clear again.

The dull, regular monotony of the rythmic clatter of the wheels sliding along the wet rails eventually lulled her into oblivion and, feeling the gentle waves of sleep slowly lapping over her she yielded to their caress, longing only to awaken to a day in which the past few months had been completely obliterated and where all doubt and pain had been washed away as if by a soft spring shower.

But when she opened her eyes from a fitful dream-laden sleep and looked out of the window at the slashing rain and the changing landscape, all the hopes and fears of the day rushed mercilessly at her like wild caged animals suddenly set free, and she wished she had taken the plane and already arrived at her destination, amongst familiar things and people who loved her, not alone and distraught in this dreary swaying compartment.

By the time the train finally drew into Perth station a dreadful lassitude and hopelessness had descended on her. But Donald's homely face and welcoming smile, the drive through the early evening countryside, ablaze with glorious flashes of rust and mauve and gold as the sun glinted in and out through fluffy clusters of clouds, and Flora's delight at seeing her again, momentarily dispelled the overwhelming feeling of gloom. So that when she walked into the room which she had shared with Alasdair for so many years and saw the photograph of the Laura who had captivated him at nineteen standing on his chest of drawers, she felt warm and secure and safe again, and a semblance of peace gradually enfolded her. She was back inside these old stone walls which had weathered many a crisis, many a violent storm in their time.

And Ardnakil once again wove its spell on her: that place where clouds never cast a dark shadow for long but were always soft and puffy and pink-tipped, floating serenely in a delicate blue sky; where the grass was always greener, the sun's rays more caressing, where nothing ever changed and life glided by in an endless summer afternoon with the promise of scones and honey and velvety raspberries for tea.

Laura peered into the small mirror on Alasdair's tallboy and saw a white, drawn face with dark circles under the eyes staring back at her.

Her eyes wandered from her reflection to the portrait of the smiling girl and she resolved to become once again that girl. She even convinced herself that she had been right to come on ahead of Alasdair, and that when he arrived at the weekend with the boys she would be that happy, laughing girl again, all the hurt and the misunderstandings between them forgotten, wiped away by the magical touch of Ardnakil.

But as the days slipped by in the quiet gentle haze which had enveloped that great house in the past few years she found herself once more slowly sinking into despair.

25

Reminiscing

On the Friday afternoon as Laura sat listlessly at the piano trying to play 'Liebestraum' the way Josh had played it, Flora came into the drawing room and stood in the doorway quietly listening.

Feeling her presence, Laura turned round and her mother-in-law walked over and put an arm gently across her shoulders.

'It's AMAZING how much you've improved, darling,' she said softly. 'Your playing has a depth and a maturity which it lacked a few years ago.'

She sat down on the stool beside Laura and ran her hands lightly over the keys.

'It's a wonderful solace, isn't it,' Flora murmured, 'music'.

Laura got up abruptly and walking over to the window stood looking out, afraid lest Flora should detect the turmoil underlying her outward calm.

Flora stopped playing but didn't look up.

'It's a lovely afternoon,' she said. 'I was just going to walk over to the Fort to see what needs to be done about it. Why don't you come with me?'

Laura didn't answer immediately. She wasn't deceived by Flora any more than she was deceived by Edwina. She knew that beneath Flora's vague exterior was a perceptiveness which was often painfully sharp and she wasn't sure whether she wanted to be laid open to such scrutiny. But Flora had another bait to cast.

'Did I tell you that I shall be going to live there very soon?' she mentioned innocently.

Laura swung round and looked at her in astonishment.

Hamish had died early in the new year whilst watching a boxing match on the television: one minute he had been sitting bolt upright, his eyes glaring, his moustache twitching ferociously, making angry comments and pounding his stick on the floor and the next moment, all had been still, the breath finally gone from his body in one exasperated roar. He had moved into Ardnakil, as Graeme had suggested, on the night of Robert's death and when Jeannie had packed up and followed him a few days later the Fort had been closed and had remained uninhabited ever since. But now Flora had dropped a bombshell.

'*You* leave Ardnakil?' Laura gasped incredulously. 'And for the *Fort*!'

'Oh, the Fort only needs a little arranging,' Flora said, still as innocent as ever, keeping the real bait dangling. 'It could be a very pleasant place to live.'

'But . . .' Laura gaped at her mother-in-law, and no words came.

'Ardnakil will soon have another mistress,' Flora said sweetly, rising from the piano stool and walking over to Laura. 'Come,' she coaxed, holding out her hand, 'let's walk in this lovely sunshine.'

They went out onto the terrace and across the lawn, Laura rather like a zombie, Flora still with her faint, amused smile as if she were enjoying a joke. Neither of them spoke. But it wasn't an awkward silence, it seemed to Laura's stunned mind to be more like a comfortable drawing together of two kindred spirits as they sauntered out of the dancing sunlight into the darkened wood and out again and round the crystal lake. Something quickened inside her, a premonition that this moment in time had a purpose, it hadn't happened by chance.

'Here we are,' Flora smiled as she opened the heavy, creaking front door and entered the hall. She wrinkled her nose in distaste. 'Smells musty, doesn't it?' And she crossed to the drawing room and began opening windows.

'Ugh,' she grimaced looking out onto a garden which was threatening to rise up and totally submerge the house. 'Malcolm is going to have a wonderful time trying to make something of this.'

Flora dragged a dust cover off a large sofa under the window and, sitting down, patted the seat beside her.

'Come and look at this view, Laura,' she breathed. 'Don't take any notice of the weeds. Isn't it wonderful? It's ALWAYS been one of my favourites, and it catches the late afternoon sun on the mountains and turns them the most beautiful shade of deep pink.'

She closed her eyes and breathed deeply.

'It's so peaceful just to look at the lake,' Flora went on, 'there's no downstairs view in Ardnakil which shows the lake, the wood hides it. But here one can sit and drink in its peace.'

She laid her head on the back of the faded damask sofa and closed her eyes again.

'I'm going to love living here,' she murmured.

She appeared at that moment to be so far away that Laura didn't like to disturb her, but after a while she opened her eyes and looked at Laura mischievously.

'Aren't you going to ask me why?' she teased.

Laura relaxed and smiled.

'Well, why?' she enquired.

Flora took a deep breath and a little smile played around her lips.

'Haven't you noticed a change in Graeme?' she remarked.

Laura had noticed very little. Graeme had been in

306

Edinburgh the evening she arrived and although he had appeared at lunch the following day, he had been immersed as usual in estate business.

'Not really,' she answered. 'Why, what's happened?'

'Like Robert,' Flora said dreamily, 'he's finally fallen in love.'

She sighed.

'And I couldn't be more pleased: it seems that in his time God works everything for good: out of evil he *can* in the end bring good.'

Laura was slightly embarrassed, and yet at the same time intrigued. It hadn't occurred to her that God ever worked at all, he was just a mystical figure way up there who did nothing for either good or evil. But here was Flora talking about him in that intimate way again, as if he were her next-door neighbour.

'Out of the tragedy of Sandy's death,' Flora went on, he HAS brought something good, something beautiful, though none of us could have dreamed it at the time.'

'But WHAT?' Laura demanded. 'WHO has Graeme fallen in love with?'

'Rose,' Flora replied softly. 'Isn't it wonderful?'

'ROSE?' Laura gasped unbelievingly.

'Yes,' Flora smiled. 'She finally came back home and Graeme met her again at a New Year's Eve dinner party in Edinburgh – her father's family come from there you know. And since then he's had many an unexplained trip to Edinburgh, especially at the weekends.'

Her eyes twinkled, and she seemed to be almost girlish, reminding Laura of Cristobel as she sat there, her lips parted in a half smile, bubbling on the edge of laughter.

'He always was the secretive one of the family,' she mused. 'Ninian was quiet, but Graeme was secretive. I had no inkling until last week when he asked me if I still had my Grandmother's ruby ring.

Laura's eyes widened.

'You had the sapphire, Alasdair especially wanted it because he said it reminded him of your eyes. Sandy gave Rose the rose diamond. She had it made into a pendant after he was killed as she couldn't bear to wear it as a ring. When I asked Graeme why the ruby, he told me that he especially wanted it because it was bloodshed which had brought he and Rose together.'

She smiled across at Laura.

'Do you remember at the funeral,' she went on, 'it was into Graeme's arms that Rose finally broke down and wept? Apparently it stirred something deep in him from that moment on. Perhaps that is why he has never been interested in any other woman since. He brought her to Ardnakil last weekend and the engagement will be announced next week: I think they intend to marry some time in October. After all, Graeme is already forty-four and Rose is thirty-two. They don't want a big wedding, just a quiet family ceremony, possibly in Edinburgh, so as not to bring back any memories.'

She looked at Laura and smiled her sweet vague smile.

'Isn't it wonderful, darling, that Rose will be my daughter-in-law after all? And that she has found happiness? It's especially wonderful to see them together: they look so RIGHT.'

Laura suddenly burst into tears and Flora put her arm round her.

'I'm sorry,' she sniffed, 'but it's such a shock.'

She gulped and putting up a hand brushed away the tears which were streaming down her cheeks.

'Such a beautiful shock,' she murmured, looking up, her deep blue eyes swimming. 'And so wonderful to think of their happiness.'

Flora slowly turned her gaze to Laura's tear-stained face.

'And you, Laura,' she said softly, 'are YOU happy?'

Laura looked up through her tears, startled.

'Of course,' she stammered. 'Why do you ask?'

'No reason,' Flora said quietly.

She got up and walking over to the window stood leaning against the sill, gazing out across the lake which the late afternoon sun had turned to a sheet of molten gold.

'Life isn't always easy,' she said as if talking to herself, 'and marriage isn't always easy either, especially when the first blissful honeymoon years are over.'

'Why do you say that?' Laura asked suspiciously.

Flora turned and smiled at her.

'Just an old woman's musings, my dear. I remember a very difficult period I went through in my marriage and I imagine it must happen in most, especially when a woman marries young. One either survives and goes on at such a time or . . . one goes under. And, if one goes under, I am sure one lives to regret it to the end of one's days.'

'Mother,' Laura cut in breathlessly. 'What do you mean? You and Father were BLISSFULLY happy.'

'We were,' Flora said, coming back to sit beside her, 'right to the end. But there was a crisis in our marriage, though I don't think Robert ever knew about it: if he did, he didn't say so. But it was very traumatic for me and, at one point, I really did NOT know which road I would take.'

'Go on,' Laura said tightly.

Flora gently took her hand.

'It was during the war. You remember I told you on the night that Robert died that the house had been turned into a military hospital and convalescent home for Allied officers?'

Laura nodded.

'I was lonely, missing Robert and I fell in love with a young polish officer who was convalescing at Ardnakil.'

Laura gasped.

'MOTHER,' she breathed, 'I can't believe it.'

'It's true,' Flora sighed.

'But you and Robert were DEVOTED to each other.'

'We were,' Flora went on, 'and I still loved Robert, that was what was so dreadful. I thought at one point I was losing my reason.'

She turned Laura's hand over in hers and sat gazing idly at her upturned palm.

'It was music which brought us together,' she finally said softly.

Laura let out a little gasp.

'Jaraslaw was a brilliant pianist. He was beginning to make a name for himself internationally when Poland was invaded.'

Laura felt herself stiffen and she quickly withdrew her hand, but Flora affected not to notice.

'He was in Paris when war broke out and he came over to England and joined the Royal Air Force. He was badly wounded in the Battle of Britain, I believe, or it may have been later, I can't remember. Whenever it was, he almost lost a leg and after a great many operations came to Ardnakil for a long convalescence.'

Flora smiled dreamily.

'I think it was his limp which made me notice him, and the fact that he was always alone. He used to walk endlessly round the lawn, at first on crutches and later leaning heavily on a stick. I used to see him from the nursery window where I spent most of my days with the children.'

She paused and Laura held her breath. When, after a few minutes Flora had not broken the silence, Laura felt that she would burst if she did not hear the end of the story.

'Please go on,' she whispered at last.

Flora looked at her as if returning from another world.

'I really knew very little about him,' she continued, her eyes now on the still waters of the lake. 'Like most of them, since the fall of Poland, he had no news of his family and he scarcely mentioned them. I think it must have been too painful.'

She looked at Laura and smiled.

'He was much younger than Robert, about my age, I believe, though he may even have been younger.'

She laughed.

'It's strange how little we knew about each other, and yet there was this irresistible attraction, this magnetism between us: Perhaps, looking back, it wasn't even love, though we thought it was at the time.'

Flora sighed.

'Why him and not one of the others, I shall never know. He was lonely, but so were most of them; and so was I. I had been ever since Robert left, a terrible aching loneliness, but no-one else had been able to fill it. Yet when I met Jaraslaw it was almost as if there was something beyond ourselves drawing us towards each other.'

She looked at Laura with a distant smile.

'We both resisted it. There was a different moral code in those days.'

Laura gazed down at her hands and said nothing.

'He used to spend hours playing Chopin on the drawing room piano, and after a while I couldn't resist creeping in to listen.'

Laura leant her head against the back of the sofa and closed her eyes, feeling as if she were watching the last few months of her life being enacted on a stage: Flora's story so closely resembled her own even to the ambiguity of being able to love two men at the same time.

'I always admired your technique when you played Chopin,' she murmured without opening her eyes. 'Did he teach you?'

'Yes,' Flora replied. 'He sat beside me on the stool and played with me. I'd never had ANYONE interpret the meaning of the music to me in the way Jaraslaw did.'

She sighed dreamily.

'They do say only Poles can really play Chopin as it's meant to be played.'

Flora lay back against the soft cushions, her eyes far away.

'It was inevitable I suppose,' she said quietly. 'Robert had always been tone-deaf, like all the children.'

Flora paused briefly and her silver grey eyes misted over.

'All except Sandy,' she murmured.

For a moment neither of them spoke. Then, as the full impact of what she had heard struck her, Laura slowly sat up and looked at her mother-in-law in astonishment.

'You can't mean . . .' she gasped. 'You're not saying that Sandy wasn't . . .'

But she couldn't finish the sentence: the words refused to come.

'Wasn't Robert's son?' Flora queried, then she broke into a light tinkling laugh. 'Oh NO, my darling, NO-ONE could deny that. Sandy was CERTAINLY Robert's son, he was so like him.'

She paused and once again seemed to be far away.

'He was the child of our reconciliation,' she went on softly, 'although Robert never knew that there was a reconciliation.'

Flora smiled to herself.

'Men are strange creatures sometimes, aren't they? They don't feel things the way we do, and mercifully don't see things, either. No, Robert never knew about Jaraslaw. He left to go back to Poland soon after the war ended, just before Robert arrived home from the Middle East.'

She looked at Laura and there was pain in her eyes:

'It was hard Laura, so hard. I was TORN, I really did not know what to do. I didn't think I could go on living without Jaraslaw, even the children seemed to fade into the background when I thought what it would mean to be without him.'

'Were you,' Laura began, 'were you . . .' and again she couldn't go on.

'Lovers?' Flora finished the sentence for her. 'No, we weren't. I don't know why; it would have been so easy. But rightly or wrongly, I don't know, something stopped us, some code which doesn't seem to exist nowadays. But I think if we had been lovers, I would have walked out of Ardnakil on the day Jaraslaw did: I wouldn't have been able to stay, and certainly not to face Robert when he came home.'

She smiled to herself again.

'Looking back, it was a beautiful idyll,' she remarked, 'which would have turned into something sordid had we let our emotions overwhelm us and take control.'

'Do you still think of him?' Laura whispered.

'Yes,' Flora replied levelly. 'I don't think I shall ever forget him, nor him me. But it is without pain now, it has been for many years: just a precious dream which, had it come true, would probably have ended as a nightmare.'

She turned to face her daughter-in-law.

'Just think, darling, had I followed Jaraslaw I'd have lost everything which gave sense and meaning to my life and gone to live in a country I didn't know where I would have been a stranger, a foreigner, perhaps ostracised, perhaps unable to adapt. My roots and everything I'd ever cherished would have been brutally torn away and, in time, I'd have ached for my children and tortured myself because of what I'd done to them. It certainly wouldn't have been the beautiful dream I imagined.'

Flora gave an almost imperceptible shudder.

'Oh NO, darling, I am SO thankful that, even in my moments of wildest despair, something held me back.'

'Was it very dreadful?' Laura asked, purposely avoiding her mother-in-law's eyes.

'Yes,' Flora replied. 'It was. AGONISING in fact. Life was pointless and empty without him. I was about your age, and the road ahead looked very long and dreary indeed.'

'But how did you survive?'

For a moment Flora remained silent. She slowly turned her head and gazed out of the window her eyes seeming to see something which Laura could not see, something far away.

'Because,' she said at last, her voice low and still, 'I believed that God had a purpose for my life and I trusted him to carry me through the difficult times.'

A deep silence fell over the room as they each wrestled with their own thoughts. Laura picked up a faded velvet cushion and her fingers began to play mechanically with the tassle.

'You speak of God as if he were a human being,' she said at last without looking up.

'Not a HUMAN being,' Flora replied, her eyes still looking into the distance, a faint smile on her parted lips. 'But a PERSON; a person who has our lives in his hands, and whom we can trust ... to bring good out of evil.'

She took a deep breath and turned towards her daughter-in-law.

'As he has brought good out of the evil of Sandy's death,' she said quietly.

Laura lay the cushion carefully back in place.

'I wish I had your trust,' she murmured.

'You can have, my dear,' Flora answered softly. 'Just look what he's done for Rose.'

Laura didn't answer.

'And, in a way, God gave me a gift in Sandy, so very much Robert's son and yet with MY love, and Jaraslaw's gift, for music. That in itself, after four tone-deaf children, was a wonderful compensation.'

Flora smiled to herself.

'Dear Sandy,' she breathed. 'HOW he changed.'

Laura looked at her enquiringly.

'Jamie reminds me of him more and more,' her mother-in-law went on, 'so mischievous, so full of life, always in trouble.'

She leaned back against the cushions, her eyes once more far away. 'Just think what a charming, delightful young man Sandy finally became.'

Laura placed her hand on her mother-in-law's and they sat together in silence, remembering.

'And Robert never knew about Jaraslaw?' Laura finally remarked.

'I don't think so,' Flora replied absently, her thoughts obviously still with Sandy. 'If he suspected anything, he never said so.'

'And Jaraslaw? Did you ever see him again?'

'Only once, about ten years later. Robert and I were on one of our rare holidays abroad: he had taken me to Venice for my fortieth birthday.'

Flora leant back against the faded cushions once again.

'It was early May, such a perfect time of the year, and the holiday had been like a second honeymoon.'

Flora sighed voluptuously, her eyes glistening.

'On our last day we were having tea at the Danieli before taking the night train to Paris.'

She turned to smile at Laura.

'People didn't travel in aeroplanes very much then, always by train. It was so much more romantic. I

315

remember we arrived in Paris in time for breakfast
then caught the Golden Arrow to London. We didn't
get home until about four days later, but it was all
part of the holiday and so exciting.'

Flora slowly twisted a large diamond ring round and
round on her finger.

'Robert bought me this ring that day we spent in
London on the way back. To mark the occasion. He was
always so thoughtful and generous,' she ended softly
and she looked up at Laura, having completely lost the
thread of their conversation. Then added innocently,
'Rather like Alasdair.'

'Did you meet Jaraslaw when you were having tea
at the Danieli?' Laura prompted.

Flora gazed at her vaguely, then suddenly remembered.

'Yes,' she murmured. 'He came in and sat down
almost next to us.'

She broke off and smiled mischievously.

'With his beautiful Hungarian wife.'

Laura drew in her breath sharply.

'What did it feel like?' she questioned. 'Meeting him
again?'

Flora shrugged her shoulders expressively.

'Just like meeting an old friend with whom one has
lost touch,' she said quietly. 'He introduced me to his
wife, she was absolutely exquisite, a violinist, much
younger than him. I introduced him to Robert, we spent
a pleasant half hour chatting and then we had to leave
to catch our train.'

'So he didn't go back to Poland?' Laura enquired.

Flora's eyebrows drew together in a puzzled frown.

'No,' she said thoughtfully. I don't believe so. I'm
afraid I didn't ask him.'

'If he had he wouldn't have been able to get out
and travel, would he?' Laura encouraged, anxious to
know more.

'You're probably right,' Flora agreed. 'I think he said they were living in Paris . . . or was it Vienna? I really can't remember.'

She suddenly laughed.

'Isn't it strange Laura? I once thought I couldn't live without him, and less than ten years later I meet him and can't even remember where he DOES live.'

She took her daughter-in-law's hand in hers and looked tenderly down at her.

'Nothing lasts, Laura,' she said gently. 'Not even the worst pain. By then Robert and I had found a new love, a less selfish love perhaps, certainly on my part. We can love very selfishly when we're young. Our love had, I think, been strengthened by my love for Jaraslaw, or maybe it was because of the war and our separation, I don't know: but it was different, deeper, stronger, more tender.'

Flora smiled mistily.

'Meeting Jaraslaw again made me realise how much Robert meant to me, how much I loved him: that *he* was the man I couldn't live without.'

Flora's beautiful grey eyes were brimming with unshed tears.

'Sandy was the living proof.'

Laura got up and, in her turn, walked over to the long low window and stood looking out at the sun reflected on the still waters of the lake: for a long moment they remained silent, each thinking their own thoughts.

'There's nothing special about me,' Flora said quietly at last. 'What I did, with God's help, any woman can do, if she really wants to.'

She paused, but Laura did not turn round. She knew perfectly well that what her mother-in-law had meant was 'what I can do *you* can do,' but her tact, her delicacy, perhaps her love for Alasdair had prevented her from intruding into their personal dilemma.

317

'That's where you're wrong,' Laura replied at last. 'There IS something special about you: something VERY special.'

'I've been very blessed,' Flora said softly. 'SO blessed. I always seem to have been surrounded by beautiful things, and beautiful people.'

She smiled across at Laura's back view almost willing her to turn round.

'You and Deirdre, and now Rose, whom I thought I'd lost for ever. God is so GOOD.'

'Perhaps beauty attracts beauty,' Laura remarked, half to herself, her eyes still on the overgrown garden.

Flora glanced at her enquiringly as she turned round and faced her mother-in-law.

'Have you never looked in the mirror?' Laura teased.

Flora smiled dreamily.

'Robert always told me I was beautiful,' she murmured, 'right up to the end. So it never really mattered to me what other people thought.'

She closed her eyes, and rested her head once more against the back of the sofa.

'Mother,' Laura ventured at last. 'Is it because you go to church that you have this inner strength?'

She paused and went back to twiddling the cushion's tassel.

'I often go with you when I'm here, but it hasn't meant very much.'

Flora opened her eyes, and slowly turned to face her.

'Going to church didn't give me the peace I now have,' she said quietly. 'It was meeting Jesus as a person, a living God, someone whom I could talk to and call upon in times of trouble, not a beautiful figure in a stained glass window.'

'But how did it HAPPEN?' Laura insisted. Her mother-in-law removed the cushion and cradled Laura's hand in her own.

'When I knew Jaraslaw was leaving and the pain was very hard to bear, one night I just called out to God and said, "If you're real, if you're really there, then show yourself to me. Come and help me".'

Laura looked at her, her eyes wide with amazement.

'And what happened?'

'He showed himself to me,' Flora said simply. 'Perhaps you'll think I'm just a silly old woman and a lot of people will certainly find some rational explanation, but I saw Jesus standing in front of me with such love and compassion in his eyes. It only lasted a few seconds but he held out his hands and showed me the marks of the nails. It was as if he said: "I suffered for you, because I love you". And such a wonderful overwhelming sense of peace simply flooded through me and, with it a deep certainty that he would help me and carry me through these deep waters. Jaraslaw left the next day. I won't say it was easy: it wasn't, it was very hard, just as it was when Sandy died. But like then, I had this absolute certainty deep inside me that I wasn't alone, that Jesus was holding me and wouldn't let me fall to the bottom of that pit of black despair.'

'And what happened then?'

'By some miracle of administration Robert arrived home soon afterwards. I told you I still loved Robert, didn't I? I don't know HOW one can love two men at the same time, but I did. And when he came back and we were a family once more, life slowly began to return to normal and I knew I had done the right thing: the only thing in fact.'

'And did the church help?'

Flora laughed shortly.

'The church, as you call it, never knew. I don't know

what they'd have thought if they had. But yes, going to church DID help. I now went to worship the God I had come to love, instead of going out of habit: and it made ALL the difference.

Laura looked surreptitiously at her mother-in-law as she lay back against the sofa, and saw that her eyes were shining.

'Jesus had shown me that the human spirit with its changing moods is not unlike the sea,' she continued softly, 'sometimes sparkling like a June morning, sometimes dull and sullen like a grey January day. But that when a person has his Spirit living inside him, although life and outside circumstances can change dramatically, like the sea, and on the surface the storm can rage, deep down all is quiet and calm and at peace.'

'I wish I could have your experience,' Laura whispered.

Flora gently took her hand again.

'You can,' she smiled. 'What happened to me can happen to anyone – has happened to many people. Just call on him and ask him to come into your heart and give you his peace ... and he will, I promise you.'

Laura studied her hands intently, but didn't reply. There was a deep silence in the dusty, cobwebbed room as each waited for the other to speak. The sun glided behind a grey cloud and a dark shadow fell across the window.

'Good gracious!' Flora exclaimed, picking up the delicate gold fob watch hanging round her neck and glancing down at it. 'It's almost tea-time and we haven't even LOOKED at the rest of the house.'

She got up from the sofa and held out her hand to Laura.

'Darling,' she smiled, 'will you ever forgive a sentimental old woman droning on?'

'I really brought you here to ask your advice about colour schemes,' she confided as they walked across the room. 'You have such *exquisite* taste.'

She opened the dining room door as they passed through the hall, and shuddered.

'I MUST have this room stripped and fumigated first of all,' she exclaimed. 'It's quite monstrous. Hamish always refused to change a thing: I think he must have liked the smell of last year's mutton.'

And she quickly closed the heavy oak door.

'Come, darling,' she said, 'we've just got time to do a quick tour and you can tell me what you think.'

As they walked back down the stairs Flora said softly, 'You're a very precious daughter-in-law, Laura. I don't know why I've always felt so close to you, but I have, ever since Cristobel brought you home as a shy schoolgirl with long golden plaits. I'm so glad you married one of my sons and have made him so very happy.'

She stopped as they reached the front door.

'I've never told anyone about Jaraslaw,' she murmured, 'not even Cristobel.'

She squeezed Laura's arm, which was resting lightly in hers.

'But I'm glad I've told you.'

Laura looked at her mother-in-law intently and understood that she had been right not to be deceived by Flora's apparent vagueness. She realised that Flora had been aware of her own inner turmoil and, in confiding in her, had tried to defuse some of the pain which she sensed Laura was feeling, and show her that she understood.

She squeezed Flora's arm in return, and as they walked out of the house into the warm late summer sunshine and the great oak door slammed behind them, she felt that its closing had concluded an episode, a chapter in her life. And with the words 'what I have done, with God's help, any woman can do' echoing round and round in her head she resolutely turned her back on the past few months and looked hopefully forward to an uncluttered, uncomplicated, unsullied future.

26

'What is it?'

As the two women sauntered in a contented silence
across the lawn towards the terrace, Laura noticed a
car round the bend of the drive and swerve towards
the front door of Ardnakil.

'Mother,' Laura exclaimed, shading her eyes. 'I think
that's Alasdair.'

Flora smiled at her in amusement.

'That's what I thought,' she replied calmly.

Laura slipped her arm from her mother-in-law's,
and ran swiftly across the lawn and up the terrace
steps. She burst into the drawing room just as the
barking and howling from the half landing (followed
by the slithering of paws and the answering shrieks of
delight from her sons and her husband's deep laugh)
echoed round the hall. Crossing the room she stood in
the doorway watching the scene.

Andrew looked up from the floor where he was
kneeling gently stroking the growling MacDuff, who
had, as usual, waddled from his turret when he heard
the excited yelps of the other three.

'Mum,' he cried delightedly and leapt to his feet as
Iain disentangled himself from the other dogs' enthusi-
astic licks and lolloped towards her. Laura held out her
arms to these two lanky young men who were her sons,
hugging them in delight. Then, releasing them, she
turned towards her husband who was standing slightly
awkwardly to one side. Alasdair slowly removed Joe's

large paws from around his waist and smiled across at her. He seemed tense and ill-at-ease, as if he didn't know how he would be received.

'DARLING,' Laura breathed, walking over to him and holding up her face to be kissed. 'How LOVELY to see you all.'

The green and gold lights began to dance in Alasdair's eyes and he took her small body in his arms and held her to him.

'But what happened?' she asked, stepping back from his warm embrace and looking up at him. 'We weren't expecting you till tomorrow evening.'

Alasdair smiled and put a protective arm around her shoulders as they followed the boys and the yapping dogs into the drawing room.

'The school rang on Tuesday to say that Iain and Andrew would be arriving back on Thursday instead of Friday, some mess-up with plane bookings I believe. So I made a superhuman effort, cleared my desk and we left early this morning. I didn't think there was any point in letting you know: we decided to give you a pleasant surprise instead.'

He looked down at her.

'I hope it *is* a pleasant surprise?' he queried.

'Darling,' she whispered. 'Of COURSE it is. It's LOVELY to have you all here.'

Flora had arrived at a more leisurely pace and now stood by the huge empty fireplace, smiling at them all.

'I've just rung for tea,' she said, holding her face up for her son's kiss.

'Splendid,' Alasdair replied, and he flopped down on to a sofa.

'Whatever time did you leave?' Laura enquired, sitting down beside him.

'Pretty early. The boys got back yesterday evening. Edwina, bless her, fed us all and we just transferred their baggage to the car and left at the crack of dawn.'

He grinned down at her.

'Well, almost.'

They all three laughed and, as tea arrived and was placed on the little table in the west turret, walked across the room and sat down.

'It's good to be here,' Alasdair breathed, looking out of the window across the expanse of green lawn to the wood. 'Especially after London. It's stifling there at the moment.'

'Has the weather changed again?' Laura enquired. 'It was pouring with rain when I left.'

'Not since,' her husband replied. 'It's been sweltering these last few days.'

'Are the boys not coming to tea?' Flora asked beginning to pour.

Alasdair grinned at his mother.

'Can't you guess where they've gone?' he said. 'Down to the kitchen to be spoiled. We stopped for an early lunch just outside Edinburgh so I imagine they're starving and,' he added, lifting the lid of a silver salver, 'I doubt whether scones will be enough to keep them going till dinner.'

'You didn't by any chance bump into Graeme in Edinburgh?' Flora asked mischievously.

Alasdair took a large bite into a scone.

'No,' he said, looking up. 'We avoided Edinburgh as a matter of fact. It's always hell in August with the Festival coming up. Why? What's he doing there?'

Flora smiled at Laura.

'Shall we tell him?' she teased. 'Or shall we make him wait until tomorrow?'

Alasdair glanced from one to the other.

'What's going on?' he asked.

Flora laughed happily and told her son the good news.

Alasdair let out a low whistle.

'The cagey old devil,' he murmured.

He picked up his cup and looked thoughtfully at his mother over the rim.

'And you?' he enquired laconically.

'I'm moving into the Fort,' she answered. 'Laura and I were on our way back from there when you arrived. We went over to see about renovations and redecorating. I wanted her advice about colours and furnishings.'

'So you'll have finally managed to get rid of all your offspring,' he smiled.

Flora smiled back.

'And mother hen that I am, I may even have all of them around me for the wedding,' she replied. 'Do you think the boys could possibly have a weekend from school to come up for it?'

'It depends when,' Alasdair hedged.

'Graeme is going to telephone Ninian and Deirdre when the date is finally settled,' Flora rushed on, 'then perhaps they will all come over too.'

Ninian had been seconded to the Embassy in Washington the year before.

'It would be lovely if they could,' she said dreamily. 'It seems such a long time since I saw Michael and Anna.'

Alasdair grinned conspiratorially across at Laura.

'Well,' he announced getting up and stretching. 'I'd better see about sorting out the stuff in the car. I very much doubt that the boys will have thought to do anything about it. When's Jamie coming by the way? Any news?'

'None at all,' Laura replied. 'He and Helen are apparently still inseparable.'

'Perhaps they could all come here,' Flora put in wistfully.

'Why don't you ring Cristobel and suggest it?' Alasdair said. 'When's the baby due, by the way?'

'Not until the end of September,' Flora answered. 'But Cristobel prefers to stay quietly at Lochincraig this year and I do understand. She's not getting any younger and it *is* her sixth.'

'She doubled our output,' Alasdair laughed.

Laura got up hurriedly.

'I'll come and help you clear the car.'

He looked intently across at her.

'It's not necessary,' her husband said quietly.

She returned his gaze.

'I know it's not, but I'd like to.'

As they entered the large, high ceilinged room they had shared for so many years, Laura walked over to the tall boy and stood looking at the smiling girl in the photograph.

Alasdair came up behind her and put his arms on her shoulders, pressing his face close to hers.

'You haven't changed a bit,' he said softly.

She reached up a hand and held his.

'Oh ALASDAIR,' she replied.

Their eyes met in the oval mirror in front of them.

'Happy?' he asked quietly as he turned her round and took her in his arms.

She hid her face against his broad shoulder and sighed contentedly as he tipped her chin towards him and kissed her parted lips. They were warm and soft, and as his brushed against them it was like being touched by a velvet petal.

They looked at each other once again, each seeing the tension drain from the other's eyes. They told themselves that they had imagined all that had gone before: it was fatigue, the end of a long summer. Now that they were relaxed and back inside these solid grey walls everything would be all right.

Then, suddenly, Alasdair's face disappeared as if a blob of acid had been dropped on it, and Josh's lean sensitive features rose up in its place, his dark eyes burning, seeming to bore straight through her. Laura stiffened and turned away.

She felt Alasdair stiffen also. He put his hands on her shoulders and turned her slowly to face him, but she dropped her eyes and, as she did so, his hands fell listlessly to his side. With a sigh he walked slowly across the room towards the open window and stood looking out over the garden. Sensing his disappointment, his bewilderment, a cry of pain broke from her lips.

'Alasdair,' she pleaded, but her voice sounded forced.

He didn't turn round, and the silence between them was heavy and ominous, like a dark cloud, threatening to completely engulf them.

She put her hands up to her face in a helpless gesture.

'I'm not the girl in the photo any more,' she said brokenly. 'But I will be . . . I will be . . . I promise you. Just give me time.'

He turned from the window and stood facing her, the lines of his face taut, the dancing green and gold lights and the laughter gone from his eyes.

'What is it, Laura?' he asked quietly.

She looked at him and his face reflected her own pain. But no words came and, with a strangled sob, she ran from the room.

* * *

The boys' excited chatter over dinner covered the tension which was obvious between Laura and Alasdair. As soon as coffee had been served she pleaded a headache and retired to bed.

Flora's eyes followed her as she walked across the drawing room then she, in her turn, excused herself and left the room.

As Laura reached her bedroom door Flora came up beside her and gently slipped her arm through hers.

'Do you remember the night Robert died?' she said quietly.

Laura nodded.

'You sensed my distress and came up and sat with me. I haven't forgotten.'

She paused as Laura put her hand on the heavy brass knob, and the two women who had so much in common, looked straight at each other.

'May I come in and talk to *you* now?' Flora enquired.

Laura saw compassion and understanding in Flora's expressive grey eyes. For a brief moment she hesitated, longing for the relief and the release which she knew confession would bring, longing to be reassured that she wasn't losing her reason, that everything would be all right, that her world, her security, all the things which meant so much to her were not about to be shattered, that life would one day return to normal, her feelings for Alasdair would become again what they once had been and she would no longer have this desperate gnawing ache, this blank despair and terrible fear.

She smiled and half opened the door. Then she suddenly remembered that Alasdair was Flora's son, and it was as if a heavy dark curtain had swiftly been drawn between them, cutting them off from each other. And she knew that the luxury which Flora was offering her was one she could not accept because, loving her as she did, she could not, would not, hurt her more. Pulling the door quickly to she dropped her eyes, afraid that Flora would see the stark fear in them.

'Not tonight, Mother,' she answered tightly. 'I'm very tired. I just want to sleep.'

Flora squeezed her arm briefly, affectionately, nodded, then turned away. The moment when Laura could have obtained relief passed. Entering the darkened room which held so many memories she closed the door behind her and, as she did so, a shaft of bright moonlight beamed onto the tall boy throwing a ghostly silver gleam onto her smiling portrait. She caught her breath and stood for a moment, unable to move. Then, quickly walking across the room, she tugged the curtains across the window, shutting out the vision of the girl she once had been.

27

Rose

Just before lunch on the following day Graeme arrived with his fiancée.

Laura had not seen Rose since Sandy's funeral and she had a shock when this poised, slender young woman, almost as tall as Graeme himself, stepped out of the car. Standing close to Sandy at their engagement reception almost seven years earlier she had appeared much smaller and plumper, altogether more bubbly.

But as she came forward to greet the waiting family gathered on the drive, her deep brown eyes, which Laura had never noticed before, had a soft velvety lustrous sheen and seemed to be almost too large for her finely chiselled face. They were now luminous with happiness but in their depths was the after-glow of intense suffering.

When Rose had been engaged to Sandy her dark hair had been short and bobbed. Now she wore it, like a ballerina, smoothed back into a soft roll at the nape of her neck, thereby accentuating her high cheekbones and the delicate bone structure of her face. Standing slim and erect at Graeme's side she was the same Rose, and yet not the same, subtly different, her former roundness and infectious gaiety replaced by a quiet tranquillity.

To everyone's surprise and delight Lindsay drove up with his family just before tea.

'CRISTOBEL!' Laura cried excitedly, rushing to

meet her as Lindsay helped his wife, weighty and cumbersome with the impending birth, out of the car. 'We never expected to see *you* this summer.'

Cristobel hugged her.

'I couldn't RESIST it,' she laughed. 'If the baby comes early, what does it matter? I can perfectly well have it here.'

Jamie crept up and caught his mother round the waist in a smothering hug, and Cristobel turned to Graeme.

'Especially after hearing your wonderful news last night,' she breathed, her eyes shining as she stood on tiptoe to kiss him. 'Oh GRAEME, I'm so happy for you, and for Rose.'

She let go of him and looked round.

'Where *is* Rose? I must see her immediately.'

Rose had been standing in the doorway slightly apart from the family reunion, but as Cristobel called her name she walked gracefully forward to be clasped in her turn to her future sister-in-law's heavily maternal figure.

The rest of the weekend was spent making plans for the wedding, which was fixed for October the second in Edinburgh. Neither Graeme nor Rose wanted the sumptuous affair which her wedding to Sandy would have been, but they were delighted when Ninian telephoned to say that Deirdre and the children would certainly come over for the ceremony and that he would do his very best to be there as well. Flora was in her element and had already started on her lists for a small reception in a fortnight's time so that everyone could share their wonderful news.

Rose watched all the excitement and planning going on around her with a certain detachment. She had about her an aura of serenity, of quiet happiness, the aura and the happiness which youthful brides rarely have, the happiness only borne of great suffering.

Seeing her, Laura remembered the time, which now seemed so distant, when she and Alasdair had first been engaged; and a lump rose in her throat.

But it was difficult to be melancholy for long. The old house had resumed its former atmosphere. The endless galleries and corridors which seemed to wander without any kind of plan through wings and green baize doors were now filled with people and laughter and noise and activity. In spite of herself, Laura was caught up in the happy swirl of events, and although she occasionally found Flora's eyes resting thoughtfully on her, there was so much going on everywhere they had little chance to be alone together again. For which Laura told herself she was grateful.

Even her relationship with Alasdair seemed to settle once again into an easy friendliness, the tension momentarily gone. He was happy to be on holiday with his sons and his nephews, with Lindsay and Graeme and the older nieces. When they all went off on their various outdoor pursuits, Laura invariably opted to stay behind with Cristobel: to all outward purposes it was quite normal that the two women who had grown up so close together and who now rarely saw each other for any length of time should want to make the most of this golden opportunity.

'I suppose you're hoping for a boy,' Laura said one afternoon as she and Cristobel sat together on the terrace, lazily drinking in the rays of the sun.

'Not really,' Cristobel answered. 'I don't mind either way.'

'But don't you want to even it up and have three of each?' Laura pursued.

'After Rob and Roddy,' Cristobel yawned, 'I'd be quite happy to have another girl. Even HELEN is easier to cope with than those two. I don't know how you manage with THREE boys.'

'Are girls so different?' Laura enquired.

'VERY,' Cristobel said grimly, 'at least mine are. It was quite a shock when Robert and then Roderick appeared. They're full of mischief!'

She laughed.

'Gorgeous, but little mischiefs all the same,' she finished.

And they lapsed into silence, closing their eyes and lying back with the sun beaming down on their upturned faces.

'You should have a little girl Laura,' Cristobel said dreamily after a while. 'Have you never thought about it?'

Laura shrugged.

'It just never happened,' she replied evasively.

Cristobel turned her heavy body uncomfortably round to face her sister-in-law, and the sagging deck chair groaned in protest.

'It's not too late,' she said quietly. 'After all, you're three months younger than I am.'

She lay back again, her sentence unfinished, and Laura felt her limbs stiffen and a chill damp sweat trickle slowly down her back.

She shivered and sat up. The sun was still shining brightly down on them but she suddenly felt cold.

'I'll ring for tea,' she said abruptly. 'It must be about time. Anyway, I'm ready for a cup, aren't you?'

She got up and stretched as Cristobel nodded sleepily.

'And then I must find Mother,' Laura went on. 'I promised to walk over to the Fort with her, they've begun painting the drawing room and we need to decide on the colour schemes for the bedrooms as soon as possible. Time's running out – it will soon be October.'

But the only response from Cristobel was a gentle purring escaping from her half open mouth. The end of her nine months was in sight and the inevitable fatigue and the warm last rays of the northern summer sun had done their soothing work. She was fast asleep.

Between the long lazy days spent idling and chatting with Cristobel, and sessions with Flora poring over catalogues and colour-schemes, punctuated by trips into Perth to buy materials for the new furnishings, the holiday passed serenely by and Laura regained her sense of peace and well-being.

The weather was unusually warm and pleasant and she and Alasdair met each evening in an atmosphere which was both affectionate and relaxed. The cousins were delighted to be together and filled the house with their laughter, and Flora was more sparkling than Laura had seen her since Robert's death as she organised her new home and made preparations for the approaching wedding.

Rose and Graeme were so obviously happy that they wove a web of joy around all those with whom they came in contact. When September arrived, with the new school term and the end of the holidays in sight, Laura too seemed to have regained her sparkle and was able to tell herself once again that all the agonising of the previous few weeks before she came to Ardnakil had been imagined.

Contrary to all the predictions and forebodings, Cristobel did not have the baby in her old home. When, early in September, Alasdair packed his family into the car for the return journey, she was still happily trotting around Ardnakil under Lindsay's watchful eye, with no sign of an imminent birth.

'We'll be on our way in a couple of days' time too,' Lindsay said as Alasdair slammed down the lid of the laden boot. 'The girls are due back at school next week.'

'Hope you make it,' Alasdair laughed.

'Oh, we will,' Lindsay replied. 'Cristobel's like her

mother: looks frail and delicate but she's really as
strong as a horse.'

He threw his arm affectionately round his wife who
had just waddled out to say goodbye.

Laura disentangled herself from Flora's embrace and
turned to hug Cristobel.

'You WILL let us know the minute the baby arrives,
won't you?' she said anxiously.

'Promise,' Cristobel replied, one hand tenderly
caressing her distended abdomen. 'And . . . Laura.'

Laura turned beside the car door which Alasdair was
holding open for her.

Cristobel leaned towards her.

'Don't forget what I said,' she whispered.

Laura frowned as Cristobel looked at her knowingly,
one hand still pointedly on her tum.

'Oh *that*,' she replied.

'Yes *that*,' Cristobel said. 'Think about it.'

And she added, her eyes twinkling, 'Why should I be
the only one in the family to spend half her life looking
like the Leaning Tower of Pisa?'

Laura turned abruptly and got into the car, and
Alasdair walked round and climbed in beside her. The
family closed ranks, and, with the boys hanging out of
the back window shouting last minute goodbyes and
recommendations to their cousins, they slowly moved
off down the drive to the accompaniment of waves and
shouts.

'Whatever did Cristobel mean?' Alasdair enquired,
putting his arm out of the window for a last wave.

Laura looked straight ahead of her as they turned
and swung out through the large wrought iron gates.

'Oh nothing,' she said shortly, feeling the peace and
happiness which had enveloped her during the past few
weeks begin to slowly ooze away.

Alasdair looked at her strangely and said nothing,
but out of the corner of her eye, she saw his lips

suddenly compress into the hard line she had noticed on that first afternoon in their bedroom. He pressed his foot heavily on the accelerator and shot along the country road with a reckless speed totally uncharacteristic of him. Laura looked down at her small feet and bit her lip in an attempt to hold back the tears which were gathering behind her eyes and threatening to spill over and cascade down her cheeks.

'Alasdair,' she whispered.

He looked quickly down at her and then back at the road, but didn't reply. A sense of desolation swept through her.

'Dad, where are we having lunch?' Jamie piped up from the middle of the back seat, breaking the uneasy silence.

'Good heavens, Jamie,' Alasdair replied irritably, 'you've only just had breakfast.'

'OK, OK,' Jamie said amiably. 'Only asking.'

But his remark had defused the tension and Laura saw her husband's hands slacken on the steering wheel as he reduced speed. He looked down at her with a half smile.

'Where would you like to stop for lunch?' he asked.

She looked up at him gratefully and smiled back.

'Let the boys choose,' she replied.

And, as they sped along in the soft late summer sunshine, past quilted fields and low stone walls with drifts of wild flowers peeping up from their crevices, she convinced herself once again that everything was going to be all right. The holiday had renewed and refreshed her, had allowed her to see things in perspective instead of out of proportion. The past few months had merely been a bad dream from which she was now fully awakened.

They were going home, the boys would soon be back at school and she and Alasdair would resume their usual comfortable existence. And as this thought hammered itself into her brain, she leant back in her seat and relaxed.

When they arrived home Laura reduced her classes at the Academy by half and, as Edwina had warned her before her marriage, stopped making music her god. After the turmoil of last minute shopping and preparations for the forthcoming term, the boys returned to school, the evenings drew in and she and Alasdair settled down once again into the comfortable affectionate silence and regular routine which had characterised their marriage since they moved to London.

And each silently watched the other and tried to convince themselves that there had been no upheaval, no crisis in their marriage, they had been mistaken and everything was as it had always been.

28

The Telephone Call

'There's a letter from Josh,' Alasdair said as he put a tray on the bedside table and walked across to the window to draw the curtains.

Laura turned over lazily then slowly drew herself up, still half asleep.

'Josh?' she queried vaguely.

Alasdair sat down on the bed beside her and began to pour the tea.

'Yes, Josh,' he grinned handing her a cup. 'You know, that pianist chap who haunted the place till he went off on tour last July.'

'You sound as if you don't like him,' Laura yawned.

Alasdair laughed as he slit open the envelope.

'You know I like him very much,' he answered. 'I just said that to startle you into waking up.'

Laura sipped her tea but did not reply.

'He's coming back to London next Saturday,' Alasdair went on, his eyes scanning the letter. 'Will let us know the time of his plane later.'

He put the letter down and picked up his cup.

'I told him before he left we'd meet him and give him a bed till he leaves for Canada,' Alasdair remarked. 'It'll be nice to see him again, won't it?'

Laura nodded.

Ever since their return from Ardnakil she had wondered just how she would react, what her feelings would be when she heard of Josh's return. She was

surprised at how little the news of his imminent arrival
seemed to affect her. She smiled to herself, convinced
that she now had her emotions under control, had
compartmented them into a little Pandora's box and
firmly shut the lid, only to be opened much later when
all danger was past and she felt like a whiff of nostalgia.
When, perhaps, like Flora, she would reminisce with
her daughter-in-law.

Alasdair looked down at her with his crooked smile.

'What are you grinning to yourself about?' he teased.

She smiled up at him, but did not reply.

'You still seem to be half asleep,' he went on, bending
down to kiss the tip of her nose. 'Why don't you turn
over and have another snooze? I can manage my own
breakfast.'

'No, I'm getting up.'

Laura turned on her elbow and looked out of the
window.

'It looks like another beautiful day.'

'That's what the weather man predicted last night,'
Alasdair replied, getting up from the side of the bed and
walking towards the bathroom. 'The boys are coming
home this weekend aren't they?' he enquired over his
shoulder as he disappeared inside. 'They'll be pleased
to see Josh, too.'

Hearing the splash of the shower Laura picked up the
letter and ran her eyes over it: but there was still no
reaction, no overpowering surge of emotion, no tangled
feelings hammering inside her for release. She laid it
on the tray and smiled to herself once again.

'It was only imagination, after all,' she murmured.

'What did you say?' Alasdair enquired, coming to the
bathroom door, his face covered in lather.

'Nothing,' she replied and on a sudden impulse
added: 'Would you like to take me out to lunch
today?'

'Sorry, darling,' Alasdair grimaced. 'Old Johnstone's

still around. I have to dance attendance on him, I'm afraid.'

'Never mind,' Laura smiled. 'I'll ring Edwina and see if she's free.'

'If not, try Polly,' Alasdair cut in.

'Yes I just might,' Laura mused. 'It'd be nice for her to get away from the children for a few hours. I believe her new au pair's very good, so there shouldn't be a problem.'

She threw back the bedclothes and pulling on her dressing gown went to draw the curtains on the landing outside the bedroom door. As she did so, the sun streamed in through the tall oblong window, casting pools of golden light onto the old polished parquet. Laura stood looking thoughtfully down upon the quiet square below and, suddenly, a feeling of intense happiness coursed through her. Having wondered what she would feel knowing of Josh's return and now having faced the situation without any undue emotion – in fact, without any emotion at all – she suddenly felt free and light hearted as if the last barrier had been torn down.

Singing under her breath she entered the small kitchen giving onto the tiny garden filled with her potted plants. As she reached for the kettle some words which she had once heard and long since forgotten floated into her head: 'God's in His heaven, all's right with the world'. Laura leant, relaxed, against the sink, idly watching the water tinkle into the kettle. She felt she had come full circle: she had run the gamut of her emotions and had survived. The last hurdle had been jumped, and all was truly right with her world.

* * *

'Give my love to Edwina,' Alasdair said as she accompanied him to the front door, 'or Polly, as the case may be.'

He laughed and, planting a hasty kiss on her cheek ran lightly down the steps and out into the sunlit square.

Edwina had already left by the time Laura telephoned but Polly was at home and delighted by the suggestion that they meet. Over lunch Laura and her niece exchanged family news. Polly's father was strangely enough now also at the Embassy in Washington and he and Philippa often met up with Deirdre and Ninian.

'It's odd, isn't it,' Laura remarked, when Polly told her how much her mother was enjoying this posting, 'how the two families have linked up.'

And, suddenly, she once again remembered Flora's words: 'I knew that God had a pattern for my life . . .'

'Do you think, Polly,' Laura said pensively, 'that it's all by chance – life, I mean – or could there be some divine hand guiding it all?'

Polly crumbled a roll thoughtfully.

'I don't know,' she replied. 'I must say I sometimes wonder. Why do you ask?'

'Oh, just the way things work out,' Laura said vaguely. 'Ninian could have been sent anywhere in the world, but he went to Washington where your parents are. It's almost weird, as if some unknown hand were guiding our lives.'

Polly didn't reply.

'As one gets older, one does see a kind of pattern,' Laura went on. 'My mother-in-law firmly believes in a God who has our lives in his hands and guides and directs them.'

Polly stopped crumbling and looked up.

'Your mother-in-law is a very special person,' she said quietly. 'I noticed it all those years ago when Daisy and I were bridesmaids at your wedding, and how old was I then? Twelve? Not more. She's got something about her, I can't quite pin-point what.'

'An aura?' Laura suggested.

'Perhaps,' Polly mused. 'Yes, I think that's what it is. She has an aura. She's somehow different from the rest of us.'

Laura nodded, and realised that both she and Polly had been avoiding mentioning Daisy's name. But when it came up, almost by chance, it seemed that the floodgates opened and they both plunged in, helpless and yet desperate to find an answer, a reason for her totally uncharacteristic, inexplicable behaviour.

There was a slight, breathless pause as if each one was waiting for the other to take the lead and brave the taboo subject.

'Pity that aura didn't fall on Daisy,' Laura remarked drily at last.

She looked across at Polly whose eyes had suddenly filled with tears.

'Whatever got *into* her?' she continued, 'abandoning her husband and child like that? She and Rupert seemed so happy.'

'They were,' Polly said miserably, 'until that ghastly man came on the scene.'

Laura shook her head in bewilderment.

'DAISY, of all people. She was always the shy, retiring one.'

She smiled mischievously at her niece.

'Now, had it been you . . .'

'In a way I feel responsible,' Polly said miserably.

'Older sister syndrome?'

'Perhaps. I was always very protective of Daisy; then when Mark and I became engaged she seemed lost.'

'But didn't Daisy meet Rupert through Mark?'

'Yes, at our wedding, don't you remember? Rupert

was Mark's best man. He and Daisy fell madly in love the moment they set eyes on each other and were married four months later. It SEEMED to be a marriage made in heaven.'

Polly sighed.

'But for Rupert it turned out to be just the opposite. And poor little Clarissa . . . she misses her mother so much.'

'I can imagine,' Laura murmured.

'I do what I can,' Polly continued, 'but Clarissa's so shy and sensitive, just like Daisy was as a child, and my boys are so boisterous and noisy they terrify her.'

Laura smiled and Polly looked at her aunt thoughtfully.

'Daisy should have been your daughter,' she remarked. 'Mother always said she was more like you than anyone else: even to enjoying piano practice!'

For a brief moment Laura was shaken. The comparison was frightening.

'How has your mother taken it?' she said, changing the subject.

'Not very well,' Polly grimaced. 'She was absolutely furious once she'd recovered from the shock.'

'I've hardly seen her since Daisy left,' Laura continued. 'Hugo was sent to Washington shortly afterwards.'

Polly cast her eyes to the ceiling.

'That's another thing,' she spluttered. 'The gutter press over there found out that Daisy was living it up with the ghastly man in his penthouse in New York and trumpeted it on every front page the minute Daddy arrived, I'm not sure the Foreign Office saw the joke.'

Laura's eyes widened.

'Oh, they had the grace to move,' Polly went on. Left New York and went to the Bahamas where he has a house. Now, as far as we can gather from the odd post-card, which is all the news we get, they're sailing on his yacht round the Greek islands.'

'But what's going to happen?' Laura enquired.

'I think Rupert will divorce her,' Polly shrugged, 'that's what she wants and there doesn't seem to be any other solution. At first he thought she'd come back, we all did, but it's been almost two years now . . . and she's apparently anxious to become the fourth Mrs. Whatever-his-name-is, something opolopolous.

Polly made a face.

'Imagine giving up a nice uncomplicated name like Haigh for that handle.'

'Poor Rupert,' Laura murmured.

'And poor Clarissa,' Polly broke in angrily. 'How could Daisy do that to her only child . . .'

She looked helplessly at Laura and groaned.

'Whatever does she see in that dreadful man? He's old enough to be her father?'

And added bitterly.

'But rich as Croesus.'

For a moment they avoided each other's eyes and stared uncomprehendingly at the white tablecloth, each immersed in her own thoughts.

'I never thought Daisy was all that interested in money,' Laura said quietly at last.

'She wasn't . . . until he started dripping diamonds all over her . . .'

Polly laughed shortly.

'Ironic thing is Rupert introduced them. I was having lunch with Daisy when he rang to say they had to have dinner with this shipping magnate. Daisy wasn't at all keen, but Rupert said he was a very important client and persuaded her to come. She went dragging her feet . . . but no doubt, looking stunning or the end result might have been different.'

She sighed.

'Poor Rupert. I bet he now wishes someone else had brokered the wretched man's yacht.'

Laura could think of nothing to say.

'Who's she like?' Polly went on. 'Have there been any other bolters in the family?'

'What do you mean?'

'Well,' Polly shrugged. 'Any other females in our ancestry who've behaved in this outrageous fashion.'

'Not that I know of.'

I suppose it sometimes skips a few generations, Polly mused. I don't remember grandmother, but she seemed to live a life of unsullied purity, and one can hardly call Aunt Edwina wanton . . . or Mother or Aunt Mary, for that matter.'

Laura smiled.

'That only leaves you,' Polly grinned. 'You COULD be another dark horse, and suddenly surprise us by bolting like Daisy did. But I shouldn't think so, you and Alasdair have a blissful marriage.'

She grimaced.

'But that's what we all thought about Rupert and Daisy.'

At Polly's words, Josh's face rose unbidden in front of Laura's eyes and, suddenly seeing the comparison, that awful fear overwhelmed her once again. She and Daisy, so very alike in every way . . .

But, at that moment, the waiter came to brush the crumbs from the cloth and, when he left, the momentary panic had subsided and Laura was able to return her niece's smile and deftly move the conversation round to other topics.

They said goodbye outside the restaurant without Daisy's or Flora's names being mentioned again, or even the subject they had been discussing, referred to.

Laura decided to do some shopping on the way home and set out to walk along the sunlit streets back to Sloane Square, her conversation with Polly momentarily put aside.

As she mounted the steps and turned her key in the lock, from inside the house the telephone started to ring. Dropping her parcels on the floor, she ran lightly across the hall and picked up the receiver, mechanically repeating the number.

'Hullo,' a man's voice with a North American lilt came down the line. Hearing it, her heart began to thunder in her chest. 'Hullo there, it's Josh.'

'Josh,' Laura answered breathlessly. 'Where are you?'

'I'm in Geneva,' he laughed and the line crackled. 'Just wanted to let you know my flight time like I promised.'

'Oh yes,' she replied briefly, 'of course.'

There was a slight pause.

'It IS OK, isn't it?' Josh's voice came anxiously down the now crystal clear line. 'I mean, if it's a bother for you to meet me . . .'

'Oh Josh, no,' she cut in, 'of course it's not a bother, we're all looking forward to seeing you again immensely. It's been so long.'

Her voice trailed away, and catching sight of her reflection in the gilt mirror on the opposite wall, Laura took a deep breath.

'Is it going to be tomorrow or Sunday?' she enquired.

'Tomorrow,' he answered. 'I'm leaving after lunch and should touch down at three thirty. I'll be on my own, the orchestra's staying on till Monday to sightsee but my rehearsals in Boston have been put forward a week: I've got to leave almost immediately.'

So it was to be hallo and goodbye. For a brief moment a feeling almost of relief surged through her only to be immediately replaced by a sudden bleakness, as if the whole world had suddenly been dyed a dark shade of grey. Since her return from Ardnakil, her life had fallen back into its tidy pattern and she had convinced herself that when Josh returned she would welcome him back as a fourth son. But, hearing his voice again and finally faced with the reality of his departure, all the old turmoil suddenly boiled up inside her as the dormant emotions churned through her body with even greater intensity than before, leaving her drowning in their flood. She felt as if loud crashing chords were being unremittingly struck on her like a death knoll. For a moment, her throat parched and dry, Laura did not reply.

'Hey, what's going on?' Josh called as the line once again crackled ominously. 'You've gone all weird on me.'

Laura tried to force a laugh through her tight lips. 'Nothing, it's just this bad line.'

'It's not only the line,' Josh insisted as the crackling ceased. 'Is something the matter?'

There was concern in his voice now, the laughter gone.

'No, nothing,' she answered dully. 'When do you have to leave?'

'Sunday morning, first thing.'

'I see.'

She bit her lip tightly to hide her emotion.

'So you'll be with us just for tomorrow night?'

''Fraid so,' Josh replied. 'Look, I have to dash, I've got a rehearsal for tonight's concert starting in five minutes. Sorry about that but I've been doing my nut trying to get hold of you since noon.'

'I've been out,' she answered mechanically.

'Don't I know it,' he said, the laughter once again back in his voice. 'And so does the hotel operator, I've just about driven her bananas trying to get in touch.'

'See you tomorrow, then, Josh, half past three,' she repeated tonelessly. 'We'll be there. The boys will be so pleased.'

Her voice sounded like an answering machine repeating a recorded message, coming out from the back of her throat in sharp staccato jerks. But Josh didn't appear to notice.

'Bye now,' she heard him say as she replaced the receiver, her dry throat incapable of uttering another word.

Sitting down heavily on the chair next to the telephone she looked up at the copper green sky which still held an after glow of summer, reflected in the tall oblong window on the half landing above her. As she stared vacantly through it a film seemed to pass over its surface, causing the sunlit patches on the parquet floor to vanish and dark shadows to flit across the hall.

The telephone jerked her back to consciousness as it began to ring again. Reaching out she picked up the receiver, once more mechanically repeating the number.

'Laura?'

Alasdair's voice came down the line.

For a moment no words came from her.

'Hallo . . . Laura?' he repeated, and stopped.

'Laura,' he went on after a brief pause, his anxiety echoing down the line. 'Are you all right?'

Laura slowly dragged her thoughts together as if awakening from a deep deep sleep.

'Alasdair, hallo. I'm sorry, my mind was on something else.'

And, as the words tumbled from her lips she realised that they were the very ones she had spoken to her husband on that May afternoon when he had telephoned not long after she had felt the shock waves vibrating through her body when Josh's hands had touched hers as he placed them gently on the keyboard.

'Darling,' he insisted, 'you sound so odd. Are you SURE you're all right?'

349

'Yes of COURSE,' she cut in testily, and immediately hated herself for her abruptness.

'I've been trying to get hold of you all afternoon . . .'

'You're not the only one, Josh has just rung from Geneva.'

'Oh?'

Laura compressed her lips into a tight line to hide her emotion.

'He's arriving tomorrow afternoon.'

'Oh GOOD,' Alasdair replied warmly. 'How long's he staying?'

'Only until Sunday morning, he has to start rehearsals in Boston earlier than expected.'

'Pity,' Alasdair went on. 'Still, the boys will see him.'

'Alasdair,' Laura cut in sharply. 'Did you ring for anything special? I've just come in, I'm surrounded by parcels and I'm longing for a cup of tea.'

'I'm afraid so, darling,' he said apologetically. 'Old Johnstone's not leaving this evening as I thought: he's decided to take Concorde back to New York in the morning and he wants us to join him for dinner.'

'Oh NO,' Laura groaned.

'Sorry about that, but he *is* my chairman, there's nothing much I can do about it.'

He paused.

'If you're too tired I'll make some excuse; but he does have rather a soft spot for you and if you COULD make the effort . . .'

'It's all right,' she snapped. 'What time?'

'Early, mercifully. I'll be back at about half past six to change and we'll go straight off. Wear your black chiffon, you'll completely bowl him over.'

Laura sighed.

'Oh, it's one of those evenings, is it?'

Alasdair laughed.

'Well, you know how he loves dressing up. Must go, darling. Bless you for being so understanding.'

Laura slowly replaced the receiver. A deep jagged crack had suddenly gashed her world, splintering it and revealing a bottomless void beneath. She felt suffocated by her own overwhelming emotions, fighting desperately to escape, yet hemmed in on every side. She seemed to be once again on the platform of that great northern railway station, a station which was so full of memories. As she sat alone in that empty echoing vault watching the black smoke rise and merge with the dirty mosaic of the ceiling, the rails streaking in every direction began to swim before her eyes; and she knew that this time she could not see where those rails were leading, or what the end of the journey had in store.

Glancing down she saw that her knuckles were white, her taut hands still gripping the edge of the dark oak table onto which a bunch of sulphur-coloured roses, drooping in their pewter jug, had moulted soft velvet petals, leaving a lingering scent of summer in the dim, quiet hall.

Releasing her hands Laura slowly picked up the petals one by one and sat gazing at their delicate dying beauty as they lay in her upturned palm. And as she sat there a butterfly wafted silently in through the half open window, shimmered momentarily above the fragile petals then fluttered languorously away in a flash of blue and gold and scarlet.

From the church in the square a tumbling peal of bells suddenly rang out, crashing, bouncing, echoing round and round the silent hall. Laura pressed her face into the fading petals, slowly inhaling their sweet elusive scent, breathing deeply in rhythm with the distant chimes. But, suddenly, the pealing ceased, to be abruptly followed by a solitary melancholy clang, like the slow beat of a dying heart.

She closed her eyes and longed to open them to a world where life was ordinary and orderly again. But when she did so Josh's face rose up before her and she laid her head on the table with an agonised groan. The momentary peace induced by the bell's hypnotic clang evaporated. As the agonised cry escaped from her lips the drawing room door was pushed slowly open and her sons' ageing Yorkshire terrier padded across the hall and settled himself on her feet. Laura reached down blindly, and picking him up in her arms, she nestled her face in his soft, warm coat, tears which up till then had been choking somewhere deep down inside spilling over onto its silky strands.

'Puddle,' she murmured, 'oh Puddle!'

His kennel name was Ulysses but her sons had discarded it soon after the puppy's arrival when they discovered his total incomprehension and refusal to comply with the most elementary house-training. And although this misunderstanding had long since been cleared up, Puddle he had remained.

The dog now stirred and growled, then settled contentedly down in Laura's arms, gently licking the tears from her cheeks. She hugged him closer, feeling security in the warmth and familiarity of his furry body, a feeling she knew would fade as soon as she turned to face the evening, the weekend and all the bottled up emotions which, at that moment, were threatening to choke her.

The telephone rang again.

'Mum?' Andrew's voice, telephoning from school, came down the line.

'Hallo, darling,' she replied automatically.

'What's happening tomorrow? Are you picking us up or shall we make our own way home?'

'Can you make your own way?' she answered. 'Josh has just telephoned, he's arriving at half-past three and we've promised to be at the airport to meet him.'

'JOSH!' Andrew exclaimed. 'Super.'

'I thought you'd be pleased,' Laura answered dully.

'You BET.'

Andrew paused.

'But can't we come to the airport with you?'

'Not really, darling. If we picked you up on the way we'd be late. Better just take the tube and be here waiting for him when we get back. With luck, we should be home before five.'

'OK,' answered the easy-going Andrew. 'Bye, Mum.'

How like his father he is, Laura thought, so uncomplicated, never any fuss. It was just the kind of reaction Alasdair would have had. She was glad it was Andrew telephoning and not Jamie. Her youngest son would have argued and wheedled and she'd have ended by giving in to him in desperation, with the result that they would have arrived late at the airport and everyone would have been in a bad temper.

'Goodbye, darling,' she said softly and, putting the receiver back, felt a hot tear fall on her wrist.

She brushed a hand impatiently across her eyes and straightened up.

'This is RIDICULOUS,' she said out loud. 'You're going to pieces, ruining everything. And for what? A young man, no, a boy, who is hardly older than your own sons.'

The grandfather clock in the hall struck six.

'You have EVERYTHING,' she went on angrily, still talking to herself as she turned heavily towards the stairs. 'A loving husband, three teenage sons, a home, friends, security . . . And you're nearer forty than thirty!'

Laura suddenly stood still, one hand on the banister.

'Yes, THAT'S it,' she murmured. 'I'll soon be forty.'

She took a deep breath.

She was being ridiculous, behaving like an infatuated,

hysterical schoolgirl. Tomorrow she and Alasdair would meet Josh and welcome him as a fourth son coming home for the weekend. That was how it had been in the beginning and that is how it would remain. After tomorrow she might never see him again.

But as that thought struck her all her careful reasoning suddenly collapsed. Laura clung to the banister for support, knowing that whatever it was she felt for Josh it was certainly not the love she felt for her sons. His voice had stirred up all the buried emotions which his letter had failed to revive: emotions she had convinced herself were all in her mind.

She reached the top of the stairs just as Alasdair's key was inserted in the lock. Crossing into their bedroom, she heard him call her name, but she didn't answer; she couldn't, her heart was too full of suppressed emotion as a feeling of guilt and shame invaded her. How could she ever look him in the face again: Alasdair who was so straight and transparently honest, who had been by her side, loving her, encouraging her, supporting her for almost twenty years.

His footsteps crossed the hall and disappeared into the drawing room. She was suddenly pleased that they were going out this evening, that she didn't have to face him, just the two of them across the table from each other. She knew that if she did she would be unable to pretend, all her anguish and humiliation would rush to the surface and come pouring out; and she couldn't bear the pain she knew she would see in her husband's eyes.

Lying on their bed gazing out over London's rooftops at the darkening heliotrope sky which was beginning to cast its cloak of twilight over the pale pink walls, she tried to shut the memory of Josh from her mind. But she was unable to: his face kept rising up and blotting out everything else. Laura remembered their first meeting on that blustery February day and she couldn't understand how it had happened. She wondered whether Josh was also aware of that change in their relationship, and as this thought struck her she clapped her hand to her mouth to stifle a cry of fear. Hearing Alasdair's step on the stairs, she took a deep breath and called out to him.

'I'm here, Alasdair. Just lying down, but I'll be up and ready soon. Run me a bath, will you, when you've had yours?'

He opened the door of their room, and coming over to her side, sat down on the bed.

'You look whacked,' he said gently, taking her hand in his.

She saw the concern in his hazel eyes, the green and gold fires which usually danced in them almost extinguished in the half light. Over her husband's shoulder she saw the oval photograph in the silver frame standing with the others on her dressing table. Daisy on her wedding day. And, once again, she was struck by the incredible likeness between them. It was true what Polly said, what her sister Philippa had always said, that Daisy was more like Laura than anyone else. Suddenly, as if superimposed on the oval frame another picture appeared, Daisy as she now was, sailing round the Greek islands with her elderly millionaire lover, her wedding vows and all thoughts of her husband and child swept from her mind. And Polly's words: 'Are there any other bolters in the family?' rang clearly in her ears.

She stifled a cry and clung to Alasdair, afraid of herself, her reactions, her heredity: afraid of this strangling emotion which she thought had drifted away with the summer clouds but had now returned to stifle her. And with a rush of suppressed feelings she knew that she was afraid, too, of the future and of that uncanny resemblance between herself and Daisy, that shy, gentle, sensitive niece who had seemingly unaccountably switched personalities, changed so dramatically and abandoned everything which, until then, had been so important in her life. And she wondered just how much any human being was ever really in control of her life, her emotions. And how much heredity and destiny played a part in the overall pattern of each individual life.

Her husband sensed her tension but mistook its source, thinking it lay in the anticipated boredom of this unexpected evening out.

'Sorry about tonight,' he said gently, squeezing her hand, 'but it needn't be late.'

He bent to kiss her forehead, stroking her hair back as he did so. Then, releasing her hand, he got up and stood looking tenderly down at her.

'Stay there quietly for a few more minutes,' he said softly. 'I'll call you when your bath's ready.'

Alasdair closed the door noiselessly behind him and, as Laura heard water splutter and gush into the bath, she buried her face in the soft flowered pillow and wept.

On the Edge of the Precipice

While she and Alasdair waited in the warm autumn sunshine for the plane to land, a light breeze caught the folds of Laura's soft silk dress, causing it to billow about her legs like gentle waves stirred by a deep blue sea. She looked up at Alasdair standing by her side, his large angular frame propped casually against the balustrade of the small airport.

'Just half past three,' he said, squinting at his watch. 'It looks as if Josh will arrive on time.'

The syrupy tones of the airport official coming over the tannoy announcing the arrival of the flight from Geneva mingled with the rattle of trolleys as they both leant forward, shading their eyes to watch the light aircraft bump down.

The plane door opened and a hostess appeared at the top of the steps followed closely by a stream of passengers, the last of whom was Josh.

Laura pressed her lips tightly together, seeing his lean figure walk down the steps and stride out across the tarmac. She looked up at Alasdair, her blue eyes scanning him anxiously. He caught her glance and smiled.

'Well, he's arrived,' he said, straightening up and taking his wife's arm. 'It'll be nice to see him again, won't it?'

Laura didn't reply but she was grateful for the security of Alasdair's arm against her side as he steered her through the waiting crowd to the reception area. Dear, kind, reliable Alasdair. Her life with him was so organised, so safe, so settled. Or it had been. Yet at that moment their years together seemed to have slipped away forgotten, and she felt like a young girl, an agonisingly young girl, in love for the first time.

Angrily Laura shook her thoughts back to the present, telling herself that she was almost thirty-seven years old and Josh barely twenty-two, hardly older than her own sons. And then she saw him standing there, his eyes wandering over the crowd, and she knew that it didn't matter.

Alasdair gripped the young man's hand in both of his and then Josh turned and caught Laura to him in an affectionate hug. She held her breath and allowed her cheek to be kissed.

'The boys are waiting for you at home,' Alasdair said as they made their way to the car park. 'How did the tour go?'

'Pretty well, I think,' Josh replied. 'Did you see the notices?'

'We certainly did,' Alasdair enthused. 'Couldn't have been more proud if you'd been my own son. Laura's kept all the cuttings.'

'Thanks, Mom,' Josh said, turning to her with a smile.

The word made her wince.

She was very quiet on the drive home through the autumn-tinted countryside. The afternoon sky was like a faded rose and in the orchards bordering the roads the trees were hanging low with rosy apples. The smell of burning leaves drifted on the still, scented air. Normally, Laura would have enjoyed the peace and the beauty of the changing scenery, but today her mind was restless.

The car slid to a standstill in front of the tall, terraced house as Big Ben struck the half hour.

'Hi chaps, he's here,' Charles called, turning his key in the lock and pushing open the front door.

Three pairs of eager feet thundered down the uncarpeted stairs like a landslide, and shot through the door.

'Josh – hi!' yelled Jamie, poking his face through the car window, as Josh collected his things together.

Josh laughed and pulled Jamie's tousled red hair, affectionately pushing him out of the way as Andrew yanked open the door.

But Iain elbowed his brothers aside.

'Good to see you, Josh,' he said warmly. 'How did it go? We read all the notices and Mum's kept the cuttings for you.'

'Good old Mom,' laughed Josh as he relinquished himself into their hands.

And again Laura winced.

Alasdair slipped his arm through hers and glanced down at her. He thought he had never seen her looking more beautiful. Her pale gold hair fell softly round her face, her eyes were moist and shining, their deep blue reflected in the simple woollen coat which clung attractively to her small, slim figure.

'No-one would think you were the mother of that lot,' he said affectionately, squeezing her arm against his side. He wanted to tell her how beautiful she was, even more beautiful than on that summer evening when he had fallen in love with her all those years ago. But there was now this barrier between them and whenever he tried to put his feelings into words, somehow they stuck in his throat and refused to come.

'More like their big sister,' he ended lamely, releasing her arm as they entered the house.

Laura smiled at him dropping her coat and bag onto a hall chair.

'Let Josh breathe,' she called to the boys. 'He'd probably like to have a shower after the journey.'

But the only reply was a burst of laughter from Iain's room.

'I'm going to see about dinner,' she said to Alasdair. 'We're later than we thought and they're all sure to be ravenous.'

She fled to the kitchen, wrapping her thoughts and her body in a large practical apron, and, for the first time since her marriage, was pleased they only had sons. In spite of Cristobel's parting shot when they said goodbye only a few weeks before, she knew that it would have been harder to hide her feelings from a daughter than from the boys. A teenage girl would probably have been in the kitchen with her and noticed the savage way she was pummelling the pastry into submission.

And for the hundredth time that day she asked herself the same question.

How had it happened?

As her hands went through the motions of washing a lettuce, Laura gazed out of the kitchen window at the sun setting over London's rooftops, remembering, until the down-to-earth smell of hot pastry rose from the oven, drawing her thoughts back to the present. The sun had finally disappeared and the rooftops were now in shadow silhouetted against a sky which was gradually changing to deep purple.

'Evenings are drawing in,' she murmured to herself as she bent to take the blackberry tart, Josh's favourite, out of the oven. 'It'll soon be quite dark.'

She put the tart down and crossed to the window to pull the blue checked curtains against the approaching night.

'Like the future without Josh,' she heard herself say, and she stood there, the thin curtain gripped tightly in her hand.

Jamie stuck his head round the kitchen door.

'Mum,' he teased, coming up behind her and grabbing her round the waist. 'You're dreaming again.'

Laura dragged her thoughts back to the present.

'When's dinner?' her son enquired. 'We're all STARVING!'

Laura smiled at him affectionately. They're all leaving me far behind, she thought, these tall sons of mine, and she took a deep breath and pulled herself together.

'It's ready, darling,' she replied. 'Call the others.'

'I don't know what's the matter with you these days,' Jamie bumbled on. 'Must be middle age, you're always on the moon.'

Laura caught him smartly across the seat with a wooden spoon as he dodged out of the kitchen.

'Idiot,' she laughed, the former tension momentarily broken.

* * *

'What a pity it's such a brief stopover,' said Alasdair, settling comfortably into his armchair when dinner was over. 'I was hoping I could persuade you to take Laura to a concert or two.'

He leant forward and took the coffee cup which Laura was holding out to him.

'I wouldn't have needed any persuading,' Josh smiled. 'But I start rehearsals in Boston the day after tomorrow.'

'You forget he's famous now, Dad,' Iain put in. 'You can't boss him around any more.'

Josh lay back in the deep chintz-covered armchair and laughed.

'"Famous" is a big word,' he replied. 'But these months in London have certainly opened the door to engagements and, of course, the tour was a wonderful bonus.'

'But now you're deserting us for the New World,' Alasdair teased, looking across at Josh with a twinkle in his eye as he filled his pipe and sucked gently, holding a lighted match to the bowl.

'Not DESERTING,' Josh reproached, 'going home.'

He bent forward and placed his empty cup on the polished walnut table in front of him.

'It'll be great to be on the same continent as my folks again,' he said thoughtfully, 'but I'm going to miss you all a whole lot and I hope that one day I'll be able to come back. It's been a fantastic experience.'

The words sank slowly into Laura's brain.

A one night stopover and then everything would return to normal . . . or would it?

She looked up and saw her husband's eyes upon her. He leaned across and took her hand.

'You're very quiet darling,' he said gently. 'Is anything wrong?'

She avoided his eyes.

'Difficult to get a word in edgeways,' she replied tightly, stretching for the tray. 'More coffee, anyone?'

'Yes, please,' Josh smiled. 'Poor old Mom, we're all talking at such a rate she's got left out in the cold.'

There it was again: that word.

And a few months earlier when he had said it for the first time, calling her his 'English Mom', she had been so touched.

'Are you very tired, Josh?' Alasdair asked, drawing contentedly on his pipe. 'If not, I'm sure Laura would love you to play something. Perhaps one of the solos we read about which were such a success on the tour. It might be a long time before she has another chance to hear you.'

His words pierced Laura's heart.

She didn't want to remember those sensitive hands

on her keyboard, hands she had so often watched and now longed only to touch, to feel enclosing her in a warm, physical embrace. But Josh had already crossed to the piano and was sitting on the long, tapestry-covered stool, his fingers wandering caressingly over the keys.

'This isn't a tour piece,' he said quietly without looking up, his head bent low over the keyboard as his fingers continued to trip effortlessly up and down. 'But it's a piece of music which has come to mean a great deal to me in the past few months.'

He looked up and across at Laura but her eyes were closed as she lay back among the cushions and prepared to yield herself to the music, willing it to flow over her, to soothe her, cleanse her.

Alasdair had seen Josh's look, the intensity in his eyes, and he glanced across at his wife, then back to Josh. But the young man's head was turned away from him and, as he struck a few idle chords, Alasdair too leant back in his chair, his fingers tips pressed lightly together, his expression thoughtful.

A log sank into its bed of ashes with a whispering, lingering sigh, sending little plumes of smoke towards the chimney as Josh leant forward and slowly, hauntingly, the first poignant bars of 'Liebestraum' throbbed their melody throughout the now silent room.

Laura bit her lip to prevent the agonised cry which was struggling in her throat for release. Then, opening her eyes, she gazed at Josh's bent head, saw his straight dark hair falling and sweeping his forehead and steeled herself to relax, to be emptied of every emotion and simply to be submerged by the now cascading notes which rose and fell, pleading, sighing, caressing and finally dying with a last whisper, a quivering sigh.

Then, subtly, quietly, before any of them had had time to recover from the cascade of notes, to even emerge from the beauty of Josh's playing and return to earth, his fingers stroked the keyboard again, the rhythm changed and, smiling over towards her, Josh broke into 'Laura', singing the words softly to himself.

A surprised murmur went through the assembled family.

'Your tune Mum,' said Iain.

Jamie leapt up and began prancing round the chairs chanting:

'Josh's in love with Mum, Josh's in love with Mum . . .'

The music stopped abruptly as Josh's hands fell from the keys. He didn't look round as a sudden embarrassed hush fell on the room.

For a moment Laura's composure deserted her then, quickly getting to her feet, she began rattling coffee cups on to the tray.

'For goodness sake sit down Jamie,' she blurted out angrily, 'and stop talking such absolute rubbish!'

'Oh Mum,' Andrew broke in, 'can't you take a joke? It's time you and Dad did something different, got out of your rut before it's too late. You've been in love for nearly twenty years, it's hardly decent.'

'That's enough Andrew,' Alasdair said sharply, and at his tone even Jamie fell silent.

Rising in his turn, Alasdair took the tray from Laura's hands and followed her into the kitchen

'Are you sure you're all right, darling?' he asked anxiously as he set it down on the table. 'The boys can be very stupid, but they were only teasing, you know.'

'Of COURSE I'm all right,' she replied tightly, and hated herself for her brusqueness. Her voice sounded hard and metallic and she hardly recognised it as her's.

She tried to smile at Alasdair but her lips were taut and the smile was forced and unnatural.

'I think I'll go to bed,' she said lamely, passing a hand across her throbbing temples. 'I'm rather tired. Say goodnight to everyone for me.'

'You do that,' Alasdair said quietly, 'I'll see to everything down here.'

Josh was leaving before six the following morning to catch his plane and the chances were that she would not see him again. But Alasdair did not suggest that she went back to the drawing room to say goodbye. She started to climb the stairs, but suddenly stopped and caught her breath as a sharp pain like a knife turning in a deep fresh wound shot through her. Clinging to the banisters for support, she heard a loud peal of laughter coming from down below and was grateful that her outburst did not appear to have even ruffled the surface of her family's composure.

When Alasdair finally came to bed her eyes were closed.

He slipped in beside her but she didn't move and, for the first time for as long as she could remember, he didn't bend over and kiss her goodnight before turning out the light.

'Josh, Josh,' she seemed to be voicelessly crying into the darkness.

The house was silent but his music was everywhere, whirling round and round in her head. Why had he played that tune?

'He could almost be your son,' that inner voice kept insisting.

She knew he could. But it didn't matter.

Laura got out of bed: she was sure Alasdair was not asleep, but he didn't stir. Pulling on her dressing gown she went downstairs into the dark drawing room and sat at the piano, softly picking out the notes. Laura. The words rang in her ears.

Had he been trying to tell her something? He'd never played her tune before.

What had Jamie meant when he said Josh was in love with her?

Abruptly her hands dropped to her lap and she found that she was trembling. Was she losing her reason? How many times had she asked herself that question in the last few months? Once again her fingers picked out the notes and, in her mind, she heard him softly singing the words.

After a while she got up and went to the window. Pulling aside the heavy velvet curtains, she gazed out at the empty square: the houses opposite looked grey and lifeless, like empty shells, and the street lamps cast an eerie glow over the trees in the centre. In the distance she heard the low hum of a car driving down the King's Road and then Big Ben chimed and struck two.

Listlessly, Laura let the curtain drop into place and turned back into the room. The fire was dead in the grate and the room was cold: she shivered and, drawing her dressing gown more tightly round her, walked wearily towards the stairs.

As she put her foot on the first step a door opened and Josh came out onto the landing wearing only his pyjama trousers.

She caught her breath and stood motionless.

He paused as if listening. Had he heard her picking out the notes of her song which had so suddenly become their song? As if sensing her presence near him he stretched out his arms, groping for her in the darkness.

'Laura,' he whispered tensely. 'Laura, are you there?'

She remained motionless, her body suddenly limp and drained. At that moment the moon glided from behind a cloud, fleetingly outlining his hard young body, the dark matted hair on his chest, the strength in his bare arms, She pressed herself against the wall, her breast heaving, until the flash of silver passed beyond the uncurtained oblong window and darkness descended again.

'Laura,' he whispered urgently, 'I know you're there: I heard you playing . . . our song.'

Tears began to slowly creep down her cheeks as the words of the song danced through her head, 'But you're only a dream, only a dream, only a dream'. The last line thundered on and on like an old gramophone record caught in a groove, until she thought her head would burst.

'LAURA,' Josh pleaded.

He paused, and a note of anxiety crept into his voice.

'Laura, you're crying.'

The tears were now flowing freely down her face: but how could he know? And once again she felt his deep sensitivity and knew that that was what had drawn her to him in the first place.

'Laura,' he whispered again, almost inaudibly.

For one wild moment she almost ran up the few steep stairs and flung herself into his arms. She longed to bury her face in that hard young chest, and her body trembled uncontrollably, imagining the touch of those sensitive hands as his arms tightened round her. Her head reeled and she clung to the banister for support.

'You're there, Laura,' he said, coming to the top of the stairs. 'I can smell your perfume: all through the tour it kept coming back to me.'

Her eyes clung hungrily to his young body once again briefly silhouetted in the long window. As darkness enveloped them Josh felt for the banister and began to walk slowly down the stairs until he was standing just above her, but she flattened herself against the wall hardly daring to breathe, knowing that he knew she was there, almost within reach of his arms.

In the shadows he could just make out her slim body

standing below him. He reached out as if to take her in his arms but she drew away and, for a moment they remained transfixed, staring at each other as the sailing moon once again fleetingly lit up the stairs.

'I love you, Laura,' he whispered. 'I don't think I realised it until this evening . . . but I love you.'

For a few tense seconds there was an electric silence between them. Every fibre of her being was throbbing and crying out for him; never before had such strong waves of emotion raged through her slim body; never had she felt this craving, this burning desire to capitulate, to completely annihilate herself in another human being. Her head reeled and she held her breath not daring to move.

'I love you,' he repeated softly, silently pleading for some response from her.

A sharp agonised cry escaped her lips and she made a movement towards him but, as she did so, she heard Flora's voice in that peaceful sunlit room: 'It was just a precious dream which would have ended as a nightmare . . . What I did any woman, with God's help, can do'. And Laura drew back. Her mouth once more resumed the taut, fixed position it had assumed earlier that evening in the kitchen with Alasdair and, although she tried to speak, no words came. Then, suddenly, she heard a harsh, metallic sound rising from the back of her throat.

'Josh,' she said, her voice cold and brittle. 'Don't be so RIDICULOUS. You could almost be my son.'

Josh's arms which had been reaching for her in the dim half light fell abruptly to his sides. He gasped and staggered backwards as if struck in the face by a heavy blow.

'LAURA,' his voice came out as a strangled cry.

And, as the moon once again illuminated the dark staircase they stood facing each other, his face hurt and bewildered, his eyes pleading: hers set and cold.

The moon slid away and darkness enveloped them again. Josh groped blindly for the banister and dragged his bare feet back up the stairs

As he reached the top he turned and looked beseechingly in her direction, his firm young body begging for some response from her. But she remained lost and silent in the shadows.

'Laura,' he cried brokenly.

Then after a few moments he heaved himself onto the landing and crossed to his bedroom door. Laura watched mesmerised as he opened it and saw it close behind him. For a few seconds there was no movement and she knew he was standing there on the other side of that closed door waiting for her, willing her to join him. But she remained still at the bottom of the stairs. She heard the gentle creak as he at last got back into bed and as life began to throb back into her aching body she had to cling tightly to the banister to prevent herself following him into the room; and she imagined the second creak as she crept in beside him.

A dull moan rose from her throat and she sank onto the stairs, burying her face in her hands as once again she heard the tune, their tune, going round and round in her head.

Would there ever again be a waking moment when Josh would not fill her thoughts? He had come into her life as unobtrusively as a pebble which, tossed into the water, drops to the bottom of the pool. And, like the pebble, he had remained there, sending out ripples in every direction.

Laura slowly raised her head and saw the doors behind which her sons were peacefully sleeping. She knew that, at the other end of the landing Alasdair, her husband, the man she had loved for almost twenty years, the man she still loved, was lying in their bed, perhaps sleepless, waiting for her. And once again words which Flora had spoken came back to her: 'Just call on Him . . .'

With a heartbroken sob Laura lifted her face and, like a wounded fawn, cried out to this unseen God to help her.

As she did so the dark staircase was suddenly flooded with light, as if a round, smiling harvest moon, so unlike the pale silver slither which had been gliding in and out of the clouds, filled the oblong window at the top of the stairs. It swept slowly across the aperture then disappeared, leaving behind an indigo sky speckled with glittering stars through which a silver radiance intermittently flashed. And as she gazed upwards into the vast velvet immensity, the heart-rending sob died in her throat. Something snapped and then melted inside her and a great surge of warmth coursed through her whole body. She felt as if she were bathed in a gentle, caressing, enfolding love, her body weightless and transparent, floating effortlessly through an immense aura of light, and as she yielded to this gentle caress, a wonderful feeling of peace and joy filled her, the tension inside her snapped, and her anguish slowly faded away.

At that moment she knew that her destiny and Daisy's were not inevitably intertwined; that she was not the slave of heredity nor of her turbulent emotions, being led blindly along a path down which she was loathe to go. She had surrendered herself to a supreme being, a God she had paid lip service to all her life but until this moment had never really believed in. She knew he would now take charge of her destiny and guide her through it into safe waters. The burden had been lifted from her shoulders, and she was no longer standing alone in the path of a roaring angry wave.

As this realisation sank into her tired mind everything suddenly became transparently clear and she sank gratefully onto the cold hard staircase, drained but at peace.

In the distance Big Ben chimed and slowly struck three.

A door opened quietly and Alasdair came and sat on the stair beside her, gathering her shaking body into his arms. Laura looked up and saw the concern, the love and the hurt in his eyes. He held her close and she clung to him as he gently lifted her to her feet and led her back to bed.

'Alasdair,' she whispered hoarsely.

'It's late, darling,' he said tenderly, drawing the blankets closely round her shoulders and climbing in beside her.

'But Alasdair,' she pleaded.

He gently took her in his arms.

'I have to be up in a couple of hours to take Josh to the airport,' he said softly, holding her close. 'Let's try to get some sleep.'

A strangled sob escaped from her throat.

'Oh ALASDAIR,' she cried brokenly.

She seemed to be slowly awakening as if from a frightening dream, and in her bewilderment she clung to him. He stroked her soft hair and held her tightly as her body shook with sobs.

'Don't say any more, my darling,' he murmured. 'Don't try to explain.'

He kissed her wet face and his arms closed fiercely, protectively round her.

He gazed tenderly down at her closed eyelids as her weeping gradually subsided, leaving her trembling body soft and limp and relaxed in his arms.

Alasdair's eyes were full of love mingled with pain. He knew that the evening had been cathartic, that something had broken in both of them. He also knew that the pain would pass and he desperately hoped that the love would remain, a love which was deeper because of the pain.

Putting up his hand he gently stroked her shining

golden hair. Her breathing had become low and regular and the lovely oval face on the pillow beside him was the face of the young girl who had entwined herself round his heart in the ballroom at Ardnakil all those years ago. And, as Alasdair gazed down at his wife, he knew that he would now be able to tell her just how much she meant to him: the words would no longer stick in his throat and refuse to come.

He bent and kissed her closed eyelids.

'You've been a long way away, Laura darling,' he whispered. 'But ... thank you for coming back to me.'

As Big Ben chimed in the still night air and slowly struck five, Alasdair gently released her sleeping form and, with a sigh, understanding now how very nearly he had lost her, he silenced the alarm clock and slipped out of bed.

30

Out of the Tunnel

Just as the tumbling peal of bells had broken in upon her reverie two days before, out of the mist of a dream they broke once again upon Laura's subconscious. Sleep was enveloping her like a grey flannel cloak as she struggled to grope her way though it, out of the phantom shadows of the night to where real life was waiting to emerge.

But, as her consciousness surfaced, memories began flooding through her mind like a turbulent stream and, only half remembering, she shivered and turned away, a part of her refusing to face the day, longing only to awaken to a world in which the past would have no place, where all regret and remorse had been obliterated.

The pealing suddenly stopped and the clang of one solitary bell took its place. With its steady, insistent boom the shadows of the night were finally swept away and the real world slowly surfaced. Half opening her eyes, beyond the shimmer of gold in the slanting beams that streamed in through the window opposite her bed, Laura saw Alasdair sitting in the deep armchair under the window, watching her.

He smiled. And as he did so, she remembered.

'Ready for a cup of tea?' he enquired, getting up and going over to a small table where a tray was laid.

Laura watched him drowsily as he poured out a cup and brought it over to her.

'What's the time?' she asked sleepily.

'Almost ten o'clock,' he replied, sitting down on the edge of the bed.

'Ten O'CLOCK?' she gasped, sitting bolt upright. 'But . . .'

Alasdair smiled and gently pushed her back against the pillows.

'It's all right,' he soothed. 'Everything's under control. You were sleeping peacefully, so I saw no reason to wake you.'

'But what about breakfast, the boys? And aren't you going to play golf?'

'Not today,' he answered quietly.

'But you ALWAYS play golf on Sunday morning.'

'Sometimes,' he replied, 'it's a good idea not to always do the same thing. And the boys have had breakfast and gone.'

'Gone?' she gasped. 'Gone where?'

'I suggested they went to Hurlingham for the day and they whooped at the idea. They'll be having lunch there and I said we might or might not join them.'

'I see,' Laura said, sinking back onto the pillows and slowly sipping her tea.

'Would you like to join them?' Alasdair asked gently. 'Or, perhaps we could have lunch somewhere quietly by ourselves.'

Laura didn't reply. Her world seemed to be whirling round her at an incredible speed, and she wasn't sure just where it would land.

'I thought I might go along to church with you,' Alasdair ended diffidently.

Laura had taken to accompanying Flora to church on Sunday mornings when they were in Scotland and, since their return, she had continued the habit.

'But Alasdair,' she gasped weakly. 'You NEVER go to church.'

Alasdair held out his hand for her cup, then walked across to the tray and refilled it.

'There's a lot of things I've never done before,' he said tightly. 'Or not done for a long time. But that doesn't mean that I shouldn't have done them or that I was right not to.'

He handed the cup back to her and she looked at him. His eyes softened and he bent towards her.

'One of the things I haven't done for a long time is tell you how much I love you,' he murmured.

Laura looked away from him, feeling the hot sting of tears rising in her throat.

Alasdair took the cup from her hand and cradled them in both of his.

'Do you remember when we became engaged I told you your eyes were like forget-me-nots?' he continued.

She nodded, willing the tears to stem their threatened flow.

'Well, they aren't any longer. They're deeper and far more beautiful, like two precious sapphires.'

Laura bit her lip.

'You've never said that before,' she whispered.

Her husband sighed and, releasing her hands, got up and walked over to the window.

'No,' he said slowly, gazing down into the tiny garden below. 'But I've thought it many times.'

He turned abruptly and she could see the tension in his face: his lips were drawn tightly together and a muscle was twitching in his cheek.

'Laura, you're the most beautiful woman I know, I've ever known. But somehow in the last few years I've been unable to tell you so.'

His wife said nothing, just sat smoothing a fold of the sheet.

'Perhaps now it's too late?' he asked hoarsely, that muscle still working agitatedly.

With a shock Laura realised what his words meant:

that he had known all along or certainly last evening about her feelings for Josh. And, suddenly, the leaden fear which had been dragging at her for the past two months, the deception which was so alien, the ache and humiliation rose before her in a great ugly wave so that she almost cried out in fear. Then, just as once before Alasdair's face had risen before her and been blotted out by Josh's lean features, so now Josh's face hovered fleetingly in front of her eyes, then slowly receded, taking with it that terrifying ugly wave which had threaten to submerge her.

In the ensuing few seconds when she lay helpless, suspended between reality and unreality, lost in a world of shadows from which she was not sure she knew the avenue of escape, it was as if veil after veil of diaphanous gauze was slowly lifted from before her eyes. And, as each one floated out of sight, a warm golden haze came dancing through until all that was left was the soft apricot light of a glorious summer's day out of which her husband's face rose, smiling his crooked, quizzical smile.

She raised her eyes.

Alasdair was looking at her. She could see the green and gold lights, not dancing lights but like consuming fires in his hazel eyes: she could see the pain and the unanswered question in them.

'Is it Laura?' he asked bleakly.

As he spoke, the memory of that flash of moonlight on the stairs and the warmth and peace which had followed in its wake suddenly flooded back into Laura's mind, and she sat up and held out her arms to him.

'Alasdair,' she cried in a voice which was more like a sob.

He came slowly towards her and took her in his arms, pressing his face into her soft silky hair, murmuring endearments.

'Oh Alasdair,' she cried again and again and, in sudden relief, she began to laugh.

He held her tightly, not sure at first whether it was a laugh or a sob.

'It's so long since I heard you laugh,' he said at last, holding her away from him and looking tenderly at her, watching the tears which had mingled with the laughter and were now meandering in little rivulets down her cheeks.

He reached into his pocket and taking out a handkerchief gently wiped them away.

'You've been in another world,' he said almost inaudibly.

It was so close to the truth, Laura felt that he had looked straight into her heart. She drew away from him and took his hand.

'Alasdair,' she whispered brokenly.

And as she did so the telephone rang shrilly at her side.

They looked at each other and neither moved to answer it.

'Let it ring,' Alasdair said tightly.

'It could be the boys,' Laura pleaded and, leaning over, she picked up the receiver.

Lindsay's triumphant voice came down the line.

'A fourth daughter,' he announced. 'Half an hour ago.'

'Oh Lindsay, how WONDERFUL,' Laura breathed. 'And Cristobel?'

'Right as rain,' he laughed. 'Sitting up in bed eating a huge breakfast. Can't stop, must go on doing the rounds. We're calling her Fenella.'

'Cristobel?' Alasdair enquired as Laura put the telephone down.

Laura nodded.

'A little girl,' she answered dreamily. 'Fenella.'

Alasdair smiled.

'After her great-great grandmother.'

Laura looked at him enquiringly.

'The one whose portrait is in the locket Hamish gave Cristobel when she became engaged,' he explained. 'Her name was Fenella. She's also hanging at the top of the stairs.'

He grinned at her and she smiled back, then they lapsed into silence. Alasdair began fiddling with one of the bows on Laura's dressing gown which was draped across the bed.

'So they haven't pinched our name,' he ventured at last.

Laura didn't reply and he stopped fiddling with the bow and reached over and took her hand.

'Don't you remember,' he said softly, 'before Iain was born we were sure he would be a girl and we decided to call him Elspeth.'

Laura nodded.

'We decided on Elspeth three times without any luck, didn't we?' he continued.

She nodded again and, leaning towards her, he cupped her face in his hands.

'Laura,' he whispered, 'is it too late?'

Laura looked at him and her eyes filled with tears again.

'Oh Alasdair,' she cried brokenly.

They looked at each other, both seeing the pain reflected in the other's eyes.

'There's something I have to tell you,' she said, her voice scarcely audible.

But he put his fingers on her lips.

'Do you HAVE to tell me?' he asked sadly.

She looked down but didn't reply.

'Do you WANT to tell me?' he murmured, drawing her back into his arms.

'Don't you want to know?' she whispered.

His arms tightened round her.

'All I want to know,' he said softly, brushing his lips through her long golden hair, 'is that you're here with me now. Nothing else matters.'

He gazed tenderly down at her. Each saw the other's eyes soften with love.

The bells from the church in the square began to peal again, joyfully, triumphantly, their rippling chimes bouncing, with the dancing sunbeams, off the pale pink walls.

Alasdair's lips sought hers and she yielded willingly eagerly to his touch like violin thrilling to the tremor of the bow. And as she did so she experienced once again that wonderful feeling of being held, suspended in an aura of peace and love which had flooded through her on the stairs only a few hours before when, in her moment of deep distress, she had called on the God Flora had promised would answer her.

And she suddenly had a tremendous longing to see Flora again and tell her what had happened. Tell her that she had met her God, that He was real, that He had made all things new in her life as He had done all those years before in Flora's.

Turning her head on the pillow Laura looked at her husband, seeing him as if for the first time and a new outpouring of love swept over her.

'Alasdair,' she whispered.

He loosened his hold, lifting one eyebrow enquiringly: and suddenly that tell-tale blush which had not stained Laura's cheeks for many years began to slowly mount until they were suffused with a soft pink glow.

Raising himself on one elbow, Alasdair looked down at her.

'We're back where we started, aren't we?' he teased.

She glanced up at him enquiringly.

'That blush of yours always fascinated me,' he smiled. 'But I haven't seen it for a long time.'

He bent and kissed the tip of her nose.

'It seems to reflect in your eyes and make them shine even brighter,' he murmured. 'They're like two deep blue unfathomable pools at this moment.'

Laura put up a hand and stroked his cheek, conscious of nothing but a tremendous outpouring of tenderness and joy, mingled in a strange way with gratitude. Gratitude for Alasdair, for Flora, for all that they both, in their own way, meant to her; gratitude that at the edge of the precipice, like Flora before her, her foot had been kept from slipping into what she now realised would have been a bottomless pit, an endless void, a world without hope or pattern where she could never have belonged or had roots.

And once again that tremendous longing to see Flora swept over her: to tell her that the miracle which had happened in her life over thirty years ago was now being repeated in her daughter-in-law's and, as she had promised, as one door closed so another was opening.

'Alasdair,' she whispered again. 'I can't wait to see your mother.'

He looked at her in surprise.

'But we've only just come back!'

That blush began to glow on Laura's cheeks again.

'I know,' she breathed softly, her fingers tracing the outline of his firm mouth, 'but . . .'

Laura hesitated as Alasdair bent and gently kissed her half closed eyelids.

'Well, you won't have to wait too long,' he murmured, 'you'll see her in October when we all go up for Graeme's wedding.'

He half sat up and looked down at her a quizzical smile on his face.

'But why this sudden urge?'

Laura slowly raised her eyes until they were gazing straight into his, smiling that sweet, shy smile which had captivated him all those years before.

'. . . I want to tell her about Elspeth.'

Alasdair looked down at her disbelievingly, the green and gold lights now dancing wildly in his hazel eyes then, as the full implication of her words struck him, a low moan escaped from his lips. But it was one of pure joy.

He drew her gently back into his arms, his heart beating swiftly against her breast. It was much more than desire which throbbed through his body, it was rather a consummation of all the lost years of longing and hoping.

As they merged together it seemed to Alasdair that all their youth reflowered and the barren silent years melted away: those years when they had each wandered alone down a long dark tunnel searching frantically for the speck of light at the end which always seemed to elude them.

Alasdair gazed down at his wife, at her closed eyes, her glowing cheeks and the look of ecstasy on her face, and he knew that they had at last found the way out of that tunnel. The light shining ahead was not only beckoning them it was flooding them, enfolding them in its rays. No matter what the future might hold, the ghosts, the misunderstandings, the dark shadowy figures which had been haunting them since Sandy's death had been finally laid to rest and could never rise up and threaten them again.

And, as this realisation dawned, he felt the wood, the lake and the rolling green lawns of Ardnakil stretch out green and russet arms and wrap them both in a vast everlasting embrace.

It was one of those rare, mystical moments that happen only once in a lifetime and sometimes never happen at all, that moment before an imperceptible sigh or a gentle word intrudes to burst the shining bubble of perfect happiness.

Laura nestled blissfully against him feeling like a balloon which has suddenly been released from a child's

tight grasp and is now buoyant, floating free, soaring
effortlessly, joyfully upwards towards a vast, beckoning
blue sky.

Alasdair's arms tightened round her and she felt his
warm breath on her cheek. Their hearts beat rapidly
in tune and, as she yielded to his embrace she sighed,
a sigh of deep contentment, all remembrance of past
pain gone, obliterated, washed swiftly away as if by a
sharp, cleansing mid-summer shower.